# QUA

Marie Browne

Published by Accent Press Ltd – 2013

ISBN 9781909624740

Cover design by Chris Mallyon

**www.accentpress.co.uk**

# Dedication

For Finley.

# Acknowledgements

The biggest thanks, of course, have to go to Geoff.   Over the past two years he has been bombarded with bizarre questions, been talked at, read numerous drafts and has always given me the right amount of kick just when I needed it most.  He is the best husband ever.

The other person who also deserves far more than a mere thank you is Dr. Ian Kirk.  He never stopped asking 'why' and took the time to discuss some of my odd theories. I can honestly say that, without him, this story would be a far more outlandish endeavour.

Thanks as well to Helen, Arwen and Sarah who did the 'big' reads at various points and pointed out some serious holes in the story.

Chris Mallyon for a wonderful cover, and Cam Field for her input.

I'm sure there are others that I have forgotten.  A big general thanks to all those who read bits, changed bits, argued bits and helped make this story what it is.

Thank you all.

Marie.

# CHAPTER 1

THE OPEN DOOR ANNOYED me for two reasons. One, the enticing aromas of meat and spices drifting through the rain caused my stomach to growl and clench. Running a hand over my wet stubble I could feel the prominent jaw and cheek bones; I'd missed far too many meals lately. Two, the triangular shaft of light that flickered, steam filled and golden through the shabby doorway made it a lot harder to find a decent shadow in which to lurk.

Hoping to spot any trouble before it spotted me I peered around the gloomy alley. A set of tall black bins, most of them overflowing, slovenly guarded the open door. Rainwater dripped from a broken gutter, slid down the greasy wall and splashed onto half-glimpsed rats that chittered and squeaked as they busied themselves in the wet shadows. I tensed as the sounds of laughter and clinking glasses drifted toward me, but the tired kitchen staff were only relaxing, slowly shutting everything down after a long night.

'Call this summer? Shut that bloody door, it's freezing in here.' At the sudden shout I pressed myself against the bricks and froze, holding my breath. A red-faced young woman, her apron smeared with the remnants of the evening's menu, staggered out beneath a large box of vegetable peelings.

'Hurry up, Kath, I want to go home.' The man behind the door forced his words out around a huge yawn. Kath rolled

1

her eyes and sighed loudly. Looking around at the bins for a moment she shrugged and then dropped the box carelessly to the ground, pushing it into the gloom with her foot. Humming tunelessly, she headed back into the warmth and, as the door closed, the laughter was cut short. I suddenly had a wealth of shadows in which to hide.

Stamping my feet in an effort to bring feeling back into my numb toes, I shuddered as my skin cringed away from the cold, wet leather of my jacket. A drop of icy water fell from my hair and ran an oddly erotic finger down my spine.

'Why don't I just insist on having meetings in a nice warm pub?' I demanded quietly of the heavy clouds. 'Why am I always ankle deep in other people's crap?' I kicked a dented carton of orange juice across the alley, huffing with irritation as it split, spraying its fermented contents across the toes of my boots.

A small black cat crept from the shadows and leapt to the top of one of the bins. It stared at me, I stared back. This silent exchange continued until I noticed that there were *two* tails wrapped tightly around its neat, white-tipped paws: Bakeneko demon.

'Erm ... Meow?' A young man, of obviously oriental origin, laughed down at me from where the cat had been perched on the bin lid, his long legs elegantly crossed at the knee. 'For a moment there I thought you were actually going to try and stroke me.'

I smiled up at him. 'I'd rather stick my hand in a blender.' I shuddered again and pulled my collar a little higher. 'Why the hell are we here? Did you actively seek out the most disreputable place in the city before or after you sent your insanely vague little message?'

He leapt to the ground, landing with hardly a splash amid the food-filled puddles. 'Horrible, isn't it?' He looked around with a big smile, his sharp white teeth dimpling his lower lip. 'However it's the best place for very fat rats.' He licked his lips then chuckled. 'It's a kind of slow-food takeaway.'

There are rules to this sort of exchange and one of the major ones is: Do not enter into a dialogue. Keeping my expression neutral I took a long, slow look at my watch.

The skinny cat demon sighed and scratched one ear before breaking into another wide smile. 'You're always in such a hurry, Collector.' He tensed and fell silent, his eyes narrowing to follow a particularly well-fed rat as it wobbled bravely toward the recently discarded peelings.

'Bakeneko!' I stamped my foot, sending the rat scurrying back into the shadows.

The diminutive demon twitched and blinked for a moment. Studying his fingernails he frowned at a small chip in the black nail polish. 'It's really not nice to treat friends that way,' he grumbled.

I hate dealing with "cats". Enigmatic to the point of idiocy, they all tend to use twenty words where five would do. They also share an odd collection of Japanese idioms and quaint phrases that, even when translated, are almost impossible to understand. The whole race seems determined to irritate anyone they talk to. Well, tonight I didn't have the time to play stupid word games. Shaking my head, more to dislodge the rain than to express any particular exasperation, I turned away. 'We're not friends.' I stuffed my hands into the deep pockets of my coat, searching for the scruffy bit of paper that had my appointment details scrawled on it. 'You're just someone that owes me a favour.' I ignored his petulant hiss at my nastiness.

I looked up as he hissed again. His rain-slick hair had lifted in a wet Mohawk across his head. 'I don't know why I try to help you.' He growled, the guttural sound was very much at odds with his slim and dapper appearance. 'You have no respect either for yourself or anyone else. Quite frankly ...' he raised a lip into a sneer, '... you're rude.'

With a wave I began to walk away.

'Wait!' Leaping forward, he grabbed the sleeve of my jacket, piercing the wet leather with razor-sharp claws that had slid in an instant from his fingertips.

I didn't even bother to look up. Grabbing his wrist I gave it a twist. The demon screeched as I screwed his arm around in a circle, his claws retracted and he yelped as I dropped him

3

roughly onto the ground. A heavy boot in the small of his back made sure he stayed there until I decided otherwise.

'You're supposed to pick up a package tonight.' He struggled to keep his face out of the puddles.

I pressed harder. 'I pick up packages nearly every night; parcels, messages, things like you.' I gave him a good prod with the toe of my boot and then moved away.

He climbed to his feet and attempted to wipe the water from his black jeans. 'Yeah, but this pickup's special, isn't it?' He peered up at me, his green eyes giving off that animal glow as they reflected the dim lights from the windows. 'This collection order has come from the top, right?'

Folding my arms I stared at him until he dropped his gaze. 'Go on,' I said.

'You mustn't pick this one up.' Bakeneko busied himself muttering over his soaked trousers.

I looked over my shoulder. 'Why?'

'It would have ...' he paused for a moment '... unfortunate repercussions for you. In fact, it would be in your best interest to take a very long holiday.' He chewed on his lower lip. 'Please, Joe, you of all people should understand. I'm trying to pay off my debts here. I could well find myself made into a fur collar for even talking to you.'

'Just tell me why.' I pushed myself away from the wall, a sudden and aggressive movement designed to make him nervous. I wasn't disappointed. I really wanted this meeting over and done with. My hair was dripping down my neck again and I'd begun to shiver. 'You worry about paying off your debts? Well, give me one straight answer and I'll consider it cleared.'

The small cat-man frowned, still chewing at his lip. I watched, fascinated, as a small bead of blood appeared. 'Whatever's in that package, the Host want it kept very quiet. They've gone to huge lengths to make sure no one knows it's here.' He licked the blood away and, for a moment, his stiletto teeth gained a red sheen. 'But it's more than that; the whole thing isn't just what's in the package – it seems to be about *you* and the package. The Host mustn't get their hands on both together.'

This wasn't making any sense at all.

'They already have me,' I said. 'What's in the package?'

He shrugged and scratched his ear. 'The rumour is that if they get it the repercussions are going to be fairly biblical. There's no way we can let them get that sort of advantage.'

I snorted. 'Yeah, very funny, it's the "Host" – everything's fairly bloody biblical.'

So, this feeble attempt to prevent me doing my job was just to obstruct the angels. Well, it looked as though I'd got soaked for no reason at all. I'd heard all this before. The never-ending power struggle between Heaven and Hell had really reached the depths of petty tediousness.

'As you say, we're all trying to pay off debts.' Checking my watch again I sighed; I was definitely going to be late. 'I pay off mine by doing as I'm told. No questions asked and get things like you back to where you came from. The only reason you're still here is that, as demons go, you're pathetic but at least you stay out of my way.' I was surprised at my depth of feeling and, keeping my hands fisted at my thighs, I studied the puddle beneath my feet. 'I don't care about you, or them, or your stupid war. I don't care which side has the upper hand. I don't care about the petty one-upmanship and the need to prove each other wrong.' I took a deep breath and glared at him. 'To me, you all seem pretty similar; you argue about the rules and change them to suit yourselves. So you just keep staying out of my way and we'll get on fine.' Irritated at having said so much I turned and walked away.

Bakeneko silently attacked. Half transformed between cat and man he was a bizarre mix of the two. Claws outstretched, long teeth bared and slit eyes wide, he twisted himself around my side and leapt for my face. I reacted without thinking, pushing my arm into his gaping mouth. It was pitiful really. Hissing, yowling, biting and scratching, the demon used every trick he had. Bakeneko was a fair bit stronger than he looked in either of his forms, but he was only about the size of your average seven-year-old. I'm six foot-two. The contest really wasn't equal, demon or not.

'What the hell are you doing?' Forcing my forearm against his face, I used it to manoeuvre him toward the wall. Ignoring the searing pain as his teeth pierced my wrist, I pushed him hard into the bricks. I could feel a warm wetness running toward my elbow and, as he bit through the flexor tendons that ran across the back of my hand, my fingers began to deaden.

I held him there, using my arm as both gag and restraint. Avoiding his kicking feet and scratching nails, I fumbled in my jacket pocket for a knuckle-duster. As I lifted my armoured hand Bakeneko caught sight of the weapon and, eyes widening, began to struggle and shriek. His movements became frantic as he sought to spit out my wrist.

'No … no … wait …' His voice was muffled. 'I had to, you wouldn't stop. You can't pick up that box. I didn't know what else to do … You never listen.'

'You backstabbing little shit.' I leant on his throat until his eyes bulged slightly. 'It was a mistake to let you go last time. So tell me, "demon", is this pickup *so* important that you feel you can just throw your life away?' I raised my bone-clad fist and watched, emotionless, as his breathing hitched, stuttered and then ceased.

Bakeneko's eyes rolled up into his head, his teeth and claws retracting as he turned back into a small black cat that dangled in a dead faint. A little pink nose could just be seen over the arm of my jacket and both tails hung limp and lifeless.

'Oh, for pity's sake.' Lowering the unconscious animal to the ground I nudged him lightly with the toe of my boot; he was completely out cold. 'You great scaredy cat, you're never going to earn that third tail if you carry on like this.' The tingling in the back of my hand informed me that my tendons were healing; it also reminded me that the kipping kitty at my feet could still be a problem. Picking up the limp form, I carried him over to the bins. Lifting various lids I coughed at the acrid and carrion stink of rotting meat that corrupted the rain-washed night. Finally finding an emptyish one, I gently placed him in the shallow puddle of noxious fluid at the bottom. Pushing the bin over to the wall, I wedged the lid shut under a stone windowsill. At least he'd be safe from the rats while he came round. I didn't think that he'd thank me though – especially as he was going to have to work to get himself out. It wouldn't take him that long, but he'd emerge stinking of garbage and very dishevelled and that, more than any beating, would upset him for days.

Pale cold light flooded the alley and I realised that the rain had stopped and the thinning clouds had revealed a huge summer moon. Running my hands through my wet hair, my fingers clinked with the sound of old dice. I still had one of my "'dusters" on and, as I wiggled my fingers, they glowed yellow-white in the moonlight. I could understand why they'd upset Bakeneko – I wasn't that fond of them myself.

I called them knuckle-dusters, but they were a long way from the metal thumping aids that bore the same name these days. An armoured half-glove would be a better description. Covering the back of my hands, the first two joints of each finger and the first joint of my thumbs, they had been skilfully crafted by some unknown artisan to fit my hands perfectly. Made from *that* ass's jawbone, the ancient weapon had been remodelled to deal with the rigours of modern-day fighting. Samson probably could have faced twice as many Philistines with these. Each small plate was elegantly etched with sigils and designs – some of them I didn't even recognise. All, however, revolved around "focus". Even a gentle push while wearing these would send an assailant tumbling away, like those balls of weed you see in old westerns. I stared at them, mesmerised as the moonlight defined individual symbols, causing them to writhe and twist.

They weren't "alive" but they certainly had more sentience than I was comfortable with. I blinked and shuddered. Holding my hand above my pocket, I waited for the 'duster to release and flow back to its dark, warm sleeping quarters. Apart from my knife, these were the only weapons I used; they'd saved me on a number of occasions. But, try as I might, I just couldn't like them. The ancient, yellowed bone always came through for me, the 'dusters never faltered and were always there when I needed them. I just got the odd feeling that they humoured me, laughed at me and were just waiting for the right time to do their own thing. Warm and faintly slimy to the touch, it was as though you'd put your hand into someone else's body. I shrugged my wet coat further onto my shoulders as I hurried back down the alley. No, I didn't blame Bakeneko for freaking out at all.

My echoing footsteps sounded intrusive as I walked along Worcester's empty high street. I spend a lot of time in wet, dark and deserted cities and they always worry me. Their watchful silence played on every ancestral fear I could dredge up.

Ghosts rustled discarded papers and spun empty bottles in my wake. The wet street reflected both the bright shop lights and the huge moon, becoming a fairytale path of silver and gold which would fade with the dawn, possibly leaving those that travelled it trapped for ever. The few dark windows reflected the city and captured the additional image of a walking man; I'd joined the ghosts and memories that haunted this place. Here and there were relics of the absent human race: bottles and empty fast-food cartons, receipts and tickets, a stolen shopping trolley and even a coat. I felt as if I was merely studying a post-apocalyptic scene and the city resented my interest. I could feel the hairs on the back of my neck straining to stand upright. Unlike those that slept soundly in their warm beds, I knew what hid in the shadows.

As I turned away from the bright lights of the high street, I began to breathe gently again. This part of town was much older and had its roots deeply anchored in history. It felt no need to bluster and threaten; passive and dreaming of days long gone, it allowed me to pass without comment. I stood for a moment, uneasy, at the bottom of Pump Street. A crossroads is always a dodgy thing. These are places of emptiness just waiting to be filled, crossing points, decision points – always best avoided if possible and especially so near sunrise. I rubbed a hand around my tense neck and took a moment to check that my "escape route" was still intact.

Long years of doing the same thing over and over again had beaten at least that much sense into me and, satisfied that everything was still in place, I headed down Friar Street.

'Make sure you have an escape route.' That was one of the first things my boss had ever taught me. 'All you have to do is pick a spot where reality is open to suggestion, protect it, grab it, fold it and then tear through the layers.' He'd demonstrated and, with a grin and a wave, just seemed to vanish. I'd been surprised at how easy it was. Within an hour I could pretty much get to wherever I wanted to go. I'd watched him leave then, flushed with overconfidence had attempted my first ever solo trip. In my haste to prove myself, I'd forgotten one vital step and hadn't bothered to cast the necessary protective circle before creating my "door".

It didn't take me long to find out why that circle was an integral part of the process. Like ripples from a tossed pebble, the tear I'd created just hadn't wanted to stop. Spreading out in all directions, I'd watched in horror as trees, bushes and local wildlife disappeared into a cloudy pool of sickening nothingness which had spread outward at an alarming rate. It had taken four angels to catch it, reverse it and then seal it up. I, of course, had been verbally kicked from here to forever and had spent years doing cover-up work. By the time I got my travelling privileges back I was sick of abominable snowmen, yetis, sea monsters and other low-level pests that occasionally need to be escorted back to where they came from. The only reason that the boss had granted me permission to use doors again was that I'd turned up in his office, covered in stinking yeti phlegm and had stained his carpet. He'd been laughing so hard I swear he would have agreed to anything.

Smiling at the memories and lost in thought, I almost missed the small sign above a darkened shop door. "The Cosy Cauldron", the cutesy name made my teeth ache. Nestled beneath the sagging overhang of a bulging black-and-white Tudor building, it looked the very place to find hemlock or a new cauldron.

I glanced around the silent street before knocking gently. A light flicked on and a face appeared, making me jump. Dark eyes glared at me from beneath heavy black brows, which in turn squatted beneath long greasy hair.

'Yes?' Her voice was clipped and deep.

Ignoring my suddenly hammering heart I smiled as best I could. 'I'm here to pick up a present for my wife.' The script I'd been sent had been very precise.

The woman, her livid lips extreme in a pale face, looked as though she could have a pretty good part-time job at being Morticia Addams' stunt double. She glared at me for a moment then gave a rapid nod. Pulling back the bolts I was ushered into the shop, hardly gaining entrance before the door was slammed and locked behind me.

'You're late.' She scowled as I made apologetic noises then raised a hand to shut me up. 'Whatever, just stay here and I'll get it.' The skirt of her long dark dress swished in time to the tinny chimes of her jewellery as she walked away.

'Friendly and welcoming: customer service at its best,' I muttered.

Feeling nervous and out of sorts, I meandered about the shop studying the stock: tarot cards, oils and incense were arranged artistically in a little nook. Books on witchcraft, demonology and a hundred other distasteful subjects lined the shelves, stacked into every available space. Crystal balls, scrying mirrors, cauldrons and even handmade brooms and staffs. I've visited a lot of these places – this one was very well stocked.

These shops have a lot to answer for. They create frauds and give the hopefully deranged somewhere to congregate, somewhere to tell their lies and enhance their fantasies; fantasies, I might add, that would cheerfully render them into component body parts if they ever actually got what they yearned for.

Leaning on a display of small packets and vials I rubbed at my neck again, rolling my shoulders to ease the tension that threatened to lock my spine. My skin felt tight and I had a headache brewing behind my right eye. After my time spent among the garbage, the smell of mixed incense was overwhelming and my stomach churned as I tried not to breathe too deeply. Picking up a packet of "Graveyard Dirt", obviously an essential in their voodoo collection, I read the instructions:

*Mix GRAVEYARD DIRT and SULPHUR POWDER with an enemy's private bodily concerns, put the mixture into a bottle with nine pins, needles and nails then bury under the enemy's DOORSTEP or put GRAVEYARD DIRT into an enemy's shoe. Mark a trail to the nearest graveyard, sprinkling a pinch at every CROSSROADS to lead the enemy to take that path.*

I grimaced. That sounded a little too specific for my taste and I really didn't want to think too hard about "bodily concerns" ... I read on and then laughed aloud at the final part of the sales pitch:

*We do not make any supernatural claims for GRAVEYARD DIRT, and sell it for interest only.*

'What are you doing?' Her voice sounded close to my ear. I jumped again.
'Eh? Oh, nothing.' I put the small plastic packet back on its peg. 'Just looking.' I took a deep breath trying to calm my racing heart. If Bakeneko's ridiculous warnings had been designed to make me nervous they were working. Maybe it was time to cut down on the coffee.

'Well, don't.' Holding a purple carrier bag out toward me, she drew her heavy brows together, her dark lips thinning. 'Just take this and go.'

'That bad, eh?' I peered into the bag. Nestled at the bottom was a small white wooden box, with protective symbols painted on each surface. I reached in and placed my hand on the lid. It was hot – very hot – and I drew my hand out quickly, shaking it to get rid of the sharp burning pains that touching a warded object always produced. I sighed with relief; obviously it was this that had set all my senses tingling.

'Just *go*.' Morticia grabbed my arm with a shaking hand and, after steering me to the door, thrust me out into the street.

'OK, OK, I'm going.' I pulled my arm from under her hand. 'Look …' I began to give her the normal spiel about forgetting she'd met me and to just get on with life but stopped to stare at her as she stepped into the light. She looked ghastly, her face clammy like the skin on a pale frog. Red, broken veins sketched lines across her cheeks and chin. Coupled with the dark shadows under her eyes, she reminded me of a junkie, albino half-demon I'd once met. Not a good look for anyone.

Obviously holding this "thing" had been hard on her – I certainly wouldn't want it around me for very long. 'I'll take this away,' I said. 'You shouldn't have any more problems.' I watched as a bead of sweat slowly emerged from beneath her lank fringe. Taking what seemed an age, it ran down her sagging face, trickling along tissue-paper creases until it finally slipped into the corner of her mouth. She stared at me in silence, her dark eyes were wide, the pupils shrunk to pinprick holes.

'Just make sure you tell him I kept my end of the bargain,' she said. Her voice was gasping and rough as though she was having trouble finding oxygen to fuel it.

'Tell who?'

'That evil, bottom-feeding scum-sucker you work for.' She coughed once then turned back toward the shop. Slamming the door behind her she turned out the lights then peered at me, her pale face pressed once more against the glass; obviously she wanted to be absolutely sure I left.

I wondered for a moment who she thought I worked for. There were many words I'd use to describe my boss: short, fat, cheery, possibly alcoholic and endlessly sarcastic but "evil scum-sucker"? I snorted a laugh as I tucked the plastic bag safely into one of the big pockets of my leather jacket. She was obviously either drugged or a sociopath. I really

12

didn't care which, just as long as I didn't have to deal with her again.

To irritate her I yawned and stretched, wasting time. Then, checking my watch, I decided that was it for the night's work; the sun would soon be up and I really wanted to be in my bed before it was. Giving her a last grin and a cheery wave I turned away.

I had only taken a few steps when an explosion of breaking glass accelerated my heart rate once more. I twisted around wondering if the woman had fallen or fainted. She really hadn't looked well.

She was nowhere to be seen but the door appeared to have been punched outward. Splinters of wood and cubes of safety glass were scattered across the street. Confused, I hesitated. Dreadful anticipation was measured out in splatters by the broken metronome of my own stuttering heartbeat; each surreal second was stretched Dalí-like into grotesque proportions before the illusion of passing time was shattered by the tinkle of late-falling fragments of glass.

A dark and contorted figure, bending low to clear the doorway, stepped through the glittering shards. Freed from the confines of the shop it straightened up to about seven foot, taller still when it extended its long neck – the better to sniff the air. It turned toward me with an odd yodelling cry, its tall ears twitching and circling, nostrils flaring.

'RUN!' The woman's white face appeared at a window and then disappeared as the demon whipped around to hiss at her through the devastated shop door.

Shit! This wasn't some pathetic little cat demon; this was a living, breathing nightmare. I did as I was told and, swearing as expressively as a merchant seaman with every step, I hurled myself into a run and headed down the street.

A Drekavak demon: hell's muscle. Powerful heavy legs, thick lower body and long prehensile tail; all of these segued upward into a lean stomach, skinny chest and upper arms. These demons are often described as being brown, or grey but, chameleon-like, the tiny scales that cover their body can change colour to match their surroundings and, when lifted,

13

create a thousand tiny points that blur their outline, adding to their camouflage capabilities. I just prayed that I could get away. I'd fought off Drekavak on a couple of occasions; they were formidable hunters and merciless killers. The huge eyes gave them excellent night vision and they also had superb hearing, long reach and incredible strength and, just in case that wasn't enough, they're armed with retractable razor-sharp claws.

This was supposed to be an easy job, I thought as I belted down the street. If that thing caught up with me it was going to rip me limb from limb, which would hurt. All this and more raced through my head as I pounded along the pavement.

'Stupid, stupid, bloody stupid.' I huffed as I searched for somewhere to hide.

Hidden behind a car, I squatted down against the wall, pausing for a moment just to work out how much shit I was in. Cautiously sticking my head around the wheel, I could see the demon standing in the middle of the empty street. Its skin glistened, changing colour as the scales reflected and mirrored the street lights. Lifting its long triangular head, the creature slowly turned in a circle, the twitching nostrils working overtime, then, snapping its head toward my hiding place, it barked a laugh. I could see cars, shop window displays and my white, shocked face perfectly reflected in those solid black eyes.

Stumbling and swearing I ran again. Should I open another doorway? No, I discarded that idea almost immediately. I still had one open at the crossroads and the chances of some innocent ending up inside it tomorrow morning were all too possible. I'd honestly rather be ripped apart than try and sort out the mess *that* would cause. I glanced over my shoulder. Despite the Drekavak's alleged speed this one didn't seem to be moving that fast and I was pretty confident that I could make it to the portal before it caught up with me.

Reaching into my pocket to check the package, I didn't break step as I careered back down Friar Street. I could feel my doorway just ahead and, trying to ignore the panic-induced images of claws about to thrust themselves through my ribs, threw myself into the rift leaving Worcester's demons far behind.

There was a moment of confusion and then, still trying to run, I stumbled out into Muntz Park in the suburbs of Birmingham. Disoriented and blinded by the sudden change from lit streets to full dark, I tripped over some unidentifiable object in the grass and tumbled gracelessly to the ground where I lay for a moment, covered in leaf mould and panting like a fat poodle that had been chasing cars.

But there was no time to lie about. I slammed the doorway closed and, without following any sort of ritual, banished the protective circle. The energy, originally drawn from my life force and denied any time to gracefully dissipate, looked for the nearest living thing through which to return to its original state. Unfortunately it was me and I yelped as the sharp pins and needles sensation of returning energy flooded through me. Heaving and retching, I leant against the reassuring rough bulk of a tree and, between painful breaths, waited for the nausea to subside. Using a low branch as a crutch, I clambered to my feet. 'Fuck!' I whined at its uncaring trunk. 'That really hurt.'

Outside the park and over the road, I could see the hall light shining through the stained-glass panel above my front door. 'There's no place like home,' I muttered then laughed. I was actually going to finish the evening alive.

A heavy weight landed across my shoulders and, as I hit the ground, I realised that the damned demon had been right behind me. It had followed me home and I really didn't want to keep it.

It pulled me upright with one paw. Huge eyes studied me as though I was some sort of interesting bug. The creature slowly, so slowly, extended its claws, then, totally expressionless, whipped them across my face.

I yowled as ebony scalpels cleaved my forehead, nose and cheek. As a rush of blood blinded one eye, I pawed at my face with dirty fingers.

Placing both hands flat on the monster's slim chest, I pushed as hard as I could. It laughed with an odd and grating sound. While it was busy being amused at my puny efforts I raked the edge of my paraboot down its shin and got ready to run again. Every living creature has fragile shins. As it shrieked I rolled away then dragged myself, pain drunk, to my feet.

Obviously the wretched thing had been merely strolling in the city because now it was incredibly fast. Within seconds it was ahead of me, warbling its doleful cry. The bloody creature actually appeared to be enjoying itself. As it turned, claws fully unsheathed, I tried to feint away; I failed and those long claws sank deep into my buttock as it snagged the back of my jeans. The demon leant away pulling me off my feet. I fell back and rolled over, raising my arm to ward off that deceptively small mouth. It really didn't matter how big it was when it was filled with row upon row of tiny, sharp white teeth. Hissing, the demon casually ripped chunks from my sleeve as it attempted to bite my face. Finally, it slipped past my arm and nuzzled the side of my face for a moment, making odd sniffling sounds; there was a moment's silence before it sniggered and tore into my ear.

I wondered who was screaming then realised it was me. Having removed what felt like a fair amount of my ear and cheek, it hovered over me, fetid breath bathing my face. Holding me immobile, it lifted its head and gave another coughing laugh. 'Take a message, lickspittle.' Its speech had an odd inflection. Obviously that tiny mouth wasn't designed for English. 'We know what's going on.'

That was the second time I'd been asked to take a bloody message and I was fed up with it. While the Drekavak was laughing I had been reaching out. Desperately fumbling around in the grass, I was hoping to find a fallen branch like they always did in films. Obviously, there was nothing that even remotely resembled a weapon. Finding a natural shillelagh capable of braining a seven-foot demon in suburban Birmingham would have been a little unlikely. Groping around desperately I searched for something –

anything – that could be used to fend it off. I flinched as I realised that I'd stuck my hand into a pile of the inner city's most lethal weapon. Trying not to think too hard of what I was doing, I brought my hand up and forced a mother lode of dog shit into the demon's face. I was aiming for the small, open mouth but was happy to smear it hard into any feature I could reach.

It had an amazingly human reaction. Retching and heaving, the tall creature threw itself backwards. Taking the only opportunity I was likely to get, I managed to get a hand into my pocket and slip on a single knuckle-duster. I didn't, however, have time to get up.

Grabbing me once again the demon held my face into the dirt with one hand while it used its other in an attempt to get rid of the stinking mess I'd created. Eventually it gave up and leant down toward me. I could feel its spit on the back of my neck. The combined smell of demon and dog crap was overpowering to say the least.

'You are disgusting.' It released one arm. 'All humans are disgusting. Don't worry about delivering the message – I'll send an email.'

There was excruciating pain as I felt its teeth close on the back of my neck. I felt the wet suck and pull as a mouthful of flesh and muscle left my neck. With another scream, I reached back and smacked the demon lightly on the thigh. Tucked under my heavy assailant I was at an awkward angle so it wasn't much of a punch but, with the 'duster lending me a huge amount of strength, the demon was flung away to roll across the grass. It landed with a grunt against the base of a tree.

Heaving myself to my feet, I staggered over to where, obviously rattled, it was shaking its head. Reaching back I ran my fingers over the warm hardness of bone – that bite had been deep. Reaching further between my shoulder blades I drew my knife. It was about time I stopped messing about.

'Hey!' I could hear a voice over the sounds of the winded Drekavak grunting as it tried to stand. 'Who's there, what's going on?'

I looked round at the figure. Backlit by a streetlight on the road beyond the park, I couldn't see the face but there was the silhouette of long hair and the tinkling sound of tiny bells. In my confused state I wondered if it was Santa.

Taking advantage of my distraction, the demon, which had finally dragged itself upright, leapt toward me. It took my head in a firm and loving grip and gave it a vicious twist. I heard bones grate, then snap and couldn't seem to raise my arms. Through the sudden red mist, I watched bemused as the dark figure took a step forward. The last sound I heard was the demon's hunting cry and then, even though I fought it with everything I had, the darkness became complete.

# REBOOT

ADRIFT IN THE SILENT *dark: a final resting place.*

*A peripheral awareness. Tiny, living flames that shyly dart and twist, in and out of being: each appearing only for a moment, each a single instant of pain.*

*They dance in my hair, blind my eyes and seal my lips with painful kisses before fleeing like startled fish to gather, nervous, at the apex of my spine. Calm once more, they amble down that lumpy track. As they pass, bones fuse, muscle rebuilds and thick blood begins to pulse through plump arteries. Confident now, they kick-start quiescent nerves, wriggling with delight at the stabbing points and searing streaks of anguish that cavort and dance in their wake, a mindless street carnival of renewal.*

*I sink stiff fingers deep into the cold earth as I'm rebuilt. I keep my jaws clamped shut, a barrier to the screams that seek to force themselves out through a larynx still under reconstruction.*

*As I'm forced toward yet another life, the darkness sends out a final seductive siren call. I twist and struggle, reaching back toward the void: I'd like to stay.*

*Eventually the flame creatures separate, then diminish and fade, their major work complete. Cuts and grazes will close soon. Slower to heal, they are left as visible reminders that I have failed – again.*

# CHAPTER 2

AS USUAL, I AWOKE. Dawn had obviously come and gone and I found myself lying in the cool green shadow beneath a dense bush. Groaning, I rolled over and forced myself to crawl out into the warm sunshine. Well, at least this time it was only my spine that had to be fixed. Apart from the puncture wound in my backside, the bites to my face and a couple of minor scratches, all the rest of me seemed happily in one piece. Even the chunk that had been ripped from the back of my neck, although still bleeding, was filling in nicely. But death comes with its own side-effects. I ached all over, the wracking shivers weren't entirely due to the damp and, as rolling waves of nausea added to my misery, I wondered again about following Bakeneko's advice and treating myself to a long, long cruise.

I dragged myself upright and, taking long, deep breaths, struggled to remain that way while I checked my losses. I was surprised to find that there didn't seem to be any. Unbelievably, the box was still in my pocket and still warm; I used it like a hot-water bottle while I tried to regain my equilibrium. Listening to the comforting hum of traffic on the Bristol Road and the cheerful birdsong that drifted on the warm, slightly diesel-scented breeze, I forced my legs to stop shaking and get moving. Staggering toward home, I had the mother and father of all headaches and my backside, quite frankly, felt as if it were on fire.

'Damn.' I studied the long rip in the arm of my jacket; there was no way *that* was getting fixed. 'Damn and blast it.' One leg of my jeans was shredded and blood soaked. 'Bloody, flaming, bloody hell.' I caught a tragic mess of wires and sparkling bits as they slipped from my torn back pocket. What had once been a top-of-the-range MP3 now resembled a tangled mass of cheap Christmas decorations. There was no chance of getting a new one on expenses; I'd happily lay a bet that my boss didn't even know what an MP3 was.

'Do try to keep the foul language down if you possibly can.' A nasally sour voice effectively silenced the happy birds and caused my stomach to roll. Gritting my teeth I turned to face the speaker and suppressed the almost overwhelming urge to stab him in the throat; even beaten and bruised I was supposed to be the good guy. I suppressed a shudder as another warm, wet trail of fresh blood ran down the inside of my shredded jeans then forced my face into a smile.

Mr Morris, my next-door neighbour, always seemed to catch me at the worst possible moment. Ice blue eyes glared from behind rimless, bottle-bottomed glasses. Thin, pale fingers plucked impatiently at threadbare trousers and, as he followed my limping progress along the pavement, frustration and disappointment thinned his dry and colourless lips.

'Love thy neighbour, love thy neighbour,' I muttered under my breath. The hinges on my gate gave a tortured squeal as I forced it open. 'Hello, Mr Morris, lovely morning, isn't it?'

He snorted. 'It's midday, you bloody layabout. When are you going to do something about those?' He pointed at the clumps of lion-faced young weeds that had cheerfully scattered themselves throughout my front garden. 'Appalling.' He sniffed and hiked his ancient trousers further over bony hips as he glared at me. 'Mind you, if you go around looking like that, I'm not surprised you don't care about your garden, you're a disgrace, just look at the state of you, staggering home from a night of debauchery, no doubt.'

I studied the small but vigorous crop of young dandelions that had muscled their way through the clover, nettles and scrubby grass that was my front garden; did the wretched things actually manage to grow overnight? 'Sorry, Mr Morris.' My rapidly healing backside was beginning to itch like the very devil and, digging my dirty fingernails into my palms as I shuffled toward my front door, I desperately tried to ignore the almost overwhelming need to scratch. 'I promise I'll deal with them as soon as I can.'

Misery Morris was obviously the price someone like me had to pay for attempting to live in one of Birmingham's quieter streets. He was a member of the neighbourhood watch, sat on most of the local committees and had taken an almost psychotic dislike to me from the moment I'd moved in.

'You always say that, young man.' He shook a finger in my general direction. 'But, as with most of your *type,* you never actually keep your promises. You drop them like litter and then some other poor bugger has to pick up your trash.' He waved a finger at me. 'That's why you and your ilk are just a waste of everybody's time.'

My *type*? My *ilk*? I managed to keep a straight face. I hadn't realised that frequently dead "collectors", currently contracted to angelic duties, were forever doomed to be bad gardeners.

Carly, my other neighbour, had recently created a "natural art garden". Slumped glass "sculptures", stacked rusty tins and artfully placed mosaics peered coyly through the long grass, nettles and bolted herbs. Wind chimes, created from twisted silver cutlery and painted bottles were suspended from every available branch of her young rowan tree. Whenever the wind blew, the resulting cacophony could be heard right down the street.

Mr Morris ignored my pointed looks. 'I can tell you weren't in the Army.' He puffed his pigeon chest out at me then jabbed a thumb toward the frayed yellow pullover he wore. 'I was, you know.'

I spoke up quickly before he could get started on his favourite monologue yet again. 'Mr Morris, I *will* get the garden sorted.' Giving him what I hoped looked like a friendly nod, I limped quickly toward my front door; I really hoped that he wouldn't notice the bloody trail that dogged my footsteps – he'd just assume that I'd mugged someone.

Or worse.

My hallway was dim and blessedly peaceful. Leaning on the door I took a moment to enjoy the silence. As I caught sight of myself in the mirror I had to accept that Mr Morris might just have a point. Even if I ignored the half-healed cuts and that really impressive black eye, I was definitely looking a little rough around the edges. My unruly brown hair, darkened further in patches by dried blood, curled toward my shoulders. A week's worth of stubble needed removing and I was positive that my eyes used to be dark brown on white, not dark brown on bloodshot pink. I turned sideways and glared at my reflection. I'd lost weight again; "skinny" was now a description to be aspired to, "emaciated" seemed to fit me better.

Rubbing at the back of my neck with one dirty hand, I indulged in a long groan. Every part of me ached, itched or stank of dog do and demon. I needed a long, hot bath – possibly two – and lots and lots of tea.

As much as I tried to ignore it, there were days when I had to admit my life was more than a little odd. I'd even go so far as to describe it as unnecessarily complicated and so incredibly unfair.

First complaint on the list? Legally and physically, I'm dead and have been for a very long time. So long in fact, that I don't remember much of the last thousand years at all, just odd flashes of faces or places. My boss once told me that this selective amnesia was a self-defence mechanism and that, if I actually had to remember all those years, I'd probably be as mad as a box of badgers. He might have been right: the hazy jigsaw of half-memories, feelings and people that I could recall when I really tried always made me feel a little queasy. I didn't attempt it very often.

Second complaint? Unlike all the films and comic books, being dead didn't give me any special powers or make me "cool" in any way. I still needed to eat, sleep and, apparently, pull up weeds. Paper cuts still stung and stubbing my toe had me swearing like a fishwife and, my absolute favourite: I still had to experience the whole glorious range of human emotions.

My third and loudest complaint? Even though I was already dead, I could die again – and again and again and again, each death as messy and painful as the last.

I'm not a vampire; if I sit in the sun for too long I end up as sore and rueful as the next guy. I'm not a ghost, a ghoul, a poltergeist or anything even remotely awe-inspiring. When I'm not dead I'm just human and when I am dead, which happens far more often than I'm comfortable with, I'm a dead human: like I said, the whole thing's very unfair.

Kicking my boots down the hall, I pulled off my blood-soaked socks and shuddered as the cold of the Victorian tile floor bit into the soles of my feet. Alternately tiptoeing, limping and scurrying, I headed off through the house toward the kitchen.

Beside the kettle was a postcard. I stared at it and swallowed hard as the familiar sinking feeling caused my stomach to roll over once more. 'Oh come on.' I whispered at the uncaring stationery. 'You have got to be kidding me. I can't face another job after last night.'

As usual, there was no stamp or address on the front, just the word "Joe" written in a heavy and florid hand. I'd never seen who delivered these wretched missives but I'd spent years dreaming of what I would do the day I finally caught up with them. This one had only one word written on the blank side: "Dark".

Placing the card back by the kettle, I grinned in relief. That meant I had most of a day before I had to go out again and I was damn well going to enjoy it. I filled the kettle and, as I waited for it to boil, stared mindlessly out of the window trying to ignore my own smell.

A small frisson of guilt crept up on me as I stared at the dustbin in the back garden. Bakeneko had been telling the truth. I wondered if he was still in the bin; I probably needed to apologise to him when I saw him next.

After a long hot bath, during which the last of my injuries vanished, I settled my knife and sheath back between my shoulder blades. Wrapping an ancient grey bathrobe around me, I squelched, still wet, down the stairs. Grabbing yet another mug of tea, I headed out into the sunshine for a well-deserved siesta.

Settling into one of my two mismatched chairs, I stuck my damp feet up onto the ancient garden table and turned my face to the sun. It was hot; the traffic was merely a faint drone in the distance and the low-level hum lulled me into an almost trancelike state. Forcing my eyes open, I watched as a plane scored parallel stripes across the blue sky. Wherever it was going it surely couldn't be any better than here. I could feel myself dropping steadily toward sleep.

'Hey, Joe!'

At the sudden shout, I spasmed and dumped most of the hot tea into my lap and, as my delightful drifting state vanished in a sudden flood of wet pain, I recognised the unsympathetic snigger that belonged to my "artistic" neighbour.

'Whoops, sorry, hun, do you want a towel?' Carly, leaning over the fence, was trying to untangle her long hair from one of my feral rose bushes. Despite what she said, she didn't look the least bit sorry. 'I heard Moany Morris having another go at you,' she said. 'So when are you going to join the Army and let them make a *man* of you?'

Her laugh was always infectious and even though I was concentrating on holding my hot dressing gown away from certain important parts of me, I couldn't help smiling. 'Hello, freckles.' Setting my half-empty cup down, I waddled, in a rather ungainly fashion, over to the fence. 'Actually, I think it might be a good idea to join the Army.' I laughed as her big green eyes widened. 'But that's only because it's safer than living next door to you.' I tore my attention away from my blistered bits and took a closer look at her. 'What the hell are you wearing?'

If possible, her smile got even wider and, stepping back, she gave me a twirl to show off the full effect of her "garment". It spun around her in a mad disharmony of sound and movement, little bells tinkled and rang, tiny mirrors sparkled and flashed as they caught the sun and bright, multicoloured embroidery combined into a riotous blur as she moved.

'It was a present from a friend who thought it would suit me for some reason.' She wrinkled her nose and studied the dress intently. 'I haven't had the nerve to wear it out of the house yet.'

There was something about the sound of those little bells that was familiar, but the connection was elusive and I gave up reaching for it – I was too tired to think. 'Probably wise, you look like an explosion in a primary school craft box.' I leant on the top of the fence and leered at her. 'Where have you stuck the fuzzy pipe cleaners?'

Carly casually reached over and gave my ear a sharp twist, smiling at my yelp of pain. 'Don't be rude, or I'll be forced to give this cake to the birds.' She went back to picking bits of rose bush out of her thick red hair.

'Cake?' Rubbing my hot, tingling ear I peered over the fence. 'That cake with the ants all over it?'

She looked down quickly then sighed; the cake was untouched. 'You know I only look after you because you're my karmic charity case, don't you?'

As she bent down to pick up the cake I had to force my eyes away from her cleavage. I've lived long enough to know that only bad things will follow if you're caught checking out the goods. Sure enough, she looked up suspiciously. I met her eyes with a grin – no expression on my face other than "hopeful cake appreciation".

She pursed her lips and then grinned. 'I bet there's nothing in your fridge except for a hairy tomato, some milk and half a can of ravioli.' She looked me up and down and then shook her head. 'I only made you this cake because you're beginning to look a lot like a scarecrow; it's getting embarrassing introducing you as my neighbour.'

'Thanks!' I know I'm tall and thin but really … a scarecrow? That was more than a little harsh. 'I'll have you know I had a right day of it yesterday, I haven't really slept yet.' Reaching over the fence, I took the cake. I didn't feel guilty lying to her, I hadn't actually slept … I'd spent some time dead but that wasn't ever particularly restful.

Carly rolled her eyes then laughed. 'Are you going to be in tonight?' She stuck a finger deep into the icing.

I remembered the card, still sitting in the kitchen and shook my head. 'Nope ... Working as usual.' I tried not to stare as she sucked the icing from her finger.

'Good,' she said. 'That means I can be as loud and disorderly as I want.' With a small wave she walked away, then, at her back door she paused and looked back over her shoulder. 'You *are* going to be careful tonight, aren't you?' she said.

I laughed. 'Carly, I'm a security guard in an abandoned factory. The most dangerous thing I have to face is the occasional lost squirrel; I don't think they're going to get that feisty.'

She watched me for a long moment then shrugged and giggled. 'You just be careful where they stick their nuts.' Blowing me a kiss, she went inside.

I smiled at the closed door before carefully carrying the cake back to the table. Drawing my knife from the well-worn sheath between my shoulder blades, I studied it as I wrestled with my conscience. Could I be bothered to fetch another from the house? I shrugged: no, I really couldn't.

Defining the whorls and eddies of the ancient Damascus steel, the sunlight seemed to slow on the blade. Flowing in hot caramel waves, it sank into the etched sigils that lined the blood gutters of the oddly shaped weapon. Grasping the worn bone handle I hesitated, then shrugged. For hundreds of years this knife had spilled viscous and disgusting fluids – eviscerating an excellent coffee cake would probably do it some karmic good.

Juggling an obscenely large and sticky slice in one hand and the last inch of my tea in the other, I made short work of both. With a full stomach I leant back in my chair, stuck my feet back onto the table and dozed the afternoon away.

As the summer sky finally darkened, I put on my jacket and then remembered that it was only good for the bin. Sighing, I transferred everything to an old combat jacket. It didn't feel right and I shrugged my shoulders inside it trying to get comfortable. I'd had that leather jacket since I'd bought it back in 1953 and I hated to see it finally give up the ghost. I put my boots on while I waited for my phone to ring and, as the final rays from the setting sun faded, the display on my phone lit up and at the second vibration I was gone.

For such a quiet, peaceful little guy, my boss certainly seems intent on making a statement with his office space. The large rectangular room was opulently decorated in rich cream and pale gold. The ceiling hung heavy with intricate plasterwork which framed a painted, central panel depicting the fall of Lucifer. The only piece of furniture was a huge oak and leather desk, deeply carved with intricate foliate faces that peered menacingly from behind lifelike leaves and flowers.

Every previous visit, I had been there for a disciplinary showdown, usually for some misdemeanour that wasn't entirely my fault. I was always threatened with negation of my existence and the sullying of my soul if I transgressed again. None of these threats had ever come to anything – my employer was nothing if not terminally patient. After these wonderful and enlightening little "chats", I would then find myself back at home, ears still ringing. It seemed a little odd to be here when I hadn't done anything wrong.

Wandering across the plush blue carpet, I had to suppress the desire to remove my boots and plunge my naked toes into its deep, soft pile. The colour had obviously been chosen to extend the sky through which Lucifer forever plunged. I glanced up at the ceiling admiring the workmanship in the masterpiece. However, it was far harder to admire the subject. Through an indigo sky the Morningstar fell toward Earth, his outstretched hand reaching back toward heaven. His beautiful face was contorted with anger and loss, his wings twisted, blackened and useless.

I shuddered as I stared at the ceiling. The whole thing was extremely … disturbing. Trying to ignore Lucifer's obvious outrage, I approached the desk and wondered, not for the first time, how anyone could work below something so sad and yet so threatening.

Upon the embossed leather writing surface, ink-spotted and distressed, there was an odd assortment of items. Boiled sweets, all red, nestled inside a tiny crystal bowl. A leather coaster supported an empty coffee mug on which the legend "WORLD'S BEST BOSS" stood out in bold black letters. I'd bought it for him as a joke one Christmas. An elegant black and silver fountain pen jutted from a red plastic pen holder, which stood to attention beside an antique curved wooden blotter. I ran a finger idly along the polished wood and wondered how old it was.

One of the two cathedral-sized windows flooded the room with a pale golden light which stretched in glowing patterns across the floor. Curious, I wandered over and stared through the glass; I'd never had the opportunity to see what lay beyond the office before.

Classic English countryside stretched far into the distance. The late afternoon sun spread final, soft rays over rolling chequerboard fields of fat wheat and lush grass that undulated in waves as an occasional breeze drifted through the crops. Each well-stocked field was bordered by luxuriant hedgerows that dripped wild roses and fat, ripe blackberries. In the far distance a strip of blue sea could just be seen, occasionally twinkling, as the sun's golden reflections rippled across its surface.

A small flock of birds dipped and wheeled above a chocolate box cottage, complete with roses around the door and bull's-eyes set into the diamond-shaped window panes. I could hear the ducks quacking as they meandered in meaningless circles on a small pond.

At the edge of the water, a man and a woman sat together. The man, who looked to be in his late 20s, his blond hair unbrushed and dirty, stared into the water as he monotonously, dropped single pebbles into its green depths. The woman, her feet bare and her long dark hair hanging in stringy, dirty locks, rocked backward and forward as she stared expressionless toward the sea. Isolated within their own thoughts, neither spoke. At first glance the scene was idyllic but as I studied the pair a frisson of unease ran along my spine. Curious now, I crossed the room to the other window. 'And what can we see through the square window?' I muttered. 'A happy beach scene, or no, better yet, a family at Christmas standing around the piano with their dog wearing a Santa hat.' I laughed and leant on the sill. Within seconds I felt sick.

Peering through the dirty glass, my hands cupped around my eyes, I could just make out a dark, wet street through which the inhabitants scuttled, their thin coats pulled tightly around thinner shoulders. Keeping eye contact between each other to a minimum, they flowed in a steady stream of expressionless sadness in and out of factories and other huge black buildings – row upon row of which formed the horizon. Each chimney breathed putrid smoke into the heavy yellow sky.

Two teenagers, creeping through ankle-deep rubbish from overflowing bins, had managed to trap a scrawny alley cat; they killed it with disturbing efficiency. I was momentarily reminded yet again of Bakeneko and winced. Was he still in that bin? Other younger children, a small group of six or seven, crept toward the pair. Where they had come from I didn't know, but it was horrifying to see the desperation on each thin face.

The fight erupted as each child attempted to possess the dead animal. Eventually, a fat security guard from a nearby factory stepped in and, without even the slightest change of expression, picked up the nearest child by the hair and casually punched her in the face.

The fight stopped immediately as the unconscious body of the girl was dropped to the gutter. The passers-by didn't even look up. Stepping over both girl and cat they hurried on.

I watched the man waddle back to the small sentry box that nestled up against a set of huge black gates. In the moment it had taken me to look away, the children had disappeared but, as I watched, one small boy appeared again. Casting many furtive glances toward the sentry box, he crept forward, grabbed the mangled body of the cat then faded like smoke back into the shadow of the bins.

'There has to be a balance, Joe, especially with extremes.' The boss's voice sounded at my right shoulder.

I jumped and squeaked causing him to laugh. 'Damn it, Metatron!' I waited a moment for my heart to slow down. 'Don't sneak up on me.' He did this so often that I was fairly sure he did it on purpose – just another of his "amusing" little habits.

My employer gave me a big smile and, putting his arm around my shoulders, led me away from the windows. 'Things can only exist in balance. The very bad.' He waved a hand at the dark window. 'The very good.' He nodded toward the country scene.

I looked back over my shoulder. 'Your "good" scene doesn't seem to please those living in it very much.'

Metatron frowned. 'Arseholes! Everything is done for them: Everything!' He ran a hand through his salt-and-pepper mop of hair. 'Yet they sit there silent and still, stupid carved puppets that have had their strings cut.' Grabbing the wooden blotter from the desk he pitched it toward the window. It missed.

Shrugging, he waved a hand at the city scene. 'Now the others, well, I really couldn't make things worse for them, yet they strive to make it better. Characters keep popping up, inciting the occupants to work together.' He shook his head again. 'I have to keep removing them.'

'You made those scenes.' I felt a little sick. 'Why?'

Metatron gave my shoulders a squeeze. 'Oh don't worry, it's just an experiment. You know, trying to understand how humans think. I like to keep up with the times.' He laughed up at me. 'It's not real.'

The sick feeling dissipated. 'So it's just an illusion then?' I was relieved. 'These are just some of your constructs?' Reaching into my pocket I handed him the bag.

He gave the contents a cursory inspection, then without even an acknowledgement; put the whole thing into a drawer. Pulling out his chair he sat down, his elbows resting on the desk top. After studying me for an uncomfortably long moment he indicated another smaller chair on the other side of the desk.

'Sit down.' He picked up his now steaming coffee mug and took a sip. 'Coffee?'

It was hard to imagine that this mild-mannered little man was the most powerful angel of the entire Host. His blue eyes, set behind horn-rimmed half glasses, shone. He looked as though he would make an excellent professor. His natural leaning towards tweed, three-piece suits complete with leather elbows and his scruffy grey hair did nothing to dispel the image.

'Sure.' I sat opposite him and picked up a mug that bore the words, "God's last name is not dammit". Taking a sip I tried not to wince; he hadn't bothered with either milk or sugar. 'Last night was a little exciting; you didn't say anything about that box being wanted by demons.' I tried very hard not to sound reproachful but my neck still hurt. It seemed to be par for the course that I only ever got partial information when I was sent on a pick-up these days.

Metatron ignored me and, as we sipped coffee, I began to get nervous. My previous visits had been short, unhydrated and usually loud. I waited for the bomb to drop.

The angel stared at me over the lip of his mug. 'Just for the purpose of this conversation,' he said. 'I want you to answer every question I ask you with absolute truth.' He raised his slightly fuzzy eyebrows. 'I promise they won't be trick questions but I have to make sure you know what's going on.'

I nodded and clamped my lips together; this obviously wasn't the time for my mouth to get me in trouble.

'Who am I?' he asked.

Ah, I knew this one. I'd learned it by rote. 'You are the physical representative of God. You and you alone can withstand the direct word of God and are tasked to relay his orders to those that can fulfil them, that his presence and voice may not cause them pain.'

The little man nodded then beamed at me, his teeth flashed white between the scraggly hairs that he called a beard. 'That's not bad actually, have you been practising?'

Reaching into a drawer he pulled out a bottle of whisky. Filling a crystal tumbler for himself, he waved the bottle over the desk with an enquiring look.

Now that was just wrong! Knowing, just *knowing* this conversation was about to take a serious downturn, I decided that it was definitely better to face whatever was coming from behind a well-padded alcoholic barrier. I nodded and pushed forward my half-empty coffee mug.

Metatron made a face and gave a huff of exasperation. 'You really are a bloody heathen, aren't you?' He lifted his glass to the light and smiled as he studied the amber liquid. 'This is a rare whisky, made in two casks. One with delicate rose petal and violet notes the other with pepper, oak and smoke flavours. It's been standing in the cool darkness for 80 years, before being combined into one special cask by a renowned malt master. It has then stood for another six months to make it almost perfect.' He frowned over the rim of his glass at me. 'And you want to stick it in a half-cold cup of coffee.' Shaking his head sadly, he obligingly topped up the mug. Then, putting the bottle away, gave me an odd look. 'What do you know about Lucifer?'

'The Morning Star?' I glanced up at the horrible ceiling. If anything, Lucifer looked in even more pain than when I'd first arrived. 'Not much to be honest, a tale here, a myth, a legend. All I know is that Christ bound him to Earth at the time of the resurrection but where he is and what he's doing now ...' I shrugged '... I have no idea.' As far away as possible I hoped.

Picking up his glass, Metatron climbed to his feet and began to wander about the office. 'After the crucifixion Jesus's body was put into Joseph's tomb and did not resurrect for three days.'

I hoped he wasn't going to preach for long. Hell, I knew the crucifixion story as well as anybody. Taking another sip of my fortified coffee, I arranged my features into what I hoped resembled an interested expression.

'In those three days, while Jesus's body lay in that tomb,

his spirit had not yet ascended, nor was it earthbound. This was the only opportunity the Son of God had to bind Lucifer, being between life and beyond. But the first created could only be bound by something very, very powerful. Jesus bound him into his own blood, a substance so pure that it could contain all that evil. The blood that was on the spear of Longinus.

Despite myself, I was finding the story intriguing. I'd always wondered how it had been done. Despite the feathers, angels aren't that much like parrots – you can't just bung one in a cage and say, 'Stay there'. I nodded. 'The Spear of Destiny.'

Metatron snorted. 'Pfah! "Spear of Destiny", my arse,' he said. '"The spear of a bored legionnaire who was fed up with death duty and wanted to go home", it should have been called. Doesn't really have the same ring to it, does it?' He took a mouthful of whisky and swilled it expertly around his teeth. 'Anyway, over the years the spear disappeared.' Metatron gave an eloquent shrug. 'Some of the conspiracy theories that you humans make up about it are quite fun actually: The Vatican has it, the Nazis hid it, it's buried in Glastonbury ...' He shook his head and smiled. 'Anyway, the spear isn't my problem, it's the disappearance of the blood that's causing my worries.'

'The blood of Christ.' I nodded.

'No.' He leant forward and shook a finger at me. 'The blood of Longinus *and* Christ.'

'What?'

'Longinus was a complete incompetent. He cut his hand on the spear, just before he plunged it into Christ's side.' Metatron stared up at Lucifer. 'Quite a bad cut from what I remember, the two bloods became mixed, which was why Christ failed to completely bind Lucifer. The blood was tainted.'

Metatron stopped pacing and sat back down. Placing his elbows on the desk, he rested his chin on his fist and stared at me, obviously waiting for some sort of insightful comment.

I shrugged. 'I ... I don't know what to say.'

'In Revelations, it is foretold that Jesus would reign for a thousand years, and then Lucifer would be released.'

I nodded again. Actually, this little bit of prophecy was open to huge interpretation and was already way, way overdue.

Metatron slammed both fists down on the desk making me jump yet again. 'Well, we can't release him if we can't bloody well find him.'

As silence fell over the office, I tried, but I just couldn't stop myself. 'You've *lost* Lucifer?'

Metatron pushed both hands into his hair and ignored me. 'We're late, we're very, very late.' He took a swallow of the whisky. 'May 21 was the point that everything was supposed to really heat up. That day should have marked the beginning of five months of Hell on Earth and in October the entire unworthy were supposed to be swept away.' Metatron ran a finger around the rim of the glass and smiled at the pure tone he created. 'The celestial armies were all tooled up and ready to go, Michael was wandering about with a huge grin on his stupid bloody face and the flaming swords had been handed out. All we needed was for Lucifer to do his part and it would have been a done deal, and where is he? God only bloody knows.'

'God isn't telling?' I raised my eyebrows at my irate boss. 'You *are* his voice, right?'

Metatron slowly raised his head and stared at me again across the desk. Clenching his teeth he hissed at me. 'Yes, I am the Voice of God and no, he isn't telling because he isn't speaking any more.' Sighing, Metatron picked up the bottle of whisky and with a slightly shaky hand, sloshed a good measure into his glass. I hopefully nudged my mug a couple of inches across the desk; he ignored it.

Taking a gulp, he got to his feet with a wince and began to prowl the office again. 'Lucifer hasn't been needed for years.' He snorted a laugh. 'Man doesn't need the Devil to help him on his way to Hell. He's doing it all on his own and coming up with more inventive ways to be evil than even the Morning Star could imagine. Mankind has gone *way* beyond just breaking the commandments. Humans have invented a whole modern book of rules and regulations then gone on to break every single one in style. Wars, murders, rape. You name it, they've done it and that's just on a worldwide scale. On a personal level, most humans are just evil through and through and the biggest laugh is that they never actually see it – most of them were upset when the Rapture didn't happen, most of them really thought they were going to get taken away.'

'So, what's going on?' I said. 'Lucifer's lying on a beach somewhere, smiling gently and just watching it all happen?'

'No.' Metatron shook his head. 'If he was doing that I could find him, he's just …' he paused and shrugged, a worried look on his gentle face '… nowhere.'

'And God?' I prompted.

Again the shrug. 'I've been waiting.' The angel turned and walked back toward me. 'These things take time. I haven't really needed to talk to Him all that much since we culled the Nephilim, I sort of got used to the silence.'

He sat down again. 'When the signs started –the floods and the volcanoes – I expected some connection, but there was nothing. So I went looking for him.' He stared through me, obviously remembering those searches. 'He just wasn't there.' Metatron shook off his worries and focused on me. 'There has to be a balance.' He waved a hand at the two windows, both awful in their own way. 'Christ failed to completely bind Lucifer but he did "reduce" him; it was the human element of the blood that did it, I think. As Lucifer became less, so God reduced as well.'

Draining his glass, he finally reached over and refilled my mug. 'This is where you come in.' He gave me a big, encouraging smile; I wasn't fooled for a moment. 'For years you've been working to pay off your sin; you've tracked down demons, escaped creatures and renegade angels. Anything, in fact, that needed returning.' He paused and his smile faded to a slight frown. 'Well, quite frankly, you're not very good at it.' He shrugged. 'So if you really want to pay off your debt, I need one final job done: I need you to find

Lucifer.'

'You have *got* to be fucking joking.' For a moment, I forgot who I was talking to.

Metatron pursed his lips slightly and raised an eyebrow.

'Sorry.' I could feel my heart pounding. 'But you're right, I'm really not very good at this – if I was I wouldn't keep dying.' I shook my head. 'No,' I said. 'I think this may be a joke, I'm hoping that it's a joke.' I looked up into Metatron's expressionless face and ignored my little voice that was screaming at me to shut up. 'I can't do it.' I swallowed hard. 'I won't even try.'

The diminutive angel smiled. 'No?' He pushed his chair back and got to his feet.

A line of sweat trickled down my spine. 'Look.' I held my hands up in an attempt to hold back the inevitable. 'You need someone better than me for this job. There's no point in sending me, I'll inevitably fail and the whole thing will just become another big clusterfuck.'

Metatron grew. At about seven foot other changes began to take place. He rolled his shoulders and closed his eyes as his face lengthened; the bone structure, so similar to humans in many ways, became more defined. High, ascetic cheekbones pushed through the stubbly, salt-and-pepper beard which in turn receded, leaving the angel's skin a smooth, pale gold. Cold, blue eyes stared at me from below slim, straight brows that were currently furrowed over a long patrician nose. His fluffy grey hair straightened and lengthened, turning white as it burrowed over his naked shoulders and down his back. Long legs, encased in a pair of simple white linen trousers, ended in elegant bare feet buried in the soft carpet.

'You know, Joe.' The expressionless angel walked slowly toward me. 'I cut you an awful lot of slack. I try to understand your pathetic limitations and I put up with a vast amount of disrespect. You really are a huge disappointment.' He ran a finger around the edge of the desk as he stepped slowly toward me. He watched, smiling gently as, all alarm bells ringing in my head, I began to back away. 'Time and again I give you chances to prove yourself and every single time you screw up. I'm beginning to think you do it deliberately, just to irritate me.'

I bumped into the wall. There was nowhere left for me to go.

With a single sharp crack his wings swept downward and we were, once more, face to face. I could feel hot sweat gathering in my hair and my heart was trying to climb out of my chest. I tucked my chin down as he gently wrapped those inhuman fingers around my throat – a vain attempt to halt the inevitable. With a snort of derision he began to squeeze.

'Wait, WAIT!' I forced the words from my compressed larynx.

'Shhh,' His smile stretched into a grimace and his eyes stared through me. 'I don't want to do this but ...' he shrugged, '... you push me too far, you make me do this.' He squeezed a little harder and, ignoring my scrabbling hands that were convulsively grasping his wrist, he casually lifted me from the floor and pressed me back against the wall.

I literally saw stars, tiny motes of light began to dance at the outer limits of my vision and, bereft of oxygen, I could feel my heels begin an arrhythmic and involuntary tattoo on the wall behind me.

Although panicking and dying I found myself in an almost Zen-like frame of mind and studied my feelings about the situation. In all the years I'd worked for him Metatron had never lost his temper, never raised a hand to anyone. The worst I ever expected from him was a sarcastic comment highlighting my incompetence. Looking into this creature's snarling features I finally realised that he was capable of so much more and it terrified me.

Eventually the stars faded and my sight began to collapse into darkness; the last thing I saw was his mouth moving. I couldn't hear what he was saying and, quite frankly, I was beyond caring. I slipped into the darkness, carried away on a blanket of white noise. My last thought was that if anyone could, Metatron could make sure I didn't come back. I left the world with a smile.

No such luck, I came around, lying comfortably on my back in the deep blue carpet, a cushion beneath my head. I looked around, swallowing hard in an attempt to get my yet again abused throat to work properly. Metatron was sitting cross legged beside me, his head in his hands.

Seeing that I was awake he leapt to his feet and helped me to sit up. 'I'm so sorry, I'm so sorry.' He handed me a glass of water. 'I don't know what happened.' He rested on the edge of the desk and regarded me. 'I have no excuse; I'm under a lot of pressure at the moment.' He hung his head then. Getting up, he brushed off the knees of his trousers before holding out a helping hand.

I wanted to ignore it but that just seemed a good way to end up dead again so hesitantly I took it and clambered to my feet.

'There is no one else, Joe.' Metatron handed me into my chair and gave an elegant shrug. 'The Host can't know, the humans can't know and, most importantly of all, Hell can't know.' He ran a shaking hand through his hair and over the back of his neck. 'I only have you, and when you turned against me I just lost it.'

Hang on a minute, I didn't actually remember "turning against him"; I just remembered saying no for once in my long life. I decided that staying quiet would be a good idea and nodded at him to show that I understood.

I swapped the glass of water for the dregs of the whisky-filled coffee that was still on the desk. I should have been used to that sinking feeling by now. Staring into the cloudy mess of whisky and coffee in my mug I took a long swallow.

Obviously I was deluding myself if I felt I had a choice in any of this so I was now going to have to find Lucifer. I had a horrible feeling that ending up face to face with the Morning Star would have me dead, then deader, then deadest (if there was such a word). Maybe it wouldn't be such a bad job after all.

I pulled myself together and took a deep breath. 'So let's get this straight.' I coughed then smiled at him, ticking off points on the desk with a finger. 'You want me to find the most powerful angel of all time. An angry, bitter, very formidable ex-angel that doesn't want to be found and you want me to tell him to come quietly, so that he can fulfil the prophecy that has him slaughtered, to enable the onset of Armageddon.' I took a huge gulp of whisky and spluttered again. 'Have I missed anything out?' Downing the last mouthful of the now sour-tasting drink, I stared up at Lucifer's glowering countenance. 'Metatron, I can't see him being pleased about that and, if *you* can't find him, where am *I* supposed to look?'

The angel, all smiles and grace once more, poured us both more whisky then, after nudging my mug toward me, wandered over to stand directly beneath the painting. 'Don't worry, even I couldn't stand against the Light Bringer at full strength.' Metatron paused and glowered up at Lucifer. 'Hell knows where you are.' He took a long swallow then smiled. 'And soon, so will I.'

There was silence for a long moment as he glared up at the painting. Eventually he seemed to remember I was still there and, without any apology, returned to the subject at hand.

'The blood of Longinus is still present and alive. His ...' He shrugged. '... Oh however many times great-grandson is still here. I'm fairly sure that's where Lucifer's hiding, in the body of a human; it's the only place that we can't see. He's just skulking there, a passenger in someone else's life, jumping from generation to generation as they're born and staying off Heaven's radar.'

'So, he's human?' I could feel my brain beginning to twinge. There were billions of humans on Earth – it would be the ultimate "needle in a haystack" hunt.

'No.' Metatron stared once more at the painting. He seemed physically unable to look away from it for very long; the antichrist glared back at him. 'He can't *become* human, he'd have to give up everything for that and there's no way he would even consider it. However, he can hide away in one since the two bloods became mixed; we just have to find the right one. You *will* present yourself for judgement,' he

40

shouted up at the mural. 'You can't hide for ever!' Metatron scowled and rolled the bronze-coloured whisky around his glass. 'Hell has been hiding this one man for eons but they will have records. All you have to do is find out who is Longinus' living descendant and I'm fairly sure we'll have our man.'

'You don't have access to the same information?' I said.

Metatron shook his head, 'No, this is a rather odd line – one male child and in each case the father dies very soon after the birth. We managed to keep track for a couple of hundred years but there were so many false leads and trails that we lost it. Hell says that they've lost track as well. They're lying.'

I could feel my mouth opening and closing like a stranded fish. 'I'm supposed to get a quick peek at Hell's records?' This was becoming surreal. 'What am I supposed to do, trot up to the gates and say "Hey, guys, I'm the new filing clerk?"'

'Oh, stop clenching.' Metatron poured me yet more whisky. 'It's not that bad. Since Lucifer's rather seditious personality has been absent, Heaven and Hell have had fairly routine diplomatic relations. They're not always cordial but there are things that need to be discussed. Tomorrow, Michael, Raphael and a full entourage of scribes are heading down there for their yearly talks. You'll be going with them – we've got a man who owes me a favour, he'll meet you and take you to the hall of records.' He paused for a moment considering. 'Just don't let Belial catch you there.'

'Why doesn't this man of yours give you the information?' I coughed to clear my throat and get rid of that whining tone. 'Is there even a chance that Belial will know I'm there?' Belial had long been the power in Hell. Lucifer's second-in-command was rumoured to be over 15 feet tall, eyes of fire, horned with the classic cloven hooves and red skin thing going on. He was way down my list of people I ever wanted to meet. Even the demons were terrified of him and spoke his name with a sort of hushed reverence.

Metatron frowned. 'He won't, he says he doesn't owe me

*that* big a favour.' He pulled his chair from beneath the desk and dropped into it. 'Belial knows nothing, just go in with the scribes, get the file and just hope that you don't run into that twisted bastard of a boss by coincidence. If you do catch a glimpse of him … Run.'

The icy look was back and I resisted my more immediate need to run. 'But Michael wants to kill me.' That horrible whining tone was back and I coughed again.

'That's because he thinks you don't take him seriously.' Metatron glared at me. 'Sometimes you can be a little dismissive of his status and that really gets up his nose.'

'But …' Well, this was just getting worse and worse. I'd rather face a horde of demons than archangel Michael any day. Lifting the mug, I downed the contents in one huge gulp; it burned all the way down my abused gullet causing me to splutter and choke.

'No arguments, you need to be back here tomorrow at midday.' Metatron stood up indicating that this meeting was over. 'I don't have the time or inclination to discuss this any further. Like it or not, you're going to Hell.'

# CHAPTER 3

LANDING RATHER HEAVILY IN the middle of my living room knocked the last of my breath away, which was the only reason I couldn't indulge in hysterical giggling. Finding Lucifer was the least of my worries: tomorrow I was going to have to face Michael again. Dragging myself to my feet I headed for the kitchen. I needed tea.

The last time we'd met things hadn't gone well. In fact, if I remembered rightly, he'd actually threatened to disembowel me if he ever laid eyes on me again. I didn't even dare to hope that he'd forgotten. Michael: "The Archistratege", field commander of God's armies. Sword swinging, sociopathic and permanently enraged, he was the one member of the Host that frightened me – no, that wasn't true, I wasn't frightened of him, I was terrified.

I hadn't realised I'd been staring at the wall, until it was obscured by the steam from the kettle. Grabbing some teabags, I threw one into a mug then opened the fridge. Bloody hell, fire and damnation: no milk.

Swapping the teabag for one of Carly's weird herbal things that she keeps giving me, I poured hot water onto the small green bag and located a sticky, dusty jar of honey at the back of one of my kitchen cupboards. After bending three spoons trying to get the wretched stuff out of the jar, I finally managed to wrestle a good dollop into the steaming, fragrant brew then headed back into the living room. The wafting scent of peppermint and ginger from my mug raised my spirits in spite of my need to mope.

I like my house and, although I'm in imminent danger of running out of shelf space, I really didn't want this to be the last time I saw it. I've had a lot of years to collect books and now they're everywhere. Floor-to-ceiling bookcases run the

43

length of the combined lounge and dining room; books are stacked under the table, in every corner and piled beneath the stairs. The funnies can all be found in the bathroom and the spare room is filled with text books.

I picked up one of my copies of the Bible, intending to read up on Lucifer and all his ways but then put it down again. I really couldn't face anything heavy and meaningful, so grabbing my tea and a well-thumbed copy of *Consider Her Ways* by John Wyndham, I killed the lights and headed upstairs. Sometimes, the only way forward is to let the world go hang.

After an uneasy night where screaming angels sliced my dreams into ribbons with flaming swords I was awake ridiculously early the next morning. Trying to ignore a beautiful sunrise I decided to spend some time putting my house to rights. I really needed to redecorate, the aging 70s wallpaper with its tiny floral pattern just made me feel tired. I was getting old – old and tired. Pushing that thought resolutely aside, I shoved a load into the washing machine, then, locating my boots and wallet, headed down to the shops for some much-needed supplies.

I smiled as I noticed Carly and Henry walking toward me. Henry was an elderly basset hound that belonged to the Morrises and Carly loved to take him out for a walk – well, more of a waddle really. He was the most ridiculous design for a dog: short, chunky legs with feet that splayed out at the ends, his knees were just a mass of wrinkles. His huge chest, droopy face and ridiculously long ears gave the impression of stupidity. However, I knew from painful experience that Henry was anything but stupid.

'Joe!' Carly bounced up to me, the arms and legs of her hairy purple monster backpack flapped as though it was trying to take off. Henry followed at a more sedate pace. 'What on earth are you doing up and about at this time of the morning?'

'No milk. My world can't start without tea. You look bright and perky.' I grinned at her. She really did look great. Her fiery hair had been dragged back into a scruffy knot, revealing a lot more freckles. Some of them had actually joined up in some places giving her a slightly piebald look; it was very cute. The denim cut-offs, sandals and a T-shirt which read "What if the hokey cokey is what it's all about?" just confirmed that cuteness. Pushing away the sudden impulse to kiss her, I crouched down to give Henry a rub. It always amused me to pull his long, flapping jowls back into a smile. 'Hello, happy.' I laughed at the indignant look on his face.

'Stop mauling the dog.' Carly slapped me gently. 'You know he reports back to Mr Morris. He actually itemises all the awful things you do to him.'

'Sorry.' I stood up and, grinning innocently, tried to surreptitiously wipe the drool off my hand and onto her arm.

Carly rustled around in her backpack then handed me a small bottle. 'Vitamins,' she said. 'She reached out and tapped the bottle I was holding. 'Take those, you're beginning to look a little waxy and for God's sake treat yourself to something green from the shop and a bottle of absinthe doesn't count. Get some proper food inside you.'

'So, my choices are: succumb to the Green Fairy or eat some broccoli? That's not much of a choice, lady.' I gave her a huge smile. 'Actually, the crockery's clean, the machine's doing my washing as we speak and I'm in the mood for apples, so I'm heading down to the supermarket right now.'

Carly frowned at me. 'Well, you're obviously sick.' She laughed. 'Look, I fancy cooking this afternoon, do you fancy eating?'

I couldn't think of anything I wanted more and was just about to give her an enthusiastic agreement when I remembered my prior engagement. 'I'm working. Any chance you might feel like cooking tomorrow?' I crossed my fingers deep in my jeans pocket; if I got out of Hell and managed to avoid being decapitated by Michael, I would definitely want to celebrate. If I didn't … well, Carly would never know what happened to me. I felt my chest tighten.

She took a step backward and held up her hands to give in. 'OK, OK, no need to look quite so sad, come round on

Sunday and I'll cook.'

Reaching over I gave her a big hug and, as I felt it may be the last one I was going to get, I may have held on for just a little longer than I should have.

'Get off me, you great twit.' Carly took another step back and straightened her hair. 'I never realised my cooking was so good.' She smirked. 'Make sure you buy an expensive bottle of wine while you're in the shop, I'm sure I deserve a treat for living next door to you. Come on, Henry.' With a cheery wave they wandered off up the street, Carly humming to herself and stopping every ten steps or so to give Henry a chance to catch up. He certainly wasn't a dog inclined to hurry; I don't think I'd ever seen him run and really couldn't imagine him even trying.

By 11.30 my fridge was stocked, my washing done and I'd even managed to unearth my ancient vacuum cleaner and had given the carpet a going over. But even with all the displacement activity, my mind kept going around and around, imagining my afternoon's trip.

Finally, I headed for the spare room and dug out an elderly book of medieval paintings that depicted both Heaven and Hell – maybe this would give me some insight. Within an hour I'd tucked it under the sofa and resolved never to look at the damned thing again. Evidently the tortures of Hell were diverse and imaginative; each picture showed variations of the same theme over and over again. There was fire, there was pain and I could only imagine the sounds and the smells. All those souls, all terrified ... I sank onto the sofa and just stared out of the window. There was nothing to do now but wait.

Midday on the dot and I was back in the boss's office.

'Joe!' Metatron's cheery greeting did nothing to dispel the icy atmosphere that appeared to be emanating from the tall, dark man standing with his back to us. The other occupant of the room was seated, his bare feet resting on Metatron's desk; he gave me a cheery wave.

'Hey, Joe.' Raphael tossed his long blond hair over one shoulder and stuck a thumb up to me.

I'd always liked Raphael. If he'd been human, he'd have probably been a beach resident and would have used words like "Dude" and "tubular". Dressed in his usual white cotton trousers and tunic he was relaxed, calm and smiling. It was a complete mystery to me why he always seemed permanently teamed up with Michael, who could easily be described as Raphael's evil twin. Dark to Raph's blond, sour to his brother's sunny, you never turned your back on Michael. He was a stickler for protocol, had a hair-trigger temper and loved nothing more than a good fight.

Archangel Michael turned slowly from the window and scowled at me. 'Metatron says you're coming with us,' he snarled. 'Don't get in my way, don't do or say anything stupid.' He walked slowly across the office, lips pressed tightly together, his well-muscled arms crossed rigidly across his pristinely white shirt front. 'In fact.' He bent down toward me and his long dark hair, tied in a neat tail at the back of his head, fell across his chest. 'We'd all be safer and happier if you didn't do or say anything at all.' Raising his hand he pushed two rigid fingers hard into my chest. 'Got it?'

'Michael!' Metatron grasped his shoulder and gently turned him away from me. I drew in a deep breath and tried to slow my heartbeat. I could see Raphael sniggering quietly as he helped himself to the whisky decanter standing on the desk. He looked at me over the rim of the exquisitely cut glass tumbler and winked.

'Just do your job and leave Joe to do his.' Metatron's voice made it clear that this wasn't a subject for discussion. 'He's not going to get in your way – just make sure he gets in with you and then he's on his own.'

Michael cracked his knuckles and stared at me, one lip seeming set in a permanent sneer. 'He's not trustworthy.' He pulled his shoulder from beneath the other angel's hand and swung back toward me. 'Why do you even keep him around, he's just a stinking, traitorous, stupid and ignorant human.' The tall angel punctuated every insult with another poke at my chest, his voice becoming deeper and more strident with each slur.

'Michael!' Metatron snapped.

Ignoring him, Michael carried on. 'I was there, you stinking little piece of shit,' he snarled down at me. 'I had to stand and watch because the "Voice of God" ...' he jabbed a finger toward Metatron '... wouldn't let us do anything to stop you. Preordained was the word he used, I called it cowardice.'

I had no idea what he was talking about – we'd only been together on a couple of jobs. Admittedly none of them had gone as planned and, yes, there were times when I'd stepped back and let the angels fight; I didn't feel this was cowardice, I felt it was eminently sensible – they were harder than I could ever hope to be.

Breathing heavily he raised himself to his full height, closed his eyes and gritted his teeth. He seemed to be struggling with some internal dilemma. As I watched, his face took on a certain pallor and tall loops of colour began to spiral slowly upward from the back of his neck, changing from pink through gold and on towards the purples. As the colours became darker, the movement became stronger. Colours leapt and circled, creating spirals which sent out pulses of light that whirled and danced before fading into invisibility. Diminutive solar flares bathed the room in ghosts of pastel light.

Crap! Out the corner of my eye I noticed that Raphael had come to his feet, his normally open and friendly face worried, his mouth open in an unvoiced shout.

Michael's eyes became a pale, icy violet and his jaw, previously darkened with a hint of stubble, cleared and became more chiselled, the lips darkening and filling. Trousers and shirt disappeared to be replaced by a thigh-length, sky blue silk tunic which only served to accentuate the muscles in his legs. His feet pointed elegantly as he rose toward the painting of Lucifer, his long toenails shone silver through the straps of his plain leather sandals.

Although the changes were pretty amazing I really didn't take much notice – I'd seen it all before. My attention was on only one thing. In his left hand a shaft of flickering red and orange light appeared. This quickly became a huge sword, fully six foot from pommel to tip. Flames licked and curled along its shining length then fell toward the floor. Scattering like a child's fumbled sweets, each drop hissed and bubbled, forming smoking black holes in Metatron's beautiful blue carpet. With no other option available, I reached up and pulled my knife from its holster. The dull, grey metal of the blade refused to reflect the terrifying light show that was going on in front of me.

The angry archangel became almost incandescent. 'You piece of rat shit,' he screamed, 'you cockroach, you viper. You'd pull a weapon on ME? He rose another foot into the air. The sword, now held high above his head, began its inevitable downward plunge, trailing silent flames that all but hid the metal of the blade. With my back to Metatron's desk there was nowhere left to go. Shaking, I raised the knife and closed my eyes. Let's see Metatron bring me back from this, I thought. It might be a bit difficult, even for him, to actually stitch two separate halves of a human back together.

'MICHAEL!' Metatron shouted and reached forward to stop the descending weapon.

'Michael!' Raphael leapt between me and the descending sword. 'This must NOT happen.'

The sword winked out of existence but the enraged angel's eyes stayed fixed on me, his chest heaving as he fought to regain control.

'Michael,' Raphael's voice rolled around the room soothing and calming. 'This doesn't help – you've got a big job to do today.'

Raphael grabbed the angry angel's face and forced it away from me. He smiled and, as he gently rubbed a thumb down Michael's jaw, the taller angel's breath became steadier. His wings faded to smoke and whirling motes of light and then disappeared completely. As he landed he was fully in control of himself, his handsome face expressionless and unforgiving once more.

Breathing a sigh of relief, and positive that I could actually see my heart beating through the skin of my chest, I slowly put the knife back into its sheath. Not at all convinced that my legs would support me, I stayed leaning on the desk.

'Thank you, Raphael.' Metatron watched Michael walk away and lean his forehead against the cold glass of a window, chest still slightly heaving. His hands, gripping the sill, alternately flexed then released, the only outward sign of his inner turmoil.

'Right.' Metatron turned to me with a bright smile. 'You know what *you're* doing.' He looked at Raphael. 'And you know what *you're* doing.' He glanced across the room at Michael then dropped his voice to Raphael. 'Keep an eye on Joe, please, I want him back in once piece. I can't stress how important this is.'

Raphael looked at me with a slightly puzzled expression and then nodded slowly. 'We'll bring up the rear, eh, Joe?'

I felt like a child being told to keep hold of his big sister's hand. Quite frankly, after Michael's little display, they could put me in gingham and tie pigtails in my hair as long as it kept me from being skewered on the giant and scary physical representation of one of the dour archangel's tantrums.

Walking through the sunny streets of Cambridge with Raphael beside me, I was indeed, bringing up the rear. All dressed alike in black trousers, white shirts and black ties, the group ahead of us looked like a collection of Mormons gathering for a pep talk. The scribes and lesser angels walked in pairs, silent and smiling, looking neither left nor right. It was no wonder that the shoppers avoided us with such vigour. Any that looked our way were treated to such a matched set of toothy smiles that they soon turned and hurried about their business.

Dressed in my usual worn jeans, Para boots, T-shirt and combat jacket I felt scruffy and far too human as I trailed behind the happy-looking group. 'If they break into song I may throw up,' I muttered at Raphael who started humming *Kumbaya* with a grin. 'So what's got The Commander of the Armies of the Lord in such a knot?' I asked the tall blond next to me; it was more to shut him up than for any real need to know.

He looked down at me and frowned. 'You can hardly blame him, Joe.' Raphael looked sad. 'He has a very long memory and he's under a lot of pressure to get things sorted out. It's not going to be long before some of those titles of his are going to get a good airing. He knows that the end's coming. I know it, Hell knows it and it's driving him mad to have to sit and wait for the "right" time.' The tall angel smiled down at me. 'Metatron isn't helping in the least. All Michael wants is a timescale and The Voice just refuses to give one; he just keeps telling us that our father says, "Not yet"'.

'God says it's not time yet?' I struggled to keep my face straight – so Metatron was lying to the Host as well. 'Isn't that good enough for him?'

Raphael nodded. 'Michael had just finished banging his head on the wall when you walked in.' He shrugged. 'Unfortunately, with nowhere else for his frustration to vent, you got both barrels.'

Hmm, I decided it was time to change the subject and looked around the colourful marketplace. The canvas tops to each stall flapped in the light summer breeze. Rows of fruit and vegetables formed a brightly coloured backdrop to cheap clothes, bags and tarnished jewellery. Spoilt students and disappointed tourists milled around the stalls, drinking overpriced coffee and eating cheap ice creams. 'Doesn't really look like "Hell",' does it?' I said.

Twenty different languages flowed and clashed over the sounds of screaming children and crying babies. Locals on bicycles wove their way through the shoppers: some didn't make it. Small battalions of desperately smiling sales people hassled passers-by, urging them to go punting or see the city from a rickshaw. It was certainly Hell to me.

Raphael chuckled, 'I take it this is your first visit?'

I nodded.

'You're going to love this.' We walked a little faster in an effort to catch up with the others who were rapidly being swallowed up by the heaving Saturday afternoon crowds. 'Come on, slowcoach.' He slapped me on the shoulder then set off at a trot.

The shining glass and chrome entrance to an exclusive department store loomed before us. A smartly dressed doorman touched a finger to his peaked cap and held the door open. Michael stopped abreast of him.

'You'll be wanting the lift, sir?' The man pointed into the store, 'If you'll accompany me.'

'Hell is a shop?' I stared around. Nothing seemed out of the ordinary. Women scuttled between the rows of clothes and shoes. Men lounged around on plush, red velvet seats looking bored and children alternated between whining, crying and wiping sticky fingers on anything they could find. It seemed like a perfectly ordinary Saturday afternoon.

Raphael shrugged. 'Everything moves with the times and just look at this place.' He gestured around the store. 'Come on, it's the ultimate temptation for anybody.' He pointed out a pretty young woman who was twisting and turning as she stared at her reflection in the mirror.

'She's just lost her job,' Raphael said. 'She's up to her ears in debt but she's going to buy that dress. She's not listening to the little voice that's telling her, "Don't do it". There'll be no food, her bills won't get paid and her husband is going to be really angry.' He clicked his fingers and a button between her breasts unravelled and fell to the floor; a dark smudge slowly bloomed on the skirt. The woman leant toward the mirror and, after a fleeting frown, began to smile.

'There,' he said. 'At least now she'll get a decent discount.'

He pointed again. 'That man over there is thinking about buying a present for a woman at his office. His wife, sitting at home and worrying about the mortgage isn't even on his mind. She's boring, she nags and he deserves young, fresh and carefree. It's his money and he should be able to do what he likes with it.' He shook his head sadly. 'It's clever: pride, anger, avarice, adultery. Every vice, every sin, all under one roof; they cater for everything.'

'Gluttony?' I quipped, 'I can't see how they'd manage that one.'

Raphael snorted as he shoved me between the closing doors of the lift. 'They have an excellent patisserie up on the fourth floor,' he said.

Before the lift doors closed, I took a last look at the men and women that smiled from behind each glittering counter and display. 'So is it all demons that work here?' I said.

Raphael laughed. 'No, they're all human; this is one of the best places to get qualifications in customer service.' He laughed again at my expression. 'Oh, come on, nobody knows how to give the customer exactly what they want like Hell. Those that really excel can expect a job for life, and beyond.'

Making sure we were all settled, the doorman used a tiny key to open a silver panel above the buttons. He depressed a switch, then closed and locked the panel again. The lift doors shut with an efficient hiss and I could feel that we were rising, which surprised me.

Being in a lift full of angels is exactly the same as being in a lift with anyone. After about two floors, feet start shuffling and everyone pretends to be listening to the banal muzak that is always either too loud, or just too soft. It was a relief to finally feel the slight jolt that heralded our arrival. I had kept my eyes on my boots for the entire ride; there was no way I was risking eye contact with Michael. The possibility of an angry angel transforming in a small metal box didn't bear thinking about.

The doors slid open and the doorman kept his finger on his cap as we all stepped out. Feeling Raphael's hand on my arm, I took a deep breath and shut my eyes. If Metatron hadn't offered me a second chance, this is where I would be. I had been told often enough that this was where I *should* be. Finally, after I couldn't put it off any longer, I opened my eyes, heart steeled for the horrifying images that I would surely have to face.

Well, "horrifying" wasn't really the word I'd have used – "boring" actually suited it much better. Brown sand stretched as far as the eye could see. A huge expanse of mostly nothing was broken only by short grasses and stunted bushes. Small lumps and humps where the sand had blown over the fallen branches of long dead trees gave the area some texture. The view stretched, unchanged, toward the horizon. I sighed in relief as I remembered the myths and legends. This wasn't Hell – this was what was known as the "plains". A no man's land through which all damned souls had to travel. The walk gave them the opportunity to contemplate their sins, time in which to really appreciate their horrible circumstances and time to build up a good reserve of guilt and contrition.

The whole vista was rendered in sepia tones. I could just make out a path, only slightly darker in hue than the sand around it, meandering away into the distance. The bushes marked the edges of the path; they had no leaves but long, deep red thorns that stuck out at all angles. Each thorn was at least an inch long – nasty things.

As earth and sky were almost the same colour it was nearly impossible to determine a clear horizon. What appeared to be hills were hazy and unfocused; they might not have been hills at all. It wasn't hot, it wasn't cold and the air had a thickened quality that muffled all sound. In the distance there started a doleful ringing, as of a bell stuffed with blankets.

Raphael looked back at me as the others moved off. 'Mind where you're treading and don't lag behind,' he said. Frowning slightly he bent toward me. 'Are you all right, Joe?'

I nodded and shrugged. I felt sick, I wanted to run and scream. I really couldn't face the horrors that squatted beyond this desolate wasteland.

'Did Metatron tell you that you were going into Hell?' Raphael put his hand on my hair, and like a cool breeze on a hot day, I felt immediately better. I nodded again.

'If you go to Hell, Joe, you don't come back.' Raphael smiled at me. 'This is the path to Purgatory where, those souls that *choose* to …' he put a huge emphasis on the word "choose", '… can pay for their sins and attempt to cleanse themselves enough to go to Heaven.'

'No seven circles?' I felt about five years old again.

He shook his head, 'Not here. No.'

'No torture chambers?'

'A few ...' Raphael shrugged. 'But those that enter do so of their own free will in the hope that mortifying the flesh may expunge their sins.' He looked over his shoulder at the line of scribes that were now moving away. 'Come on,' He linked his arm with mine. 'We don't want to let them get away.'

We must have walked in silence for about half an hour. Each step was dogged by sounds of chittering and sighing – an unnerving and worrying sound. I spent more time looking behind me than toward the trudging column ahead. However, there was never any sign of life, just shadows and shifting sands. Eventually, in the distance, what I had first taken to be a hill, or even just a different coloured patch of sky, slowly began to transform into a recognisable wall. It seemed to be a fortress, although it was difficult to be sure.

Thick at the base, the wall thrust itself into the sky, a huge wave of sand, frozen just at the very point of breaking. This colossal structure formed a solid barrier that loomed over the shifting sands below, it seemed ready to topple at any moment. Standing beneath its tip, I stared upwards and struggled with vertigo and nausea.

'JOE!' Raphael's voice cut through my musings. Turning toward him I was confused; he seemed to be dissolving, or blurring; indistinct as though standing in thick fog. He held a hand out for me to grasp. 'Joe, take my hand.' His voice was urgent and thick with worry.

Reaching forward I took the proffered help and Raphael pulled me toward him becoming more distinct with each step.

'Please don't do that again.' Raphael looked me over from head to toe. 'I don't want to be the one explaining to The Voice how I lost his ...' his voice trailed away. I couldn't blame him – I'd never been sure what Metatron classed me as either.

'You should have left him there.' Michael's voice from the front of the parade cut across the moment of discomfort. 'I'd have explained for you.'

'What happened?' I looked back in confusion.

'We have special dispensation to walk here.' Raphael stared back at the path we had taken, 'But if the group gets separated, all the "things" out there that have been prevented from molesting us suddenly find themselves with an unexpected playmate. Here have one of these.'

I shuddered as I listened to the chittering and scratching. I didn't even want to guess what would make that sort of sound. But, rebellious as usual, my mind conjured up a picture of something large, insectile and very predatory. I swallowed hard and reached into the battered white paper bag that Raphael was waving at me. Jelly babies, a red and a yellow sat in my grubby palm. I stared at them in confusion.

'Come on, you.' Raphael grabbed my shoulder and, grinning, propelled me ahead. 'I think that I'll bring up the rear – that way I can keep my eye on you.' He grinned into the bag before selecting a bright pink sweet. 'Do you eat their heads or their feet first?' he enquired.

I swallowed hard and put the sweets into my pocket.

As we approached the fortress, I could finally make out a single different feature in this land of tonal changes. A huge pair of dark wooden gates vast, old and blackened dominated the scene. The wood, dried and ancient, had splits into which I could easily have plunged my fist. Huge, square headed nails, worn and dull, each the size of my head were embedded in the wood, giving it a speckled, medieval appearance. Set deep within the sand-coloured walls, they were obviously designed to catch the attention of anyone approaching. The immortal words, "Abandon all hope ye who enter here" were missing, (obviously another urban myth). However, these gates needed no negative advertising. Anybody that laid eyes on them would immediately and irreversibly abandon any false belief that they had gone to a "better" place.

Closer now, I studied the walls. They were constructed from huge blocks of stone, each one approximately the size of a small bungalow. I wondered how they'd managed to move them into place and where they had come from. As we approached, my thoughts about the architecture were interrupted as the gates began to creak. As they swung ponderously open, I noted that they were at least 50 feet high and thicker than my body. Were they built to keep invaders out or to keep things, trying to escape, in? I wasn't sure I really wanted to know.

Between the open gates a figure appeared. A big man, on a vast black horse, trotted over the sand toward us. He was carrying a long pole which had a vicious spike at one end and an elegant, curved axe head at the other. I'd seen one before. Carly and I had once visited a re-enactment event at Warwick Castle and, if I remembered rightly, that type of weapon was called a bardiche. I laughed, I only remembered the name because I'd been messing about and had knocked it over. As it fell, it had missed Carly by millimetres; the look on her face had been priceless.

'Don't laugh.' Raphael frowned and nudged me. 'This is one guy you don't want to upset.'

'What? No, I wasn't … I was just …' Getting my mind back on the job I stared over at our approaching escort. As he neared I squinted and tried to get my brain to confirm exactly what my eyes were seeing. 'What the hell is that?' I whispered to the angel.

'That's Nessus,' Raphael said. 'I bet you never thought you'd see one of *his* kind.'

I couldn't tear my eyes away from the creature striding toward us but I managed to shake my head. 'They're not real.' I finally focused on Raphael who was obviously enjoying my astonishment. 'Next you'll be telling me that dragons and unicorns exist as well.'

Myths and legends tell us that a centaur is merely a horse and a man joined: it's not, nothing like.

Standing 20 hands at his horse shoulder Nessus looked down at us from at least nine foot in the air. His hooves, unlike horses', were cloven. Twin toes sporting shining black claws peered from beneath long white hairs like those on a shire horse. The heavily muscled legs each sported a single bone spur, which sprouted from just above the back of each fetlock. These spurs had been encased in finely worked silver which extended the natural claw and gave each a wickedly sharp tip. As thick as my wrist at the base they looked effective and brutal weapons.

The creature was a mass of well-defined muscle which moved with a silken fluidity beneath tanned human skin or glossy black hair depending on which part of him you were studying. His shoulders and neck were solid, the hefty shaft of the weapon he carried, slung casually over one shoulder, made no indentation at all.

I craned my neck to look at his face. Large dark eyes, as limpid and liquid as black glass, gazed out from between heavy brows and a broad nose. A forelock and long coarse mane sprouted in a straight Mohican across his head and continued on to finish midway down the massive spine. Each huge spinous and transverse process of his vertebrae pierced the skin and created twin spiked ridges down his back. I could easily believe that he was the outcome of a threesome between a body builder on steroids, an armoured carthorse and a small stegosaurus.

The shaved sides of his head, his shoulders and back were heavily tattooed. Prehistoric animals: mammoths, deer and other, less identifiable creatures fled into the black hair that signalled his change of genus. From here, a long line of white, cryogenically branded images of stickmen shot arrows, waved weapons and chased yet more animals toward his tail. Around his waist hung a beautiful leather bag, its flap embossed with the same creatures that decorated his skin, his tall ears were pierced with gold and silver hoops as was the one eyebrow that was currently quirked toward his fringe.

'Didn't your mother tell you that it's rude to stare?' A deep, gravelly voice interrupted my study of his physiology.

Forcing myself to study the toes of my boots, I muttered an apology.

As he walked slowly toward me I noticed that there was a wonderfully heady fragrance about him – a mixture of hot horse, sweet grass and musk. There also seemed to be a faint hint of aftershave, but try as I might I couldn't quite place the brand.

'Is this an angel?' Bending, he peered into my eyes, sniffing at my hair and face, then, with a sudden snort, he shied away. Folding his arms across his massive chest he turned to face the angels. 'That's human. Michael, why is that here, you know it's forbidden?'

Michael stepped forward to stand in front of the towering monster. 'My apologies, Nessus, he has been sent by Metatron.' Michael turned and gave me a look of utter disgust. 'To observe.'

Raphael stepped forward but a warning look from Michael stilled anything he might have been going to say.

'An observer?' Nessus stepped daintily around the archangel in front of him to confront me again. 'Then why does it have a weapon?'

Grabbing my hair, the huge horseman bent me forward and plucked the knife from between my shoulder blades. With a yelp he dropped it on the ground as though burnt. 'And such a weapon.' He cautiously kicked the knife away, using only his claws.

There was silence for a moment as Nessus regarded me before once again turning to the angels. 'That cannot go with you,' he said. 'That must stay here and wait. I would not stop the talks but that must stay with me.' His long black tail flicked and caught me across the face. 'You're lucky I choose *not* to take this as an insult.'

Michael grinned happily at me then turned a serious face to the dour centaur. 'As you wish, Gate Keeper.' He gave a small bow. 'I would not presume to know what Metatron wanted him to observe, but I know that the talks must continue. We'll be happy to leave him in your care.'

With that he turned back to Raphael and the scribes. 'Shall we?' He gestured elegantly through the gate. As they walked away, Michael turned back to me. 'Have fun, Joe, we won't be long. Don't worry, we'll tell Metatron that you just weren't allowed in.' He walked away laughing, obviously very pleased with the outcome.

Watching the angels walk away, the centaur muttered

under his breath; it was only one word and it sounded suspiciously like "Arsehole".

Looking as innocent as I could, I attempted to sidle after Raphael. However, at the first shuffling step, Nessus's huge arm barred my way. 'Stand still, little human,' he rumbled, 'I think we can amuse ourselves until they come back.' He didn't look at me but continued to watch as the party moved through the gate and away down the stone passage.

Standing in silence outside the gates of Hell, I watched as my guardian angel walked away. Just before they disappeared, Raphael turned to me with a worried look. Michael put a hand between his shoulders and moved him firmly onward. One by one they vanished into the fortress.

Eventually, Nessus turned to me. 'You'd better grab that.' He pointed toward my knife that still lay, half-embedded, in the sand. 'But put it away and keep it under control.' He shuddered, both types of skin rippling as though shedding a fly. He watched as I picked up the knife, relaxing only after it was safely between my shoulders once again.

'Nasty piece of ironwork that.' He turned away, his long tail raising puffs of dust as it dragged elegantly through the sand. 'Come on.' He looked back over one tanned shoulder. 'We don't have long so let's get moving.'

With the exit of the angels his voice and inflection had changed, becoming softer and less formal. His accent sounded suspiciously West Country. I stared around at the never-changing sand. Well, I had two choices: stand here and never know what was behind those walls, or follow a horse's arse into Hell. I shrugged and followed the horse's arse. Well, it wouldn't be the first time now, would it?

Once through the gate we turned right and entered a confusing array of passages, doors and corridors. Nessus walked with no hesitation and eventually we emerged into a large open space.

Forgetting why I was there, I stood and stared at the hustle and bustle that paraded before me. Recognisable demons and things that might have been demons wandered past chatting and laughing. Centaurs, humans, reptiles, furry things, slimy things, big things and little things, all rubbed shoulders as they wandered and laughed together around a colourful and vibrant fayre. Each stall displayed something different: vividly coloured cloth, hot food, exotic weapons, books, toys and sweets to name but a few. One stall sold tall plants which, obviously due to some unseen stimuli, occasionally opened and puffed a small amount of brown dust into the air. Smelling of cinnamon, there was the hint of sweet grit as it settled on the tongue. Another stall held nothing but small brown paper packets. Each was sealed with wax and multicoloured ribbon. I had no idea what was in those mysterious packages but the owner was doing a brisk trade.

Set on a slight hill, the market was spaced around the village green which snuggled between tall black and white houses. Each had a jetty-like first floor which was supported by carved wooden creatures that peered down at the bustling scene. Every stall had been carefully placed between trees or behind flower beds to form three diminishing rings. These gently herded shoppers toward a large fountain which stood, in pride of place, at the very centre of the green. Stone seats, set in a circle, formed the outer barrier to the water which, on closer inspection, contained a huge amount of coins. Some were silver, some bronze or copper; one or two appeared to be gold. From the centre of this wet wealth there reared a large block of uncut black stone, from which spewed a glittering, bubbling deluge. The water cascaded down the stone, leaping its natural peaks and troughs to land splashing and chuckling into the pool.

All through the fayre there were crafters hard at work, their busy cacophony served as a counterpoint to the gentle melody of the fountain. A burly metalworker sang in a guttural language as he worked on a glowing metal rod. Hammering, twisting and heating he grunted as he worked. Two jewellers chatted in their own high-pitched and stuttering language as they threaded cut-glass beads into an intricate pattern. Beside them, a gaggle of older women, containing at least three different species, sat in a circle sewing and gossiping. Their frequent outbursts of ribald laughter made me smile.

Between the stalls, jugglers and stilt walkers moved, each trying to attract the attention of a group of children who laughed and shouted as they chased a large dog puppet manipulated by two Drekavak demons. The dog would wander through the market sniffing at trees and under stall covers, occasionally it would appear to notice its little band of giggling followers and would whip around to sniff the air then pounce toward the children sending them screaming and laughing between the stalls to hide. As the hysterically screaming parade passed each stall, the stall holder would look up with a grin and shout advice either to the children or the dog. If someone had handed me a beer and made space for me between the elderly beings that smoked beautifully carved pipes while they chatted on the fountain seats, I could have sat and watched for hours.

Carly would have loved it all. I could easily imagine her exclaiming over each stall, biting her lip and pushing her hair out of her eyes as she haggled over prices. She would have had a field day.

'You coming?' Nessus's deep voice broke through my reverie and he peered over my shoulder trying to work out what I was looking at. 'What are you smiling about?'

'Nothing.' I took another long look at the madly busy fayre. The fruit-smelling smoke from those sitting by the well reminded me of Christmas and made me feel oddly sad. 'Well …' I took a deep breath as I wondered if what I was about to say would offend him. Then plunged on anyway. '… I'm having problems matching this …' I waved a hand at the folk milling around the market, '… with what I expected to see.'

Nessus rumbled a laugh. 'Let me guess.' He reached out and turned the handle on an ancient green door set deep into a grey stone wall. He gave it a bit of a push, sighing when it didn't budge. 'The bottomless pit, a place of torments and sorrows, the very centre of everlasting destruction.' His deep voice added a chill realism to the quotes he was using. 'Where men are tormented with fire and brimstone.' Flexing his muscles, he gave the door a good shove; it finally popped open with an anguished creak. Flakes of disintegrating green paint fluttered down to land on his back. Shaking himself with a look of irritation, he muttered, 'The Great Abyss, where no maintenance man can ever be found.'

So horse bum had a sense of humour? That was also unexpected. I began to relax slightly. 'So no weeping and gnashing of teeth then?' I followed him through the door.

'Only if the market traders hike their prices too high.' He looked over his shoulder and snorted a laugh. 'Then the gnashing of teeth can be heard for miles.'

As the door closed, the sounds of the market faded and I took a deep breath of the cool old air. We were in a corridor. Plain stone flags lined the floor and the walls were painted with a greenish-white lime wash. At regular intervals a door, a window or another corridor broke the monotony of the echoing, empty passageway.

'So why all the bad press?' The corridor was wide enough for us to walk abreast and, feeling particularly brave, I trotted along at his side. 'Why do people still expect to see fire and demons with tridents? I've worked with angels for a long time and they still refer to Hell as a place of sorrows and the damned.' I shrugged. 'I've never heard even one of them say, "Hey, I've run out of tea, let's pop to Hell and buy some more".'

'Hmmm ...' Nessus looked down at me. 'One, I wouldn't shout too loudly that you work for the canaries.' He grinned 'That's the sort of thing that upsets people.' He chuckled. 'Two, they don't know. The talks are held in a *very* special place. It's been set up especially for them, if you know what I mean.' He laughed again. 'It's sort of a tribute to bygone days, if you like.'

'Canaries?'

'Yeah.' Nessus's grin faded. 'Irritating little feathered things – noisy and useless.' He frowned. 'But very pretty.'

'So why keep them in the dark about all this?' I had a sudden thought. 'And aren't you worried that I'm going to tell them?'

'Keeping them in the dark is the only reason we're still enjoying what we've got now.' Nessus nodded to a well-dressed woman that was coming the other way. She acknowledged him with a smile that was just a little too wide. 'We have a fairly good thing going on here.' He lowered his voice slightly. 'They'd be very upset, if they knew. Here, there's so much space just waiting to be utilised. It really is a land of opportunity and exploration.' He laughed. 'It's driving the canaries crazy, they really can't understand why their eon-old proclamations of torture, pain and agony aren't having an effect any more. We like it that we've moved with the times and they're stuck firmly in the Dark Ages and we'd really like to keep it that way.' He gave me a long and meaningful look. 'I think you're a man who knows how to keep his mouth shut.' He turned to face me and slowly pulled one huge cloven hoof along the stone floor. There were sparks.

The threat was clear and I nodded quickly. A month ago I would have been delighted to tell Metatron everything, but now? Well, let's just say that after our last illuminating "discussion" I was open to other options. 'What did you mean about having lots of space?' I stared over my shoulder at the woman as she disappeared down the corridor. Dragging a small, four-wheeled trolley filled, almost to overflowing, with manila files she was in constant danger of trapping her long, scaled tail beneath the wheels. To save herself from the pain of being run over she had to keep it high and out of the way. She looked like an angry cat as she stalked off into the distance. 'You must be close to being full. How many thousands of years have you been taking in our sinners?' I thought about the millions and millions of people that died and as the numbers became ridiculously large, I gave up and settled for "a lot".

Nessus peered around a corner, looked both ways and then stepped out into another hall. 'This place is much, much bigger than you've been told.' He bit his lip for a moment. 'But I'm really not sure that now is the time for a deep and meaningful discussion of the merits and dangers of the alleged human afterlife.' He stopped outside a tall wooden door. 'Ah, here we are.'

I was so completely caught up with his explanation I didn't notice that we'd stopped walking. 'How big?' I persisted.

'It's complicated …' He rubbed a hand over the back of his neck. 'It's not just one place here.' He frowned for a moment and then shrugged. 'There are a lot of places all interlinked and interwoven. I suppose you would call them different worlds or "planes". Pick a place you fancy, there are all sorts: industrial, rural or forests, anything you like.' Nessus looked up and down the corridor then quickly opened the door. 'Come on, we don't have much time and you ask way too many questions.'

I wanted to talk a lot more about this. Within six hours I had gone from being terrified to almost jealous of this place. I needed to know how it all worked. I wanted to look around the stalls, try some of the sweets and the other food. I wanted to go and sit with the old folks and hear what they had to say. I didn't really want to carry on with my mission. I sighed; I really *didn't* want to go into that room.

The smell as we opened the door immediately informed me that we were buried in paper. From the parquet floor to the vaulted ceiling, shelves lined the walls – walls to which there seemed no end.

'Come on.' Nessus walked quickly away down one of the stacks.

'What are we doing here?' I asked.

'This is what you needed to see, wasn't it?' The gatekeeper cast a wary eye over his shoulder and increased his pace slightly. 'Any chance of you moving faster?' His dark brows drew together with a slight look of consternation. 'We've still a fair way to go and I don't want those bloody companions of yours turning up back at the gate and finding you not there. The last thing we need is angry angels zipping through here in a flap.' He broke into a trot.

Jogging and talking don't go well together so I just puffed along in his wake. Finally he couldn't take it any more.

'Come on, useless.' He came to a halt and waited for me to catch up. 'If anybody sees me doing this, I'll never live it down.' Reaching for my arm he threw me up on his back. 'You can hold onto those ridges.' He shook the long mane that flowed between his shoulder blades and then he took off. 'Don't pull my hair.' He shouted over his shoulder. 'That can really hurt.'

I hate horses. They kick at one end, bite at the other and are bloody uncomfortable in the middle. As my buttocks made sharp contact with his back for about the fiftieth time, I realised that if it looks like a horse and moves like a horse, then quite frankly it may as well be a bloody horse and it didn't matter how flaming mystical or mythical it was. After only two minutes, it was painfully obvious that I wasn't going to be walking in a straight line for the next couple of days.

Eventually the plunging, rocking, nausea-inducing ride stopped and Nessus slid to a halt.

I had been gripping his spinal ridge so tightly that I found myself, either unwilling or unable, to swing my leg over his back. Using pure will power, I forced my fingers open one by one and then slithered from his back to lie groaning on the cold stone floor. My backside throbbed, my thighs felt as though someone had been rubbing them with low-grade sandpaper and my fingers, although now open, were white knuckled and stiff.

Reaching down again, Nessus grabbed my jacket and hauled me to my feet. 'Stop being such a big girl's blouse.' He pushed me toward an ancient-looking set of shelves, their contents imprisoned behind ornate, black steel gates. 'Get what you need and be quick about it.' He pulled a key from his bag and opened the lock as quietly as he could. At the final click, he looked over his shoulder, his long ears twitching. 'Be *really* bloody quick about it.'

Pulling the gate open I stared at the hundreds of files on the shelves. 'What am I looking for?' I think my brain must have been shaken about with all the bouncing.

'Oh for the love of ...' Nessus gently poked a large file on the lower shelf with his foot. 'It's that one.' Turning away, he muttered, 'Metatron isn't paying me nearly enough for this.'

"LATIMER. G 1974". The file was the last in a long line marked with similar names. Although "Latimer" had changed over the years, it really hadn't changed that much: Latimarus, Latinier, Latonere, Latinarius and so on. 'This is all the same family?' I asked Nessus.

He nodded. 'These files don't exist anywhere else ... Shh ... listen.' His long ears swivelled backward and forward; a muscle twitched in his shoulder.

After placing the large file carefully into my backpack, I was just about to ask exactly what I was supposed to be listening to when something large dropped from the stacks. Landing heavily on my back it pushed me to the floor with an odd laughing grunt.

'Hello, Lickspittle.' A horribly familiar voice hissed into my ear. 'Having a déjà vu moment, are we?'

Flat on the floor with the demon on top of me, I was trapped. All I could do was watch as two armed centaurs appeared. One was chestnut, his human parts young and blond. A long, heavy chain dangled from his fist. The other was older, a flea-bitten grey, his speckled white coat scarred and dull. His grey hair and beard were long and rough-trimmed. Tanned, weather-beaten and sporting an impressive amount of chest and back hair he held a huge hammer easily in his spade-like hands. He certainly looked the more dangerous of the two.

The fight was short and brutal. As they approached Nessus reared, took a firm grip on his bardiche and screamed a challenge. The brazen roar, echoing around the huge hall of records caused the stacks to shake. Striking out at the nearest assailant he forced the shining silver shod spurs into the back of the scruffy grey. The points sank deep into its fleshy shoulder; blood welled and then ran in a vivid stream down its front leg.

The older beast screamed and twisted, retreating in an effort to dislodge the painful spikes. The grey turned and looked set to run. I quickly found out that I wasn't an expert in reading a horse's body language. Bracing both front feet squarely below his chest, the grey glanced over his shoulder, took aim then lashed out with both back feet. Fast and hard, it was a smashing blow which caught Nessus squarely in the ribs and sent him staggering hard into one of the heavy bookcases. He dropped his weapon as the shelves splintered and cracked, dropping full files and loose sheets onto the floor.

For a couple of moments I couldn't see through the storm of swirling paper.

Quick to seize the opportunity, the younger centaur raced forward, his chain swinging. Without hesitation, he gave a swift flick with the chain; lassoing the heavy links around Nessus's back feet he gave a hefty tug. Discarding his hammer, the grey turned to help and both pulled mightily as they slowly stepped backward. With his back legs useless, Nessus fell to the floor, his arms desperately grabbing at the shattered shelves in an effort to keep upright. Handing the chain to the grinning youngster, the grey walked calmly forward and wrapped another chain around Nessus's front legs. Giving the stricken centaur a judicious look, he swung his hammer and, with almost a gentle blow, brought the great metal head onto the back of my guide's neck. Nessus's eyes fluttered closed and he collapsed onto the pile of splintered wood and crumpled papers at the base of the great shelves.

In the sudden silence the demon on my back laughed. 'So, here we are again.' I had been so caught up with the fight that I'd almost forgotten it was there. Grabbing my hair it banged my face into the floor. I heard the crack as my nose broke and felt the sudden wet warmth as blood flooded my lips and chin. The sudden, sharp agony made my eyes water and I spluttered as blood and tears ran into my mouth.

'No use crying. Take a good look around.' The Drekavak laughed. 'You won't find any dog shit here.' Standing up, it hauled me to my feet. 'They tell me you can't die? I'm willing to test that theory. I'm sure even *you* would have trouble getting your shit back together if I ripped you limb from limb then put each organ into a locked box. Either you wouldn't come back at all or each bit would grow a new you. That could be an interesting experiment.' It pushed me onward by poking a razor-sharp claw into my shoulder.

The Drekavak herded me through a small door at the side of the stacks. Then, keeping a fairly fast pace, it hustled me along down a small, dark corridor. Well, this was just great. Michael was going to kill me for embarrassing him and then Metatron was going to kill me because I didn't return with his file. There wasn't any way I could see myself getting out of this in one piece. Well, if that was the case, I may as well let my mouth of its leash and see exactly how much bedlam I could create.

'Hey, Skippy!' I glanced over my shoulder at the demon stalking along behind me. 'Where are we going?'

'Shut up.' Obviously this guy wasn't much for small-talk.

'What's up with you?' I pressed on. 'Still got dog shit in your ears? Certainly smells that way.' I shrugged and dragged my feet. 'Any minute now you're going to have a flock of angels through here, I take it you're fine with that?'

I ducked and yelped loudly as it stuck its claws deep into my shoulder. Tripping over my own feet I crashed to the floor. Without any emotion the demon kicked me, raking its long back claws down my thigh.

That hurt! So I didn't feel too bad about squealing loudly and crab-walking backward, trying my best to get away from the expressionless creature.

'Damn!' The beastie studied its paw – one claw dangled at an odd angle. Busy with its broken nail the demon ignored me.

Scuttling into the shadows in a corner of the passage I pressed my back to the wall. I reckoned I had one small chance and, fumbling in my pockets, I waited, frustrated, for both 'dusters to grip my hands, then quickly reached over my head to grab my knife.

Encumbered by bone-covered fingers, I fumbled the knife and yelped in irritation as it threatened to slip.

The demon swivelled toward me. 'Are you in pain?' It hissed a laugh. 'Good!' It stepped toward me.

Twisting to one side I swung a fist and made good contact with one of its knees. There was a satisfying snap as it screamed and toppled over.

Concentrating on keeping a firm grip on my knife, I scrambled to my feet then faced the enraged creature. Favouring its leg only slightly, it came for me. As it lunged, claws out, I ducked and, stooping below its arm, brought up the knife intending to go for its throat. The knife slipped, I missed and, slashing wildly, only managed a deep graze to the flesh of its breast.

The demon screamed. Smoke and black ichor erupted from the shallow wound. Eyes wide with surprise and pain it slid slowly down the wall, its breaths coming in shallow, ragged gasps.

I didn't hang around to find out how it fared – I ran.

Once out of sight of the demon I paused. Should I try to save Nessus? I dithered for a moment before self-preservation reasserted itself. He knew the dangers; I was sorry to lose him but there was nothing I could do.

Over the last thousand years or so I've developed a fairly good sense of direction and it only took me about five minutes to get back to the market. I trotted carefully through the crowds. Head down, I tried to make myself as small and as insignificant as I could. Ahead was the exit to the passageways and, hoping I could remember all the turns Nessus had made, I lengthened my stride. I'd never wanted to see Michael so much in all my very, very long life.

The two angels were standing with a small creature that looked to be the product of a fox and a human. Its big amber eyes and long ears twitched toward me as I ran over to them then stood, hands on knees, gasping and wheezing, trying to force air back into my lungs.

'Are you all right, Joe?' Raphael put his hand on my back. 'What happened to you? Where's Nessus?'

I swear my mouth actually formed the shapes for a dozen different words but in the end I opted for silence.

Michael stared over my shoulder with a frown. 'What have you been up to?' he asked.

'What I was told.' I glanced up at him and gulped as I saw his lips thin.

'Come on, Michael.' Raphael grasped his arm. 'Metatron didn't tell us what Joe was supposed to do – don't force him into spilling the beans.' He gave me a sly wink. 'Is it time to go?'

I nodded rapidly and suppressed the urge to check over my shoulder for pursuers.

The little creature's nostrils twitched. 'It's bleeding.'

Raphael gently turned me around and studied the wet rip in the shoulder of my jacket then raised an eyebrow.

I shrugged. 'Must have caught it on something,' I said. Come on, guys, I thought, we really have to go. I imagined that I could hear faint shouting on the wind.

Raphael narrowed his eyes and stared at me, then, with a slight shake of his head he turned to smile at Michael and the other angels. 'Right,' he said. 'All present and correct, let's head for home, shall we?'

Back in Metatron's office I sighed and slumped onto the carpet, then, finding even that soft haven unstable, I collapsed onto my back and closed my eyes. I had entered the lift in Hell with everyone else but I'd turned up here alone. I wasn't unhappy about it. Eventually, I hauled myself to my feet and wandered over to Metatron's desk. Pulling the file from my backpack I was tempted to read it. Shaking my head, I kept it firmly closed. I could almost guarantee that, the moment I opened the first page, the boss would turn up and catch me with my hand in the cookie jar. Where was he anyway? This was something he wanted a great deal, so why wasn't he here? I needed to talk to him. Fed up with waiting in the silence, I placed the file on his desk. As soon as I'd removed my hand the floor disappeared and I was back in my living room. It took me less than two minutes to get to bed.

# CHAPTER 4

ARE SUNDAY MORNINGS SPECIAL because even God took the day off or did God take the day off because they were already special? That question, like the chicken and the egg, went around and around in my mind as I lay snuggled up in bed the next morning. I was desperately trying to put off that moment when I would *have* to put my feet on the cold floor. Rolling over, I stared at the clock. 10.30 a.m. ... check. Sun shining ... check. Still alive ... oh definitely check.

I ran my tongue over my teeth and grimaced. Was that sulphur? I was fairly sure a good scrubbing would take care of the disgusting taste in my mouth and, if that failed, a double-decker bacon sandwich with cheese and ketchup would do the job.

Half an hour later I was back in bed with a tray that held the ultimate breakfast: a pot of tea, the aforementioned bacon sandwich, a bowl of Häagen-Dazs' finest and a book of World War Two poetry. Pausing only to settle my pillows around me, I took a gulp of hot tea and opened the book at the first page. I fully intended to stay there till noon.

Twenty minutes later, I slapped the book, unread, down onto the bed. My ice cream had melted and the sandwich, its melted cheese oozing from the one bite I'd managed to choke down, had coagulated into a greasy mass. The image of a centaur, chains wrapped tightly about his legs, arms twisted up behind his back and blood oozing from the back of his neck just sat in my mind, blocking out everything else. I went over it again and again looking for something I missed – some way I could have helped. I closed my eyes and deliberately remembered each and every second of that fight; there really was nothing I could have done.

One little comment kept coming back to me. Something

Nessus had said about Metatron not paying him enough. Having given myself a headache, I decided that ignoring the small voice of my conscience would probably be better for my health and that I'd leave it all to the big guns to sort out. It wasn't my problem. I'd followed my orders and been successful – that was all that mattered. If Nessus was playing off both sides then that was his choice. I punched my pillows then. Pulling the quilt over my head to keep out the cheerful morning sunshine and any form of guilt-induced insomnia, I went back to sleep.

The alarm went off for a second time at 12.30 p.m. and, after hitting the snooze button twice, I had only just enough time to get dressed before I was due next door. Throwing myself out of bed, I sent the forgotten tray and its contents flying. Dragging the quilt off the bed I threw it in the corner of the room. Damn it all, I'd clean that up later.

After a quick shower and a rather perfunctory shave, I shot downstairs and, grabbing the bottle of wine that I'd bought at the shop yesterday (good God, was it really only yesterday?), I staggered toward the front door. Before leaving I did the usual checks: matching socks, flies done up, mobile and 'dusters in pocket and knife between the shoulder blades – check, check and check. I was as organised as I was ever going to get. Lying on the hall table was a small bunch of flowers; I'd forgotten to put them in water. I turned them upside down in an effort to make them look healthier. No chance. I shrugged and dashed back to the kitchen, searching feverishly for the chocolates I'd also bought. Even a girl you've known for years needs more than hidden knuckle-dusters and slightly dehydrated carnations.

Shrugging my shoulders just to make sure my knife was settled, I gathered up the slightly embarrassing gifts and headed out into the sunshine.

Hopping the fence, I wended my way through Carly's "garden art" and, pausing only to run my hands through my hair and rub a finger over my teeth, I knocked on her bright red front door.

'Hey, Joe.' My neighbour looked as gorgeous as ever.

'Didn't realise you'd be here so early.' The green towel, desperately attempting to contain her mass of wet hair, failed at that moment; one end snaked free and made a bid for freedom.

'Erm … Here.' I pushed the wine, chocolates and flowers toward her. I could feel my face heating up.

'Thanks.' She couldn't actually take them as her hands were busy tucking the towel back around her head. 'Come on in.' She grabbed at the flapping corner and tucked it into another fold, then deftly snagged the wine and chocolates with a grin. 'I think I'll take these before you decide you need them for Dutch courage.' She turned and headed back into the house leaving me on the doorstep holding the bunch of wilting flowers. 'Come on, gooseberry, don't just stand there,' she shouted from the kitchen. 'I need your views on my latest creation.'

Carly was a much better interior designer than I could ever hope to be. My house looked exactly what it was: a sleeping base for a bachelor book fanatic with a bad diet. Carly's looked … cosy, lived in and, despite the shape of the rooms being a mirror image of my own, she had made this a *home*. It was obvious that she loved and cared for her property. I'd often considered paying her to decorate mine.

For numbers, our book collections almost matched and her shelves had come from the same Swedish furniture store. That, however, was pretty much where the similarities ended. Carefully positioned between the contents of her library were little ornaments, each representing a cherished memory. No china poodles for Carly; everything was natural wood or stone. Figurines, bowls and boxes, every one lovingly carried back from far-off places by travelling friends, or found in little craft fairs. Some had even been created just for her by other artists. Each piece nestled happily in its perfect place between huge tomes of medicinal herbalism, feng shui, glass art and myriad other strange titles – each dedicated to enriching its owner's life in some small way. To complete the feeling of warmth and homeliness, the whole room glowed. Multicoloured shadows moved with the sun over the walls; pastel ghosts of the stained-glass tree that spread deep green leaves across the top of her bay window. The solitary red apple that hung from its branches created a fuzzy sniper's spot that slowly tracked across the books, sluggishly threatening each ornament in turn as the day progressed.

Carly's own paintings hid the magnolia of the walls. Each vibrant, colourful canvas expertly illuminated by a small spotlight, I studied them every time I visited. She may have been a bad gardener but she really was an excellent artist. Concentrating on alternative and esoteric urban settings, she was usually employed by big record companies or by publishing houses; her work was always in demand.

While she rattled around in the kitchen, tutting over the state of the flowers, I stared at my favourite painting, hoping to find yet another tiny detail that I'd so far managed to miss. This one had been commissioned as a book cover; the story had followed the short, disturbed lives of urban fairies. Forced to live as humans, they seemed to spend most of their time mourning the loss of a lifestyle that should have been theirs. The book hadn't really been that good but it had sold very well. I harboured my suspicions that its beautiful cover had played a large part in the sales.

The painting showed a skinny Goth girl sitting, smoking, on the edge of a crumbling and deserted quay, a half-empty bottle of whisky at her side. She stared out to sea, smiling slightly at the ghostly shadows of dolphins, sirens and kelpies which plunged through the foaming water. There was a hint of flippers around her huge boots and her expression was one of pure longing. I could look at it for hours.

'Here.' A hand holding a glass of red wine broke my gaze with the painting. 'Hey, this isn't bad at all,' Carly laughed, licking her lips, 'I take it this isn't one of those three pound bottles of plonk that you normally drink.'

I took a sip and shrugged – all wine tasted the same to me. 'You told me to get something good,' I said. 'The one thing I can do is follow orders.' Looking up at her, my breath caught and I had trouble swallowing my wine. She had changed into a long rust-coloured skirt and had thrown a man's dark green silk shirt over a black vest top. With her long red hair hanging in mad curls and spirals, she could have just slipped into any of her fairy paintings and not looked out of place at all. 'Wow. You look gorgeous.' I downed the rest of my wine to hide my embarrassment then waggled the empty glass at her. 'Very Botticelli. Any chance of another?'

'Not if you're going to compare me to a Botticelli,' she sniffed and pointedly ignored my glass. 'That's way too stuffy.'

I hunted around in my head for any other artist. Finally I grasped at a name, I couldn't remember exactly what he'd painted but I'm fairly sure that he was also a fan of redheads. 'Erm … definitely a Rossetti?' I winced, waiting for my ear to get twisted. But Carly gave me a huge grin.

'That's much better, fiery with the promise of sex.' She grabbed the glass and sashayed off toward the kitchen leaving me stunned behind her. 'I like it!' she yelled over her shoulder.

Slightly shocked, I stood with my mouth open.

After refilling my glass, she wandered over to a large easel. A paint-stained dustsheet, which billowed occasionally in the slight breeze from the open window that looked out over her back garden, covered the canvas. She lifted one corner of the sheet; her lip caught between her teeth then paused.

'Well, come on, don't keep me in suspense.' Carly wasn't usually shy about showing off her work; I must have seen dozens of her paintings over the years. 'Don't tell me, let me guess, you've decided that an abstract square is really what it's all about.'

'What? No!' Carly looked down at her hands, studying her paint-flecked fingernails. 'It's just that I got this commission to do a CD cover for a band called The Scourge. They had a very definite spec.' She wafted the sheet as she thought about it. 'Normally I would have turned it down but I got this idea which just wouldn't go away, so I accepted.' She sighed and, letting go of the sheet, twisted her hands together. 'Now I'm wondering if I've got the whole thing really, really wrong.'

I shrugged and waited patiently to see her latest work.

The silence stretched on as Carly examined her motives for accepting the job. Finally she sighed and, without another word, whipped away the sheet.

Staring at the revealed painting, I could feel that my mouth was hanging open but I just didn't have the willpower to close it.

Rendered in tones of blue and grey, a desolate and destroyed city stretched away into the distance. Smoke and dust from the burning and toppled buildings obscured the sun, giving the whole painting a hazy, foggy look. Bodies and trashed cars littered the street. Scruffy dogs nosed amongst the rubble; they seemed to ignore the young woman that was huddled in a shop doorway, eyes blank as she gazed out of the canvas, her thin fingers picking at the stitched yellow bunny in the corner of a small pink blanket. In the foreground, a mound of human dead had been piled high … no, wait, the dead weren't all human. I took a step forward and closely studied the faces in the painting – there were demon corpses in the pile as well and what appeared to be a small, dead kangaroo.

'You hate it, don't you?' Carly moved as if to bring the sheet back down.

'No! Shh, I'm trying to look.' I was probably a bit more abrupt than I should have been. Carly raised her eyebrows and stepped back.

There, just there! I leant in close to check the face. That was the demon I'd seen in the market – she'd been buying sweets, which had made me smile at the time. Her short white dress had shifted slowly as though in water and, when she'd turned to look at me, her long black hair had moved in the same way; the languid movements made her appear slightly out of time with everyone else. Her face was long and thin with lines of swirling blue tattoos that ran from the bridge of her nose down both cheeks to meet in a point at her chin. Catching me staring, she had given me a sultry smile revealing pointed white teeth which promised all sorts of beautiful pain. Then, dismissing me with a laugh, she had turned back to her perusal of the sweet stall.

In the painting, her hair hung limp and bedraggled, trodden into the black mud beneath the pyramid of dead. Her white dress was ripped, exposing one small torn breast. Open and pale among the dark tattoos, her clouded eyes stared vacantly into mine. Nauseated, I studied the rest of the dead; thankfully that was the only face I recognised.

Standing atop the mound, a spectacular angel held one fist above his head and bellowed his triumph into the whirling vortex of dark splashes that formed the sky. In the other he held a sword that dripped blue and white flame; it spread along the ground burning all things in its path. The angel's silver and white armour, battered and bloody, partially reflected both the fire and the dead. Wings spread wide and head thrown back, his hair slicked into a long dark tail, the angel screamed with a savage and uncontrollable joy. A cold finger of fear gently lifted the hairs on the back of my neck. There was no doubt at all: Carly had managed to capture Michael perfectly.

'Do you think he'll mind?' Carly looked worried, rubbing her hands together.

I shook my head. I was having trouble breathing.

'I saw him outside your house one day; he had the most amazing face and I just remembered it when I was painting.' She shrugged. 'Joe, say something, is it really that bad?'

I pulled myself together and turned to face her. 'You saw him outside my house?'

She nodded. 'Yeah, a couple of years ago, I thought he was a friend of yours.' She frowned. 'He was with another man, long blond hair, both dressed in black suits. Oh my God.' She put a hand to her mouth. 'He *is* a friend of yours, isn't he? I haven't just painted in some random evangelist or double-glazing salesman, have I?'

Swallowing hard I forced a laugh. 'I have no idea.' I needed to change the subject. 'What's the album called?'

She rolled her eyes and pulled the dust sheet back over the painting. '*Rage Against Restriction* or some such crap.'

Pushing past me she headed for the kitchen. 'Maybe, one of these days, I'll be asked to work for a band that isn't convinced the world's going to end in fire and pain.' She stuck her head back round the door. 'You know, some nice folk band.'

I laughed. 'Have you ever listened to folk music?' I leant on the door frame. 'Let's face it, a lot of folk music is all about dead sailors, mad witches, rape and fratricide. Most of it really isn't big on the cheerful stuff.'

'Hmm.' Carly stuck her head into one of the cupboards and began pulling out ingredients for a meal: lentils, beans and vegetables. I indulged in a moment's guilty reminiscence about the bacon butty I'd abandoned earlier. 'So, come on, what did you think of it?' She paused with her head still in the cupboard. 'I can take a bit of criticism, you know.' Standing up, she stood with one hip against the oven, her lip caught between her teeth; obviously she wasn't expecting a good review.

Putting my glass down, I crossed the tiny kitchen to give her a hug. 'Your painting is exactly what you intended it to be: slightly disturbing.' I thought back to what I'd seen. 'No, scratch that, it's extremely worrying. It's also beautifully painted, eye catching and will delight the record company. I can see this one being made into a poster; it will sell in its thousands.'

Carly reached up and held my face in both hands. With a smile she gave me a little shake then kissed me on the nose. 'You are a definite smooth talker,' she laughed. 'But I'm not going to argue with you. I keep it covered up because even I can't bear to look at it for long; it actually upsets me to think I could paint something that dark.'

For a moment we stared at each other and, just as I had worked myself up to take the opportunity to kiss her, she pushed me away. 'Go and read a book or something, I can't cook with you hovering about like a bad smell.'

'Gee, thanks.' Pausing only long enough to top up my glass, I scooted out of the kitchen and headed back to the living room. Avoiding the painting, (I told myself that I couldn't really see moving shadows beneath the dust sheet.) I picked up a random book and then flopped onto Carly's squishy deep green sofa with a sigh.

I tried to read, I really did, but the wine, deep sofa and the warm afternoon sun conspired against me and, within seconds, I had slipped away into the dark.

Despite my moans about the lack of protein in Carly's cooking, dinner was wonderful and, after lingering over Irish coffee, we finally headed back to the sofa.

'Fancy watching a film?' Carly asked. 'If you can stay awake long enough?' She pinched my arm.

I winced; Carly had pinched me awake for the meal and had taken great delight in pointing out the wet drool patch on one of her cushions. 'Sure,' I yawned, 'but nothing too deep and meaningful. I don't know what you put in those coffees of yours but I feel quite floaty.'

Carly pushed a silver disc into the side of the TV then, kicking off her clogs, collapsed beside me. One foot tucked under her thigh, the other pushed deep into the huge multicoloured rug that took pride of place in her living room. Leaning against me, she lifted one of my arms and draped it over her shoulder.

'Conan the Barbarian?' I whinged. 'Really? Wasn't there anything else you fancied?'

Carly laughed then put her hand over her mouth as she burped gently. 'Oh dear, in this state, I'd probably fancy anything.'

'What, even me?' I just couldn't resist pushing my luck.

'Oh I've always fancied you.' She turned to look at me; her face was very close to mine. 'I've just never done anything about it because you live next door and I didn't want to lose a good neighbour.'

'Oh ...' Tucked under my arm, she couldn't really get away. Taking advantage of that, I leant closer until our lips were no more than millimetres apart. 'Well, I certainly wouldn't want to lose all those cakes.' I chose to ignore the part of my brain that was screaming this was a bad idea for oh so many reasons. Closing the gap I pressed my lips to hers. She sighed and pressed closer, her tongue flicking out to run along the underside of my upper lip.

Gathering her up, I slid forward then turned to lay her down with her head on the cushion, still warm from where I'd been sitting. She giggled and raised her eyebrows at me. The little voice was now silent, pushed aside in a wave of expectation. Leaning forward I kissed her again, happy when she snaked her arms around my neck, pulling me deeper into the kiss. She smelled of summer: watermelons, coconut and was that a slight hint of rotten eggs?

There is always that awkward little moment when you try to work out whether this is just kissing or kissing leading to more. I was pretty confident that we were heading toward more, so sneaking my hand between us, I began to undo the buttons on her shirt.

Carly screamed: OK, I had *definitely* read those signals wrong. Leaping up, I began to apologise but she stared past me and continued to scream, her eyes wide and her fists clenched at her sides

I think I managed to say 'Wha–' before being physically ripped backwards and dumped, hard, onto the floor. Drunk and slightly confused from the overload of hormones, I rolled and managed to get to my hands and knees. I was getting fed up with being dumped onto the floor; it was happening so often that I was beginning to feel like a family dog that wasn't allowed on the sofa.

Two demons stood in the living room. One was Drekavak, the other a species I wasn't familiar with: tall, heavily built and the colour of a week-dead corpse. It had a long thin face with vaguely human features – if humans had the eyes of a cat and necks wider than their heads. Unlike the Drekavak it was dressed in an expensive-looking suit, blue with a faint pinstripe, which matched the grey T-shirt beneath. Long, thin, bare feet protruded from the trouser bottoms, the nails painted black and filed to a point.

Reaching for my 'dusters I decided that I really was the most stupid man on earth. Even though I'd actually stopped to pick up some formidable weaponry, I'd left my coat in the hall. Reaching behind me, I went for my knife.

'Don't do that.' The white demon had a deep voice. 'It's unlikely you'd get to it before he ...' he pointed to the Drekavak '... got to her.' The Drekavak smiled and ran a gentle claw through Carly's hair. Grabbing my unresisting arm, the white demon pushed me face down onto the floor. 'Stay still. We're just here to deliver a message and pick up a take-away,' he said. 'You took something that wasn't yours.' Bringing his face very close to my head he whispered into my ear. 'We want it back. We also want the box that you delivered to Metatron.'

It looked up and nodded to the other demon, who gave that little hissing laugh again. Then, grabbing a limp and traumatised Carly, he hauled her to her feet, cuddling her against his pale, scaled chest. 'That was my sister you stabbed.' It stopped laughing and ran a single claw down Carly's arm; a thin line of claret followed in its wake.

Sister? I couldn't really say much to that as my mouth was pushed into the deep pile of the rug.

'She's not dead yet, but I think she wishes she was.' The Drekavak paused to give Carly a little shake. She whimpered and kept her eyes tight shut. 'That fucking knife of yours is really something.' He reached up a paw and tenderly pushed Carly's hair away from her face. She shuddered, making small and intense mewling sounds. 'Hush now,' the demon whispered in her ear. Her eyes widened and the colour left her face, leaving her hair and lips livid.

'Go on, take her away.' The white demon nodded at his partner. 'Remember, we need her.'

Nodding, the Drekavak tightened its grip on Carly's arm then vanished.

Panicked beyond all reason I struggled to get my face off the floor. 'Noooo!'

The hand disappeared from my neck. 'You know what we want.' It felt as though it had hit me with a brick and everything faded to black.

When I finally woke up, the film credits were rolling and Arnie was heading off into the sunset – sad, hurt and minus the girl. I knew how he felt. Getting to my feet actually took three attempts as there appeared to be a large egg attached to the base of my skull; it was obviously pulling me off balance. 'I've got to stop getting smacked over the head.' I whinged at Arnie; he didn't care, he had troubles of his own. 'Eventually I'm just going to be one big lump.'

Staggering into the kitchen, I splashed my face with cold water, wincing at the bright red vortex that ran around the plughole. Holding a cold, wet tea towel hard against my lump, I spent a couple of minutes hunting for pain killers.

'What the hell am I going to do now?' Washing the tablets down with water, I shouted at Carly's little platoon of spider plants that drooped in healthy green splendour all over the top of her fridge. Sliding onto the floor I waited impatiently for the throbbing to subside.

Eventually, I could turn my head without hearing bells. I moaned a lot about being indestructible but, just occasionally, that ability to heal was a real blessing. I stared at my reflection in the window, a sick face made even paler by the darkness of the night outside. Finally making a decision, I took out my mobile phone and, with a couple of deep breaths, prepared to do something I had never even considered before: I was going to call the boss.

Metatron had always contacted me – I couldn't think of one instance in over a thousand years where I'd called him. I dialled the number and waited for it to connect. Within seconds I found myself standing in the darkness by the side of a road, somewhere out in the country. The weather certainly wasn't what it had been in Birmingham and, battered by almost horizontal rain, I squinted as I looked around.

'Joe?' Metatron emerged from among the trees. He looked surprised. 'I was just about to call you.' He gave me his usual huge smile then turned me around to face the other way. 'Excellent timing as usual, dear boy, come on we need to stop this car.'

'What?' Completely confused, I stared into the darkness. In the distance I could just make out the twin pinprick lights of an oncoming car. Wind-driven rain occasionally blurred them into bright lines but, even so, they seemed to be growing at an alarming rate.

'Metatron!' I squinted into the deluge, choking as water ran into my mouth, 'I've got a real problem. I was with my next-door neighbour and …' I stopped as the boss held up a hand as he stared off into the distance watching the car draw closer.

'I know all about it.' Metatron frowned as he studied the oncoming vehicle. 'Don't worry, it'll be fine.'

I breathed a sigh of relief.

'Right come on.' Metatron grabbed my arm and pulled me into the middle of the road. I could hear the car's engine, its note high pitched and strained as it tore toward us.

I tried to edge away but Metatron controlled my wrist and held me still. 'What are we supposed to be doing?' I swallowed hard as the lights grew bigger and bigger.

'Just standing here.' Metatron seemed totally relaxed. 'Hopefully Mr Latimer will see us *before* he runs us down.'

'Hopefully?' I braced myself for yet another death or, at the very least, a vast amount of broken bones. My brain gave me a little nudge – *Latimer* – didn't I know that name from somewhere? My rising panic stopped me from thinking clearly.

Metatron stood solidly in the centre of the road and watched with a wide smile as the big 4x4 bore down on us. I cringed behind him. I had just got to the point of screaming and ducking, when the big car violently changed direction. Unable to gain purchase on the rain-slick tarmac, it slid in a wide arc, the spinning wheels sending up a fountain of muddy water. Finally finding purchase in the gutter, it careered off the road, and plunged into the undergrowth.

'Tch!' The diminutive angel sighed and began to brush small flecks of mud from his suit jacket with a look of distaste. Looking up with a frown, he watched the car bounce and crash a trail through the bushes and grass, finally hammering into a tall tree about ten metres away. He winced, then laughed as the bonnet collapsed, allowing the crumpled wings to pull the tree into an aggressive embrace.

For a moment there was silence – even the wind and rain seemed to still. Finally, with a sort of loud "whoomph", the car exploded in light and fury sending a bright fireball high into the branches above. The burning air evaporated the rain and replaced each drop with flaming, distorted leaves from the instantly blazing tree: autumn in Hell.

Metatron gave a short laugh at the sight of the car wrapped around the trunk of the old oak. 'Bloody tree huggers.' He clapped me on the shoulder. 'Nice job, Joe, I thought for a moment he wasn't going to see us. It could have been a little embarrassing if I'd had to scrape you off the road and take you back in a jar.'

I stared at the wreckage for a moment. Still occasionally visible within the flames was the red glow of the tail lights. While we watched, these flickered then died as car and tree became one roaring beacon of flame.

The boss turned toward me and rolled his eyes as he noticed the state of his polished brown brogues – they were soaked through. 'These are never going to be the same again,' he said. Turning, he began to walk toward the wreck, stepping over small fires that were breaking out in the undergrowth as the burning rain continued. 'I suppose we'd better get him out, hadn't we.'

Ignoring the rage of flames, Metatron reached in through the shattered driver's window then, smiling, he breathed a sigh of relief. 'Well, I managed to catch him in time, look.' Surrounded by fire, melting plastic and tortured metal, a dark-haired, slightly doughy, middle-aged man slept, his face composed.

'Get him out please, Joe – and don't worry, fire won't touch you,' Metatron said. 'I'll just make another one.'

'Another what – fire?' I asked but Metatron didn't answer so, shrugging, I dragged open the door. I was about to use my knife to cut the seatbelt when Metatron looked up. 'Don't do that, please, it will look odd if the belts have been cut. It's the sort of thing that makes the police nervous and I need this death to be worry free.'

I hesitated. The flames were fierce and, although I wasn't burning, it was incredibly hot. Eventually, I took a deep breath then reached across and unlocked the seatbelt. Dragging the man from the car, I carried him to the side of the road and lay him in the smoking grass. He seemed all right – asleep, but still breathing. Leaving him there I went to find Metatron.

He was working on what appeared to be a shop mannequin. The blank grey form was rapidly filling out and becoming the double of the man sleeping peacefully in the bushes only a couple of metres away. I'd seen him create these before; he called them "constructs" – human forms with no will or personality. They always freaked the shit out of me. It stood eerily still as Metatron fussed over the finishing touches, occasionally consulting a set of notes. Finally, he was satisfied with his creation. 'There we go, the dental records will match and I've put fingerprints on him as well, just in case.' He studied his handiwork for a moment. 'Put him in the car, please, Joe.' He sniffed and stared at the pale, dead-looking human form with a look of distaste. 'It's really only the soul and the personality that makes you lot interesting, isn't it?' He paused for a moment. 'Without those, you're just lumps of putty.'

Grasping the form by the wrist, I gave a gentle tug. The being turned and looked at me blankly then followed with mute incomprehension. I felt slightly sick – as though I was being trailed by a corpse. I manoeuvred the man form into the car and then relocked the seatbelt around its chest. As I drew back, I looked into its eyes and saw fear. It turned slowly, watching the flames then, as I backed away, it opened its mouth in a silent scream.

I turned to Metatron. 'Why is it screaming? It doesn't feel anything, does it?' I watched in horror as flames filled the car. The form twisted and howled within.

'Calm down.' Metatron studied the burning car. 'Only enough that there will be some sort of emotion on its face.' He shook his head. 'Come on, it wouldn't look right if it was just sitting there looking composed now, would it?'

I spluttered and felt sick. 'Metatron, that's monstrous!' I turned and looked at the construct. It had raised both hands and was banging on the window; I stared into its eyes before they dissolved into the flames.

'Don't be pathetic,' Metatron said. 'It's really important that we get this man away from here; it was only a little pain, and it didn't last long.' He paused again, studying the inside of the burning car. 'Give it ten minutes and it will all be over, we are doing a good thing here, Joe, and if there's a tiny bit of collateral damage, well, it's certainly outweighed by the good we're doing.' He shrugged – obviously this didn't bother him at all.

As we stood, watching the car burn, I wondered who was this good for. Certainly not for the man unconscious in the bushes; certainly not for the poor created thing that was currently burning in the car. I sighed and looked up; the tree wasn't having a very good day either, so exactly who or what did this benefit?

Eventually, the boss decided that it was time to move and, stepping through the blackened and soaking grass, he headed back toward the car. Once again, ignoring the rage of flames, he reached in through one of the smashed windows. Then, looking more weary than disgusted, he hooked a finger into the jaw bone of the smouldering skull and turned it to face him. All that was left was bone and blackened morsels of skin. Eye sockets, boiled dry, contained only evil-smelling smoke and withered tissue. Teeth clenched together in pain, now parted abruptly as tendons gave way under intense heat and the probing finger. The lower jaw fell into his hand and he laughed before placing it carefully into the corpse's lap. 'Hmm, looks like I didn't actually need to worry about that thing's facial expression after all.' Metatron sniggered.

It wasn't a "that", it was a "he" – even if only for a few moments. Creating something just to torture it … My thoughts scattered; this wasn't right. I'd just been involved in causing something a huge amount of unnecessary agony and felt as guilty as if I'd tied bricks to a puppy, then kicked it into a pond. Gathering up the sleeping man I half-carried him, half-dragged him over to the middle of the road. I concentrated on pushing my treacherous thoughts firmly away as I walked. Metatron knew what he was doing and, even if he was playing it a little rough, I certainly didn't have the nerve to question his motives; I had way too much to lose.

As flashing blue lights lit the distant horizon we all stood in a line, the unconscious supported by the conscious. Then, as a slender gap slid aside in the world, we stepped through and away from the wind and rain. The fire brigade arrived just as the door closed with a slight chime; I was sure it would go completely unnoticed as the humans concentrated on Metatron's latest masterpiece.

'Put him down there.' Metatron nodded toward an elegant blue divan – a new piece of furniture to grace his office.

I placed the unconscious man on the sofa and stared as I had that "Eureka!" moment and realised why I knew his name. I studied the paunchy, mousey man. I couldn't help being unimpressed. Graham Latimer was about 40 years old and running slightly to fat. His hair – both thinning and greying – hung over a prematurely wrinkled forehead and his skin looked as though it hadn't seen the sun in about 20 years. I glanced up the painting on the ceiling. The angry falling angel – the most evil and uncontrollable of God's creations – had absolutely nothing in common with the unconscious man in the cheap blue suit. Obviously artistic licence had no limits at all. 'So this is Lucifer?' I asked.

Metatron appeared at my shoulder and we both stared down at the sleeping man. 'Not yet.' He gently picked up one of Graham's arms that had flopped onto the carpet and placed it on the rhythmically rising and falling chest. 'But I know he's in there.' He stepped forward and roughly prised one eyelid open; a blank green eye stared off into the distance. 'I *know* you're in there.' He muttered. He let the eyelid fall and stood up. 'And I know the way to get you out.'

Turning back to his desk, he pulled out two cut-glass tumblers and a decanter of golden whisky. Pouring two measures, he pushed one across the desk to me. 'What's the matter, Joe?' He took a sip and stared at me over the rim of the glass. 'You know what we have to do.'

I sat down and picked up my glass, turning it this way and that as I watched the light sparkle off the facets, turning the whisky to liquid fire. 'How many humans are in heaven?' I asked.

Metatron frowned. 'Thousands, why?'

'Thousands, is that all?' I had at least expected him to say millions. 'What do they do there?'

'Do?' Metatron stood up and went to have another look at his sleeping guest. He obviously wasn't really concentrating on me. 'I don't know,' he shrugged. 'Serve the Host, sing, they're treated like children.' He shrugged again. 'Pampered and played with.'

I shuddered. 'When was the last time a human entered the kingdom of Heaven?'

'What?' He kept staring at the unconscious man, as though his very will could drag the Morning Star from his fleshy hiding place. 'Oh I don't know, what's with all the questions?' Turning away from his studies he frowned at me.

I decided it was time for a little vacant eye widening. 'Have you been to Hell?'

Metatron shook his head. 'No thank you,' he said. 'I try and stay out of the gutter if I can possibly help it.'

'It's teeming with terrified people and all sorts of other things.' I took a sip of my drink and assumed a righteous expression. 'You know if people could only see that place, they'd be a lot more willing to make the effort to get into Heaven.'

The small angel's shoulders relaxed and he smiled. 'I know where this is going.' He laughed and settled back down in his chair. 'Stop worrying, I told you before and I won't go back on my promise. If this all goes well this will be the very last job you ever do for me.'

I smiled inanely up at him. My teeth and cheeks were beginning to ache. 'I can go on? I can finally really stop?'

Metatron nodded and, reaching over, patted me on the wrist. 'Well, you certainly deserve that "final reward", don't you?'

Metatron relaxed enough to pour another drink. 'Here look at this.' He reached into a drawer and brought out the white box that I'd collected from Worcester. He stared at me for a moment then shrugged. 'You are probably the only human to see this in the last 500 years and know – *really know* – what it is.' He turned the box to face me.

It was my knife, well … it's what my knife would have looked like if it hadn't been decorated, polished and loved. The unadorned grey metal gave off no reflection and lay in the box as though diseased. Feeling a little sick, I reached over, intending to remove the velvet that covered the hilt, Metatron stopped me.

'Not a good idea,' he said. 'It's not really a nice thing.'

'Is that …' There was only one knife in the whole of history that could ever give off that sort of sullen threat. It may have looked similar to mine, but it was so very, very different. I certainly wouldn't try to cut cake with that; it would probably reverse itself and cut the throat of anyone that tried.

Metatron turned the box then, and after fumbling around in it for a moment, closed the lid with a snap. He placed it carefully back into his drawer. 'Horrible, isn't it?' He chuckled at my reaction.

I nodded. I hadn't even touched it and I felt slightly dirty, as though I'd been walking through thick smog.

'That knife is the one artefact that can drag Lucifer, kicking and screaming, back into the light.' Metatron took a huge swig of whisky and laughed. 'Do you know what, Joe?' He topped my glass up. 'I'm suddenly in a very good mood.'

I didn't want to talk about Lucifer or the knife any more. So as he was, as he said, in a good mood, maybe now would be a good time to ask that final big question. Taking a good mouthful of whisky, I swallowed. 'So can I leave now?'

Metatron looked up and waved. 'Sure, I'll call when I need you.' He nodded. 'Go and get some sleep, you probably need it.'

'No.' I took another sip. 'I mean, now that you've got all

that you want, can I go? Really go?' I took a deep breath and finally managed to say the words. 'I want this all to stop. I want peace.'

Metatron frowned. 'Very soon.' He nodded toward the sleeping insurance salesman. 'Just let me get this business tied up and I swear that you'll be out of here.'

I sighed.

'Don't be selfish, Joe.' Metatron looked hurt. 'I've spent eons working toward this. Are you telling me you want to leave before you find out how it all ends?'

I shook my head. 'No, of course not.'

Metatron gave me the sunniest of his smiles.

My stomach turned over. That little voice was getting too loud to ignore, and it was telling me that if I asked the right questions and he gave me the answer I was expecting, my whole life – my whole campaign to pay off my debt of sin – would be proved a farce. There was a distinct possibility that I would have to face the very unwelcome fact that, for the last 2,000 years, I had been nothing but a deluded fool.

'So what happened to Nessus?' I reached out and flipped open the top page of the manila file I'd retrieved from Hell.

He reached over and put a hand on top of the folder. Then, still smiling, he closed it. Taking it away, he carefully put it in his drawer with the knife box. 'Who?' He frowned for a moment. 'Oh the gatekeeper, it was clever of you to get him to help you. Really, well done.'

OK, no clues there. He was just sidestepping ever having dealt with him. I switched tack. 'Do you remember me telling you about my next-door neighbour?'

'Some sort of mad artist type, isn't she?' He poured himself another drink and settled deep within the red cushions of his chair, then he stared at me, expressionless.

I nodded. 'They took her last night and you said you knew about it. Two demons turned up, smashed me over the head and took her as a Hostage; they wanted that file and the box.' I jabbed a finger towards his desk drawer. 'You said it would be OK. So is she at home?'

'I'm sorry, Joe, I didn't mean to give you the impression

that I'd *saved* her.' Metatron didn't bother looking at me. 'Look, she's better off where she is,' he said. 'All she's done is jump the queue a little. With all the pieces to the puzzle we're so very, very close. It wouldn't be very nice to save her from Hell, drag her back to Earth, then watch her and all the others get sucked, screaming into the void, would it?' The Voice of God ran a manicured nail across the leather of his desk. 'When all this comes together, the Earth will be made clean. He will sweep across the Earth removing it all: all the questions, all the heresy, the filth and the dirt, the false idols, the adultery, the murder.' He stopped to take a breath. 'It will be as if humans never even existed.'

I could see a small bubble of spit glistening on his lips. 'It's my job to make sure it all happens,' he said, his eyes still tracking aimlessly across the carpet. 'It's my job to keep it all moving, even in His absence.' He reached over and grasped my arm. It took everything I had not to yank it out from beneath his hand.

'I know this all seems harsh, but it's been foretold for millennia that this – the final outcome – was always preordained.' He shrugged and looked earnestly down at his desk. 'The humans know, although they swear they don't believe. They all secretly worry about each new rumour of an impending apocalypse.' He shrugged. 'Right now they're all nervous about December 2012, but I can guarantee that it'll be much, much sooner than that.'

'How soon?' Trying to sound casual, I leant back in the chair and took another mouthful of the fiery liquid in front of me.

The angel thought about it for a moment. 'Well, Michael's almost ready to go,' he said. 'And there are a couple of other arrangements to be made.' He fell silent, obviously ticking points off a mental list; he was silent for a long time.

'Metatron.' I tapped him on the hand. 'How long have we got – a month? A year? Five years?'

'Hmmm?' He looked up at me with a peaceful smile. 'About four days.'

'Four days!' I tried to imagine what this actually meant, but my mind just refused to deal with it and sauntered off into a dark corner humming to itself.

Metatron looked surprised at my outburst. 'Well, yes, as long as I succeed, four days is my best guess.' He rubbed a hand over his face. 'But only if I can get Lucifer to show himself, and with God missing it means we can't follow the prophecy exactly.' He shrugged 'So it's all up to me.' He traced circles in the desk with a finger he'd dipped in whisky. 'I wish it wasn't the case but there has to be balance.' He got to his feet. 'You head off now, Joe.' He ran his hands through his hair making it stand out in all directions. 'I've got to get started on a very unpleasant job.' He stared meaningfully at the sleeping figure in the corner of the room. 'But that's OK, I think it's a test, I'm being tested ...' He smiled. 'It's not one I'm going to fail so you just dial your own number and you'll get home.' He spoke over his shoulder as he hoisted Graham up by the underarms and simply carried him from the room.

I called after him. 'But what about me? In four days' time, what happens to me?'

Metatron turned slowly back to face me. He had no expression at all. 'Nothing,' he said. 'Nothing happens to you.'

'But you've always promised.' I was beginning to feel a certain amount of panic. 'You always said I could stop – we were only talking about it a couple of minutes ago.'

'And so you shall,' he said. 'Originally this was all "nothing" and that's what it will all go back to.' He laughed. 'What's that line of that song?' He hummed a familiar tune. 'Oh yes: "You've come from nothing, you're going back to nothing. What are you going to lose? Nothing."'

Whistling the chorus, Metatron carried the sleeping man from the room.

I could feel my heart racing. He'd never intended to keep his promise. I tried to feel angry but couldn't. There are some things that I excel at: turning a blind eye, self-delusion and I definitely have a flair for ignoring the bloody obvious. I think

I'd always known that Metatron was lying to me, but ignoring this had kept me going. I'd had to hope, hadn't I?

Four days! Dear God, four days till the end of the world. It sounded like the plot for a bad sci-fi movie. I remembered Carly's eyes, wide with terror as she was carried away by the Drekavak. My heart started pounding; if I concentrated really hard I could still taste her when I ran my tongue over my lips. And even if, as that rock band said 'Hell ain't a bad place to be' she'd still be so scared right now.

Unconsciously following the boss's example, I ran my hands through my hair and found myself pacing the room. What was the point in bringing her back? At least she'd know I cared enough to try. I stopped pacing as I reached Metatron's desk again. What if he didn't have all the pieces of the puzzle? What if one of them sort of disappeared? If I gave the demons what they wanted, it would certainly slow things down. Metatron would, at the very least, have a headache to deal with and I, quite frankly, had absolutely nothing to lose.

My head felt as though it was filled with wet sherbet. Thoughts and feelings, old loyalties and new loves, my thoughts fizzed and bounced, shying away from the knowledge of what would happen if he caught me.

Reaching forward I tried to open the desk drawer just enough to peer in. It was locked – what a surprise. I quietly checked the other drawers for the key but I didn't really expect to find one. I was just about to leave when I decided to try one last thing and, drawing my knife from its holder, I pushed it into the lock.

I twisted gently and, sure enough, I could feel the lock grate slightly. Casting glances over at the door I jiggled it quietly. 'Come on, come on!' It was no use – there was no way that lock was going to turn. 'Damn it, fucking damn it!' Frustrated, I jammed the knife into the lock for one last time and wrenched it to the side. 'Come on, you bitch … TURN!' There was a small flash of blue light and the lock gave a satisfying click.

My hand tingled and my heart was beating fast. I snatched

the box and file and placed them in my rucksack. Quietly shutting the drawer, I kept half an eye on the door as I slowly and carefully dialled my number. I hit the last button and was away.

Sweating like a hammered horse I rolled over the carpet. Not bothering to stand up, I crawled quickly across the room to reach under the sofa where my big trunk resided. Dragging it into the light I tipped everything out: a crossbow, two short swords, a small horn, some dried olive leaves still attached to a small branch, half-burnt candles, and three cans of silly string. I couldn't find what I was looking for. As I riffled through all the bits and pieces, throwing them with casual abandon about the room, I began to feel the first stirrings of panic. Eventually I gave up and, with a string of rather elderly Gaelic curse words, I threw a half-burnt smudge stick across the room and slumped down with a sigh. It took a couple of moments before I realised that I was royally uncomfortable. Fumbling around under my leg, my fingers closed around a fuzzy box and, pulling it slowly into the light, I stared at it for a moment before heaving a huge sigh of relief.

Opening the tiny blue velvet box, I winced at the creak from the hinges, as though Metatron was looking over my shoulder. Nestled inside was a small key on a long silver chain. With a fair amount of disregard for its fragility, I ripped it out of its velvet womb and dropped it over my head. The key lay hot against my skin, a burning reminder of my impending treachery. I stared at the clutter all over the floor then shrugged: it would still be there if I ever got home: Turning my back on the mess I headed outside to make a door.

'Hello, Joe.'

I must have leapt a foot in the air. I definitely said 'Glaeark'.

'Sorry, didn't mean to startle you.' An angel I'd never met before gave me a vague and insincere smile. With his crumpled linen suit, dark skin and black eyes he looked like a dodgy timeshare salesman. 'Were you just going out?' He casually stuck his hands into the pockets of his suit trousers and raised an eyebrow which disappeared under his heavy fringe.

I glanced over his shoulder. Mr Morris was studying his shrubbery; his back was to me but the tension in his shoulders told me that he had to strain quite hard to hear what was going on. I turned my attention back to the angel and returned his smile. 'Only down the shop, nowhere very important.'

He nodded. 'Good, I'd hate to have interrupted something *important.*'

I was stuck. If I invited him in, there would be no way I could hide the mess that was all over the living room. If I talked to him out here … I shuddered. Nope, I really didn't want to have that conversation anywhere near my next-door neighbour.

He smiled again. 'Any chance of a cup of tea?'

I could feel sweat beginning to gather in my hair. My scalp prickled and my upper lip tasted of salt. The stolen knife and file in my backpack were getting heavier by the moment; at any moment they would fall through the bottom of my bag.

The angel studied his fingernails. 'The boss felt that you were upset and sent me to make sure you were all right and that you weren't going to do anything …' his smile widened. '… stupid.'

Despite the summer heat I felt myself growing cold. Metatron knew. The only reason he'd sent this idiot down here was that he was too busy with his new friend to come himself. For some reason that, more than anything else, really hurt my feelings. If he was going to finally get rid of me, the least he could have done was send something more than a bloody low-level scribe. My nerves settled as an idea dropped whole and complete into my head. Calm, serene and utterly relaxed I stepped aside and waved him into the hall.

He frowned for a moment but when I looked over his shoulder again and called 'Morning, Mr Morris', he nodded and stepped past me into the dim hall.

Kicking the door shut behind us I reached for my knife. It dropped into my hand like a greeting from a friend.

The angel turned – all signs of friendly banter had disappeared. 'Give me the file,' he said.

Sighing heavily I allowed my head to droop and swung the backpack around my shoulders. I held it against my chest, using its bulk to hide my weapon.

The angel snorted. 'I honestly don't know how you've managed to live for so long. If all humans were as stupid as you we'd have wiped them out years ago.' He was obviously enjoying his moment in the spotlight. He shook his head and huffed a short laugh then held out his hand to take the bag. 'Come on, hand it over.'

It was all over far faster than I would have imagined. I shoved the bag toward him knocking his hand away and, with one straight thrust, my other hand embedded the knife in his chest.

It felt terrible. The blade sank through skin and muscle as though cutting lard. There was a slight vibration as the blade grated across the bottom of his sternum then a wet thud as the crossguard hit skin.

I whipped my hand away, letting go of the knife as, with a look of bewilderment, the angel fell away from me. Choking and gasping he lay on the floor, slim fingers plucking at the knife.

I backed against the wall breathing hard. My hand vibrated as if the feeling of ancient steel on bone was still with me – I wondered if it would ever go away.

The angel stared at me as his breathing became more and more shallow. Eventually there was no breath at all. His blank stare pinned me to the wall and, between my ragged breaths, my breakfast crashed in heaving swells against my stomach walls.

As silence fell I looked down at my still-tingling hand, covered in blood. That was all it took to breach my gastric break-waters and I emptied the contents of my stomach into the corner of the hall.

When I had finished heaving I wiped my mouth and was

surprised to find my face wet with tears. Wiping my hand down my jeans, I crept forward. I held my breath as I reached for my backpack, expecting at any moment a hand to grab my throat or a scream to erupt from those slightly parted pale lips. Nothing happened.

I threw the pack over my shoulder and, swallowing convulsively, reached for the knife. Wrapping my shaking fingers around the hilt I pulled, hard, expecting the blade to be stuck. It wasn't – it came out as easily as it had slid in and I ended up on my backside between the angel's outstretched legs. Scuttling backwards on hands, feet and bottom I came to a sudden halt as I hit the front door and collapsed in a heap on the doormat just trying to breathe.

I must have sat there staring at the body for a couple of minutes before I realised that fleeing and fleeing fast should be my next move. Using the door as a brace I climbed to my feet never once taking my eyes off the angel. Palsied and sobbing it took me three attempts to make a door. Stepping through, I imagined that, vigorous and renewed, he was a mere half step behind me. A quick check over my shoulder as my house faded into the pale haze confirmed that I was followed only by my guilt.

I appeared, in Cambridge, just behind the bus station. My abrupt presence startled a small group of teenagers who were playing a raucous game of cards. Luckily, they were so stoned that they just laughed at my appearance. It didn't take me long to orientate myself and start jogging through the city.

This time the store's security guard was nowhere to be seen and I walked quickly through the shop. It was hard not to draw attention to myself. Dressed in blood-stained, ripped combats, my hair greasy and unkempt and smelling of toxic smoke I must have been difficult to ignore, but you have to love the British public – they certainly managed quite well.

Two elderly ladies waiting for the lift stared at me and took firm hold of their handbags. I leant toward them with a ghastly smile. 'I don't suppose one of you ladies has a tissue, do you?' I looked hangdog and sniffed wetly. 'I've got swine flu,' I said. 'But it's the wife's birthday and sometimes you just have to get off your sick bed and do what needs to be done, don't you?'

The effect was fairly immediate. Both women's eyes widened and, apologising profusely for the lack of tissues, they backed away. Just to speed them on their way I began a deep hacking cough and held onto the wall for support. The performance was almost Oscar-worthy.

Alone in the lift, I pulled the key from around my neck and gave it a kiss for luck. Metatron had given this to me a long time ago. I'd had to rescue a stranded seraph from a mad clairvoyant who, believing he was her guardian angel, was desperate to prove that the "otherworldly" were living among us. The key allegedly worked on any lock. However, Metatron had specified "earthly lock"; I had really no idea if it would work on the little panel above the lift buttons, but I'm always being told to have faith and it was the only plan I had. It had to work – if this failed there was nowhere now for me to go. I deliberately pushed the image of the dead angel lying sprawled on my hall floor out of my mind.

I pulled aside the little metal cover and inserted the key. Holding my breath, I turned it gingerly to the right. There was no movement at all. Gritting my teeth and trying not to swear I tried the other direction. There was a quarter turn and a satisfying click. I opened the panel and pressed the small black button; with the first movement of the lift, I finally allowed myself to breathe again.

I had about three minutes of travel time. Dragging my knife from its holster I stared at my distorted reflection in the polished aluminium walls as I mustered my courage. The next part of my plan was going to be damned painful.

There is a particular sigil in the angelic script that, if cut into flesh, should make me invisible to demons. I hoped it would make me undetectable to *all* otherworldly creatures. Holding the knife, point first, to my forehead, I had to use one hand to still the shaking of the other. Remembering how easily it had buried itself in an angel's heart I half-heartedly scratched the first line of the simple shape into my skin – I didn't want to embed the blade into my own brain! I watched with a certain wry detachment as the cut repaired itself within seconds. Well, damn it all I should have expected that. I was going to have to cut very deep and even then I reckoned I had about three hours at the most.

Gritting my teeth, I pressed the knife down hard, whimpering slightly as I felt it touch bone. Moving slowly I created one straight vertical stroke. Sweat broke out simultaneously on my brow, my back, the palms of my hands and my eyes watered copiously. Using the bottom of my T-shirt I wiped away the tears. Only four more strokes to go.

One horizontal stroke created the base to the sigil. I swallowed convulsively, heaving chemically scented air into my lungs with a horrible gasping sound that drowned out the gentle warbling of some unknown singer that drifted through the speakers. Two down, three to go. Blood ran freely down my nose and dripped from my upper lip to patter onto the embossed metal floor. I cut a horizontal half-stroke to create an uneven capital "I". Trying to keep my rolling stomach under control I stared at my wobbly reflection in the metal; it was a ghastly mess that peered back at me. This next stroke was going to be hard, a wavy line that crossed from the top to the bottom on a left-hand diagonal. Gritting my teeth I cut slowly, going as deep as I could stand, whimpering as the salt sweat dripped into the wound. Only one figure left: a small circle above the upper horizontal line. I heaved and clamped my lips together in an attempt to stop myself vomiting. The circle actually took two agonising strokes to complete. Unable to control myself any longer, I deposited what was left in my stomach into the corner of the lift.

I stood entirely still for a while, chest heaving, convulsively swallowing again and again. I concentrated and watched each drop of blood hitting the floor with every ounce of focus I had; it gave me something else to think about other than the screaming pain in my head and the frenzied churning of my stomach. Within a short time the flow of blood had slowed and my stomach had managed to get itself back under control. Leaning on the wall I watched as my reflection dissipated. Slowly I faded away. Well, at least it had worked – but for how long? I had no real clue. The faster I moved the better it would be for everybody – especially me.

# CHAPTER 5

HAPPILY, THE SEPIA WORLD outside the lift did nothing to aggravate the headache I'd given myself. I stared around, trying to find the darker line that marked the path to the city. Everything was unnaturally still – only the sound of my footfalls broke the silence. This time there were no threatening shadows or movements, no chittering laughter. Walking through that twilight world I headed toward the tall stone structure that dominated the horizon and congratulated myself on a job well done.

As I approached the base of the walls, my congratulatory mood melted away and it dawned on me that as a strategist I sucked. So busy patting myself on the back I hadn't really considered how I was going to get into the city. As I stood, tiny and insignificant, beneath the huge black gates I finally saw the tiny flaw in my plan. All my grand ideas of sneaking in undetected, rescuing the damsel in distress and making a heroic, if hasty, getaway crumbled into dust. I stared up at the black, forbidding portal. Sitting cross-legged on the sand, studying the gates I rejected one stupid idea after another. There was nothing for it – I was actually going to have to *knock* on the bloody door. Fumbling around in my pockets I waited for the 'dusters to settle themselves around my hand. Well, if I was going to have to knock, I was going to do it very loudly.

There was a thunderous boom as I tapped lightly on the solid old wood; the vibrations shook little runnels of sand from between the stones surrounding the huge doors. Although the 'dusters bestowed a huge amount of strength, they were also slightly unpredictable. Even a slight slap tended to send any aggressor bowling away like a beach ball in a high wind. The first time I'd ever used them I'd killed a small rat demon. Intending only to catch and hold it, I'd managed to break its neck. I still broke out in a sweat every time I remembered the sickening crack, the feeling of loose bone beneath my fingers and the way the light had just faded from its beautiful golden eyes.

The door swung open just a crack. I forced myself to stand very still. Just wait, I kept telling myself. Don't move, just wait. Eventually, the door opened wider and the gatekeeper appeared, staring out into the sand with a comical look of confusion.

Nessus! I stifled a gasp. What the hell was he doing back here? Reaching out slowly I knocked again on the door: four short and staccato raps. In any other circumstances his reaction would have been funny. All four feet left the ground like a surprised cat and he whipped his head backwards and forwards looking for the source of the sound. The schoolboy, still unaccountably buried deep within me, laughed uproariously. This was the ultimate game of knock-knock ginger.

Nessus took his tall bardiche firmly in both hands then stepped slowly out onto the sand. With nostrils flared and long ears flicking backward and forward, his head moved continuously. I was going to have to be either very quiet or very fast. I decided that speed was probably my best course of action.

I broke into a sprint and, faster than I would have thought possible, his head whipped around and he brought the bardiche down. It missed me by millimetres; the force of the blow buried the blade deep into the sand and rock. Trying to ignore the hairs standing to attention at the back of my neck, I raced through the open door and, weaving my way through the twisted corridors of stone, headed back toward the market.

Once safely in the marketplace I chanced a look back. Nessus had followed me and, with the bardiche over his shoulder, was staring around with a slight smile on his face. I panicked for a moment; I couldn't be visible yet – that would ruin everything.

Wending my way carefully through the crowds I headed back toward the green door. I needed information and fast. Running down the corridor I kept an eye out for any stray demon that happened to be walking the same halls. As I neared the file room I slowed down, desperately trying to get my breathing under control.

As I stood there, sweating and panting, I realised that in a tall pile of stupid, ill-thought-out and sketchy plans this one would be somewhere near the top. I had no idea where Carly was, or how to find her. Even if I did find out where she was being held, I only knew about 500 square metres of a place that encompassed umpteen worlds, for Christ's sake. What the hell was I doing in Hell? I still had time to get out. All I had to do was turn around, walk back to the gate and get home. Metatron would never know. I'd return the file and the box to his desk and just get on with doing what I was told and, when Armageddon went ahead, maybe I'd find some peace.

I leant against the wall breathing hard. A faint breeze drifted down the long corridor, carrying with it the smell of spices and flowers from the market outside. It reminded me of Carly's bathroom. God, she must be terrified.

I'm no knight in shining armour – at best I'm an angel's lackey. For as long as I can remember all I've ever done is follow orders, ask no questions, do as little as possible and enjoy the benefits. I'm certainly one of the best at turning a blind eye to any injustice I've been part of. But if I did this, my brain screamed at me, I'd lose everything. My boss would literally disembowel me if he ever found out and, as if that wasn't bad enough, I'd have the Host on my tail. Michael would no doubt be delighted to deal with me; this was one order he'd smile all the way through performing.

I pushed away from the wall and turned resolutely back toward the gate. 'Sorry, Carly,' I whispered. 'I'm really sorry.' I took a step toward home, then turned around and marched through the file room door, firmly ignoring the voice in my head that was screaming, 'What are you doing? What are you doing? Stop! STOP!'

The file room was just as I remembered it: silent, dusty and stinking of ancient paper. The front desk, clear except for a large brown leather book, stood abandoned, the chair pushed against the desk. I lifted the cover: it was an index. Handwritten in tiny crabbed letters, each page listed thousands upon thousands of locations of other, larger indexes: surnames, first names, locations, the list went on and on. I closed the cover with a snap. To find a reference to Carly in here, I would have to locate the surname index, and then look through that to find her particular surname, find the part of the room that it referred to, then find that particular surname, then look through all the others with the same name. To a man like me, this overly organised paper graveyard *was* Hell. Never mind torments, pitchforks and fire, just stick me in here and tell me to find John Smith. I would be insane within seconds.

'What do I do now?' The best I could do would be to wander this place for years and check every file. There was no way I was going to find her by myself. I had one option: find someone in charge and offer them the box.

'What are you doing back here, Joe?' A deep voice sounded behind me.

'Aii!' I couldn't stop one small scream from escaping and, whipping around, came face to face with Nessus. How could something that big move so quietly?

'You can see me?' I coughed to get rid of the quaver in my voice.

Nessus snorted. 'Nope.' He swished that long tail of his, raising dust in a cloud around his rear end. 'But I can smell you, and you have an interesting tendency to talk to yourself when you're under pressure.' He shook his head and frowned. 'Not a good trait when you're trying to remain invisible.'

'Sorry.' I tried to bully my brain into rational thought. 'I'll keep that in mind.' I glanced up at him; he seemed in fairly good humour. 'I'm sorry I left you.'

'I'm fine, managed to talk my way out of the whole thing.' He reached out, feeling for my shoulder. 'OK this is a bit weird, whoops, sorry ...' Finally grasping it after smacking me round the head a couple of times he gave me a bit of a shake. 'There wasn't anything you could have done,' he paused. 'I hear you took Alice out rather spectacularly?'

'Alice?' For a moment I was confused and desperately ran through the events of my last visit. Finally it sank in. 'That *thing* was called Alice?'

Nessus nodded. 'Yeah, most of the time she's a real sweetie. I hear you met her brother?'

'I think so.' I remembered the sniggering, hissing Drekavak stroking Carly's hair. 'He was the one that took Carly right?'

'Carly?' Nessus's brow furrowed. 'What's a Carly?'

'She's my ...' I stopped and thought for a moment – what was she? 'Next-door neighbour.' I finished lamely.

Nessus snorted and shook my shoulder again. 'You know, you might be taking the "good neighbour" thing a little far. I don't know many people that would break into Hell for a *neighbour.*' He grinned and waggled his eyebrows suggestively.

'I have to get her back.' I waved vaguely at the huge room forgetting that he couldn't see me. 'But I can't find her in this.' In frustration, I brought my fist down on the book and a waft of dust drifted up into my eyes.

Nessus coughed then pushed me gently out of the way. 'Is this neighbour of yours about five foot-six, bright red hair with a temper to match?'

I nodded. Then remembered to speak: 'You've seen her?'

'I know where they're keeping someone that looks like that. Evidently she caused quite a bit of trouble for Alice's brother: she bit him twice.' Nessus laughed. 'He's been moaning about it all day.' The big centaur turned toward the door. 'Come on, I can take you there, but for crying out loud keep the muttering to a minimum, will you?'

I smiled. *That* was the Carly I knew. Obviously once she got over her fear she'd fought like a demon. I winced at the unintentional irony and followed Nessus's broad tail out of the file room. 'I don't have much time.'

He reflexively looked back over his shoulder, and then shook his head. Rolling his eyes he turned resolutely to face forward again. 'This is a bit freaky not being able to see you,' he said.

'That's the problem.' I jogged to catch up with him. 'I have about an hour and a half before *everyone* will be able to see me. I could hold your tail, if you like.'

Nessus flicked his long tail up over his back and out of reach. 'Don't you dare.' He stopped at a wide, heavy door and pressed a small button.

The door slid to the right and revealed a large lift. Nessus's hooves made hollow booming sounds as he entered.

I hesitated. 'Does this thing have a weight restriction?' I followed him in and watched as he prepared the sophisticated winch and pulley system.

Nessus snorted indignantly at me.

'Going back to our original conversation.' I watched his muscles move with a certain amount of envy as he heaved on the thick rope that operated the manual lift. 'Why are there so many Drekavak here? Over the years I've picked up all sorts of demons, little green ones that look like big frogs right up to one great big hairy one. But recently it all seems to be Drekavak.'

Nessus sniffed. 'Hell went through a huge upheaval a long time ago. Belial decided that we were no longer going to be used as Heaven's big stick to threaten everyone with. The lower levels were closed, all the sinners were set free and we opened the borders to other worlds.' He sighed. 'What you call "demons" are welcome pretty much anywhere, except Earth. Metatron did his best to kill every single one that set foot in the place. But the Drekavak ...' He smiled. 'Ah, you should have seen their world; it was as close to paradise as anywhere I've ever been. They were artists and craftsmen, their cities were beautiful and the things they made ...' Nessus shook his head. 'All lost, it was so sad.'

'Really, they're artists?' I remembered the snarling faces and the huge claws. 'I always thought they were just mindless muscle.'

Nessus studied his hooves for a moment. 'Well, they don't like you very much.'

'Me?' I was surprised. 'Why me, what have I done?'

'Their world was dying; the sun was slowly going dark. They approached Metatron for help, not wanting to ally with Hell.' He paused then snorted a laugh. 'For some bizarre reason they'd got the idea that we were evil – a place where you go when you're bad and they didn't want that. They were peace loving and gentle so they approached Heaven and asked for asylum.'

I had a sinking feeling I knew how that little conversation had gone.

Nessus continued. 'Metatron told them that they were demons and not fit to enter the kingdom of Heaven and if their world was dying then it was God's will and they should try to mend their ways.' He shrugged. 'Well, in desperation, some of them broke through to Earth – those were the ones you were sent after.' He turned to look in my direction, I was quite pleased he couldn't actually see me; the look on his face wasn't very nice. 'Luckily you're a pretty crap demon hunter and most of them got away, but you did manage to get a few, didn't you?'

I swallowed. 'I was just following orders. I didn't know …'

'Right.' He cut across me. 'They kept breaking through and, as their world disintegrated, they became more and more panicked, trying to get away. In the end, they became so persistent that Metatron ordered Michael to destroy them – the whole damn species. That was when Belial contacted them once more and offered them a way out. We managed to get about 75 per cent of the population away before the angels attacked.

Nessus paused for a moment, obviously uncomfortable revisiting the memories. 'The carnage was horrific; the Host just slaughtered everything in sight. It was mainly the elderly and the children they concentrated on. Easy targets guaranteed to cause the most anguish to all the others.' He drew in a deep shuddering breath. 'I don't know how they do it – the Drekavak kids are so sweet.' He laughed. 'They look like little kangaroos. But there was no emotion, no remorse, they just ...' He threw a meaningful look in my direction. 'Followed orders.' Pursing his lips he stared at the floor. 'Surely if God made everything, how could he have issued that sort of order?'

I swallowed hard. The rolling nausea was impossible to ignore; I seemed to spend all my waking hours feeling sick these days. 'I'm not sure God had anything to do with it,' I muttered, thinking that it was no wonder these beings hated me: I'd helped Metatron attempt genocide and now, just when they think they're safe, I come strolling into Hell and kill one here as well. My legs wouldn't hold me up any more and, sliding down the lift wall, I sat on the floor. It really didn't matter what my original sin was, everything I'd done since then just compounded my crime. I thought I'd been paying off my debt but here I was, deeper than ever before. How convenient that I was immortal – I couldn't even take myself out of the picture.

'You OK?' Nessus looked down at me. 'Do you realise I can see you a bit? You're all sort of shadowy. I think you're running out of time.' He frowned. 'Where was I? Oh yes, most of the people are happy to stay here. They like it – they're out of the host's way and don't feel the need to change that. But the Drekavak are still angry; they have very long memories and any chance they get to irritate an angel they take it. If they could move their whole species to Earth and start a war they would, but luckily Belial won't allow it.' He shrugged. 'That's why you see so many of them. Any time there's a call for volunteers the Drekavak fall over themselves to be the first to stick their hand up and because it keeps all the others out of harm's way Belial's happy to accommodate them.'

The lift finally bumped to a halt. Nessus tied off the rope and heaved the heavy wooden door open. I wondered just how much of the Drekavak hatred was aimed at me.

'Come on.' Nessus stuck his head out of the lift and peered each way down the corridor. 'My rooms are just down there.' He paused outside a tall, dark wooden door. 'They're keeping your *neighbour* in here.' He waggled his eyebrows again and sniggered.

If my whole life was a lie then I was sure as hell going to finally do something I could feel good about. At least I knew that getting Carly back to her life, safe and sound, was going to make me feel better – even if the act didn't even register on my grand list of crimes. My stomach rolled again: hundreds of years of committing atrocities, thinking I was doing "the right thing". Was I actually the most evil man alive or was I just the most stupid? If I was someone else I would have laughed at me. 'I always thought I was doing good things.' I could feel tears gathering. 'I was told I was doing good things and I was told that if I carried on doing good things then I'd get my just reward and my sin would be wiped clean.'

Nessus sighed. 'You never really questioned it all though, did you?' He glanced in my general direction still unable to look at me directly. 'Do you want to know what the Drekavak call you?' he asked.

I waved a hand. 'Go ahead and tell me – no, let me guess, the Destroyer or the Blade?'

Nessus brayed a laugh. 'Sorry, Joe, nothing so impressive.' He paused for a moment, his ears swivelling. 'They found an Earth term that they really love and have had great fun with it.' He paused for effect. 'They call you Metatron's Bitch.' He looked over his shoulder. 'Someone's coming, if you want to get your lady love back we need to go.' He reached down and rattled the polished brass handle. 'It's locked.' He looked panicked.

The adrenaline of the situation finally caught up with me and I pushed all my self-loathing away; I'd have more than enough time to study those feelings later. Right now, I actually needed to do something worthwhile. 'I have a key that will open it.'

'What?' Nessus backed away from the door. 'Well, bloody well use it then.'

Grabbing the key from around my neck I inserted it into

the lock on the handle and, with a quiet click, the tumblers released.

'Wait!' Nessus gripped my arms. 'There'll be wards to check for weapons. I take it you have your horrible knife with you as usual?'

I nodded as Nessus stared down the corridor. 'Hurry, put all the weapons into your backpack. I'll take it down to my rooms. Come and get it when you've got Carly, OK?'

Swinging the pack off my shoulders I dumped the knuckle-dusters and the knife into the bag then handed it to him. 'Thanks, Nessus, I'll be down in a few moments.' I looked down at my hands. I was definitely showing now. Running a finger across my forehead confirmed it – it was almost smooth again. I twisted the handle and opened the door a crack before turning back to the expressionless centaur.

'You'd better let me have that key as well,' he said. 'It isn't a weapon but it may set the alarms off as well.'

I nodded and looped the chain over my head. I paused for a moment wanting to thank him for all his help. Failing to find the right words, I asked a question instead. It was something that had been bugging me for a while.

'If Metatron's so wrong, why do you work for him?' I wanted him to have a good reason – preferably one that would apply to me, one that would make sense of what I'd been doing all these years.

Nessus shrugged. Then, raising a hand, he grasped me by the shoulder and bent down to smile at me. 'I don't,' he said. His grin widened as he pushed me, backward, through the door.

I landed hard and winced, more at hearing the lock click on the door than at any real pain. I couldn't stop myself; I began to laugh. At least I now had the answer to my question. I really was the most stupid person alive. I'd sold my soul to the biggest sociopath there was and basically acted as his dirty hands. I'd spent a thousand years patting myself on the back and telling myself that I was one of the good guys. Now, here I was in Hell waiting to see what my punishment for that short-sightedness was going to be. I rolled over and groaned. Even if I could escape, Metatron would be waiting. I wasn't just caught between a rock and a hard place – I was crushed between them.

'Joe?' Carly's voice cut through my cycle of impending doom and stopped the laughter short.

I didn't bother to get up; I just opened my eyes and rested my chin on my hands. 'Hi, Carly.' I suppressed another urge to giggle. 'I'm here to rescue you.' I frowned as I took a good look around the room.

Carly was sitting cross-legged on a huge red sofa – so soft she had actually sunk into it and was resting her knees on the bulging cushions either side of her thighs. In front of the sofa a low, heavily carved wooden table held a silver tray on which a tall stoneware jug sat alongside a plate of small pastries. A book, face down, spine broken and pages well thumbed showed that my rather sudden entrance had definitely disturbed "quiet time". She stared at me curiously over the rim of a large mug, the contents of which steamed and filled the room with the scent of cinnamon and cream.

Getting to my feet, I dusted myself off. It was a set from an Ideal Home exhibition. A calm, sea-green carpet stretched around the room, thick and warm. Shining wooden bookshelves, filled with well-read titles, graced one long wall and on the other was a heavy wooden desk upon which stood an ancient manual typewriter.

Well, well, here was someone else that had lied well and completely fooled me. I really ought to receive an award – possibly "Gullible Incompetent of the Year".

With all these thoughts whirling around my head I didn't really feel like talking. Ignoring Carly, I wandered over to the huge bay window and perched on the upholstered seat that ran elegantly around the sill. The market below us bustled with shoppers and performers. Beyond the market the city marched away in all directions.

It was surprisingly large. Buildings and streets stretched, in no sane pattern that I could determine, off into the distance. There appeared to be a forest along the horizon and

I wondered how it would feel to walk there, in the silence, to be going nowhere and to be responsible for nothing but yourself … It sounded pretty good to me.

'What are you doing here, Joe?' Carly's voice broke through my thoughts and I jumped, tangling myself in the long curtain ties that hung from the heavy green and gold swags framing the window.

'I don't know.' I shook my head and swallowed to clear the lump in my throat. 'I thought I did but I really don't.' I turned to look at her. 'So what are *you* doing here?' I gestured around the grand room. Was that a Gainsborough hanging on the wall? 'You seem to be a very contented victim.'

'Oh, Joe.' Carly wandered over and reached out to give me one of her normal hugs. She looked hurt when I held up a hand to keep her away. 'You aren't supposed to be here, you were just supposed to get the box and deliver it, not actually turn up all bloody Rambo and try and break me out.' She ran a hand through her hair, wincing as it snagged on her fingers before springing back into its usual chaotic spirals. 'How did you get in here anyway?' She laughed. 'I'll bet Nessus had a hissy fit when he saw you.'

Finally the pennies started to drop. 'These are *your* rooms.' I gazed around at all the clues: the little wooden figures that nestled among the books, the huge mirror over the fireplace with tickets and pictures stuck into the sides of the frame and the paintings – a couple were Carly's own.

I had an odd feeling at the back of my neck – a tightening, contracting feeling which spread to my shoulders and chest as though I was a tightly wound spring. I couldn't stop swallowing and was fairly sure I had developed a twitch.

I rounded on Carly who squeaked and took a step back. That twitch must have been more exaggerated than I thought. I remembered as much as I could of my past. As the images flashed past they created a colourful but strangely sad home movie. Each short clip centred on the irrefutable fact that, for as long as I'd been alive, I'd been used and lied to. Kept in the dark and fed on bullshit, I was the ultimate fucking

113

mushroom.

Taking a deep breath I waited until the fairly murderous feelings had calmed a little. 'Do you have another mug?' I asked.

'What?' Carly frowned. 'Why?'

'I want a drink.' I managed to get the words out through my gritted teeth. I walked over to the table and sniffed at the jug. 'This smells nice and I want a drink, what is this?'

'Chai.' Carly kept a close eye on me as she skirted around the edge of the room toward a tall wooden bureau. She took out a clean mug then, crossing the room she came to a halt as far away as physically possible. She leant over to place the mug carefully and quietly onto the table. 'Joe, we need to talk, there's a lot you don't understand –'

'Shh.' I put a finger to my lips and glared at her. She promptly snapped her lips together and stood in silence. 'I quite like chai.' I studied the mug. *Abstract art*' The quote flowed around the rim. *A product of the untalented, sold by the unprincipled to the utterly bewildered.* 'Funny,' I muttered and filled it.

'Joe.' Carly reached for my hand. Once again I silently stepped out of reach. Her hurt look pulled at my heart and she dropped the hand to her side. 'You don't understand,' she whispered.

Maintaining that hard shell was difficult, especially as I wasn't sure it was designed to keep her feelings from affecting me or mine from exploding outward. 'I think I understand enough.' Pushing the tray away I perched on the edge of the table and sipped at the tepid liquid. 'Let's see.' I paused long enough to get my thoughts in order. 'For the last thousand or so years I've been working really hard to make up for a crime I don't remember committing. I'm informed that mine was the ultimate sin but, as I'm told this by an angel who has continually lied to me for the whole of that time I'm not sure I believe him. But whatever my crime was, it doesn't matter because whether I like it or not I don't' really have a choice in what I do because I can't stand against a being that is so much more than I am.'

Carly drew a breath. 'So much more than you are?' She had her teeth gritted and her fists clenched at her sides. 'Joe, Metatron's nothing but a traitor and a murderer.'

'Yeah, well, I'm not that much better, am I?' I smiled and shrugged. 'Where was I? Oh yes, so, I'm told that I'm doing God's work by killing demons, which I do to the best of my ability. Luckily, it turns out that I'm actually very bad at it but I think that my *boss*,' I couldn't help spitting the word out, 'actually enjoys watching my pain. That's why he gave me the *gift* of immortality – just so he could watch me die over and over again.'

'Yeah, how did he actually do that?' Carly stood up and began wandering about the room. 'I can't see how he accomplished it, bestowing immortality on a human should have been impossible.'

'Ah, ah, ah!' I shook a finger at her. 'Questions at the end. So I'm wandering about wondering how much help I have to give Heaven to receive my final reward and it turns out that I'm actually aiding some xenophobic megalomaniac bring on the apocalypse and destroy anyone that's going to stand in the way of his interpretation of God's *big plan*.' I took a moment to take a breath. 'Which means that basically I'm compounding any sin I committed by murdering, stealing and generally turning a blind eye to what's actually going on.' I gave Carly a frosty look, my stomach churning; now that I'd actually admitted it to myself I thought the chai was going to make a sudden and explosive re-appearance. 'How am I doing so far?'

Carly pursed her lips and sighed. 'Actually, you've only got about half of it.'

I nodded. 'That makes sense, there's obviously got to be way more to this than just some mad angel torturing me for the fun of it.' My stomach churned harder. 'Please enlighten me.'

With a big sigh Carly sank cross legged to the floor. 'Firstly, and just to slot the final puzzle piece into place, how *did* Metatron make you immortal?'

'Blood.' I couldn't really see the point in holding anything

115

back any more but that episode was so painfully bright in my memory I still shuddered whenever I thought of it. 'I came around in his office after I'd died the first time ...'

'What year was this?' Carly interrupted.

I made a big show of counting on my fingers then, as my memory did its usual fuzzy blank out, I shrugged. 'A very, very long time ago.'

'What about before that?' Carly pressed. 'Before you died that first time?'

'I can't remember.' I frowned. There was something there but it was just feelings and colour – no actual memories. I gave up and shrugged. 'That's my first memory. I know I woke up feeling like crap, I remember not being able to move.'

'I bet you did.' Carly rolled her eyes. 'Probably because you'd been kept on ice for about a thousand years.' She shrugged and indicated for me to continue.

I ignored her. I really wasn't in the mood to deal with cute exaggeration. 'Anyway, this huge angel, complete with all the special effects of singing flames and booming thunder, basically lays it all out for me about why I was there and what God wanted me to do.'

Carly snorted.

'Then he cut his own wrist and mine and joined the two together.' My stomach heaved as I remembered the moment the two bloods flowed together. 'I was on fire, I burned, my skin dissolved. I've never felt such pain and it seemed to go on for ever.' I stopped and clapped a hand to my mouth as I heaved. There was no way the contents of my stomach were staying where they were put.

'Through there, quick.' Carly leapt forward and, grabbing my arm, dragged me over to a door. Kicking it open she pushed me through. I had just enough time to register that it was a bathroom before my stomach, once again, emptied itself.

After a while, with nothing left to get rid of, I groaned and looked around for a towel.

Carly, who had been holding my hair, handed me a damp

cloth.

'Sorry.' I apologised to Carly who rolled her eyes.

'No, I'm sorry.' She took the cloth and rinsed it at the sink returning with a small cup of water. 'I was just supposed to watch you, not make you cake, give you dinner and laugh at your jokes.' She waited until I'd finished with the water, then as she turned away she said, 'I definitely broke the rules when I found out that I really liked you.' Pulling me to my feet she guided me back to the sofa. 'You weren't anything like I expected.' She stared at me for a moment then, with an obvious effort, returned to the subject at hand. 'So he made you part angel – well, that makes a lot of sense.'

'If you say so.'

'Concentrate.' Carly snapped. 'Are you good at your job?' She picked up my hand; this time I didn't feel any urge to pull away.

'No, not at all, I don't enjoy killing things. I'm a fairly inept fighter and, quite frankly, it's frequently me that ends up dead.' I paused as something she'd said finally sank in. 'What do you mean, "part angel"?'

'Didn't you ever wonder about that?' Carly shuffled closer and looked up at me earnestly. 'Didn't you ever wonder why he kept asking you to do things even though you were so bad at completing tasks? Didn't you ever ask: why me?'

I shook my head and had to admit to myself that no, I never had. In fact I'd been very careful *never* to ask myself that question. In fact I'd never questioned anything; my motto had been: keep your head down.

'As lives go, mine was good, I always had money in the bank however much I spent, I had somewhere to live, a fair amount of free time, at least in the early years.' I leant forward and pushed a strand of her long hair out of her face and tucked it behind her ear. 'Then things changed, I got moved to Birmingham and this woman moved in next door and my life became even more normal. I made the mistake of allowing myself to dream.' I leant forward intending to kiss her.

117

'Bleaugh.' She pulled back with a smile. 'I think you need to clean your teeth.' She squeezed my knees and stood up. 'I also think you need all the facts before you make any moves, so hold on, Casanova.'

Making sure she had my full attention she began to pace around the room. 'I'm sorry but it's actually far worse than you think. Metatron has Lucifer's vessel?'

I nodded.

'In that box, we think, is the original spear of destiny blade. Metatron knows you don't like killing but will happily put something out of its torment. When you next see Graham Latimer he will be in such torment that the only thing someone like you could do would be to kill him – it would be a mercy.'

My brain turned over: what the hell was happening to that man? What was Metatron doing to him that would be so bad that I'd have to kill him?

'We think he's hoping to goad you into stabbing Graham Latimer with the cursed blade. That blade will release Lucifer as it destroys the Host, but it will also destroy the Morning Star – this time for good.'

'I see.' I tried to think of the implications of all this. 'So what? Lucifer's gone and he's been gone for millennia – what difference will it make?'

Carly began to pace the room. 'You have to be the most stupid man alive,' she said. 'You just don't think things through, do you?' Taking a deep calming breath she closed her eyes as she spoke. 'There has to be a balance. If you kill Lucifer, there is no Adversary and without an Adversary God can't exist; the balance would tip too far in one direction. Metatron's counting on this. With God gone he can become the power he's always wanted to be.'

This didn't make any sense at all. 'But there's still no Adversary, so the balance would still be off. That can't work.'

Carly dropped to her knees again and leaning on my knees she stared up at me. 'The Adversary will be you.'

'What?'

'You committed a huge sin.' Carly squeezed my knees again making sure I was focused. 'You have spent years committing atrocities, even if you didn't know they were atrocious.' She licked her lips. 'If you destroy Lucifer, you destroy the balance, you destroy God. An angel, even a part angel that destroys God will have fallen so far he will become the next "adversary". Lucifer only fell, because he tried to take over Heaven. You will be far worse: you will be the ultimate traitor and you will have actually killed God. Making you a far more powerful Adversary than Lucifer ever was, which, because of "the balance", will make Metatron far more powerful as well. He'll destroy worlds just because he can.'

I shook my head. 'So killing an angel before coming here probably wasn't a good move then?'

Carly bit her lip and sighed. 'No, definitely not. A new Adversary that works for a new God. Metatron gets everything, including his revenge.'

'Revenge?' I couldn't think. Carly's words just kept flashing through my head. I felt as though I was going to explode.

She gazed at me with an odd look. 'I'd have thought you of all people would know the story.' She settled back on her heels and began reciting: the Talmud says that Elisha ben Abuyah entered Paradise and saw Metatron sitting down taking notes – he was a scribe at the time. But sitting is something only God can do. He therefore looked to Metatron as a deity and said heretically, 'There are indeed two powers in Heaven!' It was proved to Elisha that he was wrong. Metatron received 60 "strokes with fiery rods" to demonstrate that he was not a god, but an angel, and could be punished.'

Carly frowned. 'Well, it's postulated that he felt, possibly rightly, that this was grossly unfair. He was only doing his job and just because some priggish visitor gets the wrong idea, Metatron gets the snot kicked out of him just to prove a point.' Shrugging, she put a hand on the pot of chai. 'This has gone cold.' Walking over to the desk she pressed a button on the intercom and spoke crisply into a little black box. 'Could I have some more tea, please?' She turned and looked back at me. 'Of course we're only guessing all this but it does seem to fit.'

'But I brought the box here.' I wanted to cry. I was pretty much backed into a corner and couldn't get out. 'Nessus has the box with the blade in it, so Metatron can't use that and, if I stay here, he can't use me either, can he?'

Carly shook her head. 'It really doesn't matter any more. Even if you don't kill Graham Latimer, your actions so far …' She paused for a moment and stared at me. 'An angel? You killed an angel?'

I shrugged.

'Well, all this has got you marked as the next Adversary. OK, without that final act you and Metatron won't be quite so powerful but it will all still go the same way.'

She pressed the button on the intercom again. 'Can someone please ask Nessus to come in?' She turned and stared at me. 'You need to somehow put this right.'

'How can I put all this right? And who the hell *are* you?' A little question that had niggled at me for a while circumvented all the big questions and popped out.

'Half-human,' she said. 'Pretty much your opposite, I suppose. Originally we'd have been called Nephilim.'

'So half-demon,' I sighed. Half-angels, angels, demons, other worlds; I couldn't take it all in.

'Argh! You don't get it, do you!' Carly stamped across the floor. 'There are no such things as "demons". The closest are the fallen angels that came with Lucifer all those years ago. A third of the Host sentenced to rot in Hell for following Lucifer. Lucifer, who I might add, who managed to get himself locked up in a human Host and abandoned his followers to suffer God's torment. The rest of them are just from different places, like the Drekavak. Metatron has just labelled us all demons. To him, anything that isn't host is either human, and they exist just to be got rid of because God loves them more than him, or they're something else: demon.'

A knock on the door interrupted her tirade. A small man, dressed in black and carrying another silver tea tray strutted into the room. He stared at me for a moment then, after placing the tray carefully on the table in front of me, he returned to whisper in Carly's ear.

'How long?' she asked.

The man glanced over at me again with a frown. 'Less than a day.' He gave her a short bow and disappeared through the door.

Carly ran her fingers through her long hair then stood for a moment with her head bowed.

Feeling the need for a mundane task I set about pouring the tea. Carly smiled at me as I handed her a mug that read: *I don't have a short attention span, I just ... Oh look a chicken!* I snorted a laugh. Mine declared: *This would be funny if it wasn't happening to me.* I laughed harder. There are times when you are so far in the shit you just can't get any deeper so you might as well just go with the flow. I turned to Carly. 'So ... a Nephilim, eh? Aren't you supposed to be 18 foot tall and built like a brick outhouse?'

Carly took a sip of tea and sighed. 'I'm in disguise.' She didn't smile.

My next laugh spilt my tea which seemed the funniest thing I'd seen for a long time. I couldn't breathe; my stomach, face and sides hurt. Every time I tried to stop, I'd look up at Carly and Nessus who'd come in while I was howling and the looks of astonishment on both their faces would set me off again. Placing my mug on the tray I flopped back into the cushions. Laying down seemed the right thing to do.

Nessus rumbled a laugh. 'You told him then,' he said.

Carly nodded in bemusement.

The big centaur stared at me for a moment then, picking up my mug, began to drink my tea. Returning to stand next to Carly he studied me rolling around on the sofa as one would a strange bug in a plate of salad. He had to raise his voice to be heard over my laughter. 'So how's the patient doing?'

Carly gave him a wry glance. 'Not very well. I'll take Sir

Giggles down there to see her, when I can get him to focus.'

'Let him laugh it out.' Nessus drained the mug; it looked like a toy china cup in his huge hands. 'It's better for him than crying and that's what I'd be doing in his shoes.'

Carly nodded again, 'I know I said he's taking it well, but this is heading toward hysteria.' She paused and nudged the sniggering centaur. 'Could you possibly ...'

Nessus nodded, then, handing her his mug, crossed the room. He picked me up by the front of my jacket then, hauling me off the sofa, held me at eye level and gave me a little shake.

Having your brain rattled around your skull is enough to focus anyone. 'Ow ... What?'

'Are you OK, Joe?' Nessus enunciated each word.

'Yes, I'm fine.' I smothered another giggle that was threatening to well up and break free.

'Here's your bag.' Nessus handed over my backpack. Nothing was missing and, after checking for the second time, I looked up at him. 'It's all here?'

He nodded. 'I wouldn't want to touch anything in there.' He studied me as I slipped the 'dusters back into my pockets and slid the knife back into its sheath between my shoulders.

'No time to chat.' Carly reached a hand toward me. 'We have to go.'

'Hang on a moment.' Pulling out the white box and the file I placed them both onto the table. There was silence. Ah well, no point putting off the inevitable ... I flipped the catch and opened the box. It was empty.

Carly shrugged. 'Well, that's not really a surprise, is it?' she said.

'But he showed it to me and then shut the box. Neither of us took it out.' I slammed the lid shut. 'I was with him all the time and there was no way he could have taken it out.'

Carly shrugged again. 'Well, he obviously has and, as I said, it's not really a surprise. How do you know that what you saw was the real knife and not just an illusion or a simulacrum?'

'I don't, I suppose. He wouldn't let me touch it.'

Following Carly and Nessus through the cool stone corridors, I didn't really notice where we were or where we were going. I just concentrated on keeping those little giggles under control. Incident after incident rolled through my mind and, with each dead or defeated demon – no, not demon, I corrected myself. Another little giggle threatened to bully its way to the surface; I pushed it firmly back down. What I really wanted to do was curl up in a corner and just let my guilty conscience roll face after face past my inner eye. How could I have been so deluded? Every stupid instruction from Metatron now made sense. For a thousand years I'd been laughing at him, thinking I was so clever to do so little work and do it so badly. No wonder Michael hated me. If I was an example of what the human race had become it was understandable why he was all for annihilating every single one of us. Maybe if I found him and called him a few justified names, that bloody great sword could achieve what I'd failed to do so many times.

That final thought brought me up short. Is that what I'd been trying to do all this time – find a way around my immortality? If I did my job badly enough maybe one of them would be able to finally kill me. Had I spent a thousand years trying to commit suicide by the application of apathy and stupidity? It was no wonder I'd failed: it was a fairly short-sighted plan.

'Hang on a moment.' I reached forward and put a hand on Carly's shoulder. 'If all you've been doing was waiting for me to "see the light" and swap sides, why was that Drekavak trying to kill me?'

Carly stopped walking and, without turning around, stared at her boots. 'She wasn't supposed to, she was just supposed to bring you to me and we were going to explain all this and let you take the file to Metatron. We were taking a huge chance but you had to want to do this.'

'But she didn't say anything …'

Nessus turned with a wince. 'We didn't realise how upset she was.'

'With what? What did I ever do to her?'

123

'Well, you'd already covered her in dog do and thrown her into a tree, then you broke her leg.' Carly ticked points off with her fingers before turning away and leaving me to my thoughts.

I still felt a little aggrieved. The Drekavak had certainly appeared to be trying to kill me. I'm not sure I can be blamed for defending myself. It seemed a little unfair.

'Here we are.' Carly stopped directly in front of me.

Still swinging between self-pity and self-depreciation I bumped square into Nessus's backside. 'Sorry,' I muttered.

'Focus.' Carly grabbed my ear and gave it a twist, smiling at the yelp of pain the familiar manoeuvre elicited. 'You actually have a chance to do a real good turn here, so basically the next 20 minutes or so will be entirely down to you. Just remember, although it feels like it, you're not actually *immortal*.'

'What?' That was against everything I'd been told.

Not giving me time to think she opened the door and pushed me inside. With Nessus behind her, I had no choice but to stagger into the darkened room.

Bulky curtains were tightly closed against the outside world and the thick, cloying scent of heavy incense made the air almost painful to breathe. In the far corner loomed a large bed, its covers ruffled and heaped, grey from long use and spotted with red and yellow stains. To one side, a pair of darkened figures, one large and one small, shared an uncomfortable-looking hard-backed chair.

Standing on the other side of the bed was a demon I recognised. Tall, heavily built and the colour of a week-dead corpse; he looked up with a smile which changed instantly to a look of panic. His yellow eyes widened and he turned, arms outstretched, as though to protect the immobile mound within the bed.

Carly put a pacifying hand up. 'It's all right, Jarroh,' she said. 'I thought he might be able to help.' She turned to face me, a serious look on her face. 'What are you, Joe?' she asked.

'What?' I'd been engaged in a staring contest with the

white demon and it took me a moment to process her question. 'I don't know ... a miserable waste of oxygen maybe?'

Grabbing the soft skin under my upper arm she squeezed hard making me yelp again. 'No snappy comments, please, not now. Come on, concentrate ... What are you?'

As I looked down into her bright green eyes my head buzzed and my tongue seemed to be stuck to the roof of my mouth. I swallowed. What was I? I had no idea: human, angel, pawn, undead? All of these labels passed through my mind, but I knew they weren't the entire story.

'Well?' Carly gave my arm another squeeze, gentler this time.

'I'm sorry.' It was the only thing I could think of that was utterly and completely true. I was sorry: sorry for turning a blind eye; sorry for myself; for others; for everything.

Carly nodded and pulled me toward the bed. The atmosphere in the room grew colder.

A flaccid, grey Drekavak lay in the bed. Thin, clawed hands occasionally clenched then relaxed, plucking feebly at the dirty sheets, its breathing arrhythmic and stertorous. The scales, dull and translucent, were wet with sweat and it was obviously just a waiting game. Sickened by the smell and the inevitable guilt, I peered into the gloomy corner where the two dark figures sat. The larger of the two sat on the chair, its body slumped and its head in an uncomfortable-looking position against the wall as though, while watching the other struggle to breathe, its own body took too much effort to control. Perched on its lap appeared to be a small kangaroo – obviously a young Drekavak who had yet to gain its scales. The youngster was crying continuously and silently, tears making dark tracks on its furry little face, one tiny, clawed paw held that of the one in the bed. Occasionally it would lean forward, a look of hope on its little face but then would sit back and sigh when there was no movement from the figure under the blankets.

As we approached, the adult glanced up incuriously then went back to watching the bed. Slowly its brow furrowed and equally slowly it looked up again, focusing on me.

'You!'

Faster than I would have considered possible it leapt out of the chair, regardless of the youngster that landed, with a squeal, on the bed. Then, grabbing me by the throat, lifted my feet from the floor and casually hurled me across the room. As I hit the polished wood floor the air rushed from my lungs and I had no choice but to lie against the far wall making sounds fairly similar to those of the patient.

Screams and sounds of falling furniture pierced my grey haze. Carly and Nessus were both shouting at the enraged Drekavak to stop. Nessus grabbed for the maddened demon then yelped and ducked as razor-sharp claws ripped across his arm.

'Keril, please wait!' Carly shouted. She ducked as the stool she was holding was torn out of her clutches and sent smashing into the far wall. Nessus pulled her out of the way as the demon thundered past, its narrowed gaze fixed solely on me. Skidding to a halt it reached down and seized my ankle then hauled me, still coughing and gasping, out into the middle of the floor. 'I'm going to rip you limb from limb,' it screamed. 'I was stopped from doing anything terminal to you; couldn't kill you, couldn't confine you. Free will, that's what they told me. You had to come here of your own free will.' Slapping a chair away, it didn't even look away when, hitting the wall, the legs disintegrated into splinters and kindling. 'Was it your own free will that gave you the right to beat up and then stab my sister?' Kicking furniture out of the way, the creature headed toward me. Its normally expressionless face twisted into a snarl, claws ripping through everything in its path.

Trying to ignore the pain in my chest I fumbled around in my pockets. The 'dusters seemed slower than usual to grip my fingers. The angels had been lying to me: the demons had their own agenda. There was nobody to back me up – I was completely alone. This time I wasn't going out lightly. I'd had enough of dying; this time I was doing it for me.

The Drekavak reared back, flicking his claws out;

obviously he really meant to make good on the threat to rip me open. Seeing a slight opening I blocked with my left and cuffed him lightly with my right which hurled him, hard, back across the room. The effect was fairly impressive. He bounced from the far wall and landing heavily on top of a table which promptly collapsed. Small containers of tablets, a bowl of water and half-empty bottles of odd-coloured liquid flew gracefully into the air, sparkling and pin-wheeling before cascading down to soak the stunned demon. He spluttered, groaned then lay still.

Finally able to breathe, I dragged myself to my feet and brushed myself off. I drew my knife. I really didn't care that this was another life I was intending to take. This was self-defence and I was fed up beyond words of people and things attacking me for reasons they were unwilling to explain. Lies – all lies.

As I stalked past the bed, gaze fixed on my attacker, Carly held on to one arm and Nessus took the other. Shaking Carly off was fairly easy; I didn't even need a weapon. Nessus, however, was another matter. I took a firm grip on the centaur's wrist and then lifted and twisted. He screamed as his legs buckled. Stepping over him I continued on toward the dazed demon who was still trying to pick himself up.

Armed as I was I could take them all out. I didn't need to be careful any more. I wanted to get rid of them all. I had no idea whose plan *that* would fit into and I didn't care. Starting right now I would rewrite myself. I wasn't going to be anybody's lackey any more.

Holding the knife loosely in my hand I stepped over the remains of the chair and headed toward the still gasping demon. One long swipe, that's all it would take, and I'd be able to see if the insides of the creature were better looking than the outside.

A small sound made me glance over my shoulder. The child that had been sitting on Keril's lap was staring at me. His huge black eyes followed my every move. His little mouth was open in a soundless scream and he seemed to be trying to burrow himself into the bed. Grabbing the flaccid arm of the patient he had wound himself into her limp caress. Catching me glancing his way, the fuzzy little thing panicked further and began a small backward and forward rocking movement. Still wailing soundlessly, he stared blindly toward me, the very picture of terrified hysteria.

All my murderous intentions vanished and I stopped and dropped the knife. I like kids and they usually like me. Whatever my reasons were for wanting to kill everyone, right now I was that child's worst nightmare and that realisation dropped me like a hammer to the back of the head.

It was actually Keril that physically dropped me. Thundering across the room he tackled me with the ferocity of a New Zealand rugby player and down we both went again. This time Nessus and Carly were there. Nessus merely picked Keril up and confined him in a bear hug. Carly kept up the barrage of shouts, standing between me and the enraged creature forcing him to concentrate on her.

'Keril, stop it! I think he can help ...' She repeated this about four or five times before the combination of her shouting and Nessus squeezing forced the pained demon to finally focus and, with a strained gasp, he managed a short nod.

Sick and confused I sank to the floor and, sitting quietly, let them all scream around me.

Gently and cautiously, Nessus let him go and Keril dropped to all fours beside me, both of us breathing heavily.

The tall white demon, Jarroh, only let the silence last for so long before he came bustling round with his hands full of spilt drugs. He stared at us all. 'No more fighting.' Each word was punctuated with a hiss. He turned to me. 'You ... if you can help, help; if not, get out and let her get on with ...' He turned and gave a quick look at the still sobbing child then sighed. The end of his sentence came out as a hiss: '... sleeping.'

'Nessus, keep an eye on him.' Carly pointed at Keril. She obviously wasn't in the mood for explanations. 'You, come here.' She pulled me toward the bed. The child squeaked and began rocking again. Carly picked him up and handed him to

Keril. 'Shh, Arden, sweetie, don't worry, we're sorry, it'll be OK.' She kept up a meaningless and calming babble as she handed the shaking youngster into the other's waiting arms.

I stared down at the bed. The sleeping patient's chest rose and fell only shallowly as though pressing against a huge weight. A dressing covered her chest which did nothing to stop the black blood from oozing through and around the once-white cotton cover. 'Is this …' I swallowed and turned to Carly.

She nodded. 'This is Alice, Keril's sister and little Arden's mother. This is the lady you cut with that bloody knife of yours. We have less than a day before Arden becomes an orphan. Incidentally his dad is also dead – killed by one of the host a couple of years ago – so he really isn't having a good time at the moment and he has angels to thank for all of it.'

'I'm sorry, I didn't know.' I watched the frail nostrils flutter; in repose the face seemed serene. 'So what … what the hell do you think I can do? Don't you think I've done enough?'

'You need to use the knife on her again.' Carly wandered across the ward and stood over my abandoned weapon.

'NO!' Keril leapt toward me, only just held back by the sheer brawn of Nessus, his muscles at full flex. 'No, please don't put her down.' Keril hugged little Arden and began to sob. The child looked surprised and raised a paw to stroke the older demon's face. 'Don't cry, please don't cry,' it whispered.

'Calm down, Keril, I'm not asking him to kill her.' Carly gently kicked the knife toward me; it skittered across the ward floor with a sound like nails down a blackboard, stopping only when it bumped against my foot. 'Pick it up, Joe.' She stood with hands on hips and glared at me till I complied. I don't know what she expected me to do but there was absolutely no way I was going to use this knife again.

'Don't think.' Carly indicated the demon whose breathing had now deteriorated into a series of short gasps. 'Just place the knife against the wound and "know" that it will undo the damage it's done.'

I shook my head and stepped forward. I had no idea what she expected me to do.

'You're part angel, Joe,' Carly cajoled. 'When Metatron gave you immortality he gave you all the other skills and powers that a member of the Host has. In fact, being one of the most powerful of the Host we're hoping he gave you more than he intended to.'

I stepped closer to the bed. My hand was shaking – why was that? Holding the knife out I stared at it but was surprised to see it disappear beneath a film of tears. Dashing these away with the back of my hand I held the knife out again.

'Lay it on her chest.' Carly walked up behind me. 'Just tell it that you want that act of violence undone. Just "know" that it'll do what you ask, OK?'

My focus concentrated on the point of the knife. I felt as if I were floating. The knife became as light as a paper cut-out and I laid it tenderly against the suppurating wound. 'Go back,' I whispered. It didn't seem quite the right words to use but I had no time to think of anything more poetic. I just knew to my very core that if I had the will to act, that act needed a word to kick-start the whole process.

There was silence as the knife started to glow. A glow that, once established, grew to a clear white light that swallowed both the blade and hilt. The light crept over my hand, up my arm and I winced as it travelled toward my face gathering both speed and ferocity as it burst over my head to cascade down over Alice, who gasped and struggled, her body rigid and her eyes suddenly wide open.

A feeling of utter peace and tranquillity came over me and, for the first time, I felt good, at ease and completely calm.

Alice blinked. This time her gaze was far more intelligent. Seeing me standing next to her bed she reacted in almost the same way as her brother had. Jarroh grabbed my arm and dragged me out of the way before physically holding the enraged Drekavak down.

'Stop it … STOP IT!' He spoke sternly and gripped her wrist.

I don't know where healers are trained but I wonder if there is one single place that teaches that stern snap of tone that brings everyone in a ten-metre radius to a complete halt. 'Right, thank you.' He checked his patient's pulse then lifted the edge of the dressing to peer beneath it. His eyes narrowed and he removed it in one quick movement.

'Ow!' Alice put a paw to her chest and jerked up, staring around at the ward and its silent occupants with a certain amount of incredulous confusion. 'What's the matter with you lot?' She asked then sniffed. Her scales took on a greenish cast. 'Is it me that smells so bad?'

'Mawmaw.' Arden struggled down from his uncle's arms and literally bounced across the room. Her thin face broke into the biggest smile that tiny mouth was capable of.

Watching the two of them I felt something heavy smack me in the backside. For a minute I thought Keril had attacked me again. Actually it was the floor. Without my even noticing, my legs had given way and I'd ended up sitting like a sad clown on the rug. The white glow that had started the healing continued to pulse and shine around me and I lifted a hand to stare at the light that glittered and flowed like sparkling smoke between my fingers. Nothing made any sense. I could see stars and there seemed to be a certain pressure around my temples. Something hit me on the arm … Damn! It was the floor again. It seemed out to get me.

'Whoa – catch him.' I felt rather than saw Carly beside me. 'Joe?' Her voice became faint and fuzzy before it disappeared in a mess of white noise and darkness.

I came to on the sofa in Carly's rooms. From the light coming through the window it seemed to be late afternoon. 'Hey, you've had a fairly major day.' Carly was sitting beside me holding a wet cloth to my forehead. Nessus was leaning his considerable bulk on the wall reading a book. He had his front legs crossed – the very picture of nonchalant relaxation.

Coughing and spluttering I heaved myself upright. 'What

happened?'

Carly stared at me for a moment then shrugged. 'Any advantages you've gained from Metatron's blood have, up to this point, been used on yourself.' She paused to take a sip of tea then, noticing my obvious look of jealousy, laughed and held up another mug– this one full. 'This is the first time you've actually made the specific link between your peanut brain and the use of power.' She paused, obviously considering my look of complete bafflement. 'It's like an elastic band-powered toy: you wind it up and up and up, everything gets tighter and tighter and the more tight it gets the more powerful the initial outcome will be; this had to be fairly powerful. Alice was so close to being dead you had to do an awful lot to heal her. Anyway, you'd built up a huge well of energy over the years and then used something to release it.' She frowned for a moment 'That's a good question actually – what did you say before all that light burst out?'

'Erm …' I tried to remember. 'Go back, I think.'

'"Go back?"' Carly looked bemused. 'Not "Heal" or "Fix" or maybe "Repair"?'

I shook my head. 'No, it was definitely "Go back".'

'Why?' She wandered over and perched on the edge of the sofa next to me and said almost to herself, 'Why not a healing word?'

Putting the cup down on the little table I yawned and stretched until I could hear my joints pop. 'Oh I didn't heal her.' I winced and rolled a shoulder. I think maybe Keril had been going for my face and stamped on my shoulder instead. 'I don't know anything about healing someone so I rebooted her.'

Carly just looked confused.

'You know … just like a computer? I rolled her back to a point she was well, or at least that's what I was intending to do.'

'You did what?' Carly's mouth dropped open. 'Nobody can do that. You would have had to drag a perfect body forward in time and swap it for her broken one.' She shook her head. 'I can't even get my head around how you did that.'

'Just call me Bumblebee.' I quipped, still nose deep in my tea.

'Huh?'

'Oh, there used to be an old myth that bumblebees couldn't fly because it would be against the laws of physics.' I shrugged.

'But they obviously can fly.' Carly looked even more confused.

'Yeah, but it was thought that they could only fly because they didn't know that they couldn't.' I took the opportunity to shuffle a little closer to her and, yawning again, stretched my arm over her shoulders; sometimes those old moves were the best.

Carly laughed and poked me in the stomach. As I squeaked, she leant over to give me a very long lingering kiss that set all the sparks off again. I whimpered as she pulled away. 'We really don't have time for this, but you can have that one on account – save it for when we have a moment and I'll redeem it.'

Standing up she reached out a hand. 'Come on, Bumble-boy, we have to get you back. I think you might have a man to save before Metatron opens him up to see if he's hiding a fortune inside that cookie.' Carly smiled and studied me for a moment. 'But before we pack you off, I think you need to meet my father.'

Nessus put the book he had been reading carefully back into the bookcase and then turned to grin at me.

A cold feeling settled into my stomach. I don't do meeting "parents". They imply a long-term relationship and, over the years, I'd avoided those in the same way most other people avoid the insane. 'Do you really think we're at the "meeting parents" stage yet?' I looked around for my backpack. 'Maybe I ought to go and sort out this thing with Metatron first.'

Carly watched me, her face expressionless.

'When I'm finished there then I'll definitely come back and have tea with Daddy.' I nodded and smiled reassuringly.

It was well past time I was gone.

Carly shook her head and rolled her eyes. 'You are such a prat,' she said. 'How exactly do you think you're going to get to Graham Latimer without my father's help? We need him to distract Metatron while you go and retrieve Lucifer's vessel.'

I felt stupid and snapped at her. 'Well, how's your father going to help with that – offer him a cup of tea and a guided tour of the gardens?'

Nessus roared with laughter. 'You do know whose daughter you been a messin' with, don't you?'

There is a certain point in any conversation like this where the penny drops and you realise that everybody else knows more than you do and they're enjoying your ignorance far too much. I felt that roiling stomach, Sword of Damocles thing start up again and shut my eyes. 'Go on, please do tell me.' I winced and waited.

Nessus's beard tickled my ear. I hadn't even heard him cross the room. 'Belial' he whispered.

I swallowed hard and sank down onto the sofa, then gave Carly a hard stare. 'You have got to be kidding me,' I said. 'You're the daughter of Lucifer's second-in-command. The Prince of Evil. Demon of utter destruction and ruin?'

Carly nodded happily. 'Daddy!' she said with a high-pitched little girl tone and then giggled.

'You do realise he's going to rend me limb from limb then burn the pieces, then he'll use my head as an ashtray, don't you?' I asked

Carly laughed and, getting to her feet, she held out her hand for me to grasp. 'You can't believe all you're told,' she said. 'He's a little "old school" but he's lovely.' Dragging me to my feet she headed toward the door.

Nessus gave me a huge grin, and then clapped me on the shoulder. 'Don't worry,' he said. 'He dotes on Carly, and as long as you haven't upset her you'll live through the next hour ...' He shrugged. 'Probably.'

There was no doubt about it: this was definitely not turning out to be one of my better days.

We walked through the city and I found myself forgetting our purpose as, around each corner, libraries and shops, communal areas, gardens, coffee houses and smiling people took my breath away. It was a beautiful place. Each statue, fountain or play area had been placed with intense consideration to the buildings around it. In one small crescent of coffee shops and bakeries, wooden trestle tables and bench seats had been set within a small orchard of about ten apple trees, their long branches hanging over the tables shading those that were eating and occasionally dropping apples which were eagerly snatched up and shared by those beneath them.

'Don't you have crime here?' I asked. 'Or wasps?'

Carly frowned at me. 'Of course we do.' She shook her head. 'Well, we don't have wasps, but we have things that are just as irritating.'

Nessus snorted. 'Tretins.' He shuddered. 'Burrow under your skin like ticks, but they're flying little blood suckers. Give you horrible blisters and, if they're not removed quickly, the skin around them starts to die off leaving patches and scars.'

'So do you have prisons and courts and things?' I ignored the quick lesson on local entomology.

'Nope.' Carly reached up and picked an apple from a tree. 'We don't need them, because we can cheat.' She bit into the fruit with a smile and pointed to a tall building across a tiled square. 'Anyone breaks the laws they face my father and Parity, or Farr, her brother.'

'Who?' I asked.

'Parity can tell if you're lying and look at any place or building and tell you what happened there, she's a ...' She paused. 'Nessus what *is* Parity?'

Nessus groaned. 'I have no idea what she's actually called,' he said, 'but the word "freaky" comes to mind.'

'She is a bit.' Carly nodded. 'Her brother Farr talks to the dead – he's a necromancer.' She shrugged. 'So between the two of them, there isn't a crime that doesn't get solved and, if the crimes are always solved, people tend to leave here before they do anything wrong. Criminals prefer to at least have a chance of getting away with whatever they want to do. Well,' she amended, 'the sensible ones do.' She looked around the square. 'Those who've committed minor crimes have to pay back in kind. They clean the city or fix things. Those that have murdered or raped get banished to one of the dead lands where they can prey on each other.' She picked up the pace as we passed a small group of laughing kids who were throwing water at one another in a fountain. One looked very much like an otter and was using his tail to create huge waves that swamped the others, leaving them soaked and gasping with laughter. 'It's not a perfect system but it's as close as we can get.'

'So no lawyers?'

'Nope.'

'Prisons?'

'Nope.' She shrugged. 'There's no point to them. Lies don't work here, and if you can't lie, you can't even protest. With Parity working for my father, offenders don't get the chance to even bend the truth. She sees *exactly* what happened, and every offence has a set punishment – they are published and displayed in the library. You come here, you commit a crime, you will be found and you will be punished. There will be no appeals, no reduced sentences; it's all very much set in stone.'

As we climbed a tall set of marble steps I noticed there was a large carved and polished wooden sign set above the impressive shining doors that read "Fiat Justicia". Under the heavy weight of that pronouncement I sidled through the door wondering what the punishment would be for trying to seduce the judge's daughter. I decided that I would avoid this Parity at all costs. I considered the implications of her "gift" then decided not to think about it any more; that would be one scary woman.

At the top of a slim and winding flight of stairs a door barred our way. Without hesitation Carly pushed her way through and, striding across an expanse of cream carpet, she skirted a huge table to the far end where a man sat frowning at a pile of paperwork. She put her arms around his neck and gave him a peck on the cheek. 'Hey, Dad.'

The man jumped – he obviously hadn't even noticed the door opening. Blinking for a moment he turned and smiled at Carly. 'Carlotta.' He stood and stretched. 'I see you're late, as usual.' Yawning hugely he dragged a hand through his dark hair and stared blankly around the room for a moment before rubbing his eyes with the heels of his palms. 'But then so is everyone else.' He nodded at Nessus. 'Hey, Ness.' He rolled his shoulders and frowned as, lagging behind, I sidled through the doors.

'Father, this is Joe.' She linked her arm into his and pulled him to his feet. Walking beside her around the table Belial didn't take his eyes off me – not even to blink – and in the 20 steps it took him to reach me I had started sweating profusely.

We studied each other. He was a little taller and a little heavier than me. Bright, intelligent blue eyes peered out from beneath dark brows that were sporting more than a couple of grey hairs. His long dark hair was dragged haphazardly into a tail at the nape of his neck. Full, sensuous lips curved in a smile. It looked genuine. I did a quick reassess – no horns, no red skin, no blazing fiery eyeballs. Check, just another lie.

'Joe.' Belial shook my hand then, taking my arm, he guided me to a seat at the table. 'I understand my daughter has been giving you a bit of a hard time.' He poured a coffee from a tall silver jug that was standing on a tray in the middle of the table. Holding up cream, he raised his eyebrows.

I nodded. 'I understand why, sir.' I bit my lip – I hadn't meant to call him that. I hadn't meant to give him any honorific at all, it just slipped out.

He smiled and passed me a delicate bone china mug full of steaming coffee. 'Well, she has her own reasons for doing what she does. I have come to learn that it's easier just to let her do her own thing.' He looked rueful. 'In fact, on the few occasions I've tried to interfere I've been scolded quite soundly.' He looked up at the large clock that was hanging from the wall then clapped me on the shoulder. 'When this is all over we'll talk, but for now ...' He left the words hanging as the door opened and a woman stepped through.

I stared at her. This had to be the dreaded Parity. She glided through the door, her tall stilettos making no sound on the thick carpet but leaving a series of punctures in the pile that followed her progress like a dotted line on a map. Immaculately cut black trousers and matching jacket made her business like and her bearing left you in no doubt that you'd better be very, very respectful.

There was no way that she would ever be described as pretty, or even beautiful. This woman looked dangerous but there was something about her that made you want to linger on her features – even if it caused offence, which was almost guaranteed to cost you dearly. High cheekbones and full lips certainly caught your attention, but once you'd looked into her eyes you were lost. Larger than any humans and almost completely circular the blues, purples and pinks of the iris moved like oil on windblown water – the unnerving colours lapping around a slit pupil that reflected no light at all. Her brows, slim and high, only served to add to her severity – as did her hair. Drawn back into a ruthlessly neat bun she had trapped the shining black strands in an elegant cage of silver then locked and impaled it with an elegant, carved wooden stick from which hung two silver bells on black ribbons. She moved with feline grace, sinuous and powerful and, belled like a naughty cat, she gave off warnings that you would be wise to heed.

Nodding to Belial she smiled around the room. Her bright red lips moved apart in a slow and sensuous curve which framed her white teeth; each one as sharp as a dagger, they speared little dimples into her lower lip. Taking a seat on Belial's right she stared at me for a long moment then spoke in a soft sibilant hiss. 'You must be Joe,' she said.

I swallowed and nodded. I felt about ten years old and desperately suppressed the need to wipe my sweating palms down my trousers.

Eventually she looked away, those unnerving eyes sweeping the room 'Hello, Carly.' She grinned and her face

138

softened a fraction.

'Melusine.' Carly's smile looked a fraction forced.

I shook my head. 'Melusine?'

The woman laughed – a gentle girlish sound which caused yet more sweat to break out on my brow.

'Just stop it, will you!' Carly frowned. 'There's no way he'll be able to concentrate if you carry on like this.'

Melusine's bow lips formed a little moue. 'Oh all right.' She huffed an exaggerated sigh. 'You spoil all my fun.'

Nothing seemed to change but suddenly she wasn't so attractive any more. I shook my head again causing her to laugh – a proper laugh this time. 'Sorry, Joe,' she said – her voice had lost the sexy sing-song huskiness. 'That was mean of me.'

I didn't get time to answer as the door burst open and a man and woman scrambled through, arguing heatedly as they walked, jostling and pushing each other in a raggedy drunken course across the room.

'Well, if you didn't try and run my life for me …' A small woman with short flame red hair, a riot of rings in her nose, eyebrow and lip shouted at a tall skinny man. Her cheeks were red with fury and her lips set in a straight line. As the man tried to grip her arm she whipped it out of his reach then, with a sharp turn, stared up at him, hands fisted at her thighs. 'You're my brother, Farr, not my bloody father, so just fucking well back off!' Raising a hand covered in rings she pinched the bridge of her nose and, rolling her eyes, turned again and stamped across the room. Pulling the chair beside me out with a vicious tug she slumped down into it and closed her eyes.

'Parity.' The tall man, his unstyled dark hair awry and his glasses askew, pulled out the chair beside her and settled astride it, his arms resting on the back. 'You just push it all the time, and I'm the one that has to pick up the pieces.' He frowned and was obviously about to carry on with his lecture when Belial held up a hand.

'Children, if you please,' he said.

Parity and Farr both looked a little guilty. 'This is Joe.'

139

Belial extended an elegant hand toward me.

Ignoring her brother, the small woman turned to me. 'Hi.' She gave me a huge beaming smile. She had bright green eyes, one of which was hidden under the shocking red wave of fringe that flopped over her forehead. Farr nodded as he resettled his glasses, his face as closed as his sister's was open.

With her mad hair, leopard print tights, huge boots and short skirt, Parity was an enigma – her appearance totally at odds with her reputation. Unfortunately, I didn't really have time to consider this as three figures appeared in the open doorway. Taking a deep breath I pushed my chair away from the table and stood up in order to talk to the new arrivals.

Keril was followed in by Alice who was carrying Arden. They all approached slowly, each eyeing me with the same blank look. I walked over to meet them and held out my hand to Alice. 'How are you feeling?' I asked. Arden whimpered and hid his face in his mother's shoulder.

'Fine, thank you.' Alice spoke in a dead voice. Staring at me, she ignored my hand.

I took a deep breath. If I didn't get this off my chest now, I doubted I ever would. 'I'm sorry, really very sorry.' I licked my lips – they'd dried up and my throat felt slightly restricted. I tried not to look at Keril who was looming over his sister obviously waiting for me to make one false move.

'I'd been lied to. I didn't know what was going on.' I didn't know what to say; there was either too much or just not enough. 'I'm sorry.' I shrugged. It was a lame finish but it was the best that I could do.

Alice looked at me for a moment, her long face expressionless. The only hint of her feelings was broadcast by her scales as they rippled and changed colours in quick succession. Eventually she shook her head and allowed a small smile. 'It was almost worth being stabbed just to feel like I do now,' she said. 'What did you do to me? I feel 60 years younger.'

Carly smiled at Alice and then tickled Arden who giggled into his mum's neck. 'I think Dad's waiting to get on,' she said.

Belial nodded and stood up. 'This is a very quick meeting.' He gave a mock glare at the brother and sister who sat pointedly ignoring each other. 'Very quick, so no arguments – we'll do all that later.' There were nods around the table. 'I'll hand you over to Melusine to tell you what's going on.'

The sultry businesswoman stood up and walked over to stand behind Belial. 'As you've been told, we have to make this quick. He,' she pointed at me, 'needs to steal something from Metatron and we need to get "The Voice" out of the way.' She paused. 'Really simple, really effective. I need suggestions.'

'Attack Heaven?' Parity drawled with a laugh. 'That should bring the mouthpiece out of his hole fairly quickly.'

Melusine shook her head. 'Thanks for that, Parity, but I'd really like an option where every citizen of Hell and the surrounding worlds don't actually end up as dust before the gates of Heaven.' She looked around then began walking around the table. 'Come on, people, we only need him out of his office for a short amount of time.'

Keril frowned then looked around the table. 'Are we really just going to trust him?' He nodded toward me. 'Just like that – no ifs, buts or maybes?'

Belial shrugged. 'You ask that knowing that there really isn't any choice.' He pushed his chair away from the table then began to wander around the room. 'Metatron has Lucifer's vessel and is currently trying to work out ways of getting him out of it. We only have a very limited time before he realises that he's not as well equipped as he thinks he is and then he's going to come looking for the last thing he needs. We have, at the most, about 12 hours before he starts taking his failure badly.' Belial slumped back into his chair and stared down at his nails.

Parity huffed a short laugh. 'Release Gabriel?' she suggested. 'That would get The Voice's attention.'

Melusine sniffed. 'If we knew where he was we just might. However, I thought we'd established with your last

141

suggestion that we didn't all want to die in new and fascinating ways.'

Parity just stared, straight faced, at the other woman. 'Well, that wouldn't bother me now, would it,' she said.

Farr looked up from where he'd been drawing perfect circles, freehand, on a piece of paper. 'The host have just been here for the talks, haven't they?' he said.

Melusine nodded. 'Just a couple of days ago.'

'Have we signed the accords for this period yet?' He chewed nervously on a clean fingernail.

'Not yet,' Belial said.

'What if we needed to argue over a big point?' Farr pushed his glasses up his nose and ran a hand through his hair, shaking his head when it flopped back. 'Make a stand – a stand on some issue that only God can pass a judgement.' Farr shrugged and looked slightly embarrassed. 'For that we'd need The Voice, wouldn't we?'

'Why would he come?' Parity studied her nails. 'Why should he?'

Belial jumped up with a snort. 'Because he can't afford not to.' He grinned at Carly. 'As far as he's concerned we have no idea what's going on and he really needs to keep it that way.' Getting to his feet, he slapped Farr on the back. The necromancer winced. 'I knew that geeky exterior of yours hid real brains.' He trotted over to a tall bookcase and drew out a leather scroll case which, after extracting the contents, he tossed casually aside. 'I think I know just the clause.' He looked around at everyone as he unrolled the scroll. 'As we keep saying, we need to do this *now*.' He pointed at me again. 'Mr Latimer doesn't have much time.' We'll pick up this meeting again when Joe's collected the artefact in question.' He paused and looked over at Carly.

'You have one hour, then get him over there.' He shrugged. 'After that we'll just keep The Voice occupied as long as we can.' He smiled around at everyone again. 'Isn't this exciting! Come on, people, let's go and argue petty points of order, shall we?'

Greatly daring, I gave a sort of half-hearted wave in

Belial's direction.

He raised his eyebrows at me.

'Aren't we already too late? It's been hours since I left.'

Belial shook his head and walked over to me. 'He's still alive, although he probably wishes he wasn't. If Metatron kills his Host, Lucifer might move on but as there are no further descendants of that line he could end up anywhere and he'd have to start the search again.' He looked around. 'Good luck, people – let's go.' He stared at me for a moment. 'Don't let us down, Joe. I know you can do this and, if you don't, billions are going to die. No pressure.' He gave me a huge grin then slapped me on the shoulder. He was much, much stronger than he looked and it took everything I had to nod and grin around the pain.

Everyone trooped out leaving Carly and I alone in the office. 'I'm not sure I can do this.' My legs felt shaky and I sat down in a rush.

Carly sat on the edge of the table and looked down at me. 'You have to get Graham Latimer away from Metatron.' She held my face firmly by the chin and shook me slightly. 'If Metatron succeeds in separating the Morning Star from his protective body, we are all finished. The world is finished – in fact, let's be honest, all the worlds will be finished.' She frowned and gave me a slightly embarrassed look. 'In fact, I'd go so far as to say it really will be the end of everything until that time as Metatron, who will be God, decides to remake it all again to *his* plan. Of course, by that time it will be far too late for the billions of creatures who will have been swept away into the utter negation of some voidic melting pot. They'll just simmer away and wait to be reformed into something this new God finds acceptable.'

'Oh.' I swallowed hard and stood up. 'Why me?' I leant on the table and stared at my hands. 'I can't do that. I'll just mess it up – there's got to be thousands of people that can do this better than me.'

Carly slid off the table and grabbed my face with both small hands. 'It has to be you.' She stared at me. 'You're the only one that can get into Metatron's office.'

143

'Then you'd better send someone with me.' I pulled my head out of her hands and waited for my sudden wave of nausea to subside. 'Preferably someone with intelligence, common sense and a good fighting ability, because I'm beginning to think I don't have any of those things.'

'You'll do just fine.' Carly grabbed my hand and pulled. When I was upright she kissed me surprisingly hard. 'You know, we were getting on really well that day I made dinner and I feel like we missed an opportunity, don't you? We never really got to finish that date successfully.' She pressed herself against me and kissed me again, then stood back with a look of disappointment. 'When all this is over ...' She left the promise dangling enticingly.

As far as certain parts of me were concerned, the end of the world had suddenly become a trivial issue.

Back at Carly's rooms we repacked my rucksack. Reaching over she removed my mobile before I could stow it away. 'You won't need that any more.' Dropping it casually to the floor she stamped on it. There was a loud crack, a spark of red light and the phone disappeared leaving a gently smouldering spot on the carpet.

'Great,' I said. 'So how exactly am I supposed to move around now?'

'You don't need it, you great goof.' Carly tapped me with one stiff finger right between the eyebrows. 'Everything you need is in there. All the Host can just move from one place to another on a thought – and so can you.'

'But I don't know how to do all the stuff they can do.' I coughed. I hate it when my voice comes out in a whine.

'Bumblebees, remember?' Carly leant over to give me a kiss then slapped me hard around the back of the head. 'Don't think about it, don't analyse it, just bloody well do it.'

I gulped and nodded. She made it sound so easy but I felt hot and had difficulty taking a breath. To my knowledge I'd never had anyone show that much faith in my ability to do anything; I wasn't sure I liked the feeling.

'I reckon you've got two hours at the most.' Nessus brought a heavy hand down on my shoulder and looked surprised when I shrieked. 'Good luck.'

I swallowed, hard. If a nine-foot horse-man-thing could sneak up on me I was fairly sure I was doomed. I nodded again and, with a last look at Carly, I closed my eyes and told myself, very sternly, I was somewhere else.

# CHAPTER 6

METATRON'S OFFICE WAS DESERTED. I took a deep breath. This was probably the last time I'd ever see this place and I wandered about, gently running my fingers over the desk. Metatron's mug still stood in pride of place on his blotter. *World's best boss.* Well, there you are – can't believe everything you read on mugs. I could hear the ducks quacking as they swam around the pond behind "that" window, the happy sound completely at odds with the cool, reflective peace of the office.

'Come on, think.' I spoke to Lucifer's painting. Had that changed? I didn't remember his face being so devoid of emotion. Expressionless, his eyes seemed to follow me around the office; it was unnerving.

As the ducks finally fell silent I could hear a soft sobbing, intermittent and sporadic as though someone were trying hard, but ultimately failing, to restrain themselves. I walked slowly around the walls, trying to trace the sound. It was a terrible thing to hear – each gulping sob sounded as though it were being ripped physically from the weeper's lungs. There would be silence for a moment then another sob or a small moan would erupt to disturb the silence.

After what seemed an age, I finally decided that the sound was a little louder on one side of the room. I hovered by an innocently blank wall and listened hard. Placing both palms flat against its surface I rested my ear between my hands and closed my eyes.

'Please.' A sob, a grating breath. 'Please, God help me.' A gurgle as though someone were trying to breathe through water, then another small whisper. 'Please.'

Bumblebee time. Closing my eyes I concentrated then, *knowing* that I was leaning on a door that would lead to that

146

terrible sound, I reached out blindly for the handle. It would be just to the right of my hand. Ah yes, there it was – just grasp and turn. With my eyes still shut, I pushed open the nonexistent door and stepped through.

When I opened my eyes I wished I'd kept them closed. There are times when a sight is so vast, so dreadful, so utterly abhorrent that your brain just shuts down and sits in the corner of your skull with its eyes closed and its fingers in its metaphorical ears shouting, 'I can't see this, I can't hear this, la, la, la.'

I'd stepped into a world of pain.

In the centre of the room a large crucifix had been raised, its wood old and blackened. In the neon glare of the overhead tubes the whole scenario looked like a film set. Hanging from the cross was a man, naked except for a pair of once white boxer shorts.

My mind gibbered on and refused to accept what my eyes were seeing. I had a sudden flash memory of a similar scene. A cross on a hill, women weeping and a man begging forgiveness for those that had done this to him – no doubt from some film I'd watched. My stomach joined forces with my brain and refused to work, churning over and over like a washing machine set forever to spin. I pushed the image away. Thanks for that, Hollywood, I thought, I think I can see the similarities without needing it in glorious Technicolor as well.

Staggering toward the agony, I felt as though my legs were being controlled by a trainee puppeteer. So when I tripped over a chair that had been placed before the cross, obviously a ringside seat, I wasn't really surprised. Beside the chair was an open tool roll which held a hammer, some long iron nails and the "knife", all of which were covered in blood giving hideous testament to how much they'd been utilised. Blood dripping and spraying had made strange patterns of sweeps and lines across the floor. The dark liquid had pooled around the bottom of a coffee mug which read: *Don't piss me off, I'm running out of places to hide the bodies* and had an inch or so of coffee at the bottom – still

147

warm. I was honestly surprised not to find an empty popcorn box; obviously Metatron had been enjoying himself. Finally, I forced myself to look up at the man on the cross. I couldn't imagine how long he'd been there, nor how he was still alive.

Hearing me gagging, Graham Latimer moaned. 'I don't know what you want.' He sobbed and tightly shut the one eye that wasn't a swollen red and purple mess. Even this small effort was obviously too great a strain and, as his head slumped forward onto his chest, his sweat and blood-soaked hair flopped forward to cover his lacerated face.

'Jeez!' I hurried toward him, not really noticing the irony of my exclamation.

Tears had washed lines of blood away from his cheeks and down his chest. His underpants were soaked with blood and urine; there were pools of both on the floor beneath his crossed and impaled feet. Huge iron nails had also been driven through his palms and blood trickled from his hands. I watched, almost mesmerised, as it ran down into his armpits then travelled slowly down his body to drip onto the floor. Each drip echoed in the otherwise silent room. I couldn't stand it. I had to get him down.

I tried to study him objectively. There were two deep wounds in his chest and one in his thigh – it was so close to the artery that a couple of centimetres to the side and he would have bled out within seconds. How wonderful that Metatron was so well versed in the art of torture – another small skill of his that I knew nothing about.

Unable to bear the smell and the taste of the air any more I spat to clear my mouth. Then, realising time was running out for us all and not just the poor soul up on that wooden monstrosity, I dragged the chair over to the bottom of the cross. A second trip armed me with the hammer and a pair of large pliers. 'Sorry, mate,' I muttered to the nearly unconscious man. 'This is really going to hurt.'

The extraction of the first nail caused him to scream so loudly that the sound brought a mouthful of bile up my throat and I had to swallow hard to clear it. However, after that first scream he passed out and became, mercifully, silent.

Working as swiftly as I dared, I ripped out the other nails leaving him hanging only by his wrists tied securely with rough twine around the wood.

Throwing the hammer and pliers away I took a deep breath. I wasn't strong enough to lower him down gently – all I could really do was hope to steady his fall. I cut the first set of ropes. Thrusting my shoulder into his chest I pushed him up against the cross while I prepared to cut the other.

As we fell, I gripped him hard and decided that we were at home.

It wasn't a graceful landing and we rolled, a cartwheel of arms, legs, blood (his) and curses (all mine), across the floor. Desperate to disengage myself from the tangle of limbs I pushed him away and staggered to my feet. Everything was as I'd left it: my open weapons box was still sitting by the sofa and all else seemed to be intact. I allowed myself a small sigh of relief.

A drawn-out groan reminded me that I had a guest – a guest who was currently making a severe mess of my carpet. Thick, dark blood oozed from the deep wounds in his hands, feet, his side, his leg and his left eye. It had mostly scabbed over the hundreds of cuts, scrapes and scratches that had been systematically placed to cover his entire body. They were shallow wounds, specifically placed to cause maximum pain and discomfort yet minimum blood loss; it seemed that when these had failed to elicit the required response, only then had Metatron moved on to inflicting more direct pain.

Taking a closer look I realised that various bones had also been broken: three of his fingers were at odd angles; his right wrist felt grating and wobbly; one shoulder was so out of alignment it could only have been a dislocation; and there was an odd depression in his side that was almost certainly indicative of at least two snapped ribs. I could only speculate what internal injuries there might be.

Sitting back on my heels I studied the man. He obviously had to have medical help as soon as possible. His breathing was shallow, a line of blood and spittle dribbled, bubbling, from the corner of his mouth to join the growing and diverse pool of bodily fluids that were rapidly spreading across my floor. That carpet really was never going to be the same again – and I'd only had it put down last year.

Dragging my mind away from mundane idiocies I dithered. I couldn't heal him; those injuries were far too serious. I wouldn't even know where to start. I had to get him to someone who could help him. Frustrated, I dropped my head into my hands and tried to still my circling thoughts.

I had to get him to Hell. I was fairly sure that Jarroh – Alice's doctor – would help me out. At least he'd be able to identify the bits that were broken. As I stared, Graham Latimer twitched slightly then, with a rattling sigh, his chest fell and he stopped breathing.

'No, no, no, NO.' It seemed to be the only word I could think of and I screamed it at him over and over again as I patted and shook the inert body. Well, now I really didn't have any choice: I had to try and heal him here and damn the consequences. Things certainly couldn't get any worse. Reaching over my shoulder I dragged out my knife and, quickly running through the steps I'd taken with Alice, I prepared to try and repeat the procedure. I'd done it once – surely I could do it again.

Taking a deep breath, I took the knife in my left hand and tried to recapture those feelings of building energy. I couldn't do it. A little voice just kept telling me that even if I healed him, I'd be so drained and exhausted Metatron would just walk in, take him and there'd be nothing I could do about it. I wouldn't even be able to get him away. Ignoring my screaming little doubts I managed to convince myself that I'd stored enough energy and, making sure I kept my eyes closed (I certainly didn't want to see that there was no glow to my knife), I held my shaking hand against Graham's chest and whispered, 'Return.'

There was nothing. Deep down I knew it wasn't going to work. Almost sobbing with frustration I opened my eyes and tried again. 'RETURN!' I screamed down at the body then waited. Still nothing. As the miserable lump in my throat grew, I realised that I was crying. I'd screwed up yet again. I took a huge shuddering breath and, trying to still my palsied knife hand, I pressed it once more to his chest and whispered, 'Please, please heal.'

My shaking hand dragged the knife in a haphazard jagged scratch across the already tortured flesh. Fresh blood welled into a long line of shining, ruby spheres. As usual, all I'd managed to do was make things worse. I took the knife away and thrust it back into its sheath. 'Oh come on, don't die on me, what am I going to tell Carly?' Wiping my eyes with the back of my hand, I knelt back on my heels and wondered what I was going to do.

I checked the man's pulse. There was nothing, all quiet; he was almost certainly dead. It was odd though, the blood from the scratch I'd inadvertently given him had begun to creep *up* his chest. That was impossible, wasn't it? Unable to stop myself I leant forward to watch its progress.

Graham Latimer sat up in one swift movement and screamed. Throwing myself back out of his reach I screamed with him. His undamaged eye opened and he stared blindly at a point behind me, his expression both pained and terrified. The lights blew out leaving us in darkness. With only that never-ending scream for company and my heart beating like a madman playing a steel drum I paddled backwards until I hit the wall then, unable to go any farther, I began to edge along it hoping to find the door – anything to get away from that terrible sound.

The small shallow cut extended in both directions, its progress marked by silver light that fizzed and hissed as it moved. Up over the collarbone it ran like a ladder in a pair of tights, along his chin then around towards the left ear. His filthy hair stood away from his head, a dark dandelion of static electricity. The other end of the cut extended down, doglegging around his stomach, disappearing as it plunged beneath the waistband of his soiled underwear: The screaming continued.

As much as I wanted to run, I found it impossible to look away and stifled the urge to hide under the table as Graham Latimer began, quite literally, to split in half. It was as

151

though someone was using a cutting torch on him. Through the crack in his body tiny but brilliant lights began to erupt into the stinking, thick air of my living room. Electric blue, neon purple, white and deep red all burst from the gaping wound to flicker and rotate – mad fireflies born from human skin. The lightshow spun round and round. Occasionally one small light would be flung from the body where it would flicker and die as another took its place.

As the travelling crack reached his throat Graham's voice cut off mid-wail. The sudden silence was even more terrifying than the screaming. He began to shake, twisting and turning, his split mouth open in that soundless agony. I still hadn't moved. I couldn't move.

Distantly, I heard a banging on the door, then the letter box flapped – a jarring metallic noise at odds with the insane and silent lightshow taking place before me.

'I know you're there.' Mr Morris had his face to the letter opening. 'My wife's in hospital, you know. I need my sleep and you – you inconsiderate prat – are watching horror films! Turn it down!' The flap banged shut, then immediately opened again. 'You turn that down or I'm calling the police.'

Ignoring him I kept my horrified gaze on the glowing figure, noting each change with a morbid curiosity. The crack, having reached the limits of its journey, suddenly erupted into a frayed crazy paving of glowing slashes and curves, a lit map of every vein and artery in the human body. The lights ran like water over every inch of exposed skin, even separating his hair into many sparkling partings. The swiftly changing colours became a pulsing glow, so bright it hurt. Then, still in almost absolute silence, the whole thing rose toward the ceiling. Hanging about two feet from the ground the figure began to rotate. Small splashes of light, flung from the body, landed on the floor where they inched away like worms before silently exploding in little starburst flares. The figure turned. I watched and, as my initial terror began to ebb, I struggled to my feet to get a closer look.

Before I could move, the body hanging before me exploded violently and silently outward throwing me once more to the floor. A mixture of fast travelling light and what appeared to be small pieces of burnt paper erupted outward in a wave, each dark mote flared for a moment burning quickly and brightly before it blinked out. The very air tasted greasy. Throwing my arm across my face I squeezed my eyes shut and watched the after images of lines and curves dance in red patterns across the inside of my eyelids. When I opened them again the room was in semidarkness.

I blinked as my eyes adjusted to the sudden twilight. I tried to make out the details of the man's silhouette that, despite having literally exploded only seconds before, still hung, rotating slowly, suspended in midair. Its slick, wet skin glistened dully, showing reflections from the streetlights outside; those safe, yellow balls of light, a solid and physical reassurance that all was well in the "normal" world. The man – it was quite obviously a man – hung in space, eyes closed, his head resting on his left shoulder and his long arms dangling at his sides. Pushing myself away from the wall once more I peered at the figure, trying to work out if he was alive.

Single tongues of flame at his head, heart, groin and hands burst simultaneously to life. These tiny dancing motes of light multiplied and accelerated until bright wheels of fire span freely over his body. As the burning figure rotated, the skin at each shoulder blade bulged outward – small volcanic eruptions pulsed and bubbled, becoming brighter and brighter until the flames glowed white.

As the skin on each shoulder finally split, he flung his head back and an unearthly sound issued from the open mouth. A thousand fog horns, the crash of a massive storm, the sound of lightning hitting an unstable mountain, an avalanche – all of this and more heralded the slow unfolding of huge, trembling black wings. The first beat of these wings sent out a shockwave rather stronger than the flap of a butterfly. Finally the silence was broken.

The sudden howling wind that swept around the room pinned me to the wall. Picking up books and other small items it swatted at me as I struggled to get away. Putting my head down I leant into the tempest and tried to hold onto the wall. Breathing was becoming difficult as my chest was compressed by the energy being flung from the figure that hung in perfect serenity, wings aloft, twisting gently in its own pool of light.

Taking as deep a breath as I could and, borrowing what I needed from the howling maelstrom, I attempted to create a barrier. It seemed to work and, having created it, I pushed it away from my body to act as a shield. But as I pushed forward I felt the wall behind me shudder and, even over the howling wind, heard a rather sickening creak. Ignoring the interplay of the forces I was creating, I gave my barrier a final thrust in an effort to protect myself.

I felt the bricks behind me first bow then crumble and, in a rain of falling masonry, pictures and dust, I was hurled backward through the adjoining wall to land winded and gasping onto the flower-patterned carpet of the Morris' front room. My shield vanished.

As I lay there, coughing occasionally to clear the dust from my protesting lungs, I realised that although I had a ringing in my ears and there was the occasional sound of a late brick tumbling to join the rest of the rubble, general silence had finally fallen. The assault seemed to have finished and, apart from something sharp in the small of my back and a rare first-edition copy of Grimms' Fairy Tales on my chest, I seemed to have come through the whole thing pretty much unscathed. I carefully looked around.

Kicking away various bits of masonry, I rolled over and began to drag myself out of the mess. Clambering to my feet, I blew the dust from the book and placed it carefully in one of my deep jacket pockets before beating dust out of the rest of my clothes. I futilely rubbed streaming eyes with the back of my hand trying to work out if it was dust or concussion that was causing my failing eyesight. Staring through the gap I realised that the dark figure in the living room had also fallen prey to the book and brick whirlwind that had felled me. No longer floating in his quiet paranormal bubble, he had fallen heavily into the mess and was currently lying on the carpet, unconscious and covered in what appeared to be the "C" and "D" authors from my fiction collection.

Mr Morris appeared in his hall with Henry at his heels. They both stared, horrified, into the living room. 'What the hell have you done?' he shouted. 'You … you … you …' His mouth hung open. 'What happened?'

I rescued the Prince of Darkness, then he exploded and cursed both our houses. I shook my head – nope, that wasn't going to wash, and I couldn't really claim innocence as I had one leg on my side of the wall and one leg on his. I searched desperately for something to say and came up with the oldest excuse in the book. 'Gas, I think.' My voice sounded like a can of rusty nails being shaken about. I coughed in an effort to clear the dust from my lungs. 'Definitely gas.'

He spluttered and advanced. 'You're paying for this, you useless layabout.' He stared horrified around the room. 'You'd better have insurance.'

I didn't have time for this. I staggered toward the book-covered figure. I was just about to reach out to him when a sudden crash from the hall made me turn to face yet another threat.

'Joe!' Carly shot through the front door. 'We have to go – now!' She stopped and stared around. 'What the hell happened here?' Shaking her head she tripped and staggered over the rubble to grab my arm. 'It doesn't matter. Joe, he's coming, we have to go NOW!'

'Who?' I couldn't think. I was still coughing, my eyes were still watering and a recently dead man on my floor looked as though he might be breathing again.

'Metatron!' Carly shouted as she tugged on my arm. 'He's coming.' Releasing me she hurdled the rubble to stare at Graham. 'Joe! We have to get back!'

It was too late. With the sound of splintering wood and tortured hinges the front door was ripped away and Metatron, as I'd never seen him, swept into the house. No serenity, no halo, no pristine white wings – this was a being of pure fury and revenge; a true angel of the host. Eyes blazing and hands hooked into claws it came towards us at a frightening speed.

Howling and screaming, there seemed to be very little of my old boss behind those hard yellow eyes.

Grabbing Graham with one hand and Carly with the other, I didn't even think about what I was trying to do – I just tied a knot in the world and opened a doorway straight to Hell. Metatron's howl of fury followed us right up until I slammed the door shut.

'– id you do? What did you DO?' Carly was screaming as we appeared in her apartment. Wrestling her arm from my hand she collapsed onto the sofa gasping, her eyes wide and her hair on end.

I slumped and staggered as Graham's still unconscious body sagged toward the floor. Ignoring Carly's hysterical babbling I took a good look at him. The man was clean, completely naked. There were no cuts, no torn skin; he wasn't stabbed, he wasn't bleeding and he wasn't broken; he also wasn't Graham Latimer.

Letting him slide gently to the floor I backed away. I tried to get Carly's attention by flapping a hand at her but she was still ranting about close encounters and narrow escapes. This man was taller than the poor insurance salesman, well muscled but slim, younger. Even in repose he was handsome with his strong jaw, high cheekbones and full lips. Graham's dark hair now sported a single white stripe that ran from crown to jaw; his hair had also grown long – the razor-cut fringe flopped over his slim, defined eyebrows.

'Joe!' Carly snapped at me and, when I took no notice, she snatched a mug from the table and threw it at me. I jumped as it sailed past my head to smash against the door.

I tried to look at her but my eyes kept sliding back to the man on the floor.

Infuriated, Carly thumped the sofa. 'Joe, JOE.' She looked around for something else to throw. 'Don't ignore me – you could have killed us all! What did you do to make Metatron go all psycho?'

'He's changed.' I pointed down at our unconscious guest.

'What?' Carly raked her fingers through her hair and then leant forward and peered over the coffee table. 'What the hell do you mean he's changed?'

'That's not Graham Latimer.'

'What? You grabbed the wrong guy?' Gritting her teeth, she ran another hand through the dust-filled haystack of her hair fluffing it into some mad lion's mane.

'No!'

'Then what?' Carly stamped around to stand in front of me. 'Who is he?'

'I don't know.'

'Where's Latimer?'

'He exploded.'

'He did what?'

'I tried to heal him but I cut him by accident and he just cracked up then exploded.' I shrugged. 'That's what knocked the house down.'

Carly just stared at me with her mouth open. 'What the fuck are you talking about? I don't understand a word you're saying.' She closed her eyes for a moment, exhaled and then started again. 'Who did you take from Metatron?'

'Graham Latimer.'

'And who did you cut?'

'Graham Latimer.'

'And who the hell is this?' All semblance of calm vanished and her voice rose to a bellow.

'I don't know!' I screamed back at her.

'Well, who do you think it is?' Carly gave me a shake, forcing me to tear my eyes away from the floor and focus on her face.

I thought for a moment then, gently disengaging her fingers from my jacket, I held onto her wrists. 'Carly, I think it's Lucifer.' I'd managed to get my voice down to a shaking whisper.

Carly shut her mouth with a snap and stared down at the unconscious man. Her face paled.

'It is.' The deep voice from behind us caused us both to jump and scream like a couple of spooked nine-year-olds.

Belial looked mildly surprised at our reaction then, shaking his head, he crossed the room to study the unconscious man. 'That is definitely Lucifer,' he confirmed.

Carly stared at the sleeping man. '*This* is the Morning Star?'

Belial nodded. 'I remember him well.' He focused on the Lord of Hell for a moment. 'I don't think I ever saw him asleep though and he used to have white hair.' Belial picked up the one white lock and, rubbing it between his fingers, murmured to himself, 'I remember him being taller.'

Carly grabbed his hand and pulled him round to face her. 'Father, how did he get out? What's Metatron going to do? When's he going to wake up and what are we going to do when he does?' She finally had to stop to take a breath.

'Hey.' Belial gave her a quick hug. 'One problem at a time.' He turned to me. 'Joe, how did this happen?'

'I don't know.' I flopped into an armchair with a sigh. Carly winced at the cloud of dust I created; I really needed a shower. I explained everything, from leaving Hell to getting back here again. Belial and Carly stood in silence throughout.

When I had finished, Belial took another long look at Lucifer. 'Did you say Metatron had used the knife on him?'

I nodded then took mine out from its sheath. 'It was that one from the box – similar to this but it didn't have these markings on it.' I pointed to the sigils carved deeply into the blood gutters.

Belial nodded. 'Can I have a look at that, please?' He held his hand out.

Carly threw a cushion at me. Catching it with the side of my face, I laid the knife on top of it then passed the whole thing over. Belial reached gingerly for the cushion and, being very careful, he studied the knife for a long while. Then he began to laugh.

'He never had it.' He laughed loudly and passed the cushion back. 'He thought he did, but you had it all along. We hoped that was the case but nobody could get near enough to your knife to tell for sure.'

'What?' I stuck the knife back into its sheath. 'Had what?'

'Where did you get this from?' He settled back into the

sofa and elegantly crossed one leg over the other.

'I've had it almost as long as I can remember.' I thought hard. 'It was one of the first jobs I did for the host. I had to deal with an escapee for the first time. Metatron sent Gabriel with me.' I shrugged. 'I got pretty beat up and Gabriel had to step in and help. He gave me the knife after I healed – said it may keep me out of any future trouble.'

Belial nodded. 'Well, it doesn't surprise me that we can blame Gabriel for this.' He snorted a laugh. Taking a moment, he rested his elbows on his knees and his chin on his knuckles. He stared at the still sleeping man for a long, silent moment. 'There were two spears.' Belial spoke slowly as though giving himself time to remember details. 'Longinus was using his own to finish off any poor souls that were still suffering and he broke it. He wasn't very careful with his killing and a badly aimed thrust snapped the head off as the spear hit the wood of his cross. The blade flipped back and cut his hand. Weaponless, he tried to get a friend to put an end to Jesus, but his friend refused, although he did lend Longinus his spear. The bloods became mingled when he picked up both spears. Gabriel collected both weapons afterward and obviously made sure that Metatron got the wrong one.' Belial frowned. 'I don't know why but he never really trusted Metatron. He must have laughed himself sick that you got the real one.'

My mind reeled. These petty enmities had been going on for time beyond thinking. 'Gabriel knew even then that Metatron would try and take over?' It didn't seem possible that I'd been embroiled in these events and had never known.

Belial shrugged. 'Who knows?' He watched Lucifer sleeping peacefully on the carpet. 'Gabriel became really paranoid after the crucifixion – wouldn't talk to anyone, kept disappearing. I think he just decided to keep anything dangerous out of his reach. Metatron wouldn't know the difference between the two weapons. Both had the same amount of blood on them but only one performed the actual deed.'

I gingerly put the knife back into its sheath. My shoulders

itched – I could almost feel it as an entity, sitting there just waiting. The most contentious weapon in the whole of history and I'd used it to cut coffee cake! I'd also opened boxes with it, dropped it in the bath on numerous occasions and used it to clean my fingernails. I smothered a nervous giggle with a cough.

'So what happens now?' I tried to ignore the metal's heavy warmth. 'Metatron did *not* look happy when we last saw him.'

'We need *him* awake.' Belial leant back, his hands in the pockets of his waistcoat. 'Lucifer's the only one with the power to oppose The Voice, and he'll only do that if he wants to. He could wake up and just say, "I've had enough" and let it all end. That's certainly how he was feeling just before he disappeared.'

'So where exactly does that leave us?' Carly frowned. 'Neither of those options really work, do they?' She began ticking points off on her fingers. 'Lucifer wakes up and does nothing, Metatron's plan goes ahead and we all die. Lucifer wakes up and is back to his old self and we're stuck with the Morning Star in all his angry glory and we probably all die just because he's pissed off. Lucifer wakes up, stops Metatron then takes power for himself and pretty much carries out the same plan ...' She shrugged. 'Any way you look at it there's just no outcome that's going to be good for anyone.'

'Well,' Belial began, 'we're either the proud possessors of a paddle or we're not. Either way we're still up shit creek.'

My stomach did a slow roll.

'The question is, can we swim?' Belial pushed himself to his feet with a grunt. 'I'd better go and rally the other bathers.'

'Hang on a moment.' Carly had been staring into space for a while now. 'How did Metatron know that Lucifer had returned?'

Belial shrugged and reached for his overcoat. 'I don't know – maybe he can feel him.' He waved his fingers about in magical passes. 'You know, changes in the force or some such shit.'

Well, that was true but I was positive we were missing something.

Carly stood up to help her father on with his coat. 'On balance I suppose it doesn't really matter, does it?'

Balance, status quo, everything equal. Metatron was always going on about balance. 'Were you still talking when he took off?' I asked.

She nodded. 'We'd been going round and round for ages about the meaning of God's words regarding the ultimate destruction of Hell. Metatron got fed up with all the arguing and said that God would have the final say.' She paused to remember. 'He went into one of those trances of his then opened his eyes, screamed 'No' and disappeared like a cat with a rocket tied to its tail.

Suddenly it all made sense. 'Wouldn't you?' I said.

Carly and Belial both looked at me. You could easily see they were related – I was faced with matching frowns.

'Metatron has been pretending to talk to God for years but there's been no answer – no one on the other end of the line, no one to give him guidance or answer his questions. Eventually he gets fed up with the Host becoming restless and starts issuing his own orders with God's stamp on them. The first time he did it he probably shit himself waiting for retribution, but there was nothing, so he does it again and again and he enjoys it. He enjoys the power, enjoys the notoriety and enjoys the control. He decides that he doesn't want to give it up and, as possession is nine-tenths of the law, he's going to bloody well keep it.

'So here come you lot bitching about the rules and the way things are going. Just to shut you up he goes off to contact God knowing that all he has to do is feel about in the darkness for a while, take the time to come up with a God-like proclamation and that will be it. You lot will all sod off with your collective tails down and his plan will continue unhindered. This time, however, there *is* something there. Just a tiny sliver of consciousness, but its growing and it's enough to send him into a panic the like of which hasn't been

161

seen since Sodom and Gomorrah fell.'

Belial's jaw dropped.

'There has to be a balance. Everybody keeps telling me that.' I looked down at Lucifer lying supine and happily asleep. I jabbed my finger toward him. 'He rises and basically drags God with him. The last thing Metatron wants to face is God; he would have too much to answer for. Suddenly he sees his time running out – he has to bring things to a head before God's strong enough to stop him.'

Carly looked at her father, her face stricken 'We're even more screwed than we thought,' she muttered. 'If he wakes up, God comes back and the whole of Armageddon goes ahead on schedule. If he doesn't wake up Metatron will just come and take him.' She rubbed her hands together and bit her lip. 'Either way, Hell gets wiped out and takes us with it.' She glanced up at me. 'Will you stop doing that!'

'Sorry.' I removed my finger from my ear where I'd been poking and probing. 'I think that being hit by half a house has given me tinnitus – I can hear bells.'

'Bells?' Belial gave me a wary look. 'What sort of bells?'

There was one long chime followed by four short deep bongs as though someone were hammering a gong; this sequence was repeated again and again. I tried to beat it out on the table. 'It's really making me feel tetchy,' I said.

'We have to go.' Belial walked toward the door and, sticking his head out, bellowed for someone to come. 'That's a recall. Michael's calling the entire Host back. They're getting ready for war, and somehow I don't think their attention is on Earth any more.' He bit his lip then turned to Carly. 'Get hold of Nessus and get him organising things right away. We have to clear the city immediately.'

162

# CHAPTER 7

IT TOOK A SURPRISINGLY short time to think up a plan of action, although admittedly it was a very simple plan: run away. Run away, as fast and as far as possible. Clear Hell, get everybody that didn't want to fight out through the gates and onto other planes, then the gates would be closed. Anybody that stayed would almost certainly die. The Host numbered hundreds of thousands and Hell these days was populated by families, tourists, traders and refugees. The only two races that said they'd stay were the centaurs and the Drekavak. Even they acknowledged it was suicide – they just didn't have anywhere else to go. The Drekavak felt that taking as many angels with them as they went would be nothing more than a gift to everyone else. And the centaurs? Well, all I could get out of them was a sort of embarrassed mutter that they'd rather face a billion angels than what waited them at home.

'There must be something more we can do. I don't want anybody to die.' Carly wrung her hands nervously together as she stared out over the city.

The Drekavak seemed to be enjoying themselves and there was a lot of huddling and whispering. There were a couple of disagreements but, eventually, one tall male stood up and shouted over to Belial.

'We think we have a solution,' he said.

Belial's eyebrows went up and he indicated for them to continue.

'The angels are going to attack in force. They'll do what they always do. By dint of sheer numbers and that bloody horn of theirs, the walls will fall and they'll just stamp in and kill or capture everything in sight.'

Belial nodded.

'You have to hide Lucifer somewhere until he sorts himself out, yes?'

Belial nodded again. 'Well, it's a bit more complicated than that, you see …'

'Right.' The Drekavak ignored him and, taking a pencil from behind one of his tall ears, began to draw diagrams on the wall. Belial winced as the intricate silver shot wallpaper became a whiteboard. 'The one place the angels won't go and Lucifer will be safe is Old Hell – specifically the Throne Room.'

Belial came to his feet. 'Whoa, Gallard, you're mad! There's no way we'd get there, not any more.'

'Hear me out.' The tall demon held up a paw. 'If you take Lucifer and a small group you should be able to get through the lower levels. You'll just have to be careful.' He turned back to his drawings. 'But first, we're going to raze the city.'

'No!' Belial looked anguished and sat down hard, his legs apparently feeble.

Carly sighed and placed her hands on his shoulders. 'I don't think we have a choice, Father.' She squeezed gently.

Belial reached up and held one of her hands. 'But all the people … There's hundreds of years of work here.' He stared out of the window at the buildings and flags a long way below.

'I'm sorry.' Gallard sighed. 'If we don't, then the Host almost certainly will and I think we can take most of them with it when it goes. At least it will die in glory.'

The Devil's second-in-command frowned. 'That's not glory. A few falling rocks isn't going to stop an angel.' He shook his head again. 'It may slow them down if they have to dig themselves out but they'll just keep coming.'

The Drekavak smiled. 'We're not going to pull the buildings down, Belial – we're going to make the city fight back.'

'The city will stay?'

Gallard looked over at the small group of Drekavak that were still muttering among themselves and shrugged. 'Maybe. It could fall just from the fighting, or, by the time we've finished with it, it may be uninhabitable. You might not be able to come back. This has never been done before so we just don't know.'

Carly leant forward. 'Father, we don't have time for this. The Host are going to be on their way, Nessus says most of the people have already gone, but we have to move Lucifer – and quickly.'

Her father puffed out his cheeks then patted her hand. He looked over at the tall Drekavak. 'Will it work?' He shook his head. 'I don't need to know the details – just give me the bare bones of the idea then we'll leave you blasted clever folk to do your worst.'

'Right.' Gallard nodded to the Drekavak. They all turned as one and trooped out of the room.

Belial winced again.

'Once everyone's gone we close and dispose of all the gates.' Gallard pointed his drawing of the city in the market square; a cross marked the position of the fountain. 'We set up another gate here.' He pointed to the left of the cross. 'We open both gates, you and your little lot head downwards into the lower levels. We'll wait to see you gone then we close it behind you.' He pursed his lips. 'We need one person to stay behind to set off the traps, and that person will have to wait till the very last moment to make sure we take out most of the Host.' He frowned at his drawing. 'At the very last moment I will set the city off and make a run for it through the last gate.'

'The Host will follow you.' Carly stared at the sketches. 'And what do you mean – "set the city off"?'

'No, they won't follow us. By that time there will be so much screaming and dying they won't worry about one small *demon*.' He spat the word out. 'Or at least I hope they won't. Even if they do, there'll be another gate on the other side of this one that will be closed by the others as soon as I pass through it. Any angel seeking to escape the city's wrath by coming through that gate will just find themselves trapped with no energy to use. They'll be stuck.'

I noticed he hadn't answered her other question.

'Which world are you going to use?' Parity asked, her voice quiet and gentle.

'I'll be going home.' Gallard stared, unseeing, at the wall. 'I really hope that bastard Michael follows me through. I'd dearly love him to be stuck on a dead world.' Gallard spat vindictively onto the carpet. 'Let's face it, he helped to read its final rites.'

Getting up from her chair Parity walked over to the sad creature. 'Make sure *you* don't get stuck there.' Wrapping her thin arms as far around him as she could, she hugged him hard. 'We only just got you out last time.'

Gallard smiled at her. 'Been there and done that, my little fire top.' He ruffled her candyfloss hair with a huge yet gentle paw. 'I'll be off that world as quickly as I can.'

Belial stood up and looked over at me. 'How are those bells of yours, Joe?' he asked.

I rubbed my temples. The ache was not fun. 'Still there.'

'Louder?' Belial pressed.

I shook my head then wished I hadn't. 'Just really insistent.' Talking was beginning to set up a counter vibration against the toll of the bells. I resolved not to do it any more than I had to.

'Right.' Belial nodded over at Nessus who had just walked in. 'We have about six hours. Open as many gates as possible – get the last of the citizens away. Chase them out, don't let them hang around for possessions, pick them up and throw them through the gates if you have to.' He looked at the clock on the wall. 'We'll meet at the fountain.' As we all began to move he held up a hand. 'One last thing ...'

The group of centaurs that had been heading for the door stopped and turned back with enquiring looks. 'We can't take everyone with us, so who wants to see the lower levels of Hell?' He raised his eyebrows and looked around. 'Volunteers only. Well, except you, Joe – you're conscripted.'

'Gee, thanks,' I muttered.

'I'm coming.' Carly stated.

'No, you're not.' Her father refused to look at her.

Carly snorted.

'Absolutely not.' Belial was adamant. 'You're going with the rest of the refugees. I want you safe.'

Carly continued to look at him, her face devoid of expression. 'My life isn't about what *you* want, so don't be irritating.' She smiled, taking the sting from her words. 'I'm coming and you can stamp your feet or hold your breath until your face turns purple.' She pushed her chair back under the table. 'Just give in now, Dad. There is no way – no way at all – you're going without me.'

Belial threatened to turn puce; small whorls of dark energy suddenly erupted from his spine.

Carly looked on, unimpressed. 'Stop pouting, Father, just suck it up and let's get on with it, shall we?'

Her matter-of-fact tone took the wind out of his sails and the energy dissipated into harmless fog.

Belial turned resolutely away from her and carried on taking names.

Nessus was one of the first to step forward and turned almost crimson when Belial shook his head. 'Nope, not you either.'

'What do you mean, not me?' Nessus roared at Belial. 'Who else has got my muscle? Who else can look after you all? Who else has got my speed?' Obviously mortally insulted the huge centaur was almost frothing.

Unable to make himself heard over Nessus's ranting, Belial stayed quiet and waited. Eventually, like a wind-up toy that's used all its spring, Nessus ground to a halt.

Belial stood up and, wandering over to the enraged horse man, slung an arm over his back. 'I need you to do something for me.'

Nessus turned his torso and frowned down at him.

'Whatever happens ...' Belial looked thoughtful and wiped his nose on his sleeve with a sniff. '... we're going to need a way out. I can almost guarantee we won't be able to make it back out the same way we went in. I need you to open the Fae Gateway.'

Carly gasped. 'Father, no!'

Melusine looked up from quietly polishing her knife. 'That's a shit idea, Belial.' She shook her head and went back to her weapon.

'Find Cu Sith.' Belial frowned, ignoring everyone. 'I can think of other Fae that would help, but he owes me a favour.'

Nessus canted away from Belial's arm. 'Cu Sith?' he raged. 'That mouldy dog! There's no way – no way at all – I'm dealing with him again.'

Carly snorted and Nessus whipped around to stare at her.

'I didn't lose.' He crossed his arms over his chest and glowered at the room in general. 'That lying, conniving, owl-eyed fleabag cheated.'

To say I was confused was, at the very best, an understatement. I nudged Carly. 'What?' I grimaced as the word disappeared in a hail of bells and vibrations.

'Cu Sith is a barrow hound,' she said as if that explained everything. With the noises in my head I just didn't have the strength to pursue a proper answer.

'Look, we don't have time for this.' Belial stood in front of Nessus. 'I've got two of the Fae I can talk to about opening that door for us, so it's either Cu Sith or we talk to Morrigan.' He shrugged. 'Your choice.'

Nessus stamped and flattened his ears, his tail swished over his rump. Throwing his arms to the ceiling he pushed Belial by just walking forward. 'Fuck that, Belial,' he huffed, 'that's no bloody choice at all, you and I both know that Morrigan would have a saddle on me and be riding me to some insane war before I even had chance to open my mouth.' His head dropped and he sighed. 'Isn't there anyone else that could go?' He looked vaguely hopeful – a look which fell as Belial shook his head.

'Sorry, old friend.' Belial clapped him on the shoulder then turned back to the table. 'You're the only person that could even get into Mag Mell without being killed on the spot. We're not really on talking terms with the Fae at the moment, are we.'

I pressed my fingers hard against my temples; it seemed to deaden the ringing for a little while. 'We are talking about what I think we're talking about here, right?' I couldn't understand all the hushed tones. 'Tinkerbell, little wings, fairy dust, granting wishes.' I laughed. 'The whole of Hell is populated by creatures that are heavily armed, moving muscle and ten foot tall.' I pointed at Nessus and laughed again. 'And you're all scared of *fairies*?' I ignored the look on Carly's face. As usual my mouth was on a runaway course that no amount of warnings was going to stop. 'Why don't you just buy a job lot of fly swatters, or a can of Raid?'

Melusine, her face totally expressionless, jammed her knife into her boot and stood up. Carly opened her mouth but Melusine ignored her and came to stand in front of me. We stared at each other for a moment and I realised the room had become very, very quiet. Carly shrugged and shut her mouth with a snap.

Melusine began to change, her eyes becoming huge and golden, long white teeth sprang vampire-like from between her lips and, as she opened her mouth, others popped up to fill the spaces created by her rapidly lengthening jaw. Tall nostrils quivered as they sniffed at me and short tufted ears swivelled showing the fine golden hairs within. As her skin toughened and hardened, scales rippled across her face; each was a shade of bronze or green polished to an almost mirror finish. Her body dropped to all fours and filled out with huge muscles that ran from shoulder to foot in a movement that looked like ferrets leaping around in a scaly sleeping bag. Her long and beautifully manicured red fingernails turned black and lengthened to miniature scythes, so polished I could see my shocked face reflected in each individual claw. Melusine drummed each one in turn and they clicked on stone as they gouged rents in the carpet.

I noticed Belial rolling his eyes at the sound of his priceless rugs being shredded.

Melusine rolled her armour-plated shoulders then sat up on her back legs. She used a 15-foot tail to aid her balance; the creamy bone spikes on the end dug yet more holes into the carpet. Her stomach was a pale green and, despite what all the stories say, there didn't seem to be any unarmoured

169

spots at all. Taking a deep breath she turned her long face to the painted ceiling and casually blackened a 30-square-foot section with a jet of fire and smoke that ripped the oxygen out of the air and sounded like a jet engine. While she was cremating the decorative plasterwork, tall, claw-tipped wings opened with a crack. Long bat-like "fingers" created the support to these wings. The grey skin between each finger was so soft and translucent I felt I could just poke a hole right through – it looked like gauze.

Dropping back to all four feet she flipped her wings closed and they settled neatly to lay like huge folded umbrellas along her crested spine. She laid her head on the ground and glared at me. Nostrils that were on the same level as my throat puffed clouds of carrion-scented smoke with each deep breath. I sank to my knees, coughing and choking. She gave me a long look out of one huge golden eye and spoke in a deep yet still feminine voice. 'So go on then … Bring on the fly swatter.'

Wondering if I had any eyebrows left I found myself staring at the perfect row of tiny glistening scales that lined her eyelid. I opened my mouth to make some smart comment but all that came out was 'Meep.'

'Melusine.' Belial, one hand over his mouth, tapped her on the nose with a rolled-up magazine. 'You're killing my decor and no one can breathe. Really, dear heart, you shouldn't do that inside, eh?'

She snorted and, as Belial coughed and flapped his hands in an effort to get rid of the smoke, she sank once again into the form of a humourless woman with long dark hair, multicoloured eyes and a bad attitude.

As she completed her change she cracked her knuckles, then, reaching out she patted me gently on the cheek, her long fingernails scratching just enough to make me worried. 'Just keep thinking happy thoughts.' She snorted a laugh then went back to sorting out her personal arsenal.

'Great! Thanks, Mel.' Nessus shuddered. 'I really needed that display about now.'

She snorted another short laugh and then ignored him.

'So ...' Belial stared at me for a moment then obviously decided to ignore my sweating and trembling. He tapped his magazine against his hand to regain Nessus's attention. 'Can you do it, do you think?' He looked worried. 'I don't like to ask but we're going to need that door open and, even if we get through it, we're going to have to run like ...' He obviously couldn't think of an analogy. '... A very, very fast thing.'

Nessus sighed again then, with a shrug, completely changed his attitude. He let out a huge bellow of laughter and clapped Belial on the shoulder, causing him to drop his magazine. 'Of course I can do it.' He roared and stuck his chest out. 'I'll be waiting in the Throne Room for you. I'll be the one leaning on the tourmaline throne with a pox-faced barrow puppy at my feet carrying my slippers.' He looked up. 'Belial, I'm serious ... Don't leave me standing in the Throne Room with only that useless mouldy dog for company, OK?'

'Mouldy?' I asked Carly.

'He's green,' she said.

I could feel my mind trying to bend like a willow twig.

Belial pursed his lips and rubbed his chin. It was obvious that he wasn't happy about any of this. 'Just stay out of the way of the other centaurs.'

Nessus rolled his eyes and nodded. 'You don't need to tell me, I know.' He shook himself and settled his bardiche onto his shoulder. 'If I stay to the wooded ways I'll be fine and no one will stop me.'

'What about the angels?' Carly wandered over and gave Nessus a hug, squeaking when he picked her up and gave her a tight squeeze.

'Angels aren't welcome in Faery, you know that.' Nessus placed her carefully back onto the floor. 'They can't cross the Acheron and have made themselves pretty unwelcome everywhere.' He gave her a kiss then pushed her gently toward her father. 'I'll be fine,' he said.

Belial rested his arm casually around her shoulders, then studied Nessus for a long moment. 'Good luck,' he said quietly.

Nessus nodded then, with a wave to the rest of us, he headed out through the door. I kept waiting for him to look back but he never did.

The group ended up with seven participants: Parity and her brother Farr, Melusine and Belial, Keril, Carly and me. I didn't count Lucifer; still unconscious most of the time he seemed to be just part of the luggage.

Incredibly it had taken less than three hours to clear the city. With so many gates open, everyone just abandoned whatever they had, rounded up their families and ran. No one wanted to be there when the Host turned up. Most of them talked about Sodom, Gomorrah, Jericho and others with names I didn't recognise. There was no question that if the Host wanted to get into a city there really wasn't much that could stop them.

Standing on top of the city wall Carly and I watched the last trickle of occupants as, laden with bags and packs, they disappeared into the grey haze beyond each gate. Each tall iron gate would slam shut and then, like a map, fold itself up to fall into the sand where it glowed white hot before cooling rapidly to resemble a small metal badge with a depiction of the world it opened onto etched in enamel on the surface. Centaurs with bags slung over their great shoulders were trotting about picking up the shining squares.

Keril, Alice and Arden stood in an entwined group. 'Where will you go?' Keril pressed his forehead to Arden's. The little boy pressed back – he looked solemn and scared.

Alice shrugged. 'We're going with the engineers. They're stopping in Karonet to pick up supplies then I think they said Pathern after that.'

Keril smiled at Arden. 'Pathern, eh? You'll get to see the sea.' He took the child and gave him a long hug. 'You'll love it, you can dig holes and paddle and make sand cities.' Keril swallowed hard and buried his head in Arden's shoulder. Eventually he handed him back to his mother. 'I'll see you both again.' He pressed his forehead to his sister's and added a swift hug. 'Be safe.'

Alice nodded then, with a deep sigh, pulled Arden up onto her hip. 'We'll see you soon.' They headed toward the city square with many backward glances as though wanting to keep Keril in sight for as long as possible. The big demon leant over the wall and watched their tiny figures disappear with a flash and sparkle as a big group of Drekavak vacated the city.

From our high vantage point on the top of the wall we saw the last public gate fold. I glared at Carly. 'You should have gone.' This argument had been going on for some time and Carly was obviously fed up with the whole thing.

'Oh just shut up, will you,' she said. 'What's the matter with you? I thought you'd like the company.'

I ignored her smiles. 'So what happens now?' The bells in my head were beginning to obliterate thought. The sound had changed to a fairly rapid clanging – like an over-enthusiastic student with the school bell calling in the others from play. I could feel my eyeballs pulsing with each clang and dong. My hair hurt and my teeth had been gritted against the noise for so long that my jaw felt as though it were carved from wood.

'Joe?' Carly touched my arm.

I couldn't help myself. I jumped and yanked my arm from under her hand. Every inch of me was hypersensitive. Nauseated and shaking I felt as if I could fly apart at any second. Pressing the heels of my palms to my eyes I couldn't stand up any longer and slid to the floor. I was convinced my brain was melting.

'Joe? Joe!' Carly bent over me. I glanced up at her then closed my eyes. It was too painful to keep them open.

'I can't breathe,' I gasped. 'I can't think, I can't move.' I eased over to rest my back on the wall and then slumped to rest my forehead on my knees. My eyes were actually melting; I could feel the water running into my hands and down my arms. I would have screamed if I could have stood the sound of my own voice. 'The bells won't stop, just won't stop.' I heard a voice that sort of sounded like mine.

'You idiot!' Carly knelt down beside me. Reaching forward she took one of my hands away from my eyes. 'Look

173

at me!'

When I refused to open my eyes – I really couldn't, they would have fallen out – she shook me. 'Look at me!'

I managed to lever one eyelid open a fraction and peered at her from between the wet lashes.

'Think of a switch, a volume knob or anything you would physically use to change the volume of a sound.' Carly stared at me. 'Come on, Joe, concentrate. Full angels have to answer this call or it eventually drives them insane. You don't – you can choose to tune it out. Turn it up or down as you feel like, but you have to find a way to visualise it.'

It was so difficult. Every time I managed to hold an image another toll of a bell would shatter it in a wave of pain. 'I can't,' I gasped. 'It keeps driving everything out of my head. I can't hold on to anything.'

Carly stood up. 'Sorry about this,' she muttered. Then, pushing the sleeve of her baggy green jumper up to her elbow she made a fist, hauled back and hit me as hard as she could.

'Ow!' I slammed back, banging my head on the ground.

'Now!' Carly screamed at me. 'Do it now!'

The physical pain was actually much easier to ignore than the psychic pain of the bells. I hurriedly constructed an off switch and flicked it up in my mind. Blessed, blessed silence. I breathed out cautiously and listened: nothing. There's a lot of truth to that old saying that the only good thing about banging your head against a wall is that it's lovely when it stops.

Licking my lip I tasted blood then, wiping my nose on the back of my hand, I pouted and showed the smear of red to Carly. 'I still hurt.' I sulked.

'So do I.' Carly had stuck her right hand in her armpit. She took it out and examined the grazed knuckles with a rueful face.

'I hurt more.' I was damn well due some sympathy.

'Not as much as you could.' Carly licked her knuckles.

Taking her hand I kissed each knuckle. 'Thank you, thank you, thank you.' Each graze deserved a kiss of its own, I worked my lips over her wrist, up her arm and attacked her ear.

She giggled and, holding my face between her hands, planted a heavy kiss on the bridge of my nose.

As I winced she laughed. 'Have you considered telling me when something's wrong?'

'It's beginning to occur to me,' I whinged. 'But next time you probably don't have to hit me quite so hard.'

'If you'd told me earlier, I wouldn't have had to hit you at all.' She gave me a smug smile.

Keril coughed to get our attention. 'It looks like they're opening the lower levels – we'd better get moving. I'm not sure what those engineers are up to, but if I know them, when this city goes there's every chance it's going to end up one huge pile of rubble, despite what they say.'

Carly sneered. 'Yeah, 'cos the lower levels are going to be so much safer.'

At my questioning look she sighed. 'When Dad closed them up years ago, he released all the occupants and told those that lived down there to come up and actually live a life.' She shrugged. 'Some of them did – quite a lot of them did actually. But there were some …'

Keril finished the sentence for her. 'There were some that wouldn't leave and some that weren't allowed to leave. They've been down there for eons with nothing to do but worry each other. It could be interesting to see how they've fared.'

Carly nodded. 'They'll either be a thriving little community,' she paused, 'which would be worrying in itself, or they'll be … different.'

'Different?' I was confused again.

Keril shrugged then looked over his shoulder as Parity trotted toward us, grinning as usual. She seemed to be having a great time. Farr ran behind her, his duffle coat over one arm. Sweat dripped from his head, sticking his long mousey hair to his glasses. Nodding to us, he left Parity to do the talking while he knelt down to tie his laces.

I wondered how he managed to keep his trainers so white

with all the rubble and dust that was around here.

'Belial and Melusine are moving Lucifer,' Parity shouted. 'We have to go. Everybody is meeting at the centre gate and Gallard's getting very excited.'

Carly nodded but was obviously distracted. 'What's that?' She pointed at some flashes that had started over the sepia sand dunes. We stared out over the walls. Sparkles began to blink in the distance – first one or two fairly far apart, then tens, then hundreds. Eventually the entire plain in all directions was hidden by flashing lights; it was like looking out at a million photographers. A low drumbeat climbed the walls and the lights began to close in on us like some huge glowing sphincter.

I peered over the walls desperately trying to see what was making the lights. 'What is that?' I wished I had some binoculars or a telescope; if we ever came back here I'd make sure they installed those telescopes you find at the seaside.

'The Host.' Keril turned slowly to look at all the approaching lights. 'Thousands of them. The last time I saw this many they were invading my home.'

'Thousands?' There looked to be a lot more than thousands.

Keril stared at me for a moment and then shrugged. 'Whatever, there's a fuck of a lot more of them than us.' He turned and left the wall.

Farr also turned away. 'Come on, Par.' He held his hand out to his sister who was waving over the walls at the Host and giggling. 'Let's get out of here and hope that the Drekavak are as creative as they say they are.' Reaching back he grabbed her hand then began to run, dragging her, stumbling behind him. Her long combat jacket and her untied boots caused her to stumble and trip over the discarded possessions of the fleeing citizens; she didn't slow her brother down at all.

We ran through eerily empty streets heading toward the very centre of the city. I wished I'd had time to explore. Every race had brought the best of its architecture and ideas to the city and had made it home. Long, tree-lined boulevards joined odd little suburbs. It was like looking down on one of those pictures made from thread and pins that were so popular in the 70s. Each pin was different. A small group of wooden houses nestled beneath a tall glass structure full of steel and light that reflected the multicoloured umbrellas and canopies of the cafés and curiosity shops on the far side of the cobbled street.

I didn't want to dwell on what this would look like after the Host had trampled it underfoot. As we ran through the book district Keril suddenly stopped, his long ears twitching. 'You go on.' He darted off down a small alley. 'I'll catch up.'

It didn't take long, his claws made running on the cobbled streets far easier for him that for any of us with our boots that slipped and slid, threatening to break an ankle at any moment. I heard him bring up the rear and, glancing over my shoulder, was surprised to see that he carried a small child in his arms. The child was filthy, tear stained and hanging on to the panting demon with fingers that were leaving dents in his scales. Having no breath for questions I turned my eyes back to my troubled footing and carried on running.

The sounds from beyond the wall became louder and clearer. The very beat spurred us all on to greater exertion – even Parity had finally quit grinning and was running hard alongside her brother. Our feet beat an alternative tempo to those thousands hitting the sand in unison just beyond the great oak gates. Great clouds of dust obscured the weak sun.

We arrived out of breath and rather wide eyed at the very heart of the city in a wave of heaving chests and dripping backs. Standing beside the fountain Belial raised his eyebrows at our appearance then, nodding to Carly, raised his arms above his head. With a single word the big black stone in the centre of the pool split with a crack that echoed around the empty buildings. Iron-work tendrils hastily scrabbled to break free of the stone, pushing it aside. The creeping metalwork crumbled chunks to dust as it surged upward like a tree root through concrete. Twisting and writhing, the tendrils wound themselves into a metal depiction of desolate, winter-stripped trees, their branches, trunks and roots linking to form a huge gate. Pitted with rust, the hot metal steamed in the centre of the pool as the rapidly evaporating water hissed clouds of vapour into the air.

Off to one side two smaller, simpler gates stood open. One by one, those who had been working on the city's defences filed through to disappear into the shimmering void beyond. Eventually, all that were left was Gallard and his apprentice Gart, a skinny young Drekavak, who was still sporting fur in various places through his newly grown scales. Gallard turned to him and gave him a gentle push toward the gate. 'Go on.' He smiled. 'Go with the others – I'll meet you on the other side.' He gave the young demon another gentle push. 'Go on.'

Gart hesitated, twisting his paws in small circles in front of his stomach. 'But what if …' His voice was much higher than Gallard's gruff rumble, giving him a certain whining tone.

'What if … What if?' Gallard gave a huge roar of laughter. 'If we stand here discussing what ifs, we'll never get away.' He gave the youngster another, firmer push. 'Go.'

Gart sighed and, with a final look at his mentor, stepped through the gate. Gallard stared after him for a long moment then turned to Belial. 'You'd better go as well.' He pricked up his long ears. 'Any time now they'll be getting those bloody horns out and starting a Jericho on us.'

Belial looked troubled. 'I don't like leaving you here alone.' He reached out a hand. 'I hope you know what you're doing, old friend.'

Gallard threw back his head and gave a howl of laughter then, shaking Belial's hand strongly, he pulled the surprised steward of Hell into a bear hug. 'Well, if I don't it's going to be the shortest last stand ever.' Then, as with Gart, he turned Belial toward the steaming black gate and gave him a little push. 'You've got your own problems from here on. If there's any justice, we'll see each other again soon.'

Melusine, standing with a sagging Lucifer at her side, hoisted him higher with the arm he had around her neck.

'Look,' she gasped. 'I really hate to be the party pooper but this guy is heavy – can we get on, please?' She dragged him up by his wrist again.

The man draped around her neck raised his head and stared at the gate for a moment then he looked over at Belial. 'Home?' he asked. Then, as he passed out again, his knees buckled completely and Melusine, irritated, dropped him unceremoniously into the sand.

'Great,' Keril muttered and, handing the child to Carly, picked up the unconscious Lord of Hell. He looked as though he'd picked up something toxic.

Silence fell, then a moment later an eerie wail began, softly at first but gathering tone and intensity. The ground shook beneath our feet and sand started to trickle from the cracks between bricks. The hooting, screaming cry sounded like a million children all screaming at different pitches. My teeth began to ache and I wanted to vomit. Ceramic flowerpots fell from a nearby wall, exploding as they hit the ground, strewing dirt and bright blue flowers at our feet. The gate in front of us shuddered, flakes of rust fluttering to the ground.

'Shit! We have to go – *now*!' Belial raised his arms and began a tongue-twisting and guttural recitation. Slowly, so slowly, the gate started to open, creaking and groaning in protest with every single inch.

With a thunderous roar, the cloud of dust above us thickened and blocked out the weak sun completely. The choking dust began to fall and around us buildings started to disappear into the thick, gritty fog. In the gathering dark the sounds of wings almost blocked out the wailing of the horns.

Parity turned toward the dust cloud. Her eyes rolled back into her head, the whites showing a surprisingly large number of tiny red veins. 'They're in.' Shaking her head and blinking, she threw her backpack onto her shoulder and linked arms with her brother who nodded slowly.

Belial, breathing heavily, dropped his arms as the gate finally opened enough to allow access and grabbing Carly pushed her through. 'Come on!' he shouted.

Keril, carrying Lucifer, went next, closely followed by Parity and Farr. I stared in horror at the angels that had appeared out of the fog to hover all around us. In ranks they stood in the air as though on invisible plinths then, at a shout, each drew a sword which was sheathed in flame. The light and heat from each burned through both my courage and my resolve.

I took a quick look round. I really hoped I'd be able to walk these streets again one day.

'Joe!' Carly screamed, sticking her head through the now closing gate. 'Joe – come on!'

I stared at her for a moment then back at the angels. Angels had been my life for a very long time and I was torn between running back to them for protection or plunging into the unknown with a group of "bad guys". A little voice kept telling me I was making a horrible mistake.

'Joe, you stinking, putrid pile of dog shit!' Michael's voice roared above the sound of crashing masonry. 'I told him you were a liar. I told him you were a traitor.'

Well, that certainly helped me come to a decision. Michael raged on. However I felt about them, obviously the angels didn't feel the same way about me. With a final salute to Gallard who was crouched behind a wall, a large black box in his paw, and a much ruder final salute to Michael, I ran for the gate. I only made it through by sneaking sideways and pulling in my gut. I grinned as the final clang of its closure was slightly muted by Michael's scream of rage.

'Run!' Belial looked around the vast entrance hall. The walls – damp stone for the most part – showed small patches of dirty mosaic sickly spotting the walls. In the dim light it was almost impossible to tell what it had originally depicted, but it looked very much like lines and lines of people all wearing chains. As the group raced off into the dark I hung back, curious. Hidden behind what had once been an elegantly carved pillar, I peered out through the thick, pale ivy that had grown up and around it. If Gallard failed, those angels were going to come through here like a swarm of bees. Well, at least they'd have to get past me. I drew the knife from between my shoulder blades and slipped on both knuckle-dusters. Holding the knife was now a little difficult but at least the weapons made me feel better. I might actually slow one or two of them down.

Michael gripped the long black bars and rattled the gates, screaming into the dark through which his quarry had now mostly disappeared.

'Sir.' Another angel approached and laid a hand on his shoulder. 'Sir.'

Michael whipped around and casually punched him in the face before turning back to the gate.

Raphael carefully stepped over the angel as it was spitting blood and teeth out onto the sand. 'Michael.' The tall blond was eating a custard doughnut and grinning as he covered himself in sugar. 'Michael!' He wiped the last of the confectionary from his lips. With a grin he ducked under Michael's raised arm then turned and stood up within the circle of the raging angel's arms as he rattled the bars of the gate. 'Hey!' Raphael brought his face to within a few centimetres of Michael's and smiled. 'This really isn't getting anything done, is it?'

Michael dropped his arms, chest heaving and stared at his smiling friend. 'But Raph ...'

'Nah ah!' Raphael waggled a finger in Michael's face. 'Our orders were: get into Hell and flush out everybody, kill everything and drag Graham what's-his-face back to see Metatron.' He stuck his hand into his pocket and pulled out a bag of marshmallows. 'I don't recall anything being said about screaming like a banshee, frothing at the mouth, behaving like a lunatic or punching out your own troops.' He pulled the bag open and took out two pink and squashy sweets. 'Want one?' He popped one into his mouth and offered another to Michael who stared at it as though it were poisonous. 'No?'

Michael stepped around Raphael and leant his forehead on the bars of the gate. After a couple of seconds he turned to face the massed angels that were hovering in glittering ranks all the way back to the ruined walls. He raised a hand then

181

brought it down. One by one each battalion stepped elegantly out of the air to stand around him in a huge fan. Blazing swords were sheathed and silence fell as Michael considered his next move.

'Report!' he bellowed. After a couple of seconds five angels who had been flitting around the buildings had arranged themselves in front of him. 'So what's the situation?' he asked.

The angels shuffled then one stepped forward. 'It's deserted. There's nothing here – everything has gone.'

Michael screamed again, his face puce, pulsing veins a map across his temples. Dragging his sword into being, he sent molten fireballs bouncing and careering from every wall. Before him angels ducked and threw themselves out of the way.

Breathing hard, Michael waited until order had been restored then he spoke in a quiet dangerous tone. 'You're incompetent and you're wrong.' He stared at the angel who had given him the report. 'They're just hiding and we are going to find them and kill every single abomination.'

Silence fell. The ranks looked at one another then down at the ground.

Careful not to be seen, I peered around the corner wondering what Gallard was waiting for. He was unfortunately in full view, the huge hand of a tall dark-skinned angel wrapped around his upper arm

'Sir!' It shouted as it dragged the struggling Drekavak to the front of the Host. 'Look.'

'Deserted, eh?' Michael spat viciously into the dust.

The scout who had spoken shook his head and took a nervous step back.

God's commander turned toward the grinning demon. 'What are you laughing at, shitface?' he bellowed.

Gallard's smile got wider and he relaxed into his guard's grip. 'Nice weather, eh?' He laughed and then pressed the button he was holding.

Michael looked confused as it began to rain. The first few drops helped to lay the dust to rest. It didn't take long before it became a deluge.

Water cascaded from roofs and spat from every building; it jetted out from windows and doors soaking all those that stood around. Mouths open as they looked heavenward.

For a short while there was shocked silence then the screaming began. Each drop opened skin and burnt flesh. Within seconds the Host had broken. Some ran, some tried to fly, taking off with a panicked flurry of wings only to crash down among the buildings melting, smoking and sobbing.

Raphael, obviously a lot quicker than he looked, clutched Michael at the first scream and pulled him back under the huge stone lintel that overhung the great gate. They stood together, open mouthed, bleeding from shallow gouges, watching as the Host screamed, split, bled and wept. One by one angels hit the floor and failed to rise again. Through all the devastation Gallard danced in the rain, his mouth open, his big clawed feet splashing in the muddy puddles. He laughed with delight at the damage he had caused.

I felt sick. Backing from the gate I stared as the city became littered with crawling, pleading and dying angels. Raphael, hearing me move, looked around and through the gate. We stared at each other for a moment then he smiled through the tears that coursed down his beautiful face. Turning back he returned to comforting Michael whose screams of outrage and bewilderment almost outdid those of the dying.

Something touched my elbow. I jumped and tried to pull away.

'It's me, you idiot.' Keril's face appeared out of the gloom. 'What the hell are you doing? Come on, Carly's almost beside herself.'

Dragging me with him he turned and began walking purposefully away from the gate.

'Keril?'

'What?' He obviously wasn't in the mood for a chat.

'What did Gallard do?' The sounds of screaming angels still echoed down the tunnel.

'I'll explain later to everybody.' He lengthened his stride

and, without pause, headed back toward the group.

'Keril?'

He sighed. 'What now?'

'I'm sorry I stabbed your sister.' I really needed him to know that.

He looked back over his shoulder and stared at me. 'You've already said that.'

The silence stretched on. I just waited.

Eventually he sighed and gave a single curt nod then, increasing his grip on my arm he pulled me into the darkness and away from the dying creatures of the light.

About 20 minutes later we caught up with a rather nervous party of travellers who had stopped to take stock. They were all sitting on fallen blocks of stone or collapsed statues. Belial was studying Lucifer who was still unconscious. Parity and Farr were playing a complicated-looking game; Parity slapped cards down onto a pile, laughing at her brother's rueful expression. She looked up as we approached. 'A rain of angels,' she giggled, 'and here's me without an umbrella.' She went back to her game.

Carly jumped up from where she and Melusine were talking to the little girl and walked over. For a moment she just stared at me, then after giving me a perfunctory hug reached up and gave my ear a vicious twist.

I screamed but didn't stop her. She'd obviously been worried so, just to make sure she knew I was sorry, I screamed again and added a little whimper for good measure. 'Sorry, sorry, sorry,' I yelped through gritted teeth.

Mollified, Carly let go of my ear and gave me another hug. Melusine, sitting with the child on her lap, just laughed. 'I like a man who knows when to grovel.' She went back to wiping the child's face. 'Hey, there you are.' She smiled. 'I knew there was a little girl under all that dirt.'

The child stared at her for a moment then, clambering down from her lap, wandered away to study the mosaics.

'I have such a way with children.' Melusine sighed and threw the tissue onto the ground. 'She must be able to sense my mothering instincts.'

'What's all the screaming about?' Belial sat down on a block of stone next to the grinning dragon.

'Just Joe getting his arse kicked.' Melusine picked up the discarded tissue and placed it carefully into her backpack then, looking down at the dust marks on her immaculate khaki trousers, she raised a lip. 'I love camping trips with you, Belial.'

He snorted a laugh and then turned to face me. 'Parity told us what was going on.' He glanced back up the passage toward the gate. 'What did *you* see?'

I slumped down onto another fallen block of stone, not sure how I felt about what I'd just witnessed. 'It rained acid and they fell out of the sky.'

'Not acid.' Keril had come up behind us.

Belial raised an eyebrow. 'So what was it?'

Keril looked slightly embarrassed. 'Qeres.'

Belial gave a low whistle. 'Where the hell did Gallard get that stuff from?'

I was confused. 'What's qeres?'

'Perfume,' Belial said. 'It was developed by Egyptian embalmers and was called "The first breath of the afterlife" or some such idiocy.' He shrugged. 'Somehow they found out that while angels were in mortal form it could kill them.'

'And under what set of bizarre circumstances would you find that out?' I asked.

Belial shrugged. 'I don't even want to guess.'

'When our world died, we knew the angels were coming. Gallard got it from Egypt where it was developed,' Keril explained. 'The plan was to find out how it worked, change it so that it would work on the angelic form and use it. But they turned up so fast he just stored it and ran with the rest of us. He's been working on it ever since.' The tall Drekavak fumbled in a bag and brought out a bottle of water from which he took a long drink. 'Gallard always said he would get his revenge.' He looked over at me 'Was he all right? Did he get away?'

'I don't know.' I had to smile at the memory of Gallard dancing and giggling in the deluge of perfume. 'He seemed very happy – he was dancing in the rain but it didn't seem to affect him at all.'

Keril snorted a laugh. 'Nope, it only affects the Host. Gallard changed it to hurt angels, whatever form they were in but he was very careful to make sure it wouldn't affect any other species.'

Belial frowned. 'Will it kill them?'

It was easy to forget that, as one of the fallen, Belial had once been part of the Host. This was the death of his family we were discussing so casually.

'Don't worry.' Having finished his drink, Keril waved the bottle at the little girl and, with a hopeful look, she came hopping over. 'We had one tiny vial of real qeres but Gallard has always been irritated that he couldn't change it into what he wanted. That stuff he used in the water supply will seriously incapacitate them but they shouldn't actually cease to exist. It'll take them a while to pull themselves together but they'll be all right eventually.'

Belial breathed a small sigh of relief.

This seemed a good time to give them the bad news. 'Michael and Raphael were standing by the gate. The water didn't reach them and, of course, there may be others.'

'Not good.' Belial heaved himself up off the rock. 'We'd better get moving, because eventually they'll call Metatron and come looking for us.'

Carly called over. 'He's awake.' She was backing slowly away from Lucifer.

'Great,' Belial murmured. 'What wonderful timing.'

'Keril?' I sat down next to him. I still wasn't sure if and when he was going to try and twist my head off. 'How exactly did Gallard get it to rain?'

He stared at me for a moment then, just when I thought he'd decided to ignore the question, he looked away. 'Each building has a water tank on the roof,' he said. 'We just added the perfume to the water tanks and ran perforated pipework all over the city. Down every street, inside every building. When Gallard pressed that button it increased the pressure in the tanks and pushed the water down the pipes.

Voila!' He spread his arms wide. 'Instant rain. The best ideas are always simple.'

'But what if the angels hadn't landed?' I thought it was a decidedly ragged plan. 'What if they'd all flown above the pipes?'

Keril laughed. 'What if, what if, what if.' He shrugged. 'You of all people should know not to dwell on what ifs.'

'Why me?' I didn't understand. I didn't dwell on anything – I always thought I was pretty upbeat.

He watched the little girl run her hands along the damp wall. 'If you hadn't healed my sister you'd be in a large amount of very squelchy pieces by now.' He stood up and clapped me on the shoulder. 'But you're not, so that's OK, isn't it?' He stared at me for a moment. 'But *what if* you hadn't been able to save her?'

As he wandered off to see what the little girl was up to, Carly hopped up on the rock next to me. 'You OK?'

I wasn't sure to be quite honest. I watched Keril walk away and wondered what would have happened if I hadn't managed to save his sister. None of the scenarios I concocted came out well for me. I turned to Carly, put my arm around her and, as she leant against me, I kissed her hair. Even in this dank, gloomy place it still smelt of flowers. I loved Carly's hair. 'Not really.' I gave her a squeeze. 'Better now though.' We sat like that for a couple of moments while everybody got themselves together. Belial and Melusine seemed to be having an argument with Lucifer. Eventually Belial turned and pointed to me then began waving his arms as he tried to explain something.

Carly looked rueful. 'And along comes another problem …' She gave me a kiss. 'Guess we'd better go and see what the old man is setting you up for this time.'

I nodded and, getting up, I reached down a hand for her to grasp. 'Carly, are you OK?'

She pulled me toward her father who was now running his hands through his hair in frustration and beginning to bellow at the man who was sitting below him and just laughing. 'Don't really have a choice, do I?' She frowned down at her dusty purple Doc Martins. 'Stay in the city, we die. Stay on Earth, we die. At least here we have a small chance.' She looked at me and bit her lip, tears glimmering on her lids. 'A very small chance.' She dropped her head and her hair slid over her face. 'So if those are our choices I'm really fine with being here.'

We both looked up as Lucifer told Belial he was mad and staggered away from the group. He began screaming incoherent insults at Melusine as she caught his arm and stopped him. 'And if *he's* our only hope,' Carly nodded toward the weakly struggling Prince of Darkness, 'then, quite frankly, we're really up shit creek without a paddle but at least we're not dead.'

I sniggered as Lucifer tried to kick Melusine in the shins. Then groaned as she casually twisted his arm behind his back and used it as a lever to press his face onto the boulder he'd recently vacated. 'I don't think it's going well,' I observed.

Carly put on a bright smile as we approached her vastly irritated father. 'You OK?' she called to him.

Melusine looked up as we wandered over and, taking her knee out of Lucifer's back, gave him a sharp push. He rolled off the rock and onto the dusty floor. 'You try and talk some bloody sense into him.' Standing up, she busied herself by tying her long dark hair up into a knot on the top of her head. Viciously pushing the two wooden spikes through the dark mass, she stalked away to stand, breathing heavily as she alternated between clenching and unclenching her fists and kicking at the ground.

Finally getting herself under control, she walked over to where Belial was sitting head in hands. 'We have to get moving, old man.' Putting one booted foot up onto his rock she pulled two small knives from a holster on her ankle, examined them and shoved them roughly back in again. 'The angels are going to be coming down and shit knows what's going to be coming up.' She stared off into the darkness. 'You sitting there like a great big lump isn't helping.' She began checking all the various pockets in her canvas jacket. Weaponry appeared, was checked and put back again:

knives, small vials, a length of chain and other less recognisable things appeared and disappeared into the coat. 'Keril!' she shouted over to the Drekavak.

Keril wandered over with an enquiring look.

'Do you have any more of that "queeries" stuff?' She didn't look at him, concentrating instead on checking a small handgun.

'Qeres.' Keril corrected her. He blanched slightly as she stared at him from beneath lowered brows.

'I don't care what it's called.' She turned slowly to face him, unblinking. 'I just want some.'

The Drekavak hesitated for a moment, shuffling his big feet as he considered her request. Eventually he reached into one of the many pockets on his black waistcoat. 'One touch of this stuff and you can do some serious damage.' He sighed and handed over a vial. 'Just make sure you know what you're doing, all right?'

The tiny bottle glittered, sitting in Melusine's hand like a tear. She stared at it expressionless.

'There's enough there to take out about ten angels.' Keril turned away shaking his head. 'Please don't make me regret giving this to you, Melusine.'

Melusine closed her eyes and her hand then sat down with a thump next to Belial. 'I can't believe I'd use this stuff.'

'Really?' Belial looked up at her. 'Strange – nobody else would have any trouble believing that you'd use it.' He stared back down at the floor. 'But listen to me, Melusine, daughter of Pressyne. Keep in mind that these were once my brothers.'

She pursed her lips, 'I'm not big on family as you know,' she said. 'But I will keep that in mind if and when I decide to use this.' She reached over and placed a hand on Belial's shoulder. 'Needs must when the Devil drives, eh?'

Belial shook his head then laughed as he looked over at Lucifer who was now sobbing on the floor. 'You know what?' he said. 'I'm beginning to think this wasn't one of my better ideas.'

A dull boom made us jump and we all looked back toward

the gates. There was another and another, getting louder with each repetition.

'Shit!' Melusine jumped to her feet. 'Time to get out of here, I think.'

The whole party rushed around gathering bits and pieces.

Carly pushed me toward Lucifer. 'You'd better get him up and moving.'

'Why me?' Dealing with the Morning Star again was the last thing I wanted. I felt I'd done my bit and now someone else should be put in charge of Mr Wimpy.

'You can tell him what happened.' She gave me a strange look. 'You've been with him every step of the way.' She hit me on the arm. 'Don't roll your eyes at me and don't sigh either – just get on with it.' Reaching up to give me a kiss she went to help Keril dress the little girl in something warmer.

Lucifer, Abbadon, The Great Accuser, The Father of Lies and the owner of many other titles was currently sitting in the dirt. His legs stretched out ahead of him, his arms were wrapped around his torso and snot covered his face. He was the very picture of a man in deep, deep misery.

I squatted down and studied him. He didn't look much different from when I first carried him from the car crash. I studied him harder; I was sure he'd changed far more when I'd dragged him out of my house. 'Lord Lucifer.' I lowered my voice so as not to startle him. 'We've got to get moving, you need a hand up?'

The man hunched his shoulders and stared down at his feet. 'I don't understand,' he whispered. 'I'm dreaming?' He looked up at me hoping for an agreement of some sort.

'No.' I figured this wasn't the time to get into a major theoretical discussion about what was and what might be real. The booming sounds had taken on a monotonous regularity and now shouts could be heard.

'I'm not Satan.' He shuddered and began to cry again. 'I'm an insurance salesman, I'm Graham and I'm just …' His voice trailed off.

Grabbing him under the arm I pulled him to his feet. 'We can talk about this as we walk, but we do have to walk.' I grimaced as a particularly loud thump was accompanied by a cracking sound. 'There may also be some running.'

Parity, shouldering her pack, stopped next to us. 'They're nearly through the gates.' She looked worried. 'We have to go now! Do you need any help with him?' She stared down at the still crying man. 'He's not who you think he is, you know.' She frowned. 'Not now.'

I shook my head at her enigmatic statement and pushed Lucifer toward the rest of the group. 'It's OK, I've got him.'

Half-walking, half-carrying the man, I followed the rest of the party once more into the darkness. As this became absolute Melusine broke out a powerful torch for herself and distributed smaller ones among the party including a tiny one to the little girl. The child was delighted, and amused herself by creating moving spots that highlighted the rugged old walls of the tunnel, laughing and talking to herself in a high singsong voice.

Carly jogged beside me. 'She doesn't know her name.' She nodded toward the little girl who, sitting high on Keril's shoulders, was now shining the torch on her fingers and giggling. 'What do you think she'd like to be called?'

I shrugged. 'Ask her.' I grabbed Graham's arm as he tripped over some loose stone.

'We need to keep walking.' I put a hand on his shoulder and gave him a little push. He promptly tripped over and fell to the floor. Carly sniggered quietly and wandered off to catch up with Keril.

The man remained on the floor breathing hard.

I handed him a bottle of water. 'Sorry.' I hunkered down beside him. 'I didn't mean to push you that hard.'

He took a long drink then, after pouring the last of the water over his head, he raked both hands over his face and through his hair. Taking the hand I offered he climbed to his feet. He shuddered as he ran his hands through his long hair again. 'This is all wrong.' He tried to look at himself – his hands, his body – but it was too dark. 'I need a mirror,' he said.

We walked in silence then he nudged me. 'Humour me,'

he said. 'Tell me what happened – can you do that?'

'Yes, I can, but you'd better make sure you really want to know before I tell you.' I carried on walking, waiting for him to make up his mind. The silence was broken only by the echoing footfalls of the party and the occasional soft giggles of one little girl.

He squared his shoulders. I was surprised; when he stopped hunching and whimpering, he was taller than Belial. He nodded. 'Keep it short, keep it simple.'

I thought, for a moment, that was a fairly tall order. Eventually I just plunged in. 'You, Graham Latimer, are the last in line from the man that killed Jesus. Lucifer has been hiding in your lineage since Christ's death. If one particular angel gets his hands on you he's going to kill you, which in turn will kill God. Power can't be destroyed so God's power will go to him.' I hesitated then sighed. 'And yours will evidently go to me.'

Graham paled. 'Stupid religious nonsense,' he muttered.

I couldn't repress a snort. My whole life had been dictated by stupid religious nonsense. I'd tried to get away from it but it kept coming back and biting me in the bum. 'I don't want to be the "Great Adversary",' I said, 'so we're keeping you out of the hands of the angels and trying to get you back to being who you're supposed to be.' I paused. 'But you seem to have taken some of Lucifer's looks but none of him, so now we're all at a bit of a loss.' I paused trying to work it all out then gave up. 'Oh, I don't know.'

Carly looked back at us and frowned.

I hurried on. 'So we're taking you to your old Throne Room in the hope – and I stress the word *hope* here – that this will bring it all back to you because that was your place of power and where you sat for a long time.'

Graham shook his head. 'What a load of shit.' He snorted. 'You can't even get your supernatural creatures right. Demons are bad and angels are good – they're nice, they look after people.' He frowned. 'I used to have a client with angel cards – she used to give me readings. Gabriel, Michael, Raphael and all the others. I think she said that Michael was my guardian angel.'

Coming to a junction we stopped while Belial tried to remember which way to go. 'Anybody recognise anything?' At the silence he shook his head and turned left.

'Gabriel is currently nowhere to be found. Allegedly he completely lost it and tried to kill a city full of people somewhere in Brazil. Michael is looking to kill everybody on Metatron's order. This is because Metatron wants all humans dead so that he can scrap the blueprint and start again. And Raphael ...' I paused 'I think all Raph wants is doughnuts, a quiet life and a beach where he could learn to surf.'

I ground to a verbal halt. He was right: this was complete crap. Even to me this all sounded incredibly improbable and I'd lived through it all.

'Rubbish.' Graham laughed. 'I just can't understand why you'd tell me all this. Is it money you want?' He shook his head. 'You've kidnapped the wrong person. I don't have much, I don't have any family or friends, I don't have any influence ... Are you a terrorist? Why would you try and make me believe this?' He stumbled again then cursed as he hopped about getting his footing back. 'I remember the card for Metatron. He had all these circles above his head, a beautiful purple aura and he loved children.'

I coughed remembering the children squabbling over the body of a dead cat. 'Metatron was the little guy that nailed you to that cross then tried to find out what was in your gooey centre.'

Graham came to a sudden halt, his face in the torchlight ashen and stark. 'But that was just a dream – how do you know my dreams?' He swallowed convulsively, his eyes darting back and forth. 'This man just kept smiling and saying that it was for the good of everybody.' Turning away, the tormented insurance salesman was suddenly and violently sick. All the water came back up and splashed over the walls and floor turning the dust to mud.

Parity ran back toward us shouting and waving. 'They're through the gate. We have to go, run ... *run*!'

I stood and listened. 'I can't hear anything?'

193

'Don't argue,' Carly said. 'If Parity says they're coming through then they're coming through. Get him – let's go.'

We ran. It was difficult holding on to Graham who, still suffering the effects of sickness and a sudden deluge of regained memories, kept stumbling and tripping. We staggered along together in a horrible drunken parody of a three-legged race.

There was a sudden flare of light and the crack of beating wings. The tunnel behind us lit up as huge balls of fire exploded onto the walls. Burning droplets bounced then exploded again as they hit other parts of the tunnel.

'Come on!' Belial screamed. 'We've just got to get to the Limbo Gate then we should be able to hold them off for a bit.'

'What is that?' Graham panted as he ran, eyes wild as he stared at the rain of fire that blasted molten lumps from the walls and trickled along the floor in ever-deepening runnels and valleys. Rocks crackled and snapped as they heated up then immediately began to cool. The air made humming sounds as it fried in Michael's righteous fire. 'Is that some sort of weapon?'

'That's your "guardian angel",' I said in a rush, out of breath. It was difficult to talk and run at the same time. I had to concentrate hard to keep from breaking an ankle. 'That's Michael and I'd say he's almost terminally pissed off.'

Graham looked over his shoulder as the sound of wings intensified. 'Bloody hell!' Ripping his arm out of my hand he bent his head and, pumping his arms and legs, put on a turn of speed that Nessus would have been proud of. He disappeared toward Melusine's bobbing torchlight.

Wondering what had caused the sudden change in attitude I looked over my shoulder. Michael was bearing down on us from the glowing and flickering tunnel. With wings spread wide and teeth bared he forged the way with sword drawn, its howling flame a comet's tail behind him. Spittle glistened on his chin and his eyes were fixed open. Blood dripped from an open wound on his face – the result, no doubt, of one of Gallard's "raindrops". He was screaming incomprehensible invective and each time he stopped for breath he would punctuate his rant with another volley of fireballs.

I copied Lucifer's example and, grabbing Carly as I passed, we ran like hell.

'Joe, you traitorous little shit!' Michael screamed. 'I always knew I was right about you. A leopard can't change its spots.'

Carly, despite the situation, snorted then looked horrified as Farr and Melusine walked calmly past us. They were going the wrong way. 'Farr!' she screamed.

Belial stopped her. 'Watch,' he ordered. Farr placed himself in front of the frothing angel and held up one hand.

I felt a breeze wash past me.

Melusine stepped around Farr and confronted Michael.

'Don't bother, lizard.' The angel laughed as he landed. 'Shouldn't you be sleeping under a rock, somewhere warm?'

Melusine said nothing – she just drew a short sword and a wicked-looking knife, then faced him, expressionless.

I could see the muscles jumping slightly in her throat as she tensed, ready to move.

'Hang on to something.' Belial warned sidling over to the wall.

'I have no issues with the Fae so just get out of my way.' Michael stepped lightly toward her, his sword held low and ready.

Melusine spoke quietly. 'But this Fae has issue with you,' she said. Bringing up both weapons, she held the sword out in front of her, the knife above her head. Bending her knees slightly she stilled, waiting.

Keril picked up the little girl and, holding her tight, hid behind a pillar of rock.

Michael turned to the tall necromancer and laughed. 'I remember you little sorcerer,' he snarled. 'Thou shalt not suffer a witch to live.' He raised his sword slightly as he glanced warily at the dragon.

The wind began to gust: dust and small pebbles lifted and bounced from the floor all rolling toward Farr as he focused on Michael.

'We drowned the wrong sibling it seems.' Michael laughed as he casually brushed away the dust and debris that was now whirling around the two of them.

'Heads down!' Belial barked.

Without question we all obeyed – even Graham. The sound of rushing wind grew, then screamed past us like a panicked herd of cattle: uncaring, unheeding, just blindly intent on simple movement.

The wind hit Michael like a sledgehammer and, with a look of surprise, he staggered backward.

'Pathetic,' he screamed into the maelstrom. 'If that's the best you can do …' He frowned as he was, once more, pushed back, his feet slipping on the dust and shale of the tunnel floor.

Farr took a deep breath. 'That's not even a tiny part of what I can do,' he said quietly. Raising his arms above his head, he rolled his eyes back into his skull and began to chant. The wind dropped for a moment as though it were listening to the strangely hypnotic words.

I watched the dust and grit swirl silently around Farr, creating set patterns which changed and shifted. As his chant strengthened the swirling dust became more agitated, rising and falling with the cadence of his voice.

Michael pushed hard against the wind but it held him fast. With a grunt he shrugged and pulled his sword. Sending one carefully aimed ball of fire toward the howling necromancer he waited with a superior smile. His face fell as he watched a hand of dust reach out from the swirling mass; it casually smothered the fire and bore it down to earth. Alarmed now, Michael began to struggle in earnest, his face grim as he finally realised he was held fast.

Melusine cracked a slight smile.

Eventually Farr's chant switched to overdrive. His voice became commanding and impassioned. The dust gathered in a huge ball that twisted and seethed between him and the struggling angel.

With a sudden movement of his hands Farr sent the whole thing rolling toward Michael. More rushed past us, dragged up from the depths of the tunnels and the wind seemed to be rising from the floor.

Michael drew his sword again and began slashing at the air around him. Finally the wind grew so strong that he could no longer stand against it. With a scream of rage that echoed around the walls, the archangel was steadily pushed back toward the gate.

Watching through slit eyes I held on to my rock. I thought I could see hands and faces in the wind – ethereal bodies that wrapped themselves around the silently struggling angel. Gripping the walls, Michael's face twisted with effort as his fingernails gouged rents in the stone.

Melusine frowned, then, sheathing her weapons, she carefully removed the wooden spikes from her hair. Loose and uncontained it rose in a dark cloud around her face. She gripped both belled spikes in one hand then, as the wind dropped for a split second, she took aim and, with a deft flick of her wrist, flipped them toward the struggling angel.

Both spikes entered Michael's chest with a sound like wet washing falling from a height. He howled and stared down at the tiny bells that still hung from the ends of the wooden spikes; they tinkled as they rolled back and forth across the front of his tunic.

As though crucified, Farr brought his hands out to his sides. He was now screaming his chant into the howling gale. With a swift, decisive movement he brought both hands together in a single clapping motion then, without pause, extended them toward Michael, palms flat. Around us the air became still and silent as everything – wind, rocks, sticks and dust – headed toward the gasping angel.

Distorted faces stretched up to scream into Michael's face, while hands clutched and grasped at every part of him. The wind twined around him, tying him up in a cocoon of movement and shadowy body parts. Without hesitation the whole entity fled toward the light, dragging Michael with it. His scream faded away and all became quiet. The cheerful tinkling of tiny silver bells was the last sound that echoed back down the corridor.

It was that type of quiet that follows snow – a deep peace in which nobody dared move or even breathe. As Farr crumpled toward the ground we all jumped as Parity screamed his name, her voice breaking into our shocked immobility. She pushed past us, then scrabbled over the fallen rocks to reach her brother.

'Farr!' She gently lifted his head. 'Farr, please wake up.' She shook him slightly. 'You have to wake up. I need you, I can't exist without you.'

Belial moved before the rest of us. But before he could reach them Farr lifted a hand and cuffed his sister gently round the head. 'Stop screaming at me, Parity,' he muttered. 'Even if I'm not dead, I'll be deaf.' He coughed and sat up with a groan, his hair bedraggled and grey. Small spots of blood appeared, seeping through the dust that caked his face. Grit and small pebbles rolled from his jacket and coat as he moved.

Parity sat back on her heels, her head in her hands. 'Please don't do that again.' Her voice, muffled by her palms, sounded creaky and drawn.

Farr took Belial's proffered hand and clambered to his feet. After retrieving his glasses from the pocket of his duffle coat he dusted himself off a little then pulled his sister into a cuddle. 'I'll try not to.' He winced. 'I have got such a headache.'

His last words sounded so pathetic after what we'd witnessed that I laughed. Melusine, who was standing behind me, hit me across the back of the head. 'Don't laugh, you,' she said. 'Wow! I thought I was past being impressed by anything these days.'

I turned to her and rubbed my head; she'd hit me a lot harder than Carly always did. If these women didn't stop smacking me, I was going to end up with permanent brain damage. 'You're impressed by wind,' I leered at her. 'Well, I can give you some of that.'

'Don't be gross.' Melusine continued to study Farr and Parity. 'That wasn't wind, you idiot.' She shook her head. 'That was the dead.'

'The what?'

'The old dead.' Melusine turned to look at me. 'And I mean really old – thousands and thousands of years old.' She was enjoying my obvious confusion. 'After a time the dead don't bother with a body, they just sort of exist as a thought or a memory – but they do still exist.' She shook her head, obviously awed by what Farr had managed to do. 'He gathered their memories together, made them remember their old forms and gave them a target. Then he dragged them out of their resting places and gave them the desire to head for the light. He told them that Michael was the only thing standing in their way ...' She gave a delighted laugh. 'Belial always said that boy was a much more talented necromancer than everyone thought.' She paused. 'He's been keeping his light under a bushel. I wonder what else he could do if he wasn't using most of his power keeping Parity happy.' She trailed off into thoughtful silence. I wasn't sure I liked her smile.

Carly told me he was a necromancer. 'Isn't that someone who makes zombies?'

Melusine frowned. 'No, they usually just talk to the dead but they can reanimate, if they had to.' She tailed off and looked speculatively over at the young man and his sister. 'Although I can't see why anyone would want to.' Getting to her feet she slapped the dust from her trousers. 'Can you imagine what life would be for all the living if the dead were just allowed to wander aimlessly?' She took a long look up the passage. 'We'd better get out of here before old feather fart brushes them off and comes back for us,' she said. 'They'll only be able to hold him for so long.'

The air still felt very passive as we walked down the tunnel. Graham seemed deep in thought, but I decided that if he had questions he'd ask them and left him alone.

Eventually another set of gates blocked our path. These huge silver works of art stood floor to ceiling and seemed almost entirely out of place in their dusty cave-like surroundings. Animals, plants, humans and astral bodies climbed or hung from delicate silver chains. The whole thing was welded together to form a complex and chaotic scene. Above the gates, ornamental metal letters spelled out: *Relinquite omnem spem, vos qui intratis.*

'Abandon hope all ye who enter here,' Carly translated. 'Well, that's what it means even if that isn't entirely what it says.'

'Oh that's very bloody cheerful.' Graham stared up at the gates.

I watched him carefully. He wasn't showing anywhere near the amount of hysteria I'd expect from someone who found themselves in such an odd situation. I'd had to start thinking of him as Graham again as he was so human, overweight and frightened that there was no way I could think of him as Lucifer.

'I hate to upset your apple cart,' Carly leant in and gave a loud stage whisper into Graham's ear, 'but *you* put it there.'

'Did I?' Graham frowned then put a hand to his forehead and closed his eyes. 'Why do I remember these gates being created? I was forced to stand and watch. I was on the inside and the angels were out in the passage. They wove the gates from the silver chains that all the fallen had been forced to wear when they were escorted out of Heaven. They decorated them with the animals and other glorious works of God's creation. Metatron said it was to remind me what I'd lost and what I'd forced so many of the Host to lose.' He pressed his fingers to the bridge of his nose. 'I unravelled a swathe of flowers and birds to create those letters.' He opened his eyes and stared at the gates. 'I did it to piss Michael off but he just laughed and agreed.'

'Well, some jokes fall on stony ground,' I intoned. 'Ow!' Carly trod on my foot.

Graham seemed to be able to access certain snippets of Lucifer's memory and I wasn't sure if that was a good thing or not. I turned to say something helpful and supportive but stood with my mouth open. The message above the gates now read: *Per libido dei.*

I struggled for a moment. 'By God's sex drive?' My Latin was as rusty as an old can.

200

The man beside me shook his head slowly. 'It's actually whim. By God's whim.' He stared at the gates. 'Or caprice. It covers both really.' I noticed that his eyes had become darker, his jaw a little more defined. When he quirked a lip, in what could have been a smile, he looked like a snake hiding in a sleeping bag. 'Well, at the very least that really *will* piss Michael off.' He held up a hand and the gate swung open at his touch. We all passed through in silence.

Behind us the gates swung closed with a clang. There was a click, a whirr and a dull thud as various locks re-engaged. As silence fell, the man I had only recently stopped thinking of as Lucifer grinned at me. 'This will piss him off even more,' he said. He turned and stroked the gates, He had the manner of someone who has found a well-loved toy from childhood hidden in a box of grandma's old cooking equipment. 'Stand firm.' He whispered to them. 'Give me time. Hold them back for as long as you can.'

I could have sworn the gates shuddered at his touch.

I felt a tug on my jeans and, looking down, found our little party crasher staring up at me.

'What's your name?' I knelt down on one knee to bring my face in line with hers.

'Hungry.' She smiled. All four of her top front teeth were missing and her tongue poked through the gap when she spoke, giving her a slight lisp.

'Hmm, I don't think that's a suitable name but I might have a magic pocket with something interesting in it.' I pretended to search through all my pockets.

She giggled and looked hopeful.

'Aha!' I produced a chocolate bar from one pocket and an apple from another and held them both high above her head. She jumped toward them – a futile gesture. 'Now then,' I mused. 'I have a chocolate bar to give to someone.' I studied both apple and chocolate carefully. 'They both look good.' I gave her a sad shake of the head. 'But I can't give a gift to someone I don't know – that would be rude.' I scratched my head. 'Now, if I just knew that person's name then I'd know them well enough to call them back if I found anything else

201

that was nice.' I waved the food just above her head.

The little girl stared at me for a moment, her lower lip caught between tiny white teeth. 'Una,' she said eventually.

'That's your name – Una?'

She gave a short nod then reached again for the food.

I offered her the chocolate and the apple. 'Well, Una, because I know you now, you get the choice – which one would you like?'

Grabbing the chocolate, she rushed off laughing. I looked at the slightly scrubby apple and sighed. I suppose it was too much to hope for that she'd take the healthy option. 'Hello, lunch,' I muttered at it.

I was just about to take a bite when Carly appeared and, with one swift move, stole my apple and bit into it. 'What's going on with, Graham?' She chewed thoughtfully as she stared at the man still admiring his gates.

'Do you know, I'm not sure that *is* Graham any more' I pinched the apple back and took a bite then shook my head as I watched the man trip over a rock and stagger into the wall. 'Well, it certainly *wasn't* Graham – now it seems he's back again.'

'Oi!' She'd stolen the apple from me again.

'What do you mean it *wasn't* Graham?'

I couldn't explain, but just for a moment, there at the gates, I was positive I was looking into the eyes of something far older, far deadlier than a middle-aged insurance salesman. I shrugged and made a swipe for the apple, laughing as she snatched it out of reach. 'I don't know.' I patted my pockets hoping there was something else lurking in a corner. 'Maybe I'm just starving and it's beginning to unbalance me.'

Graham wandered over to us with a cautious smile. Sitting down on a large rock he sighed. 'I feel quite out of sorts,' he said. He took his boots off and emptied out a small stream of stones and dust.

I sat next to him. 'Was it that thing with the gates and changing personalities?' I asked. 'I can see how that would freak you out a little.'

Graham looked up at me and frowned. 'What?' He looked

202

surprised. 'No no, I've spent 20 years in a suit and now, well, this really isn't me.' He looked down at the black jeans and leather jacket that someone had donated. 'I think this may be the first time I've ever worn jeans.' He shuffled around on the rock. 'Why are they so popular? They're really not that comfortable.' He frowned and hesitated. 'What *thing* with the gates and the personality?' He had a completely blank look on his podgy pale face; his watery blue eyes just looked puzzled.

'Never mind.' I stood up. 'We'd better get moving.' I watched as he shrugged and wandered away. He seemed completely and genuinely oblivious. I found it impossible to believe that he had no idea of the changes he'd just experienced. 'Hey,' I put a hand on his shoulder and looked carefully into his face. 'Are you OK now?'

Graham blinked and then shrugged. 'I should be screaming and running and terrified.' He frowned, his expression blanking slightly as he obviously explored his emotions. 'But I'm not.' He brushed dust from his knees in a slow, careful motion. 'All the panic is still there if I go looking for it hard enough.' He looked up at me with a smile 'But if I don't look very hard it just sort of evaporates.'

Well, that didn't sound good. I watched his face for some hint of a lie or deeply controlled panic but there really was nothing there.

'Maybe I'm going mad.' He brushed the dirt from his hands. 'Nobody's happier than he that fools himself, eh?'

I nodded and resolved to keep a much closer eye on him.

Belial stepped elegantly up onto a rock and gave a shrill whistle. As we fell silent he coughed his throat clear. 'When we closed these levels nearly 2,000 years ago, we only left those that either refused to move, believing themselves deserving of the suffering they were dealt, or those whose crimes and attitudes were so terrible that we just couldn't let them out.' He looked around, making sure he had our full attention. 'I honestly don't know what's here now, so when we go through those doors, I'm as clueless as you.

'Hopefully,' he looked meaningfully at Parity, 'we'll get

some forewarning before something happens.' He paused again. 'Of course it could be completely deserted and all of the occupants have decided to just let go.' He turned and stared at the double wooden doors that barred our way. 'I, however, find that extremely unlikely so let's be careful. Even here life is worth hanging on to.' He paused again to let all that sink in. 'We're going to have Michael and company chasing us. They will do whatever they can to stop us before we get to the river because they can't cross it. Whatever happens we have to get there before them.

'Don't leave the path, don't fall behind and don't get caught on your own. All the old myths are true here. With the gates charged to keep out all comers we should be OK until we cross the river, but that is really just a hopeful guess.' Turning away from the silver gates he took a deep breath and stared down a small incline toward another door set within huge stone pillars that supported what looked like the main wall of a church. 'I haven't been here for a very long time,' he muttered to Melusine who nodded and rolled her shoulders, her face set.

As we walked toward the wooden door, the dusty, natural stone floor turned to tiles beneath our feet. The first few were cracked and broken. Farther in, they became beautifully complete. Some of them depicted stylised trees, some showed knights on horses and some had just letters or a single circle. This tiled path, with its plain black borders, created a very clear walkway that moved between carved pillars of stone and slid under the dark wooden arch.

Clinging to the pillars, the door, the roof and carved into the natural stone of the tunnel, dark gargoyles stared down at us in malignant silence. In any space they could fit, fantastic animals crept and hid. Tiny winged lions, lizards with human faces and a dog with a dragon's tail and wings stared at us with cruel fascination. Small goblin-like creatures – each carved in a pose designed to shock – hung from the stonework or sat, feet dangling, watching us from the lintel. One had its finger up its nose. One had its cock in its hand, an expression of utmost satisfaction on its face, while yet another was concentrating on pulling the wings from what looked like a terrified fairy. These gruesome sentinels lined the doorway and stared out with matching smug condescension.

Melusine studied the doors with their stone guardians. 'I'm going hunting.'

'What?' Belial stopped, his hand reaching for a metal dragon.

'There is no way they're going to let me in there.' Melusine glared up at a group of potbellied fox things that lined the lintel of the doorway. They seemed to stare back at her.

'But ...' Belial looked around and then nodded. 'Yeah, I suppose you're right. We'll meet you on the other side.'

Wings burst from Melusine's shoulders and she jumped into the air. 'Just try to stay out of trouble,' she said to Belial who nodded.

Sixty feet in the air Melusine completed her change and, flapping hard, flew vertically up the walls until she was no more than a black smear against the sky. I watched as she flew over the church and disappeared into the distance.

As irritating, rude and condescending as she was, the group seemed diminished without her and, as we all stared in silence at the display of bodily functions arranged before us, Belial dragged his eyes from the sky and gave a small cough. 'Well, this wasn't here before,' he muttered. 'I think we can say things have changed a little.' He grasped the tail of a sleeping metal dragon and pulled.

# CHAPTER 8

DEEP WITHIN THE BUILDING we heard a bell begin to chime. Feeling a little hand in mine I looked down expecting to see Carly but it was Una. Thumb in mouth she looked worried. 'Don't worry, they're just stone.' I tapped a particularly ugly cat thing. She nodded, muttering around her thumb, 'Now they are.'

The door swung open and a young woman studied us with a slightly confused expression. 'Hello?' She gave us a wide smile. 'Where did you come from?'

She looked to be in her mid-20s. Long, mouse blonde hair hung in well-washed shining waves down to her waist. It was almost impossible to see any of her other curves as her shapeless but soft-looking dark green robe hid almost everything. She wore no make-up except for nail polish on her bare toes and, with her big green eyes, her face looked open and friendly. There was an almost universal sigh of relief as we all studied her. Obviously she wasn't what any of us had been expecting.

Belial stepped forward. 'We need entrance for reasons of solace and sanctuary.' He spoke the words in a formal tone and the woman rubbed her nose as she glanced around at the gargoyles then bowed.

'Follow me.' She walked away, her bare feet making no sound on the tiled floor.

Angling away to the left she opened a well-used door and ushered us all inside. 'If you'll just wait here, I'll bring you some refreshments.' She paused for a moment regarding us all. 'I think the Abbess will want to talk to you.'

'Abbess?' Farr looked askance at Belial. 'This is a church?'

'Not really, no.' Belial shut his mouth with a snap and

Farr, with a worried glance at the demon lord, wisely let the subject drop.

'Well, so much for the hideous torments of Hell.' Keril moved across the room to study a huge tapestry that almost covered one wall. It depicted a woman in armour, bathed in light, surrounded by a vast army of both angels and men. She had no visible weapons, yet there were bodies beneath her feet.

He looked up as the door opened and the young woman stepped back inside carrying a large silver tray. She was accompanied by an older man dressed in loose-fitting blue trousers and tunic. His unkempt dark hair flopped over one eye; this seemed more from a lack of brushing rather than a statement of style. He carried another tray, holding it carefully with his enormous hands. Placing it on the table he nodded in happy satisfaction and treated everyone to a huge laughing smile which was vague, childlike and completely innocent of any deeper reasoning. Shunning introductions, he bolted as soon as he could.

The young lady rolled her eyes. 'I'm Sarah.' She placed her tray down. 'I apologise for William's rapid disappearance – we don't ever get visitors by *that* door and he's shy.' Checking the food on the table she dusted off her hands. 'The Abbess will be down as soon as she can, however she may be a little while as she's in ceremony.' She gestured to the trays. 'Please relax and have something to eat and drink. If you go through those doors you'll find baths – please feel free to use them.' Her relaxed look slipped a little. 'Not that I mean to imply that you need to or anything …' She stuttered and her thin veneer of adulthood fell away. 'If you want me just ring that.' After pointing out a tasselled bell pull she also bolted, her cheeks aflame. The door slammed shut behind her.

Farr walked over and gently opened it again; it wasn't locked. He nodded then looked around. 'Well, you can't blame her.' He sniffed. 'You are all a bit ripe.'

'A bath.' Carly stretched and smiled. 'Well, I don't know about you lot but I'm certainly heading for that.' Checking the pots and plates she poured herself a cup of tea, then piled a plate high with bread, fish, fruit and what appeared to be some sort of dark cake.

'Hang on a moment.' Belial held up a hand. Carly froze with what looked like a huge grape halfway to her mouth. 'Parity – would you, please …'

Parity walked over to the table and closed her eyes. Silence fell as we all waited for her verdict.

'It's fine.' Picking up another plate, she piled it high then carried it over to her brother who was still a little pale from his exertions. 'Eat!' She pushed the plate at him. Then, irritated when he shook his head, she physically held the plate in his hand. 'You'll feel better if you eat something.' Eventually Farr nodded and began to eat, his colour improving with each bite. Parity looked on like a proud mother occasionally brushing bits of gravel out of his hair.

'What's the matter with you?' Carly asked.

'This isn't right.' I stared around the room.

She frowned around a brown roll filled with pink meat and some sort of unidentifiable greenery. Obviously unable to speak with a mouth that full, she raised her eyebrows and shrugged. 'Waff ifffnt wight?' she mumbled.

'These are people,' I said.

Carly swallowed. 'What are you talking about?' The rest of the conversations had fallen silent; the only sound was the occasional clang as Una played with the huge fire irons.

'These people are alive, they're breathing and talking and walking about.' I demonstrated by doing the same. 'They're supposed to be dead – this *is* Hell, isn't it?' I leant on the wall and stared round at them all. 'This is where the *dead* go.'

'Oh.' Carly flicked a glance at her father who just shrugged. 'Look.' She paused for a moment then, with a sigh, flopped down into a chair and placed her plate of food on a small table beside her. 'Dad, would you like to go through this?'

Belial shook his head. 'No.' He turned away.

'Well, thanks.' Carly sat for a moment in silence. 'The first thing that God created was Lucifer.' She shrugged.

'We're not sure why – as a servant, a companion? We really don't know, but whatever the reason it didn't work out. Lucifer asked too many questions and had far too much power. He disagreed with many of God's plans and eventually God created another: Metatron. This time he made some changes and, unlike Lucifer, who was never given a task, Metatron was charged with documenting and organising. One of his first tasks seemed to be documenting the arguments between God and Lucifer.

'Eventually the other four archangels were also brought into being: Michael, Gabriel, Raphael and Uriel.' She glanced up at her father.

Belial stared stonily into the fireplace.

'Nowhere near as powerful as Lucifer, they were charged with different tasks. Raphael heals – he was created as a calming influence on the others and was someone they could talk to when God wasn't around to guide them.' She glanced again at her father. 'He certainly seems to be the most sane.'

Belial snorted and shook his head.

Carly continued. 'Gabriel was known as God's strength.'

'Hang on.' I held up a hand to stop her. 'Isn't that Michael's job?'

She shook her head. 'I said strength, not might. Gabriel gave inner strength to those facing adversity. He was the angel that supported Jesus in the garden, he visited Mary. He was the one that was the messenger. He certainly had the most congenial dealings with the humans when they turned up.

'Michael …' Carly snorted. 'Well, we're all fairly au fait with what Michael was. He was God's wrath, his discipline.' She sighed. 'Really, you should feel sorry for him: it's always Michael who has to wipe out civilisations, clear up messes and generally be the bad guy. He used to complain and agonise about it a lot, but over the years he seems to have really got to grips with his role.'

Picking up her plate she took another bite of her roll and chewed in silence for a moment. 'Then of course there was Uriel.'

'Uriel?' I wracked my brains. I'd heard the name but certainly not from the angels.

'Hmmm.' Carly studied her bread. 'Uriel was a bit of an enigma. It was said that he stood guard at the gates of lost Eden. He was the angel of peace and ministration. His biggest crime was to speak on the humans' behalf when God had decided that all life needed to be wiped from the face of the Earth in one big flood. It really wasn't a coincidence that Pope Zachary had him wiped from the list of *acceptable* angels.' Carly poured herself another cup of tea and stared over the rim. 'I think I may have gotten a little off track here. Anyway, we finally get to the humans.' She sighed. 'God created the world, but we don't think he created man.'

'What?' This went against everything I'd been taught.

Carly shrugged. 'Man already existed.'

'Where?' I asked.

'Hell,' Carly said matter of fact. 'Here.' She looked around at the room. 'Hell was once – and we're talking so long ago that the mind boggles – a "normal" place. Trees, soil, evolution – all that sort of thing. But it all went wrong, we don't know why but the ice crept in. Anyway, the beings that lived here were dying by the million and to save themselves they had begun to search for another home. They moved to another place, another land. However, the land they chose was already home to a large lizard population. The lizards were incredibly happy to see them – they'd been running out of food.

'Anyway, God had created Heaven and all his angels but something wasn't right – or at least that's the theory – so he created the Earth and populated it with the final beings from this plane. All they had to do was aspire to perfection and man could become the ultimate being. Nirvana.

'Well, it went wrong. Humans are feisty, argumentative and selfish. Left with free will they did exactly as they pleased. You know your own history – it all went downhill from there. But by then God had other problems. Lucifer was becoming increasingly unhappy with the way things were going and had started gathering a following. The humans

210

were engaged in all sorts of wars and seemed determined to wipe each other out. God's infinite patience finally became demonstrably finite and he gave the humans an ultimatum: "Be better or go back where you came from. Here are the rules that I need you to follow." He sent the angels down to sort them out and that's when the Nephilim were born.' Carly stared into her teacup. 'Evidently the angels liked the humans a lot and, despite the blanket ban on getting together, children with all sorts of odd powers started cropping up due to the mix of human and angel blood.' She paused to drain the last of her tea.

'Well, basically a lot of the humans stuck two metaphorical fingers up at religion and worshipped power and things instead. The angels were fighting and arguing among themselves, Lucifer was stirring up a civil war and eventually God said, "Enough!"' Carly sighed. 'When he finally got the angel uprising under control he kicked all the dissenters out of Heaven. Those who had fought with Lucifer he sent to Hell. Those who had refused to fight became the Fae. He told the fallen angels that henceforth they would be known as demons, but if they could convince the humans to change their ways through punishment and torture they stood a chance of getting back into his good graces and so the concept of Hell's torments was born.' Carly glanced at her father who refused to look away from the flames. 'Those humans that showed an aptitude for what you call "magic" got forcibly relocated back to this plane and that's because only those with angelic blood can do the things that are considered magical. The angels collected those that survived the flood and shifted them here. Slowly they winkled all of them out. Occasionally the old mixed blood will crop up again but it's a poor watered-down blood now which is why, slowly but surely, any sign of magic disappeared on Earth. "Thou shalt not suffer a witch to live" was the decree from on high and now you know why.

'This is not an *afterlife* – it never was. It's not a place you go where you die – it's a place you go because you won't conform to God's will. If you die here, you're dead; if you're injured, you die.' She paused. 'Even we don't know what happens after you die. Angels can't cross the Acheron because they obey God's law and he forbade it so there is a sort of block – a geas or spell, if you like. Only those who chose the status "demon" are released from that compulsion and it has to be by choice.'

She lapsed into silence and no one else spoke. This turned everything I'd ever believed on its head and it certainly put the angels in a new light. Unwilling to even look at each other we all busied ourselves with other minor concerns.

I still didn't really understand.

Eventually we were all clean and fed. With the others sitting in quiet conversation by the big fire I took the opportunity to have a good look around the room. It could have been any room in any old house. Big stone flags supported huge bookshelves that were filled to overflowing with leather-bound books, files and richly decorated leather and copper cylindrical scroll cases. Around the room, couches arranged in no particular way were so comfortable that I hardly noticed when my eyelids began to droop. I was so close to sleep that when the door swung open for a second time I jumped, my heart beating wildly.

'I'm so sorry to keep you all waiting.' Sarah smiled at us. 'Mother Abbess has asked to see three of you – if you would come with me?'

Belial stood up and, holding on to Graham's sleeve, he pulled the surprised man to his feet.

Carly nudged me. 'You have to go too,' she whispered. 'You can't let Dad and Graham go on their own. Dad can take care of himself but Graham is just a liability.' She nodded meaningfully toward the alleged Lord of Hell who was currently fumbling with the buttons on his jacket. He'd misaligned them and couldn't seem to work out what to do about it. I watched as Parity wandered over to him and, with a gentle smile, deftly sorted everything out. They stared at each other for a moment then Graham smiled.

It seemed Carly had been watching them as well. 'That could be a bit of a problem,' she said.

Belial made no comment as I joined them and we walked in silence through the cathedral. The familiar church aura of dust, incense, smoky candles and old books wrapped itself around us. The familiar smell caused a sense of displacement and disquiet. What was a cathedral doing here? I remembered that this wasn't true Hell until we passed the River Acheron and I wondered if this had originally been a last bastion of prayer – a place to finally confront those sins before the damned headed off toward their personal torments.

No, from what Carly had been telling me there was no point in repenting ... I mean, what's the point of being sorry that you'd been born different? It seemed a little unfair.

Through the nave, our footsteps echoed around the cavernous space and bounced off a ceiling that must have been over a hundred feet above us. The sound echoed back as the ghosts of our own passing selves, as though a hundred supplicants passed through. At the end of the nave was a five-sided room, its roof a magnificent stained-glass pentacle. Now that was something you'd never find in a church. Standing in the very centre of the room I turned slowly as I gazed up through the glass. Weren't we underground? I stood for a long moment staring up at the sky. It was just slightly the wrong shade of blue.

'This way, please.' Sarah smiled and indicated a small dark corridor. Beyond the pentacle I could see a large, heavily carved wooden structure – an altar. Dressed in a deep red cloth and shrouded in smoke from the permanently burning incense, it was difficult to make out any features on the two large figurines that stood, side by side, at the very centre. The figure on the left was a priapic man, with a full set of antlers and a face that was definitely more than a little deer. He stood on cloven hooves and carried a staff. The statue appeared to be carved from a slab of black basalt and the light from the candles placed around him just highlighted his heavy muscles and the arrogant set of his brow.

On his right, carved from glowing alabaster, was the figure of a heavily pregnant sheela-na-gig. Smaller than her male counterpart, she had long hair and heavy breasts. From the exaggerated slit between her legs tumbled fruit, flowers, children and animals; she was depicted as a veritable cornucopia of a woman. Her face was gentle and, unlike her male consort, she seemed to be permanently amused. Both figures appeared to shimmer and warp in the heavily scented smoke from the sensors. As if in a fog, they could be seen only occasionally and never materialised together, solidifying then fading away as the fey breezes decreed. Other items on the table – a dagger, a skull, a horn and a sword – also made brief appearances as the smoke swirled and eddied. I shook my head and tried to look away. There was something disturbingly mesmerising in the interplay of symbols. I felt like a child that could see a biscuit barrel but couldn't reach it. It was all there for me; all I had to do was find a way to get at it.

I pinched the top of my nose and closed my eyes, but the images continued to throb behind my eyelids: the sword, the skull and the deer-god, then the sword, the horn and the dagger. Each group meant something but I couldn't work out what it was. Staggering a couple of steps away from the altar I picked at the soft skin under my bicep and pinched – hard. The pulsing images disappeared into the pain and I was left in blessed darkness, with only my rapid heartbeat for company. Opening my eyes, I heaved a sigh of relief and resolutely turned away from the altar.

The smoke, once it had finished gently caressing the devotional items, cascaded in a silent silver grey fall to the cold floor. Moving in tendrils, it crept along the ways and byways of the triskele-shaped labyrinth set into the tiles before the altar. All the paths through the maze seemed to terminate at the centre. Here four trees – roots intertwined and their branches reaching out to honour the quarters – seemed to be the focus of the entire room. It was an eerie and unsettling sight and left me feeling exposed. I backed away until I felt a wall at my back then turned and fled.

Hurrying after the rest of the party I plunged into the gloom of the small side corridor. The smoke tugged at my ankles. Every so often I was sure I could hear laughter. I stopped at the end of the corridor where the sunlight splashed across an open doorway. The scented miasma caught up with me then twisted and writhed in the shadows, rolling and billowing. Just through the door was a garden – all colour and light, warmth and safety. By the open door the smoke twisted and curled back on itself. Individual tendrils would test the light then pull back. Refusing to cross the threshold it sulked on the doorstep. After only a moment's hesitation I kicked through it. As I stepped out into the rich, sunlit garden full of roses, herbs and other less recognisable varieties of plant life, I realised I'd never been so pleased to see the sun – even if it was the wrong one.

'Wow!' Graham was sitting on a wooden bench enjoying the garden. He looked around at me, his mouth open. 'So what were you saying about this being Hell?' He shook his head. 'Hardly fire and brimstone, is it?' He peered at me. 'What's the matter with you?'

'Nothing.' I resisted the urge to turn around and stare back at the smoke. I could feel it watching me from the shadows of the doorway; the hairs on the back of my neck still stood to attention.

'Zephaniah?' Belial had taken off down a winding path toward a tiny woman who was sitting on a flat rock, trailing her hand in the shallow pool beside her. She looked up from the book she was reading and shook water droplets from her hand.

As though designed that way, her clothing harmonised and enhanced her surroundings. Her long skirt, woven from a multitude of earthy-coloured threads, was decorated with beads; its home-spun charm matched the beige blouse that she wore. Her only jewellery was a large necklace of a stylised mother holding a child on her lap. This appeared to have been created from molten silver, the rapidly solidified runs of metal giving the piece its abstract detail.

Her long dark hair was striped with strands of grey. She shook it all back and took a long look at the man walking toward her. The blood drained from her face as recognition took hold.

'Oh no! Belial?' Jumping up, her book tumbled to the ground and, holding one hand up to keep him away, she stuttered and stammered, 'Not now. Not after all this time – it's not fair.'

'Wait!' Belial stopped just short of the pink flagstones that ringed the stone edge of the fountain. He reached out toward her.

'What for?' The woman stared at him. 'For you to close us down again, for you to leave again, for you to force people out of their homes and away from what we've built here?' She shook her head, her eyes furious. 'Why should I be surprised? Have you just been waiting for us to fall? Did you hope that this time we'd come with you and you could lay waste to everything we've built just like you tried to last time?'

With every word, she stamped forward until she was chest to stomach with the stuttering Duke of Hell. Belial looked like a man facing an angry cobra.

'No.' Belial looked stricken. 'I'm not here to do any of that.' He paused. 'I didn't do that last time.' He bent slightly to face the tiny, furious woman. 'You never knew what was happening over the river – all you ever saw was your little world here. You took care of your children and looked after your followers; you never saw the pain, the misery, the utter degradation of all the people in the lower levels.'

Graham and I wandered a little closer.

'But you left the very worst here,' she shouted at him. 'You left us without protection. You left the worst murderers, the worst conmen, those that used their powers to control others. You left the monsters behind. And you left me.'

Belial turned purple. 'You wouldn't leave.' He bellowed into her face. 'We had a place for you and your children – a place for your followers– but you just kept banging on about the children and the women down in the city.' He paused and looked at her. He studied each of her features, blinking only occasionally as if he feared she might disappear. His voice dropped almost to a whisper. 'I waited to close the gate.' He reached for her again. 'I waited for a very long time but you

216

always had just one more person you had to save.' His arms dropped to his sides. 'In the end I just couldn't wait any more and there were some really bad things coming through that gate. I had to close it.' Stepping around her, he stole her place on the rock and sat down with a thump, his head in his hands. 'I'm sorry.'

Silence fell. Eventually the woman moved her gaze to stare at us. Her eyes widened and she put a hand to her throat as she bowed. 'Lord,' she acknowledged.

Graham looked embarrassed and, unsure what to do, gave her a short nod.

At his silence she looked up, confused. Walking over she took a closer look at him. He turned pink and his eyes darted this way and that as he tried to avoid her direct gaze. She turned to Belial. 'This isn't right. What's happened?'

Belial opened his mouth but she held up a hand. 'We obviously need to talk.' She looked at me and her eyes widened for a moment before she shook her head.

'Ma'am.' I nodded and held my breath. I really didn't want her piercing gaze resting on me for too long.

'Where one goes, the other follows.' She sighed and turned to Belial. 'Get some sleep.' She frowned then gave him a grudging smile. 'I need to do a lot of thinking before I talk to you.' She paused. 'I always thought that if I saw you again I could treat you with the contempt that I felt you so very much deserved. I hoped I could walk past and not acknowledge you.' She sighed. 'We'll talk more tomorrow.'

Belial looked up, hopeful for a moment, then he shook his head. 'We can't stay. We have to get over the river.' He stood up with a grunt and straightened the cuffs on his shirt. 'We may have brought some trouble to your door.'

'Oh? Now there's a flaming surprise.' Zephaniah spoke over her shoulder as she turned away. 'You'll be safe here. Sarah will find rooms for you and I'll see you all in the morning. Just call if you need anything.' As she headed back into the building, at the doorway the smoke parted to let her pass then turned and flowed in her wake like a protective snake.

217

Carly and I were too tired that night to do more than hold each other and it only seemed a moment before Sarah was once again knocking at our door. She was carrying another tray filled with goodies: teapots and mugs, pastries filled with an unidentifiable spice, small rounds of toast, thick with butter and a type of jam that tasted like a cross between raspberry and quince – all good things that heralded the morning. Looking around the opulent room, with its four-poster bed, heavy rug and crimson curtains, it didn't take too much effort to imagine myself in a high-class hotel. Dawdling over my second cup of tea and listening to the sounds of running water from the small bathroom, I wondered what it would be like to have a life – a *real* life. To never know or care anything about gods and demons; to have the choice of what to believe instead of having it chase me around with flaming swords or turn into a fire-breathing lizard once in a while.

I hadn't had nearly enough time to enjoy myself when Farr stepped through the door. His hair was neatly brushed and his jeans pressed into a single crease. Keril, his scales slightly out of skew from an obviously troubled night's sleep, lounged behind him eating a pastry. 'Parity says the silver gate has been torn down.' Farr swallowed, his large Adam's apple bobbing in his thin throat. 'I think we need to tell Belial.'

It only took me a moment to process this statement.

'Where's Belial?' I shouted at Sarah. She jumped, her eyes wide and dropped a mug. I watched as it tumbled slowly through the air to smash on the flagstones beneath the small table.

'With Mother Abbess in the garden.' The girl looked at the shards of crockery for a moment and then turned and ran. I ran after her, Keril and Farr at my heels.

As I raced after Sarah, I heard the tolling of a bell. There was someone at the door and I could almost guarantee it wasn't the Avon lady.

Chanting junior acolytes, walking in a long line through the nave, exclaimed as we raced through them. In the

218

distance I could see a shambling figure in blue heading toward the door. Keril had stopped and was screaming at the girls to run, get away. Terrified by his strange appearance they'd scattered like startled chickens.

'William! No!' I screamed. The strange acoustics of the cathedral took my voice away, flinging it up into the painted forest that was the ceiling and speeding its descent, splitting it and sending it spiralling away to echo around the nave.

William glanced up as I bore down on him but, fixated on the door, he turned back to the job in hand. 'Farr!' I shouted as I ran. 'Get Belial.' Farr skidded to a halt and then turned and pelted off in the opposite direction. Watching with a dull fascination I saw William smooth his tunic and reach for the door handle. Keril shouted 'Shit!' behind me. I pulled out my knife and put on a turn of speed.

There was no way we could have stopped him. Smiling serenely, William took a deep breath and lifted the heavy latch before stepping back with a clumsy bow to admit those who requested access.

The door swung open and Michael, wings aloft, stepped into the nave. His sword was drawn and behind him I could see small piles of pebbles, stones and smashed concrete. In amongst the rubble, here the head of a dragon or a cat, there a hand with a finger extended. The protective gargoyles had obviously put up a good fight. William glanced up then dropped into an even deeper bow – his smile shaky, his face pale.

His head bounced from his toes and rolled across the floor. The clean cut smoked and blackened.

'Nooooo!' I felt my stomach roll.

Michael stepped over the body, fastidiously wiping his blade on the fluttering tunic as he went past. Six minor angels followed him in through the door and also stepped over the body. Fanning out, they moved to surround Keril. One of them laid his sword across the demon's arm and smiled as Keril gritted his teeth against the burning flame.

'Stay very still, demon.' The angel smiled; it wasn't anywhere near as real or joyful as William's had been.

I slithered to a halt in front of Michael who was dangerously calm. I sheathed my knife. There was no way I could fight him. All I had was the vague hope that he wasn't as bright as he looked. I gave him a cheery grin. 'Michael, about time you got here,' I said.

'Joe.' He lifted a lip at me. 'You've given us somewhat of a run-around. I am so looking forward to cutting you into tiny, tiny pieces.'

I stared at him. 'Really?' I shrugged. 'Well, I don't think Metatron will be happy about that. I know I wouldn't be but Metatron's a better man than me, so maybe he'll forgive you.'

'Vlad Tepes was a better man than you.' Michael took a step toward me, studying his nails. 'If he'd confessed he'd probably have had his sins forgiven.' He paused. 'You on the other hand are unforgivable.'

I shrugged. 'What is there to forgive?' I folded my arms and studied him. 'I just wanted to prove that I could do something right. There were all those comments about me being useless. Now look: Lucifer's out, Hell's open and, if you hadn't been so bloody hell bent on killing me at that gate, you could have had him. I wasn't going to hang around for you to cut me in two.'

Michael stepped forward and put his hand on my shoulder. Bending slightly he gave me a long look. 'You expect me to believe that all this was done by you to prove yourself?' He laughed. 'That is the most pathetic thing I've ever heard.' He drew his sword and yawned. 'Honestly a child could make up a better story than that.'

Pulling my shoulder from under his hand I glared straight into his cold lilac eyes. 'I really don't care what you believe, but Metatron said if I could find Lucifer this would be the last job I ever had to do.' I pushed my hands into my pockets and then turned to Keril. 'Bring Graham here.'

Keril rocked backward. 'What?' He winced as the gently smiling angel applied pressure with the sword. There was the smell of burning metal as the flame licked over the scales on his arm.

I glanced at Michael. 'I'm not taking you to him because I don't want you anywhere near Carly – I don't trust you – but I will bring him to you. Just let Keril go and get him.'

'Fuck off!' Keril struggled in the firm grip. 'Just have them kill me here and now – I'm not *getting* anyone.'

'Well, that's no fun.' I stared at Keril. 'But having you watch your sister and nephew die would be fairly amusing.' I shrugged. 'You *will* get him or I'll tell Michael where he can find Alice and Arden.' I stared at the struggling demon. 'I heard which worlds they were heading for and I'm sure that two less Drekavak around would please the Host greatly. They already consider you vermin. But you bring Graham here and they stay safe.'

'You bastard.' Keril slumped.

My heart ached at the defeated tone in his voice. We'd come so close to being friends.

'Yeah,' I shrugged. 'I think we already ascertained that.' I turned away from him and faced Michael. 'Right, first they were heading for Karonet ...'

Michael frowned. His sword dimmed and the flame went out. He didn't believe me – that much was obvious – but he glanced up to watch Keril's reaction.

'No!' Keril shouted as he struggled against the angel's arm. 'I'll get him – just wait a minute.' He faced me, his scales lifting and dropping – a sure sign of deep distress. 'How do I know I can trust you?'

'You don't, no one can trust me. I'm completely self-centred and only interested in me. I'd give you my word but you know what that would be worth.' I laughed. 'You can have it though, if it makes you feel better.'

Michael stood back with a look of deep disgust. 'You really are a traitor through and through, aren't you? You have no loyalties whatsoever.'

I swung round and poked Michael in the chest. Gritting my teeth I screamed up at him. 'I've had enough! I want what Metatron promised me.' I shook my head. 'I've had enough of you, the demons, the intrigue ... I'm done with it all. Metatron promised that finding Lucifer would be my last job – that's all I want. As soon as the boss has what *he* wants I'm out of here and I hope to never lay eyes on any of you ever again.' I rubbed a hand over my face, surprised by my stinging eyes and the lump in my throat. 'I don't care if the world's ending – I just want a lifetime where I don't know any of you.' There are times when the truth just leaks out all over.

Raphael walked through the door. After taking a long look at the headless body still smoking on the floor he studied the situation that was playing out between Michael and I. Silent, he leant on the wall beside the door, rolled his eyes and shook his head slightly. He was far more intelligent than Michael could ever hope to be. I didn't make eye contact with him.

Michael chewed his lip then shrugged. 'Now that I can *almost* believe.' He waved a hand and the angel stepped away from the distraught Drekavak, who edged back across the floor toward the altar.

'Keril?' I looked over my shoulder at him. 'You've got about a minute to get him back here before I start drawing maps.'

Keril gave me one long mutinous look and then turned to leave.

Fumbling in my pocket, I watched him walk away. Although it sounded as though I was harrying Keril, in my head I directed my next comment toward my knuckle-dusters. 'Faster, please!' I called.

Michael watched with a big grin. 'Joe, you just ooze with all the best human qualities, don't you.' He turned to look down at me. 'However, I'm mortally insulted that you'd think I'd fall for this crap but it's been a real joy watching you try and fool me.' His sword appeared in his hand once more. 'I've always promised myself that I would get rid of you.' He shook his head and gave a small hitch of his wings. 'I'll apologise to Metatron, of course – he had other plans for you and I may have to apologise a lot, but I'm sure he'll understand.'

As he raised the sword, I pulled my 'duster-covered hands

out of my pockets and punched him in the face. His sword winked out of existence as he fell back spluttering and cursing. Weaving my way through the other angels I started racing in Keril's wake. Michael's shouts and Raphael's laughter followed me across the floor. As I ran past I grabbed the Drekavak's arm and towed him along with me

'You bastard!' Keril pulled his arm away then reached over and thumped me as we ran through the cathedral and back toward the bedroom. 'You told him they were headed for Karonet.'

'Don't worry,' I panted back at him. 'I heard Gallard tell them not to bother going there – they had enough supplies, they were to go straight to …' I shook my head 'Gah, I can't even remember the other one they said they *were* going to.'

'You nearly gave me a heart attack, you shit!' Keril huffed as he tried to run, shout at me and get over the after effects of a horrible fright.

'Sorry I didn't tell you, but I really needed an honest reaction.' I concentrated on running.

As we ran around the altar and through the pentacle room, Belial and Zephaniah approached, leading 12 women in long black robes, with deep hoods covering their faces. Belial reached out to stop me as I attempted to run past. 'Where's Carly?' he shouted.

'Just going to get all of them now. Where's Farr?' I bellowed back at him.

'I sent him back to look after them. Get them out. Take them outside. I'll join you there,' he said.

'You go too.' Zephaniah swung around and put a hand on his chest. 'We'll hold them.' She gave him a gentle smile. 'Get out with the others.'

Belial snorted. 'Have you become so adept over the years that you can perform the ritual while under attack?'

The Abbess shook her head slowly and stared at the ground. 'We'll buy you some time at least.'

'No! I won't allow it.' Belial brought his wings and his sword into being. 'The only way to buy us enough time to escape is for all of you to die.' His huge charcoal wings lifted as he shrugged. Rolling grey matter dropped silently from the tip of his sword, hit the ground and then crawled away to dance with the smoke that drifted from the altar. 'I have enough nightmares haunting me already – I don't need any more.' Pushing her gently aside he strode away toward the altar room.

Zephaniah watched him walk away then, gathering up her priestesses, they followed in his wake. I noticed that she was smiling. The women began a musical, lilting chant.

Keril and I skidded to a halt outside Carly's room. She opened the door, her face pale and worried – each freckle stood out in sharp relief.

'What's happening?' She stared past us down the corridor.

I leant on the door frame and winced as I clutched my side; how can someone with my healing abilities get a stitch?

Keril spoke round my wheezing and gasping. 'Angels,' he said. 'They're here. Belial told us to get everyone out.'

'How did they get through the gate?' Carly gripped the door. 'Where are they?'

'Heading for the altar room,' Keril replied as he moved down the hall, banging on doors. 'They destroyed the silver gate.' He winced. 'Lucifer is going to be *very* upset.'

'So how do we get out?' Carly looked at me in a panic.

'There's a passage beneath us.' Sarah appeared. She fumbled at her belt for a moment then handed a ring of heavy metal keys to Carly. 'Take these.' She pointed down the corridor. 'Through the door at the end you'll find stairs. Go down and follow the passage through the blocks. You'll find an old black door in the corner of the big room. It'll take you out.'

'Come with us.' Carly grabbed the girl's hand. 'You'll be safe with us.'

Sarah gave her a hug then, pulling her hand gently away, pointed her in the direction of the door. 'I need to be with my sisters. I couldn't leave now.' Her gaze rested on each of us as she intoned, 'May you find your true way and may those with need find their way to you.'

'No.' I gripped the elbow of her robe. 'I can't let you go back in there.'

'Let go of me.' Her voice cracked on the last word. 'I'll be fine.'

'No, you don't understand, they will kill you without even thinking about it.' I turned to face her. 'Look, you're coming whether you like it or not – we don't have time to argue.'

Sarah stared at me for a moment and then placed her hand on top of mine. She said nothing but within seconds smoke began to pour through her fingers.

I yelped and ripped my hand from beneath hers. The skin across my knuckles was blackened and blistered.

'I'll be fine,' she repeated, turning and walking away.

The sounds of shouting and the clash of weapons hastened our departure. Running through darkened passageways, I kept a firm grip on Graham's sleeve while I listened to Parity who, guided by her brother, kept up a running commentary.

'The women have surrounded the altar. Michael's telling them that they are pure evil and that they should be wiped from the face of the planet. Belial has stepped out and Michael is laughing, taunting him.'

She stumbled slightly and Farr grabbed her, holding her tight to his body as we hurried along.

'The smoke from the altar is dancing, getting thicker. The women have cut themselves and are pouring blood into the chalice. The deer-god moves …'

'What?' Graham stopped walking and turned around to face Parity. When there was no recognition in the seer's blank white eyes, he turned toward Farr. 'What did she say?'

Parity spoke on. Her dreamy voice gave me the chills.

'He grows; he carries the statue of the mother with him. The women are still chanting. He is now tall, so tall. The smell of the forest fills the hall. Belial has challenged Michael who's laughing. They fight but the archangel's just teasing. He's faster than this – he's enjoying the pain he's causing too much to want it to end.'

Carly stumbled. 'Oh Dad,' she whispered.

'Belial is managing to keep him away from the women

and Michael's getting angry – he's telling Belial that he's a traitor, that he deserves everything that's happened to him. He's asking why he's still alive – asking why he's too much of a coward to end it all. Oh!'

'What? What happened?' Carly grabbed Parity's arm, trying to find out what had caused the seer to stop. Farr gently removed her hand. 'She can't hear you at the moment,' he said.

'Belial's hurt. He falls. Michael's laughing.'

The seer fell quiet for a moment, her face astonished. 'The Forest Lord is awake and angry. He screams and the angels concentrate on him. Sarah is pulling Belial behind the altar. The priestesses are using magic to still the angel's wings, but it's hard – they're so strong. The women are becoming exhausted.'

Parity came to a complete halt. We all bunched up behind her and stood silent and still in the darkness.

'The god is ignoring the angels even when they attack him. He's marking the figurine with blood from the chalice. He has placed her at the very centre of the maze. There's a lot of smoke.'

Carly whispered, 'What about my father – is he all right?'

'Carly?' Holding her gently by the shoulders I turned her around. 'I need you to get everybody out. I'll go back for Belial.'

'What can you do?' She wiped her eyes on the back of her hand.

I shrugged. 'We can't get Lucifer to where he needs to be without him and if he's hurt …'

Carly chewed on a fingernail, distressed.

'Go on.' I gave her a quick hug then pushed her gently toward the Drekavak who nodded at me. 'You and Keril get everyone a good distance away and hunt out Melusine. We'll find you, I promise.'

'The figurine is changing; it's losing its glow as something comes from within, growing and … Oh it's a woman. She's laughing and she's matching the Forest Lord in size and height. They're huge – he's black, she's white –

226

two halves of the same coin.'

'Come on, Carly.' Keril nudged her, forcing her to look at him. 'If he says he'll meet us outside, he'll make sure he does.' The Drekavak gave me a long look then extended his paw, claws completely retracted. 'See you in a little while.' He nodded then laughed. 'Go and slither your way out of yet another mess.'

I quickly grasped his paw but I didn't really have time to answer that and I certainly wasn't going to hang around to study my motives and refused to even think about them as I headed back along the passage at a quiet trot. Even before I was halfway there I could hear screams and the cracking sound of breaking wood.

As I stepped through the door, the beautiful pentacle roof shattered, showering me with glass. I hugged the side of the room and watched as a beautifully lethal rain of coloured glass shards tinkled and bounced around me. The huge deer-headed man casually plucked an angel out of the air, then slung it through the broken glass ceiling. The big grin that showed through his huge beard just confirmed this wasn't the first angel to exit that way.

Michael was performing strike attacks at the white goddess. His flaming sword would open deep wounds on her huge hands and arms as she swatted at him like a wasp. He wasn't happy when they closed again moments later. Raphael hung back and watched Michael batter away at the giant woman. He didn't seem to be taking part in either the attack or the defence.

I looked around for Belial. Sarah was with him behind the altar – he lay still and pale and my stomach flipped. Another angel hurtled past, trying a surprise attack by leaping out of the rafters. With an almost lazy movement the stag-like god twisted his head and impaled it on one of his antlers. It dangled there screaming, blood trickled down the huge horns and over the god's face and he glared wildly through the gruesome wet mask.

Sarah watched as I slowly paced along the wall. Keeping low I wasn't noticed amid the noise and smoke. She nodded as I knelt down beside her. 'How is he?'

'He's not going to be jogging for a bit but I think he'll be fine.' She smiled at me. 'I'm glad you came back.'

'I'm not.' I ducked as one of the priestesses hurled a barrage of electric blue orbs across the altar toward the angels; each ball screamed as it flew overhead blowing chunks of masonry from the walls wherever it hit. 'It's terrifying in here.' The ground shook as the horned Forest Lord screamed in fury. 'What *is* that?'

She peered over the edge of the altar and stared up at the huge deer-faced being. She had such a look of devotion that I felt momentarily jealous. 'We don't really have a name for him.' She smiled as, muscles bulging, he casually smacked an angel, sending it spinning into the wall with a puff of feathers.

I winced.

'Some call him Cernunnos, some call him Baphomet, the Green Man or the Forest Lord.' She seemed to be as proud as a mother watching a son and smiled again as she watched him casually flip a screaming attacker away from the forest of his horns. 'But to us he's just "God".' She watched the huge woman, her face twisted in contempt, batter angels into the rafters. 'We don't see *her* very often at all. She's the real power – he's her consort and changes with the turning of the year. She's everlasting. They're never seen together.'

'But ...' I looked between the two; they were very obviously here together.

Sarah laughed. 'That's not really her. When her vessel animates it's actually one of the priestesses that appears, infused with her spirit. I don't know what it would take for *her* to really appear on this plane. It's a huge honour to be chosen as her host.'

The avatar of the mother goddess created a tight, spiralling miniature tornado that picked up rubble, bricks and glass and sent it twisting toward two angels that, watching the devastation, had sensibly stayed out of the way. The wind, its voice echoing hers, gathered them into its spinning embrace for a moment then callously flung them into the wall. Feathers joined the debris that marked the wind's course. Its task complete, the twister collapsed and vanished, leaving a couple of tattered, grubby feathers drifting through the smoke and dust.

Michael, taking advantage of the distraction, made his move. With a quick snap of his wings, he shot between the howling avatar and the angry Forest Lord. Snatching up the lifeless white statuette from the maze he headed toward the rafters. He held the vessel between both hands as he surveyed the destruction below him. As he dropped like a falcon from the rooftree, Zephaniah realised what he was intending and gasped 'No!'

Three feet above the ground, Michael raised his arm and flung the statuette to the ground with all the force he could.

It exploded into a thousand tiny pieces that spun and glittered through the still rolling fog. Zephaniah screamed as the avatar, her effigy shattered beyond repair, became smoke. The women watched in shocked silence as Zephaniah, beyond reason, attacked Michael with her bare hands.

The archangel regarded the shrieking woman curiously for a moment, shaking his head in amusement as she pummelled and kicked at him. Eventually he became bored and with one backhand swipe knocked her from her feet. Zephaniah, her lip bleeding, struggled to rise to the attack once more.

Belial woke up with a grunt and fought against my restraining hand.

Michael laughed. 'Thou shalt not suffer a witch to live.' Kicking the Abbess back to the floor he continued to kick her as she curled into a foetal ball.

Without the stability of his other half the god had begun to lose form. He shrank and I could see the outline of the altar through his body. The dark statue still on the altar began to tremble. As Michael dealt with his shrieking high priestess, the Forest Lord looked toward Sarah and there was a moment that passed between them.

Without hesitation she stood and, head held high, walked confidently toward him.

Michael, engrossed in his subjugation of Zephaniah, ignored her.

'Lord.' Sarah called up at the towering figure. 'I accept your offer with all my heart.'

He stared down at her. Slit golden eyes reflected the fog and the candlelight, while his huge horns cast strange branching shadows onto the wall of the altar room.

Sinking to her knees, Sarah drew a long curved knife from her belt. Taking it in both hands she drew a deep, shuddering breath. The horned god gave her a gentle smile then leant forward to kiss her gently on the lips.

The priestesses, obviously realising what was coming next, pulled themselves together then threw everything they could at Michael. Balls of blue fire hissed as they rained from the ceiling, whirling stone blades and simple symbols that glowed white, so bright it was almost impossible to look directly at them, sped from the hands of the women to strike at him.

As she pulled away from his lips Sarah thrust the knife deep into her breast. Blood flowed over the god's hands. He stared at it for a moment before catching Sarah's body as it crumpled. Lifting her in his arms he held her gently as her body began to shimmer and shrink. Within seconds he was, once again, holding the white figurine of the sheela-na-gig that was the vessel of the goddess. Laughing and young, renewed by the sacrifice Sarah had made, the Forest Lord solidified and expanded once more. He placed the new statue carefully onto the altar then turned to watch Michael who was still viciously kicking Zephaniah every time she tried to move.

The look on his face made me very glad that I was hidden behind the altar. Michael, feeling the deity's attention on him turned incredulously to face the renewed, perfectly healthy and vastly irritated Forest Lord. The archangel's gleeful grin fell quickly away but even under that baleful gaze Michael drew his sword and attacked. Laughing, the deer-god waited until he was within reach then merely caught and held him. As Michael screamed and cursed everyone else became still and watchful. The furious archangel struggled and howled, spitting curses and threats into the god's face. The ground shook as the giant form stepped toward the altar. Picking up the white statue he folded Michael like clay and gently pushed him through the opening of the white vessel he had just created.

The sudden silence that took most of us a little by surprise was broken only by the occasional shifting of rubble, the tinkle of falling glass and the heavy breathing of 13 rather shocked women. Nodding in satisfaction, the Forest Lord turned and surveyed the damage to his home.

Raphael stepped from behind a column and walked slowly through the devastation. He looked neither left nor right but halted in front of the god who raised his eyebrows in a question.

Deer-faced deity and classically beautiful angel regarded each other in silence for a moment. Eventually Raphael tilted his head in a deep nod of acknowledgement. First to the Forest Lord, then to Zephaniah and then to the women still crowded behind the altar. 'I think we're finished here,' he said. The angel gazed around the devastated hall. Broken lesser angels groaned and stirred in the rubble and glass. 'There are some wounded that I would like to take, if I may?'

I feared the deer-lord would refuse, but after a moment he slowly nodded and with a wave of his hand indicated that Raphael was free to take the angels and leave. We all watched as, with the mobile supporting the more seriously injured, the little group headed toward the door. Raphael stopped at the headless body of William and bowed – he seemed to be struggling with his thoughts. As the last angel departed Raphael turned to face the Forest Lord once more. 'I'm sorry,' he said. Without another word he walked into the dusty sunlight. The great door swung shut behind him.

Zephaniah, finally confident that all attacks had ceased, groaned and climbed to her feet, dabbing the blood from her split lip with the hem of her robe. The Forest Lord began to shrink. At about eight foot he rolled his shoulders, stroked the new sheela-na-gig vessel then began picking his way across the rubble toward Zephaniah who, her hand to her mouth, was staring at William's smiling severed head with tears in her eyes.

Standing beside her, the deity stroked her hair. He turned and nodded to two of the priestesses who went to deal with the body.

The deer-headed being turned Zephaniah to face him and patted her hand, then led her to the altar where he pointed at the jar.

Zephaniah took a sobbing deep breath and nodded, running a gentle finger down the new vessel. 'Congratulations, Sarah,' she whispered.

Walking among the silent women, he touched each lightly on the forehead and smiled. Eventually, when standing before us, his smile dropped away as I helped Belial to his feet.

'I really don't know what to do with you two.' The deep voice surprised me. I'd been under the impression that he couldn't or didn't talk.

The dark being reached up and scratched at the base of one of his antlers. 'You're trouble.' He glared at us. 'You brought them here. You started all this.' Rolling his shoulders he grumbled slightly. 'You're no better than them – you don't think about what you do, or you don't care.'

He didn't seem to move or change in any way but the room became darker, colder. Shadows chattered in the rooftree and the women gathered closer together, an air of readiness about them.

There was nothing I wanted to do so much at that moment than run. Running seemed the best option – preferably running and screaming. There was no doubt that this being had more power than anything I'd ever encountered; it rolled off him in waves. I don't usually offer obeisance to anything but, like Belial and Raphael before him, I bowed my head and waited.

'Lord?' Zephaniah stood beside Belial and faced the god, drawing his gaze. 'I would like them to carry on.' She smiled. 'If it's time for a change then just maybe these two can stir things up enough to start the ball rolling.'

He reached forward with a smile and cupped her chin in his huge hand. 'Possibly.' He shrugged. 'If that's what you wish, then I'll let them chart their own course. However, have no doubt, I'm just as happy to stop them if I have to.' Folding his arms he stared at Belial for a long moment, his dour expression changing slowly to compassion. 'You can't be two things at once.' He ducked his head to look into the fallen angel's face. 'This is something you have to choose to do. For far too long you've been pulled two ways: one side of you has dreams, the other's in chains.' The deity ran a heavy hand over his face. 'You fell because Lucifer talked you into it; you took on Hell because Lucifer left you to it. You let everyone go because it stopped them being your responsibility, then you built a city and hid in it and now you're here because, if you succeed, you can hand all this to someone else and wash your hands of everything. If you fail, nothing will matter anyway. This has to stop, Belial. Until you find something to commit to you will always be half of what you could be.'

The odd golden eyes, with their horizontal slit pupil, regarded me next. Even though I tried very hard, I couldn't stop myself swallowing convulsively.

'You.' The silence after that single word stretched on for what seemed like for ever. Eventually the huge being threw back his head and laughed. 'You, we're all watching very closely. You're like a mad viper – no one knows which way you'll strike.' He clapped me on the shoulder. I felt something crack and staggered into Belial. 'I'm glad I don't have to kill you just yet; you're quite entertaining for a little man.'

He gave a huge yawn and turned toward the witch. 'I'm tired, Zephaniah. Being here is wearing in the extreme and I have a new host to get to know.' He glanced over at the woman-shaped urn then, with a last smile, began to shrink again. 'Sorry about the mess but it was fun.' Within seconds he was gone and the black statue on the altar once more became the only representation of his presence.

Zephaniah stared at the twin statues for a moment before giving them a deep bow. Turning toward us she ran a tired hand through her hair and then looked around at the bricks, rubble and piles of shattered glass. 'You'd better go.' There were feathers everywhere; it looked as though a group of eight-year-olds had had an extreme pillow fight. 'We have some clearing up to do.'

Belial nodded then staggered with a gasp.

'You're hurt?' Zephaniah caught his arm.

He shrugged. Moving his hand, he looked surprised as, lacking that pressure, the wound in his leg began to bleed once again. Within seconds Belial was standing with one foot in a bright red puddle. 'I'll be all right,' he said. 'It'll heal soon.'

'No, it won't.' Zephaniah began undoing the tiny bone toggles at her cuff. 'Michael's blade can hurt you, I know that. Any of the angelic weapons can hurt you.' She rolled her sleeves up then, closing her eyes, placed her hands on Belial's leg and began to chant. Like my knife, her hands began to smoke and glow. I watched as the deep wound slowly knitted, becoming soft, pink skin again. Only a small white scar half hidden within his ripped trousers indicated that there had ever been any damage at all.

'There.' Zephaniah surveyed the healed wound then stood back with an air of satisfaction. 'You're OK now.'

Belial looked a bit sick.

'You.' Zephaniah turned to me. 'Have you finally chosen a side then?'

I nodded and wished people would stop referring to me as "you".

'Good. One small and genuine step toward redemption has been achieved.' She moved away to begin marshalling her women then stopped. Turning she looked at Belial. 'Don't come back unless you have good news.' Leaning forward, she gave him a lingering kiss and then walked away.

Belial watched her leave, his expression slightly haunted. 'Come on.' He headed toward the door. 'We'd better catch up with the others. They'll be wondering what's happened.'

'No, they won't.' I fell into step beside him. 'Parity's giving them a moment-by-moment monologue.'

'Ah.' Belial blushed. 'Well, that's just great.'

For a while we walked in silence. Eventually, I couldn't stand it any more and turned to the expressionless fallen angel. 'What did he mean?' I knew I was grubbing around in some very personal stuff here. 'The Forest Lord said, "You'll only be half of what you could be." What does that actually mean?'

Belial stopped walking and turned slowly to face me. 'It means that I'm cursed.' He spoke through gritted teeth. 'When we were kicked out of Heaven, we had a lot of our abilities dampened when God's grace was taken from us.' He carried on walking. 'We were told that as we obviously no longer wanted to be part of the Host we would always be inferior.' He fell silent.

I couldn't let it go. 'So that means that even though you were an angel, you're not like them any more?'

Belial nodded slowly. 'We still have our wings, we can still travel and some other bits and pieces, but compared to them, we're mud. We're really only one step up from humans.'

I ignored the insult. 'What about Lucifer?' I was confused; faced with something like this I would have at least been a little bitter but Belial sounded as though he was commenting on the weather.

'Lucifer is all he ever was.' Belial coughed out a short laugh. 'Or, at least, he would be if we could get him back. No one, not even the Morning Star himself, was ever quite sure what he was or how much he could do, but he certainly didn't lose much when he fell.'

I nodded, still not entirely sure what was right and what was not. 'I have one last question.' I glanced over at Belial who was rolling his eyes.

'What a surprise.'

'That was a god, right?' I asked.

Belial nodded. 'Yes, both of those were gods.'

'How?' I'd been turning this over in my mind and just

235

couldn't grasp it. 'God is God – how can there be other gods? What are they – demigods or undergods? How does this work?'

Belial stopped walking again and, leaning on a wall, he stared down at his boots. 'Have you ever seen a man do something almost impossible?' he asked.

I thought back to some of the Iron Man television shows that I'd watched and nodded.

'Did that man have supporters?' he said.

I nodded again.

'Do you think, if he had just been standing in a field, on his own, that he would have been able to do all that he did?' Belial looked up from the floor and stared at me.

'No, probably not.'

'Well, that's how it works.' Belial turned and began walking again. 'The god and his goddess have risen here because a whole population believe in them. They believe in them because they can see them and see what they do; because they can deal with them directly, the belief becomes absolute. That god and goddess hold all the power here. Even Lucifer himself might have a problem if he pitted himself against the Horned Lord. It's possible that only God himself has that power.' He paused for breath. As he moved away from me he spoke quietly. 'Then again, it's quite possible that he doesn't.'

We walked in silence through the passages until we came to where I'd left the party behind. Opening a door he ushered me down some stone steps into what appeared to be a cellar. It was clean, dry and empty except for some large stone blocks that seemed to have been dropped haphazardly around the room.

'Where are we?' I stared around the huge basement.

'The room of sleeping angels.' Belial kept walking. 'We'll come out farther down the hill away from the orphanage. I'm not welcome there so it's better if we just move along a bit.'

Sleeping angels? I looked around. I couldn't see anyone sleeping anywhere. There were a couple of words in that sentence that didn't make sense. 'Orphanage?'

Belial stopped walking with a frown and stared around the huge room. 'That's what Zephaniah does.' Belial ran a finger along one of the huge stone blocks. The heavy lid had broken and the stone box was empty; it looked as though the lid had been exploded outward. He sighed. 'She looks after children.' Taking hold of the stone with both hands he pulled himself up onto the side then peered into the darkness of the dusty box.

'Well, I haven't seen many of them around.'

Belial frowned 'Would you consider it normal then to keep kids in a church?'

I shook my head. 'Well, no, but …'

'There are hundreds of them.' Belial navigated his way around two blocks that were leaning together; he seemed distracted. 'There's a school, a working farm and housing just on the top of the hill.' He shrugged. 'Only those that have the ability to become acolytes come here – most of them are looked after at the orphanage.'

'Why?' I hurried to catch up with him.

Belial sighed. 'Zephaniah had two children – both were killed. Since then, she looks after any child who turns up at her door and she guards the boundaries of Limbo.' He stared unseeing at the walls. 'I can't imagine how many children have come and gone through those halls.'

'How did her kids die?'

Belial stopped so suddenly that I almost ran into his back. 'I killed them.' He walked away from me, without looking back.

I was full of questions but, staring at his bowed back, uncharacteristically I swallowed them all and changed the subject. 'So are these what I think they are?' I tapped one of the stone coffins.

'If you think they're tombs, then yes.' Belial answered shortly. He was concentrating on forging a path between them; I noticed that he seemed reluctant to touch any that were still whole.

There were no carvings, no names and no thoughtful little

messages.

'These are the tombs of some of the other angels that fell with Lucifer. They couldn't stand the thought of being separated from God. They couldn't go back to Heaven and all other options just didn't seem right to them. They willed themselves still and there they've stayed.' Belial stopped for a moment and looked around at the hundreds, possibly thousands, of blocks that littered the great cavernous cellars. 'They're not really dead, but it seemed better than just having piles of bodies all over the place.' He looked around the room. 'Some of these are now empty ...' He shrugged and carried on walking again. 'I wonder where they went?'

Up another flight of steps and we emerged blinking into the daylight. Carly and Melusine were there to greet us. Both looked hurt and confused when Belial ignored them and stalked off down the hill.

# CHAPTER 9

As WE WALKED, I tried desperately to work out why this place seemed so familiar. The hills were toothed with sharp rocks that pierced the short, yellow-green grass. Una seemed happy trotting along in the herb-scented sunlight and, apart from the pall of dust that hung above the stricken cathedral, it was difficult to believe that we were somewhere *else.* If the hills had been supporting stunted olive trees we could easily have been on a Greek island. Scrubby, potbellied, goat-like creatures grazed on the tough grass. With floppy ears, tinkling bells, scruffy brown and white coats and little tails they looked exactly like the goats that had eaten my packed lunch on a holiday I'd once taken in Kos. If it hadn't been for the blue human eyes that crinkled when they smiled, I would have had trouble believing they weren't entirely natural. One trotted past and grinned at me. I shuddered. Carly, having finished an obviously unsatisfactory conversation with her father, dropped back toward me and linked her arm in mine. It seemed as though we were just a simple couple enjoying a walk in the sunshine – idyllic.

Melusine seemed to be looking for something. She had positioned herself on a rock and was squatting down with a piece of meat in her hand.

I looked askance at Carly who shrugged.

A tall cream and brown spotted goat sidled up the track and stood in front of the motionless dragon. She stared unblinking into its eyes. The two of them stayed like that for a moment. Eventually, the goat stepped delicately forward and gently took the meat from her hand.

As it trotted off into the trees Melusine sauntered over to walk beside us.

'What was all that about?' Carly asked.

'The goats are omnivores.' Melusine shuddered. 'Zephaniah uses them as dogs. They attack anything that doesn't belong here – it's a form of protection.'

I glanced nervously around. There seemed to be suddenly hundreds of the scruffy little things browsing among the bushes.

She noticed my worried looks. 'I think we'll be all right. They have a sort of rudimentary telepathy system and I think I've managed to explain to them what we're doing here.' She looked over my head and winked at Carly who laughed. 'It helped that Zephaniah has a word that she uses so they leave travellers alone.'

'Carnivorous, telepathic goats.' Now I didn't have any trouble believing them supernatural. I stepped away from one that was standing in the shade of a short tree. It sniggered.

'Carnivorous, telepathic *attack* goats.' Melusine corrected me with a certain amount of glee. 'Zephaniah had the Forest Lord "change" them slightly. So they really are quite an abomination now.'

'Great,' I called after her as she wandered down the track. 'What would have happened if you hadn't explained to them what we're doing here?'

'They'd have eaten you.' Melusine laughed. 'Oh, and don't bleed.' Her voice echoed up the hill. 'Blood sends them into a feeding frenzy and no amount of safe words or explanations will stop them. They'll keep attacking until there's nothing left – they're really fuzzy little piranhas.'

'What's the word?' I shouted after her.

'It's a secret.'

I could hear her laughing all the way down the track.

'Don't worry.' Carly sniggered at my horror. 'I think we'll be safe. Father was telling me that it takes quite a lot of blood to set them off.' She waved at a goat that fluttered its eyelashes at her then smiled happily as it minced down for a scratch behind the ears. She happily complied. 'They smell a bit but I think they're quite gorgeous. If we ever get home I might take one with me as a pet.' She paused for a moment.

'It might just convince that bloody postman to stop opening my letters.'

'Hmm, well, I'm happier knowing that I'm not going to get swarmed if I cut my finger.' I dragged my arm across my forehead; the day seemed to be heating up.

'Why is there a sun?' I stared up into the blue-grey sky. The sun wasn't quite the right colour and looked as though it was sporting a sort of haze but it was close enough.

'Is this some sort of existential question?' Carly frowned and squinted up into the sky.

I shook my head. 'No.' I tried to put my thoughts into words as I navigated the rough stone track. 'People always say, "down into Hell" – surely we should be somewhere in the bowels of the Earth by now. Isn't that where Hell is?'

Carly looked at me as though I were some sort of child. 'You still don't get it, do you?' She paused and tried to think of a way to explain the obviously unexplainable. 'Think of a bubble.'

I nodded.

'Now attach another bubble to it.' She looked up at me to make sure I was still following her.

'Right, two bubbles.' I could see them shining pink and blue like clear glass in my mind.

'Now attach another, and another and another all over the first bubble until the first bubble can no longer be seen.'

I nodded.

'That's how these planes, or dimensions – or whatever you want to call them – work.' She stared up into the sky. There were no birds, no clouds and the sun seemed to be slightly redder than I was entirely happy with. 'At each point the bubbles touch, there is a flat spot and that's where we can cross – that's where the gates are.' She looked around at the goats and grinned; a couple of them grinned back at her. 'This is a very tiny bubble – one of a group of seven that didn't so much join up as cluster, like Russian nesting dolls. So each one is a world in its own right but getting smaller and smaller and we're heading for the very centre – the tiniest of all. God gave Lucifer exactly what he wanted: an

241

entire world to himself.

'That's why you can only get in and out of Hell through Limbo – the first bubble – because that's the one that contains all the others. It's an odd place really.' Carly looked around. 'Earth is similar. It's a bubble on the very outside of the cluster, so it only touches three places: Limbo, Heaven and one other.'

'What's the other?'

Carly looked at me and began to clap her hands. 'I do believe in fairies,' she sang, 'I do … I do.'

'Oh,' I said. 'And that's another thing. I don't understand this whole fairy business.' I paused, trying to remember what Belial had said in that meeting. 'Who's Mag Mell?'

'Phew,' Carly stopped for a moment, breathing hard. This was quite a steep climb – she wiped sweat from her top lip. 'Mag Mell … huff …' Carly swallowed trying to get her breath. '… isn't a who, it's a place … puff feowff ... There are three areas, or continents, in Faery and Mag Mell's one of them. The most accessible to other races it's very, very dangerous.' She stood up then ran a hand across her brow, before dragging her long red hair up into a scruffy ponytail and securing it with a band she always kept around her wrist. 'I'm so out of shape.' She bent over and put her hands on her knees while she waited to start breathing normally again.

'So what are the other two –' I stopped as she held up a hand.

'When this is all over – *if* it's ever over and we haven't died from being used as daisies by the angels or Lucifer's "thanked" us for saving him.' She shuddered. 'Or we get caught out in the city, we'll sit down over a vat of coffee, a good bottle of wine and I'll talk until your brain runs out of your ears.' She pulled herself upright and glowered at the rest of the hill we had yet to conquer. 'But right now can we concentrate on walking? I really can't climb, breathe and talk at the same time.'

I had to laugh; her face was almost the same colour as her hair. I held out a hand to her and we resumed climbing. I was having real trouble thinking of myself in Hell, even if it was

242

just the suburbs. A strong smell of citrus and rosemary filled the warm air. Off in the distance I could hear someone singing. As we panted to the top of the steep hill I had to stop and take a breath – the view was stunning. Farmland quilted the landscape as far as the eye could see. Neatly hedged or fenced fields surrounded small farmsteads, pools and copses. I was reminded of the window in Metatron's office but here there seemed to be a huge amount of work to do. The owner of the deep singing voice was currently walking behind two beasts that looked like fat little oxen with flat faces. They plodded contentedly along through deep furrows of dark yellow earth, shaking their huge pale horns and pulling an odd contraption in their wake. With whirling arms and nets it seemed to be harvesting the tops from some sort of green vegetable.

It was no good, I had to ask. 'Daisies?' I frowned. 'How would the angels use us as daisies?'

Carly coughed as she drank from a bottle of water then laughed as she placed it carefully on the ground by her feet. Searching around in the grass she finally pulled up a flower. With a thin stem and long green tendrils for leaves it certainly wasn't a daisy. She held the flower in one hand then began pulling the dropping yellow petals off with the other. 'He loves me, he loves me not,' she intoned.

'Oh.' I realised what she'd meant. 'Oh … euwww!' I gave her a gentle push. 'You're sick – how do you think of things like that?'

The smile fell from her face. 'I didn't make it up, Joe.' Picking up her bottle she put it in her backpack. 'I've seen them do it.'

So, Michael hadn't been just blustering when he'd threatened to pull my arms and legs off and beat me to death with them. A cold breeze chose that moment to waft between us; it was time to change the subject. I looked out over the fields.

Through all this peace and tranquillity a wide river ran its course, a thread of silver embroidery across the patchwork quilt. I noticed that the banks were beautifully tended;

someone kept them almost bare of vegetation.

'Well, at least they're not short of water here.' I wondered where the source of the river was and where it ran to; I'd never heard of a sea in Hell.

'Eh?' Carly peered in the direction I was looking then clouted me on the arm. 'That's the Acheron, you idiot.' She laughed and shook her head. 'No one in their right mind would use it for watering their crops. There wouldn't be any crops left if *that* got onto them.'

'It seems a long way away.' I shaded my eyes with my hand and stared down into the valley.

Carly sighed. 'About two days.'

'Can't we all just "go" there?' I made a swooshing movement with my hand intending to imply my normal mode of travel.

'Some of us could.' Carly laughed at a baby goat that was playing king of the castle with the other kids.

'You, me, Dad.' She frowned. 'I think Melusine as well although she prefers to fly if she can.' She winced as she rolled her shoulders. 'But the others can't, which is a shame.' She bent to pick up her pack and, with a theatrical groan, threw it over her shoulder. 'It would be great to just pick them up and carry them.'

'Can't we?' I laughed as the tiny goat got pushed off its perch by some of the others. Within seconds a scrap had broken out and I could feel my smile fading as I watched the rolling ball of bleating legs and teeth bounce off down the hill leaving a trail of blood and fur in its wake.

'Nope.' Carly frowned at the long downward slope toward the river then shook her foot. 'I think I've got blisters,' she muttered.

'Why not?' I persisted

Carly held my hand and began to follow the others down the fairly steep and gravelly slope 'Your mind knows you.' She bit her lip as her foot slid on some shale. 'You can disappear and reappear the same. Do you know how to remake Parity? Can you even imagine how something like Keril goes together?'

I shook my head and, reaching over, took her backpack from her shoulder and put it on my own.

She smiled at me and, unencumbered, made better progress down the slope. 'At best you'd end up with a life-sized doll with nothing inside; at worst you could end up with a pile of quivering, bleeding body parts and you'd be exhausted. It takes just as much effort to move something like that as it does to physically pick them up and carry them. Remember energy can't be lost or destroyed, it has to *go* somewhere and that applies to all energy – all things, all weight, all mass: everything. There's this whole $E=mc^2$ thing; you can turn mass into energy so you can move it, but then you've used the energy so even theoretically you can't get the mass back.'

'But I've already done it.' I still didn't really understand.

Carly gave me a sharp look then tripped. I managed to catch her forearm and steady her. 'You moved Graham out of your house, didn't you?'

I nodded.

'But that's just not possible.' She turned to face me. 'How did you do that?'

'Well, I certainly don't know how I did it.' I wished she would stop telling me that the things I did were impossible – I was beginning to panic. There would certainly come a time when I tried to do something and it failed and all I would be left with was a pile of what looked like pulsing paella and a very guilty conscience. I swallowed hard; there was no way I'd attempt moving someone again.

She frowned and cut me off with a wave of her hand. 'Oh! It's all too complicated. I just take the easy route and if I'm unsure or not actually being attacked with sharp, slashing things I tend to do it the old-fashioned way. Don't even ask me to explain how healing works.' She was silent for a moment as she navigated a particularly steep bit of the path. 'I asked Father once, "How do we get from one place to another?" He went all quantum on me: it was all about joining strings together and making a tear – whoops!' She tripped, righted herself and then stood, breathing heavily.

'Honestly it made my head spin.' She paused then reached up for a kiss. 'Now for God's sake shut up or I'm going to fall over and I'll be down at the river in about 20 minutes – in pieces.'

That was a bit disappointing. I'd resolved that as soon as I'd got a spare moment I was going to see what I could achieve. Now it seemed I was going to have to have a degree in advanced theoretical physics first. Nothing's simple. With a deep sigh I began to trudge down the slope after Carly. I was beginning to ache and it wasn't just from the walk.

It took us about half an hour to reach the rest of the group and, as we arrived, I noticed that Graham and Parity were sharing a bottle of water. Graham was bright red in the face, and fumbling almost everything he touched. Farr, sitting a little distance away, was glowering at both of them.

'Oh dear,' Carly whispered. 'It looks as though brother and sister aren't on the same wavelength for once.'

I laughed. 'One must learn to swim with the tides.'

Carly gave me a strange look then shook her head and flopped into the shade between Melusine and Belial. 'I am exhausted,' she said. 'Where's Una?'

Melusine rolled her eyes. 'Limitless energy, that one,' she grumbled. 'Half a plate of food and she's off exploring up there.' The dragon pointed to a cave set in the rock a little way down the trail.

I followed Carly's example and, grabbing half a loaf and some cheese, I found myself a shady rock to sit on. 'Will she be OK on her own?' I studied the cheese, which had orange veins through it. It was good, pungent, sweet and sour all at the same time. The aftertaste left my tongue tingling. I wondered what milk was used to make it, then catching the eye of one of the smiling goats I decided I didn't want to know. The goat batted its long lashes at me and gave a high-pitched, bleating laugh.

'No,' Parity spoke up. 'She won't.' Her voice was dreamy and quiet. Farr and Belial looked at each other then jumped up and shot down the hill with Keril in hot pursuit. 'She's walking to the back of the cave. It's very high; the ceiling is so far up she can't see it. It's dark and she's woken something up. It's watching her, trying to work out if she's dinner …'

Carly gave a little scream and leapt up spraying food in all directions. 'Una!' She shrieked down the trail. 'Una!'

Well, so much for food. Swallowing my mouthful I rushed after them. 'What's in the cave?' I shouted back at Melusine who was a mere pace behind me.

Melusine ran past me, with no effort at all. 'I don't know,' she called back.

'Great.' I drew my knife and fumbled around in my pocket for my knuckle-dusters.

Screams and shouts were erupting from the cave mouth and, trying desperately to see in the almost pitch blackness, I fumbled toward them as I waited for my eyes to adjust from the brightness outside. I ducked just in time as Keril flew past me and slammed into the rock wall, the scales on his arm and side smoking and stinking. He crashed to the floor and then rolled over in the sand, beating at his arm with his other hand which also began to smoke.

'You OK?' I yelled.

'Yeah!' He headed toward the mouth of the cave. 'Got to find something to wipe this off with. Be careful in there.'

'What is that stuff?' I shouted, but he'd already run outside.

Una shot past me, running at full tilt, her eyes wide. Carly grabbed her, placed her on her hip and hurried away. I thought about following her out but the sounds of battle were still coming from deeper inside the cave. I sighed and pressed on.

'What the hell is that thing?' I screamed at Belial as I caught sight of the animal they were trying to corner.

'Cave dragon.' He ducked as a wet white orb whistled over his head. 'Don't let its spit get on you.'

Again, the huge, greenish-black creature took a deep breath, raised itself to about ten feet and coughed. A large ball of grey-white phlegm splattered, then rolled across the cave floor, smoke trailing in its wake. The creature stayed pressed against the back wall, obviously not a great fan of sunshine, using its wings, teeth and snot to keep its attackers at bay.

'Belial.' I stopped him as he was about to dive into the fight. 'That's a bat!'

'It's called a popobawa.' He pulled his arm from my grip then turned back, furious, as I grabbed it again. 'What now?'

'Una's safe – why kill it?' The creature was now making a sad huffing, whining noise as it turned this way and that, looking for an escape route. The tiny black eyes were wide and its long ears flicked backwards and forwards as it tried to divide its attention between Melusine and Farr. Slashing at them with its long claws, it attempted to climb backwards up the cave wall. It looked terrified. I lowered my sword. 'I can't kill a frightened animal.'

Belial sighed and roughly turned me toward the wall. There, stacked neatly in the corner was a pile of bones and guano; the bones looked very small.

'It flies silently, comes at dusk. These are children that Zephaniah has lost. It waits on the rocks until there's only one or two, drops down and they're gone.'

'Oh.' I looked at the pile of stinking effluent. In among the shit, bones and old cloth, there was a tiny shoe with a pink butterfly stitched into the toe.

Belial walked away toward the "bat" drawing his sword as he went.

It really didn't take that long. A couple of strokes, one sharp thrust and the ugly creature crashed to the floor. Melusine wiped her sword on its leathery wing.

'Disgusting damned thing.' She looked around the cave. 'Good place to camp for the night though, don't you think?'

Farr sniffed. 'It stinks.'

'Go and get everyone together.' Melusine cast a speculative eye around the cave. 'I'll clean up here.'

'I'll give you a hand.' I put my knuckle-dusters back into my pocket and sheathed my knife watching as she reared into her other form.

'I'm going to burn it clean.' Melusine changed. Her voice

sounded strange coming out of a dragon's mouth – especially a dragon's mouth that was full of bat. 'I don't think you want to help with that, or be anywhere near me. You could easily end up as deep-fried lackey.'

I looked away, slightly disgusted at the crunching and slurping noises that were issuing from the busy goings on between her forelegs.

'I die a lot.' I shrugged and stared out of the cave mouth. 'What do *they* want?' Goats of all sizes and colours had gathered around the cave entrance, where they bleated and jostled.

'Bloody vultures.' Melusine casually ripped off both forelegs from the bat's body. Straining to keep her head held high, she waddled outside and placed them on the rocks in front of the cave. The goats, standing in a respectful semicircle around the entrance, watched her with their knowing eyes. They were now entirely silent.

'I always thought they eat grass and knickers off washing lines and that sort of thing,' I said.

'Not these.' Melusine gave an odd bow of the head then backed into the darkness.

Once they were sure she had gone back to her grisly meal, the goats pounced. Tiny, delicate mouths full of pointed teeth ripped at the two legs finishing them off in a very short time. I felt slightly sick. Soon there was nothing but bones. With their faces covered in fresh blood, the small herd moved off to carry on browsing among the scrubby bushes that grew up the hillside.

I was still staring after the goats when Melusine re-emerged and belched thunderously. She shook out her wings and, none too gently, pushed me aside. 'Stand clear.'

Sitting up on her haunches, she drew in a deep breath and, spreading her wings for balance, leant forward and shot a long stream of orange and yellow flame into the cave.

I was amazed; she just kept breathing out and out. Eventually, when I felt I might faint in sympathy and the rocks around the entrance were glowing a dull dark red, she stopped. Panting, she folded her wings shut on her back.

'I need to go and digest,' she muttered.

'Can't you change back?' I stared at the cave. Although the red had gone you could feel the intense heat emanating from the rocks.

'Joe.' Melusine burped again. 'I've just eaten the best part of 200 pounds of raw meat. If I change back now we are going to be dragging my distended stomach around on an ox cart.' She sniffed and gave me a long look. 'You really do need to start thinking, and you need to start being useful.' She poked her long nose at me and smiled which revealed a great many long shining teeth. 'Everyone in this party has a use, except you and Una.' She ran a long purplish tongue around her teeth probing for any stuck meat. 'If you can't fight and you can't do anything else, what use are you? Una, at least, has the potential to become something interesting.' Closing her jaws with a snap she turned and, heaving herself to her feet, moved a couple of steps down the trail. Stopping for a moment she looked back over her shoulder. 'However, if you want to be useful, I've always room for dessert, my sweet.' With a final smile she was gone, but like the Cheshire cat in Alice's adventures in Wonderland the toothy smile remained fixed in my mind.

By the time we'd moved the party down to the cave, the wind had blown all the ashes from the floor. With the addition of a cooking fire and the walls still radiating a little heat it was extremely cosy.

'Shouldn't we keep going?' I stared out of the cave mouth but it was too dark to see any farther than a couple of metres.

'Una's tired. Hell, *I'm* tired,' Belial said. 'We should be safe enough here for the night. Anything that's out to get us is being seriously inconvenienced at the moment.' He clapped me on the shoulder and wandered off.

Unconvinced I gazed up at the stars. Then wished I'd looked at the stars more at home – I couldn't tell if these were different or not. Little points of white sparkle are obviously similar wherever you go. One night, many years ago, I'd been sitting on a hilltop with Raphael staring at the stars while we waited for a demon to appear. I had been drinking beer and he had been sucking a barley sugar twist. 'For my part,' he'd quoted, 'I know nothing with any certainty but the sight of the stars makes me dream.' More than a little drunk, I'd laughed at him and pointed out that Van Gogh probably wasn't the best person to give sane commentary on life. Raphael hadn't turned his face from the sky. 'Perhaps he was more sane than any of us,' he'd said. Feeling suddenly cold I turned back to the warmth of the cave. I wished I'd asked Raphael what he dreamt of.

Carly was cooking something that smelt rather good. Keril, Farr and Belial were cleaning weapons. Parity and Graham were talking quietly, their heads close together; everything about them said "Do not disturb". I thought about what Melusine had said. Maybe she was right; maybe I had no place here. I poked the blackened floor with a stick. What the hell *was* I doing here? I gasped as a small form leaped into my lap.

'Hello, Una.' I gritted my teeth and waited for the pain in my groin to subside.

'Hello, man.' She stared up at me. 'Chocolate?'

I shook my head 'Sorry, baby girl, no chocolate left – it's all gone.' I poked her gently in the tummy. 'Somebody ate the last piece.'

She giggled, frowned, then sighed as she snuggled up to me.

'You smell,' she muttered.

'Sorry about that.' I peered down at her and pretended to sniff a couple of times. 'You smell nice though – you smell of apples.'

'I don't like apples.' She gave a huge yawn. Then, picking up the sleeve of my jacket, she wrapped my arm around her shoulders and promptly fell asleep.

'Hmm.' Keril's voice drifted over the crackling of the fire. 'There may be hope for him after all.'

Carly gave him a slight shove. 'Don't be nasty, bouncer.' She nudged him with her hip. 'I always knew he was completely gold beneath that frivolous, useless front he puts on.'

'But it's such a thick front,' Keril chuckled.

'Hey!' I called over. 'I *can* hear you, you know.'

They subsided into giggles and went back to making the meal.

The next morning, I awoke in pain. Sleeping all night on a pile of rocks does nothing for either your posture or your mood. I had a headache, a full bladder and one hip felt as though someone had spent the night chewing on it.

I was just about to head out and find a convenient bush when Melusine padded into the cave. Dropping the deer-like creature she was carrying, she barked a roar to get everyone's attention.

'Michael's coming,' she shouted at the top of her voice. 'He managed to get out of wherever the Forest Lord put him and he's on his way. You have to go.'

'Just Michael?' Belial paused in the process of grabbing his bag.

Melusine nodded. 'He's fairly battered.' She shrank back to her normal size and form.

There was a fair amount of hasty packing and within seconds we were all standing in the cave mouth. 'Shouldn't we be running?' Graham kept casting nervous glances back up the path.

'No point.' Belial stared at the ground. 'There's not enough time.'

'How does he do this?' Carly glared up at her father. 'How does he keep catching up to us. The silver gates were supposed to keep him out and he's been trapped by a god … How the hell does he keep getting back on our trail?'

'The gates didn't let him through,' Belial said. 'He demolished them. Michael would have had to dismantle them to get through after Lucifer spoke to them.' He paused for a moment. 'The Forest Lord is powerful but he's all instinct and he's a bit forgetful. He's got a new goddess to get to know and if Michael waited patiently he would have been able to just walk away.' He blew his cheeks out in a long huff of exasperation. 'Maybe we ought to staple one of his feet to the floor. That might work.'

'So what do we do?' Carly grabbed her bag and slung it up on her shoulders with a wince. 'How far do we have to run?'

'Too far.' Belial stared around; there was nothing that could help us. Everywhere was gravel and stone, scrub and stunted trees. 'We have to get to the ferry. Once we're on the Acheron he can't follow. He can't get into Hell, and he knows it – that's why he's making such a huge effort to get us now. Once we're over the river we're home free.'

Melusine gave a derisive snort.

I felt a nudge on my leg and looked down thinking it was Una. The big blue eyes of a happy goat looked up at me. When it was sure it had my full attention, it turned and looked deliberately at the dead animal that Melusine had dropped onto the floor, its neck broken. Obviously it had been meant for our breakfast. The goat nudged me again and, looking beyond the trail, I could see at least another dozen lurking in the shadows, waiting like hyenas. I wondered how long they'd smile for if I didn't give them what they wanted – these things were voracious. A mental image sidled into my mind and I couldn't stop a snigger from leaking out. Oh, that was a bad idea. A really, really bad idea but it made me laugh. 'Anyone got a balloon?' I asked.

I explained my plan to Belial and he looked horrified. 'That's a terrible thing to do.' He shook his head and chuckled. 'I like it.' He stared at the hovering goats for a couple of seconds. 'I just can't see where you're going to get a balloon from.'

I swallowed hard and, reaching into my pocket, pulled out a condom still in its silver wrapper.

Belial raised one eyebrow, looked over at Carly then shook his head. 'At least it's still in the packet,' he muttered.

I blushed.

After some rapid organisation we were as ready as we could be. Melusine had offered to stay and help but had been sent on down the trail with the rest of the party. Even in her dragon form she was no match against Michael. That sword of his would dissect her like a frog laid out for a biology exam. Even with Michael wounded and exhausted, the only one who had a chance was Belial, so he stood, calm and poised, his tall grey sword drawn and at the ready. From the tip of the blade dark smoke trailed, twisting and writhing across the ground.

Before she left, Melusine had shaken my hand and, ignoring the amusement of the others, she had leant forward to whisper in my ear, 'Don't tell him.' She glared at me and gave my hand a hard squeeze. 'I don't like this idea. The whole success rests on *you* and that makes me very nervous.' She squeezed harder. 'Fuck up and you're dead.' Dropping my hand she walked away to gather the rest of the group.

Shaking the blood back into my fingers as I watched them go, I studied the small, tear-shaped vial of qeres that she had pressed into my palm. Could I bring myself to use it? I watched Belial as he stood firm in the road. This was Carly's father and for her, yes, I could use it. Deftly untying the knot in the condom I snapped the fragile neck from the vial and poured the contents inside.

I crouched in the undergrowth, the stretched condom resting on my knees. My ears and the back of my neck were being nibbled by impatient goats. One was definitely more persistent than the others and the gentle love nips were becoming quite painful. Eventually, I turned around and gently squeezed one of its long, soft and floppy ears. 'Just wait and be patient, will you?' I stared into the wide blue eyes and tried to "tell" it what I had planned telepathically. The tall black and white animal glared at me for a moment. Turning, it faced the rest of the herd which, within seconds, had melted away to stand behind shrubs or to munch unconcernedly on the short grass, the very picture of an innocent group of grazing dumb animals.

I watched them go. It was a little unnerving to talk to a goat, especially when they smelled as terrible as that one did. I just hoped they'd be back when I needed them.

Michael, his face scratched, his arm hanging limply by his side and his feathers seriously awry, landed with a staggering thump in front of Belial. I crouched lower behind my bush and balanced the condom carefully. I couldn't screw this up. For once I needed a plan to succeed and make sure that Melusine knew about it. I *was* a worthwhile member of this group. I did have a right to be there. I couldn't face the possibility that she was right and that all I was good for was covering in cream, wearing a cherry for a hat and becoming a dessert for an overfed and slightly rude dragon.

'What do you think you're doing this time, you useless old bastard?' Michael, obviously too tired to indulge in his usual elegant sarcasm, stared out of the one eye that wasn't swollen. 'We've already played this game so what's this – a last stand or has it all become too much and you've decided to commit suicide?' He staggered slightly and used his sword to steady himself. 'That's a sin, you know – suicide – because you know you can't outmatch me.'

Belial said nothing, just raised his sword. The dark matter leapt from the tip and swirled around his legs as though he stood in his own personal dark fog.

'I don't want to destroy you, brother.' Michael sounded tired. 'When I saw what you'd created ...' He shook his head. 'I can't believe you fooled us into thinking Hell hadn't changed. That must have taken some doing – it really *was* a beautiful city. So if you just give me Graham Latimer, we can all go home.'

'Home?' Belial took a step sideways then another, beginning a slow circling motion that would present me with Michael's back. 'You dare to talk to me of home?' He laughed, a cold stilted sound. 'Did you call me *home* when Lucifer fell, did you speak up for me when I was judged – did you try to help me? No, you saw me, you walked by with your head up Metatron's arse, his little guard dog. God's perfect commander, just do as you're told and ask no questions.'

Michael screamed with rage. 'I ask no questions because all this is *His will*!' Taking two quick steps he spun and planted his boot into Belial's stomach, watching with a smile as the demon crumpled to the ground choking and retching.

'Whose will?' Belial planted his sword into the ground

and, using it as a crutch, hauled himself back to his feet. 'This all seems like Metatron's will, not our father's.'

'You haven't changed.' Michael staggered slightly as he raised his own sword but taking a deep breath he pulled himself upright and glared at Belial. 'No faith, always questioning, always arguing. You deserved what you got and I didn't acknowledge you because I was ashamed to call you my brother.' He snorted. 'You couldn't even do what you were told when you and Lucifer were consigned to Hell. No, you had to walk away from it and make something of your own – something you considered better.' He stepped forward with a snarl. 'You have no honour, no backbone; you are pathetic and irresponsible. I'm surprised that our father didn't deal with you long ago. He should have just wiped you out of existence.'

Belial's face twisted and, presented both with Michael's back and the very real possibility of Belial doing something infernally stupid, I quietly stood up. With three quick steps I was right behind him. I lifted the condom and, like a water balloon, exploded it on Michael's back. Blood from the slain deer thing cascaded over the furious archangel then, feeling the initial bite of the qeres, Michael began to scream. Grabbing Belial's arm I dragged him away from the shocked, blood-soaked angel.

Goats poured out of the hills. Melusine had been right: just like piranhas they attacked, standing on each other's backs as they attempted to get to the blood. It didn't take very long before Michael collapsed under their sheer numbers. He disappeared beneath a writhing mass of shaggy hair, fleas and a thousand biting teeth.

Belial watched with a horrified expression, then he turned and ran; I was a single pace behind him. 'You're sick, you know that, don't you?' He shouted over his shoulder. 'Only a bloody human could come up with something so utterly degrading. When he heals, and believe me he will, he's going to make you his top priority.'

I didn't answer. I needed to save all my breath for running, but I had a horrible feeling that Belial was right. I was fairly high on Michael's list before – now he would make it his mission in life to make sure he ended mine. For the first time in an eon that possibility no longer seemed like a good thing. I shook my head and kept running.

Finally sure that Michael wasn't going to get up from his goat and perfume-induced trauma anytime soon, we stopped running. Breathing hard, Belial slumped onto a rock.

'Can we jump to catch up with the others?' I sat down next to him.

He winced and shook his head. 'I honestly don't think I have the energy.' He pulled his hand away from where Michael had kicked him; it came away bloody. 'Damn it all!'

Reaching over I pulled Belial's shirt aside. A deep gash in his side looked painful.

Belial grunted as he tried to move.

'Michael did this just by kicking you?' Grabbing my pack I hauled out an old T-shirt and began ripping it into strips.

The demon struggled out of his shirt and shook his head. 'No, I fell onto some glass at the cathedral.'

Wrapping the strips of T-shirt around the wound I tried very hard to bring the edges of the gash together. 'Why didn't you get Zephaniah to fix it?' I tied the makeshift bandage with a bad knot and sat back to study my handiwork. 'She fixed your leg.'

Belial winced and grunted as he struggled to his feet. Looking down at the bandage, he said, 'Thanks.' Putting his bloodstained shirt back on he began walking stiffly down the path. 'I didn't ask her because I have no right to ask anything of her – not after all the pain I caused.'

I studied Belial's bowed back and decided to change the subject. 'Why did he call you "brother"?' I called. 'Is this some angel thing: are you all siblings?'

Belial stopped walking and stared, over my shoulder, back to where Michael was presumably still having problems with the local wildlife. 'No, we really are brothers,' he said. 'There were three of us. Gabriel was the oldest. I joined Lucifer because of Gabriel's apparent madness – I tried to find out what was going on but he wouldn't talk to me; he

257

just kept saying I'd find out one day. Lucifer said he could help. Michael's older than me but younger than Gabriel; it's always the middle child that causes the problems.' He snorted.

'So do you have a mother?'

Belial shook his head. 'Not that I know of.' He rolled his shoulders and a look of pain crossed his handsome face. 'It's difficult to explain.' He carried on walking.

'So why are you brothers?' I couldn't get my head around what connected them.

'Our father told us we were.' Belial shrugged. 'We were always together.'

We trudged on in silence for a while. Finally, I decided that one last question would either cause him to kick my backside into the bushes, or I might get a straight answer. 'Were you always called Belial?'

'No.'

'So, you're Uriel?'

'Not any more.' The demon stopped walking for a moment and stared at his feet. 'Belial is who I am. Who I was doesn't matter.'

That was the end of *all* conversation. We didn't speak for the rest of the day and, as twilight fell, the rest of the group came in sight. Unable to go any farther, they were standing beside the dead, desolate banks of the greatest river in Hell, the Acheron.

Parity shook herself and waved to us. 'Torment by Goat,' she laughed, 'I bet no Host has ever been taken out like that before.' She skipped over to a tumble-down wall on which Graham was sitting, and sat down beside him on one of the fallen rocks. He looked up with a smile as she approached, then blushed.

'How long have we got?' Farr was busy sorting out warm clothes for Una. A chill wind had started to whisk around, causing goosebumps to rise on exposed skin.

'We should be OK for a while.' Belial rummaged in a pack and dragged out a hip flask from which he took a generous swig. He lowered it coughing, his eyes tearing.

Carly took it away from him with a frown and a roll of her eyes, then, looking at it for a moment, helped herself to a mouthful, despite her father's feeble protestations.

'The ferry should be here soon.' She choked out the words around a fit of coughing brought on by whatever was in the flask. Her face twisted into a look of disgust and she deftly capped the flask and thrust it back into the pack. 'Farr?' She nodded meaningfully at Parity who was laughing at something Graham had said.

Farr sighed. 'I suppose there's no other way?'

Carly, Belial and Melusine all shook their heads.

With a facial expression that spoke volumes, Farr wandered over to his sister and, taking her hand, sat down and began telling her something obviously important. The more he spoke, the more panicked the pink-haired woman became. Even from where I stood I could hear her repeating over and over, 'No … No … I can't, I really can't.'

'What's going on?' I asked the big Drekavak who was standing beside me.

'I have absolutely no idea.' He looked as confused as I felt. Melusine, sitting on a nearby rock, yawned. 'Parity doesn't do water.' She looked over at the corpse-grey river. 'Not that that stuff can be classed as water.'

The argument over by the wall was growing. Graham and Farr were nose to nose and Parity, white faced and wide eyed, had started a continual gentle rocking movement.

'Shit!' Belial went to break them up. It was a fairly simple job; he just caught Graham by the shoulder and dragged him over toward me. 'Hold this.' Belial snapped at me then went back to deal with an almost catatonic seer and her enraged brother.

Graham swung round and ripped his arm out of my hand. 'She's scared of water,' he said. 'You lot can't make her do anything if she's this terrified.'

I was too tired to be gentle. 'So what would you prefer we do – leave her here for Michael to vent his anger on or stay here with her?' I looked over the river. In the distance a black indeterminate shape appeared to be heading our way. 'We have to get across. Once we're off this bank, we're safe.' The little voice in my head told me that I was lying – in truth, there was no knowing what we were heading toward.

'She shouldn't have come.' Graham looked over at Parity, who was now screaming and hitting her brother. 'Not if you all knew she'd have to face water.'

'If we'd left her behind Metatron would have her by now and he'd know exactly what we were doing and he'd probably already have his hands on you,' I said. 'I can't imagine that you enjoyed his company so much last time that you'd wish it on someone like Parity.'

Graham stared at the ground and his face burned a bright red. 'As long as he let her go he could have me.' He spoke so softly I had to strain to hear him. Well, this was an unexpected development ... I was just about to say something supportive and empathetic when Graham looked up at me, his eyes dark. 'She's useless to us like this.' His voice had changed, deepened and smoothed. He sneered in Parity's direction. 'This is what you get when you put your trust in witches.'

Keril and I took a step back, shocked by the change. Graham had obviously gone and we were now facing the Lord of Hell.

Parity began weeping and Graham shuddered. His eyes changed again to light blue and he looked fraught. I noticed that his hair had developed another white stripe.

What had just happened? I was almost positive I'd been talking to Lucifer. I stared at Graham as he wrung his hands, almost hopping from foot to foot in his desire to comfort Parity.

Keril who had been standing quietly next to me all this time nudged me and frowned a question. I shrugged – I had no answers. There seemed to be no reason why Lucifer popped up occasionally then disappeared again just as quickly. As Graham seemed to be in charge of the walking and the talking at the moment, I turned my attention to the river.

No more than 50 feet away, a long black boat was slowly

approaching, with a lantern illuminating the way. It was a hideous, damaged vessel, patched with hundreds of haphazardly cut plates of what appeared to be rusted steel – none of them the same size or shape. The original boat was long gone and it was now a thing of rags, patches and more than a little hope; a tatterdemalion of a craft. The metal at the waterline hissed and bubbled as it emerged on the crest of each thick grey wave.

'What's with the water?' I asked Keril. 'It looks like milkshake.'

'Acid,' he said. 'You can only get the ferry across. No bridge will stand, the supports get eaten through, and so does anyone that falls into it; they just disintegrate within seconds. That's why it's called the River of Pain and Tears.'

'Do you think Parity will be OK?' I changed the subject.

Keril shrugged. 'She's an odd one,' he said. 'It's like she's not really here, sometimes she just stops.' He shrugged. 'Her brother's odd as well. He's so tired all the time but I've never seen him do anything that looks particularly stressful. I just don't know what to make of them.'

'How do you think Alice and Arden are doing?' I broached the subject carefully; this was the first time I'd talked about them since offering them to Michael at the cathedral.

Keril gazed at his toes. 'She's not much of a fighter, but she's a mother through and through. I think she'll be fine as long as she stays with the engineers. Arden will have a great time – he'll be spoilt rotten. We don't have many young any more. Alice will just make sure he eats, stays warm and things don't get too crazy.' He smiled. 'Well, I say she's not much of a fighter: she can crack a punch occasionally and she's very lithe on her feet.' He looked at me and grinned. 'But I'll tell you this for nothing: she is never, ever going to forgive you for throwing that dog shit in her mouth!'

I laughed, finally feeling happier. 'I couldn't find a club and that interesting handful was just luck. If she'd been trying, she'd have ripped me open before I even had chance to get at her.' I looked at him. 'I'm really sorry.'

Keril reached over and, grabbing two large handfuls of jacket, picked me up off the floor with no physical effort at all. 'It's done. You're sorry, I know – I forgive you. Now please shut up about it! I don't like talking to you because I know you're just going to apologise again and again ... and again ... and again.' He shook me with each repetition.

'Bleaurgh!' I gripped his forearms until he put me down. 'OK, I get it, I'm sorr ...' I stopped and grinned at him as he shook his head and placed me gently back onto the dried mud of the riverbank. We stood in silence for a moment, both conscious of the rest of the group staring at us. 'Soooo ...' I stared out over the sluggish white water. 'Do you think that boat looks safe?'

'Safe?' Keril laughed. 'You do realise this is Hell, don't you?' He rubbed his long chin fleetingly, picking at a loose scale. 'Maybe you were hoping for a trip boat – you could wear sandals and a knotted hanky.' He stared out over the water. 'Hey, I know, maybe we could hire some pedalos and pedal our way across Hell's great river.'

I snorted. 'So, there was this demon, a half-angel and a goat in a pedalo ...' I began.

Keril and I looked at each other then he sniggered. By the time Carly wandered over with a look of worry, we were leaning on each other and howling with laughter. 'What's so funny?' she asked.

Keril looked at her through tearing eyes. 'Pedalo ... Goat ...' he gasped. We both started howling again. Carly, with a look of disgust, threw her hands up in the air and stalked off to talk to more serious people.

Eventually, probably due to a lack of oxygen, we couldn't laugh any more and Keril dragged himself upright just as the ferry ground itself against the dead whitish dirt of the bank. The hooded figure, leaning on a long steel pole at the end of the craft, said nothing but stood motionless, his face hidden behind a long waxed canvas cape that reached down to about an inch from the bottom of the boat. With a start, I noticed he had no feet – he just hovered. Now *that* was just freaky.

Belial stepped aboard and handed the ferryman a small

bag which clinked and rattled. 'Passage for all,' he intoned.

The hood dipped once and, as the ferryman moved, I noticed that he was actually standing on a raised box. I mentally kicked myself – of course he was, if he stood in the acid in the bottom of the boat all day soon he wouldn't have any feet left. I smiled and shook my head at my idiocy before stepping aboard.

As I took my seat, carefully making sure no part of me was in danger of getting splashed, I listened to the commotion on the bank.

'No, no, no – no!' Parity twisted and struggled, kicking out at Melusine and Farr who each had hold of one arm. Graham trotted behind them with the backpacks.

'Parry!' Farr grunted as her boot caught him just below the knee. 'You have to get on the boat. I promise it will be OK.'

'That's what you said last time.' Parity, her normally placid expression replaced by one of utter fury, spat the words into her brother's face. 'Last time they put me in a boat, last time they threw me in a river and just kept me under until I couldn't hold my breath any more.' She clawed at Melusine's face and screamed in frustration as the dour dragon merely moved her head out of the way.

'I held my breath for as long as I could.' She twisted and tried to sit down, obviously hoping that going limp would stop the inevitable. 'I could see you through the water. You just kept talking to the inquisitor and he laughed at you.'

Parity finally stopped struggling and began to cry. 'You brought me back and now I'm dead.'

Graham looked up at this, his face pale.

'But you're not God. You can't really bring me back so I'm just a doll, not real. I'm a toy and you're my battery. If my battery gives up I'll just go away again.' Her voice became quiet now; she was utterly traumatised and past making any sense at all.

'We're all dead, Parity.' Farr grunted, bright red in the face, as he attempted to pour her limp form over the side of the ferry. 'Some of us just haven't started decomposing yet.'

Belial caught the sobbing seer as she finally fell into the boat and sat her down next to Carly who wrapped a shawl around her shoulders.

'I'm not a witch.' Parity spoke quietly and her words had no emotion. 'They say I am but I'm not – I just see things. If I'd been a witch I'd have turned them all into toads.' She giggled and stared up at the sky. Even in her panic-stricken state there was no way she was going to look at the water. 'Put me in the water and see if I die. If I die I'm innocent.' She whipped around and glared at Belial. 'That really doesn't make sense, does it?'

Graham stepped over the bench seats and sat down next to Parity. Blushing furiously he gently picked up her hand and gave it a cautious pat.

Parity focused on him and smiled, then began to cry. He put a gentle arm around her and smiled. As she turned her face into his shoulder and huddled there, Graham sighed and looked entirely like a cat that had been locked in a chicken coop. Farr looked furious.

The Acheron is wide – very wide – and after about an hour we were still in midstream. Carly, cold and shivering in the icy wind, had tucked herself under my arm and was sharing my leather jacket.

'So, what's the story with the brother and sister duo over there?' I nodded toward Farr who was still throwing irritated glances at Graham. 'I mean, I get that she was drowned as a witch.' I paused. 'What was all that stuff about dolls and emptiness?'

Carly frowned, scratching the back of her neck as she pondered her answer. 'Well, she's right really,' she said. 'I don't entirely understand it myself. After her trial – I think it was in 1465 – Farr took charge of her body and reanimated it, but it was too dead.' She paused and looked confused. 'Can you actually be *too* dead?'

I shrugged again. 'Nothing really surprises me any more, Carly.'

She laughed, genuinely amused at my cynicism. 'Oh, you poor confused thing.' She giggled. 'Anyway, Farr brought her back, but it takes constant effort on his part to keep her alive. His main skill is to *talk* to the dead, or he can place a spirit into a clay body – he can make golems. He can call up the dead like he did in the tunnel, but keeping Parity alive takes an awful lot of power. It goes against every rule there is and if he were ever to go away, she'd just come to a halt – her body wouldn't be able to contain her spirit.' Carly stared out over the pale swells of the Acheron. 'She'd just become empty, I suppose.'

'Have I mentioned that you lot are all a little odd?' I looked over the ferryman's shoulder, but the far bank didn't really appear to be getting any closer.

Carly laughed. 'Well, Graham seems to be happier,' she said.

'Yeah.' I studied him for a moment. 'But sometimes he *seems* to be Lucifer and I just can't work out what triggers the change.' I smiled as Graham whispered into Parity's ear.

Parity, eyes wide, listened to what Graham was telling her with a big smile that slowly faded to be replaced with a look of horror. She stood up in the boat and stared down at him. 'That's not true!' she screamed.

Farr stood up and, placing one hand on Graham's chest, gave him a hard push. 'What did you say to her?' He recoiled as Graham smiled at him; it wasn't a nice smile.

The long, thin ferry rocked alarmingly as Parity struggled to get away. Holding one hand out to ward him off, she staggered back tripping over seats and feet.

Graham stood up and stepped casually toward her. Then, as she tripped, he caught her with a smile. The smile broadened into a laugh as he, quite casually, pushed her over the side and into the oily waters. Even before she hit the water he had both hands in his hair and was screaming. 'No! Parity!' Graham leant over and thrust his hand into the water, whipping it back out again with a scream. The skin dripped and ran as though made of hot wax.

Farr, pushing the ferryman aside, had taken his pole and was moving it through the water in an attempt to give his sinking sister something to hold on to. Parity spluttered to the surface only the once. Her face was a fright; blinded and boiling, her skin bubbled and collapsed. Through the smoking tendrils of her once luxurious candyfloss hair, glimpses of bone could be seen.

Graham just screamed and screamed.

Melusine stood up, then holding Belial's hand for a brief moment, began to change. Her hair disappeared and her face flattened out, an expressionless disc with two slits for nostrils. A set of long gashes appeared below her ear, which fluttered in the open air. Her body elongated, becoming scaled and sinuous, her fingers lengthened, growing a tissue-like web of skin between each digit. As she dived, she shimmered green and purple where her legs had fused into a long, silver-tipped tail.

Within seconds she was back on the boat, holding a jumble of bones and flesh. Dumping her cargo into the bottom of the vessel where it continued to deteriorate, Melusine changed rapidly back to human, breathing heavily as she tried to keep the scales on her body for as long as possible.

Carly rushed over with a water bag and poured the whole thing over the parts of the grimacing fairy which were melting and fusing. Farr, oblivious to all else, knelt in the bilges chanting and pulling his sister together with what seemed to be a web of pale blue light.

'I can't control it,' Melusine said as she rubbed furiously at her arms and stomach. 'It's still going inward. I haven't got long and I don't want him to do *that* to me.' She pointed at Farr then turned to Belial. 'I'm sorry, I have to go.' She whimpered and gasped as Carly tried to wring the last of the clean water from the bag. 'I'll come back if I can but I need to get this stuff off.'

Belial reached for her hand. 'Where will you go?' His face twisted. 'Don't leave.' He took a deep breath and pulled himself together. 'Where will you go?' he asked again.

'Home.' Melusine panted as the acid ate deeper causing the damaged scales to lift and dull. 'I have to go, Belial – now! I'll heal but I don't know how long it will take.'

Stepping away from his outstretched hand, she partially changed; the dragon wings erupted from her shoulders and allowed her to leap high above the boat; 20 feet above us she became fully dragon and fled back the way we'd come.

We all watched in silence. It didn't take long for her to become a dot in the distance then disappear entirely. Belial studied the empty sky for a long time before whispering, 'Be safe.' He sat down again, his face expressionless.

Parity, restored once again to her normal form, sat up and looked over at Graham. 'Why?' she asked.

That was a question to which we all wanted an answer. The silence continued as we waited for him to speak.

'I don't know.' Graham slumped beside Belial. 'I can see what I'm doing, hear what I'm saying, but I can't stop it. It's like being in a big, warm black box.' He shivered and wiped his face. 'But then things change and I can push myself back out of the dark.'

'What sort of things change?' Carly said.

Graham stared at Parity, his hand clenching as though desperate to reach out to her.

Catching the movement from the corner of her eye Parity recoiled with a look of horror and revulsion.

Desolate, Graham shrugged. 'I really don't know,' he said. 'It only happens if I feel something very strongly.'

Carly bit her lip – a tell-tale sign that showed she was thinking hard.

The boat rocked and Parity screamed. But it was only gently running aground on the far bank. As we climbed out, the hooded captain of this despicable vessel held out a hand and gripped Belial's shoulder then, without a word, pushed the pole deep into the white mud, propelling the ferry back out onto the water.

In silence we watched him disappear. Only after he had merged with the river fog did we finally take a look around. Standing on a dead finger of land that ran beside the torpid river we were the only living things in every direction. Nothing grew here. The earth was cracked, broken and as grey as the river. With every movement the dust fluffed up around our feet before settling in every crevice and crack causing a burning, itching sensation. We walked for about 20 minutes, each of us coughing and struggling to breathe. Eventually Belial pointed downward. 'Welcome to Hell,' he said.

The ground vanished. It would have been nice to describe it as a cliff or a hill but it was neither of those things – the land just stopped. Edging closer to the lip of the sheer precipice I peered over and swallowed hard as my stomach performed little flips. A long, long way below us was a mass of black rock. 'Where are we?' I tried to see details but from this far it was impossible.

'Over there is the city of Dis.' Belial pointed to a grey smudge in the distance. 'Somewhere in amongst all that rock are the ones that got left behind.'

'Will they still be people?' I racked my brains thinking of all the people in history that I could end up meeting.

Belial gave me a strange look 'I don't know,' he said. 'In some ways, they weren't really "people" to begin with. Remember we let all the decent ones out – all that was left here were the dregs of society. Of course, just to make them extra special they were dregs with one or more magical powers, but even that wasn't their real problem – they were just bad through and through. People that beat their kids, husbands that hit their wives, then tell them, "Look what you made me do." Those that laugh at others' misfortune and never raise a hand to help; those that quietly kill dreams and stamp on ambitions then offer condolences when that person comes to them for help.' He focused on the horizon. 'Murderers, torturers and those that have no bloody morals whatsoever. It's their descendants – that's what we're going to find down there – and I can't really imagine they'll have got any better.'

I nodded. This was probably the longest speech I'd ever heard Belial make.

'The worst thing any person can do is lie to themselves – those that look in the mirror and don't see what stares back at them.' He laughed. 'Most of them probably think they're in

Heaven.' He shook his head. 'They like it here, this deplorable city with its depraved and power-hungry inhabitants: it suits them well.'

Graham was standing beside me. 'Of course, there's those who should be here and aren't.' The paper-dry voice echoed back at me as though pushed back by a wind that wanted nothing to do with it at all.

We all took a step away from the edge and left Lucifer, his black and white striped hair blowing in the breeze as he gazed out over the void. He turned and laughed. 'You should be down there, Joe – it would be home for you.' He turned his black eyes away and smiled. 'Home is where the heart is and yours should be here.' He paused. 'Preferably on the end of a spike.'

I seemed to have upset the Morning Star quite badly. I shrugged. Well, "People Mad at Me" wasn't a very exclusive club – I'd upset a lot of people. I should have been terrified but I found that all I could do was laugh. Lucifer himself wanted me dead. Michael, in comparison, faded somewhat into insignificance.

Out the corner of my eye I could see that Carly was explaining something to Parity. There was a lot of urgent whispering and hand waving going on. Parity kept shaking her head. Carly was almost pleading.

Eventually, although she didn't look happy about it at all, Parity approached cautiously.

'Graham?' she said. 'I know it wasn't you that pushed me into the river. I know that you'd never do something like that.' She hesitated, waiting for a reaction then, as none was forthcoming, reached out and put her hand on his arm.

Lucifer frowned and balled his hands into fists. Closing his eyes, he seemed to relax. When he opened his eyes again Graham looked at Parity with a hopeful smile.

Parity nodded then walked away. Understandably she seemed uneasy. Carly, on the other hand, looked incredibly smug.

Keril glanced at me with a raised eyebrow; all I could do was shrug in reply. One day everything would become clear.

Today, however, obviously wasn't that day.

The wind at the top of the precipice was cold. A rude wind I've heard them called – too rude to go around so they go right through you. It was impossible to tell from which direction it originated as it swirled around and about, blowing colder and harder then dropping away to a chill breeze.

Carly shivered and began handing out clothes to anybody that needed them. 'Come on, Father,' she said. 'If we're going, can we actually go? We're beginning to freeze our bits off up here. She put an arm around Una who tucked herself as far as she could under Carly's coat. The small girl's lips were beginning to turn blue.

'How do we get down?' Farr asked. He took a cautious step toward the edge of the bluff and peered over. 'Unless Carly has a hidden cache of parachutes somewhere in those packs, we certainly don't go down that way.' Huffing, he retreated back towards his sister who was sitting mournfully on a rock determinedly ignoring everybody.

'We have to climb down the waterfall.' Belial pointed off in the distance. 'It's not really that far.'

Carly looked up. 'We have to climb down a waterfall of acid – with a child?' she asked.

'No,' Belial said. 'Well, yes … but there are steps cut into the rock face beside the waterfall and they're beneath an overhang that keeps off the acid.' He paused for a moment obviously trying to remember. 'It's not an easy climb but hopefully it's still possible.' He shrugged. 'I haven't been here for a very long time. So we'll just hope, eh?'

Carly gave him a look and Belial stared past her with a small smile. 'Have some faith,' he said.

We all snuggled into whatever we were wearing and ducked our heads into the wind. On a couple of occasions, people tried to speak but the wind just picked up the words and blew them away. Eventually we walked beside the sluggish Acheron in silence.

After what seemed an hour but was, in reality about ten minutes, Belial held up a hand. We all staggered to a halt and squinted into the wind, trying to see what he'd indicated.

The Acheron simply vanished. There was no roar or rainbow, no mist or spray. In fact, there were none of the signs that would normally be associated with the suicidal leap of a big river. It just fell over the edge in silence.

Belial did the same. One minute he was there, the next – gone.

Carly, head down and jumper pulled up around her mouth and nose, staggered over to where he'd been standing and cautiously peered over the edge. 'Dad?' The wind, funnelled up the side of the escarpment, howled and whistled, sounding like an animal in pain. 'Dad!'

Belial's head appeared over the edge of the rock. 'It looks OK,' he said. 'Bits are broken away here and there but I think we can get past.' He stared up at his daughter's furious face, looking confused. 'What?'

The descent was unpleasant, to put it mildly. For hours we crept, slithered and crabbed our way around rocks that had fallen from above and holes where steps had slid out into the silently falling river that plummeted vertically beside us. Continually buffeted and pushed by vindictive winds, our fingers were numb, bloody and scraped raw by the need to hang on to any protrusion we could find. Little Una suffered the most; she was in permanent danger of simply being blown off the side of the steps. Cold and shivering she clung on to Keril's paw, her knuckles white and her eyes wide, hair blown into a candyfloss blob that stood out around her head like a blonde halo. Eventually Farr and Carly fashioned a sling out of a blanket and tied her to Keril's back. She was so light she didn't impede him at all and, snug in her blanket, she dropped into a deep sleep against the warm scales on his back. Graham looked jealous. I knew how he felt.

Belial, leading the way, tested each step. It made for slow progress but he was meticulous in making sure we could pass safely. One particular step looked solid and stood against his tentative foot for a moment, before giving way with a sharp crack under his full weight. He spiralled away over the edge of the steps with a yell. Falling fast, he was a black speck in sharp relief to the thick white liquid that flowed in an unbroken stream, before splashing into the pool below. It sounded like a dog's diarrhoea as it hits the pavement and smelt almost as bad. Carly gave a small 'Hmph' of irritation as she watched her father spread his huge wings and skim the ground then pulled her head back from staring out over the break, her sleeve crushed against her nose.

'Bleugh, I can't take that smell any more,' she groaned. 'It's getting stronger, what is it?'

Belial shot past us on an updraft, his charcoal grey wings spread wide to catch the howling winds. He turned and pirouetted far above us before spiralling slowly back down to the steps, smiling. 'Whoops,' he said. 'I'll try not to do that again.'

Carly nudged him. 'It looked, just for a moment, like you were actually having fun.'

Belial frowned at her. 'Certainly not,' he blustered. 'I don't have "fun" – it would be against everything I stand for.'

We carried on down the uneven steps. Some were tiny, most were between 12 and 18 inches high, but others were several feet tall and we lost valuable time dropping down onto unsure footing. There was also the constant worry that the whole thing was going to give way at any moment. We rested frequently, lined up with our backs against the cliff face, looking like a small flock of starlings on a telegraph wire. Una slept on and Graham was becoming surly. The tiny stars far above us lent no light at all.

Six hours later the sun rose and, in the pale pink morning light, tired and sore, all of us bleeding and scraped, we finally staggered down from the last step and the wind dropped. The sudden absence of sound was almost deafening and most of us whispered, not willing to be the one to crack the deadened blanket of silence.

Una, however, had no such restrictions. After her long sleep, she ran around like a terrier with a ball, jumping and smiling at people, chattering about the smell and asking why we were all so grumpy. Farr, tired and miserable, was pushed beyond all endurance and raised his hand to slap her away.

Grabbing his wrist, Graham stopped the blow as it descended. 'I don't think so,' he muttered. The young necromancer stared at him for a moment then, ripping his wrist from the other man's hand, turned and stalked away. Graham looked quite pleased with himself.

Belial frowned and surveyed the surroundings. 'I think we'll stop here for some rest,' he said.

If we'd been any less exhausted we may have argued. The smell from the pool was terrible – a mixture of ancient eggs, carrion and effluent; it caught in the back of your throat and made your eyes water.

'What makes that smell?' Carly asked again.

Belial pointed to another smaller river that flowed both to and away from the pool. Before the pool it was merely clear water, beyond the pool it still ran fast but was milky and churning. 'The Styx,' he said. 'The meeting of those two rivers creates water that causes madness and blindness and those that drink it hallucinate terrible, terrible things.' He smiled. 'Back in the day we found out that one of the demons, in an attempt to start a side business, sold it to the Etruscans and convinced them it would aid them in their big battle against the Romans. Sadly, it didn't turn out that way. The liquid certainly made them formidable fighters, but unfortunately they couldn't tell the difference between the Romans, trees, each other and their own horses. It didn't take long for the Romans to work out that the easiest way to win was to just stand back and watch them destroy themselves.' He stared over the pool toward the incoming river. 'There is a very strong possibility that Caligula was descended from one of the women taken as slaves.' He shrugged. 'You can drink it on that side,' he said. 'But most that actually get as far as here can't get over there, so they're tormented with thirst, the offer of relief and no way to get it.'

Gathering bottles and skins, he closed his eyes for a moment then leapt into the air and disappeared over the river. A short while later, wet and dripping as though fresh from a bath, he settled back onto the ground. He lost the wings and began handing out the water.

We all looked at it. No one drank.

'It's fine, really,' Belial said taking a long swallow from the clay bottle he was holding.

Still no one drank.

Eventually Una trotted over and took my bottle. 'Thirsty,' she said and, before Carly could stop her, tipped the water down her throat then shuddered. 'Cold,' she said. Handing the bottle to me, she trotted back to Carly. 'Hungry,' she said.

We didn't need any more convincing. The liquid was ice cold and almost sweet – without a doubt the best I'd ever had (although I'd have given my shoes for a cold Coke at that point – preferably with a generous shot of rum in it).

Moving farther into the tumbled rocks at the base of the cliff blocked out most of the smell. Carly and Farr unpacked the little stove and began laying out lots of odds and ends: a bag of beans, some dried meat, lots of little packets of what looked like dried bits of grit but were actually vegetables. Farr, obviously feeling guilty about his earlier reaction to Una, kept giving her little titbits to munch. Within an hour the smell rising from the cauldron was heavenly and Carly had begun to slap people with her spoon in an effort to keep them away. 'We're going vegetarian after this meal,' she told us. 'This is the last of the meat.'

When we'd finished eating, she gathered all the dirty pots and plates and handed them wordlessly to Belial.

'What do you want me to do with these?' he asked.

'Wash them,' Carly said. 'You're the only person that can get to the clean water so you're nominated.'

Belial stared at her, his mouth open, then, putting the plates on the ground he stepped forward and thrust his face close to that of his daughter. 'I am Matanbuchus of the three nets, the North Crown of Hell, I am vice itself to whom no altar has ever stood and you want me to *wash the dishes*.' He stared at her with a slight smile. If he'd ever looked at me like that I would have probably needed some clean underwear.

Carly, however, folded her arms and glared right back.

'Well, Mr North Crown of Hell.' She raised an eyebrow and a lip. 'I'm pissed off, I have blisters, the smell from that river is making me sick, I'm tired and have a miserably cold child to take care of and I'm in no mood to take any crap.' With a big smile she bent down, picked up the plates and deposited them back into his hands. 'From anybody.'

Belial looked back at her expressionlessly, then, with a slight twitch of his right eye, spread his wings and flew away. As he took off he made sure to cover us all in dust.

Carly watched him go, a faint smile still on her face. 'Tetchy,' she muttered.

Keril coughed and spluttered a mixture of dust and laughter. 'I can't believe you just did that,' he said. 'He's going to be livid – those dishes are going to come back in pieces.'

Carly stared over the river. 'He might consider it,' she said, 'but he won't do it.'

Keril stopped laughing. 'Why not?'

Carly sighed. 'He's the last of the Fallen, he's out of his depth and he doesn't know what's going on with Lucifer.' She nodded toward Graham who was trying to talk to Parity. 'With Melusine gone, Dad needs to think of us as his backup and at the moment he isn't thinking of us at all. If he doesn't get some humility and stop thinking of himself as the big *North Crown of Hell* we could all end up very, very dead or worse.' Her gaze explored the barren landscape. 'This is not the Hell he left behind. He's not the big cheese here any more – others are – and they're going to resent being threatened with, "I am Matanbuchus of the three nets".' She scuffed the toe of her boot in an arc through the dust. 'It's as dangerous for him as it is for us. When Lucifer disappeared Dad had the power of reputation to fall back on; now he doesn't even have that, he really needs to be a little more cautious.'

When Belial came back with the dishes, all still in one piece, nobody said a word.

Later that evening, when Una was finally asleep, we all sat around a small fire, warming our toes and passing around a packet of dried apple pieces. Belial had flown miles

275

looking for wood and hadn't been very successful. He'd come back grumpy and had to ask Carly to pull out a splinter which she'd done with a smile. Just to make her point she'd stuck a plaster on the wound; it had little smiley crosses all over it.

'Just remember,' Carly had said. 'We're all in danger here – even you. None of us are really immortal.' She walked away to check on Parity, leaving Belial to stare at his hand.

Sitting around our entirely unfulfilling fire seemed like the right time for talking, and Farr asked the question that had also been bothering me for some time. 'Why did you close Hell, Belial?'

The former angel leant back against the rock face. 'One single woman,' he muttered, staring into the flames.

'Ha, the downfall of us all.' I glanced over at Carly who smiled, reached over and twisted my ear. 'Ow!'

Belial frowned. 'She was an Adoptionist called Ælywytha,' he said.

'A what?' I'd never heard that word outside childcare circles before.

Belial took a deep breath. 'The Adoptionist theory popped up two or three times since the second century when it had been declared heresy. The theory was that Jesus became the Son of God at his baptism by John and the Virgin birth wasn't the real story.' Belial snorted a laugh. 'The Church did *not* like this theory at all.' He looked away from the fire and stared at the silver line of the river. Eventually he went on. 'Well, because of her heresy, her upbringing and her slight power of clairvoyance she was sentenced to the sixth circle where she should have endured eternity trapped in a burning tomb.'

Carly shuddered. 'Seems a bit harsh.'

Belial nodded. 'Funnily enough that's what Ælywytha thought as well,' he said. 'She'd been dragged through Dis in chains with all the other sinners and dropped off with the demon in charge of that area, along with other heretics. They were stood in a line and informed of their punishment then told to turn and await their sentence.' He laughed. 'Poor

Cresil was in charge of that section and when this woman stepped forward, stared him in the eye and said she wanted to talk to Lucifer, he almost had kittens.' Belial smiled at the memory. 'Well, with Lucifer not around, they called me and I turned up to face this angry woman who said that she shouldn't be there.'

Belial frowned. 'It's a strange thing about religion. People believe what they're told and if they're told this is what they deserve they seem to just accept it – even welcome it. But this woman was furious. She screamed and raged that it wasn't her fault and that she'd been brought up in an Adoptionist community – she'd had no choice but to believe what she'd been taught by her parents. Surely it couldn't be heresy if she'd never had the chance to learn anything else, could it?

'Well, I did the normal thing,' Belial continued. 'Grew ten feet, turned red with horns – you know, the classic medieval demon, and she just stood and looked at me. She made me so angry I hit her – sent her tumbling away over the circle.' He picked up a stick and poked at the fire, making it collapse and flicker. 'Well, she picked herself up, brushed herself down then calmly stood before me again. "I've done nothing wrong," she told me. "I won't be punished any more." With that she turned and started walking away.'

Belial stared at nothing as Keril rebuilt the fire. 'Cresil watched her go then said, "She's got a point, you know. Come to that, what about me?" I wasn't sure what he meant.

"I've done nothing wrong either," he'd said. "Yet I stand here day after day, me and my boys spend our lives tormenting these poor sods." He threw his whip on the floor. "Why am I being punished as well?" The others around him nodded and threw their whips on top of his and three more sinners made a break for it and ran after Ælywytha.' Belial shrugged. 'It was like a crack in a dam – before I knew it I had demons leaving, sinners walking the streets of Dis with banners and horns. There were riots, kidnaps and murders. In the end I got a small council together and we opened a gate. All the upper levels and the ditches were cleared, the sinners were pointed at the gates and just told to leave. Any demon that wanted to could also leave. It was a little surreal watching them all depart Hell side by side. All they had to do was walk through the gate after describing their sin and they were gone.'

'Where did they go?' Graham asked.

'Wherever they wanted to,' Belial said. 'Although I doubt any of them got into Heaven.'

Belial prodded the fire with his stick again. Keril reached forward and took it off him. 'Belial, it will never burn if you keep poking at it like a sore tooth.'

None of us were particularly convinced that he was talking about the fire.

Belial nodded, then reaching over took the stick back; it seemed as though he needed something to hold. 'We were really concerned about the lower levels though. There were some very nasty characters down there so we had to set some guidelines. Some we released. Some had killed by accident or incompetence, others had just had no choice; each story we heard, judged on its merits and made a decision. It went on for months.' Belial gazed into the flames. 'We were exhausted – hadn't slept for days – but that was no excuse for what happened.' He closed his eyes and sighed.

'What happened?' Parity asked.

Belial opened his eyes again and for a moment I thought he wouldn't answer her. Then with a decisive movement he threw the stick into the fire and watched it burn. 'A man accused of mass murder came before the court. He was a fire starter and had burnt a school to the ground in the middle of a sunny day. He told us his story, he said that he had never intended for anyone to get hurt – a fire that he had started as some petty revenge shouldn't have spread, he'd set it up badly. He cried for all the children that had been killed and said how sorry he was.' Belial shrugged. 'Well, there was a bit of a debate, but in the end the vote on the council was split and the deciding vote came down to me. Well, that very morning I'd been accused by another member of the council of being too harsh – that I wasn't taking into account how

278

much time these people had already spent paying for their sins. In short I was accused of still enforcing God's will and not taking this revolution seriously.'

Belial frowned and picked up another stick. 'I was tired and heart sore. This was the last man to be offered even a hearing and a chance to leave Hell and even though I had grave doubts about him I decided, what did it matter? He was just one man, so I gave him the thumbs up and out he toddled into the sunshine. I felt pretty good and so relieved that it was all over. We sat in that council room congratulating ourselves on a job well done, drinking fine wine and laughing. We'd only been there an hour when a scribe came in to tell us that there'd been trouble. The man we'd let walk free had killed two children.' Belial gritted his teeth and squeezed his eyes shut as though to block out that terrible memory. 'Zephania's children.' He whispered.

'Oh, Dad.' Carly reached over and gave him a hug. 'It wasn't your fault.'

Belial nodded. 'Yes it was,' he muttered. 'I knew his story didn't feel right. He was a fire starter, he would have been able to control any blaze he started. It wouldn't have got "out of hand". Eventually all that were left were stored in the very lower levels. Caina, Antenora, Ptolomea and Giudecca; they held the very oldest prisoners. None of them were really there any more. We released a few but they were so confused and terrified that we decided to leave the others where they were, submerged in ice. The only place left untouched was the Throne Room and that was obviously empty.'

Belial looked up at us and shrugged. 'That was it, we all emerged blinking, metaphorically speaking, into the sunlight and waited for God's wrath to fall upon us, especially me, but it never came. So we built a new city and tried to forget what we'd left behind,' he said. 'And believe me it's never as easy as it sounds.' He stood up and stretched. 'I think we all need some sleep.' He turned and walked away.

Carly looked at me and winced. 'Right, like that's going to be possible now,' she said.

I shuffled toward her. 'I could help you sleep.' I gave her

a deliberate leer.

'Oh, that's a good idea.' Carly gave me a huge smile. 'Go and see if Farr has got any milk, then you can warm it up and I'd like it with a little bit of sugar and cinnamon.' She smiled and rolled herself into a blanket then, pulling the hood of her jumper over her head, ignored me.

I got the message.

Sighing, I tramped back to the fire to sit with Parity, Graham and Farr, where the conversation was stilted and polite. It was going to be a very long night.

I woke up cold, tired, confused and slightly nauseous. 'We're somewhere completely different, aren't we?' I said to Carly.

'Yep,' she said. 'The barrier's in the middle of the Acheron. That river spans two worlds, which is probably why it takes so long to cross.'

I stared out over the cracked and featureless plain. 'So how many "gaps" are there from here to the Throne Room.'

Carly thought about it for a moment. 'There were seven worlds if you counted Limbo, but now there are only four,' she said.

'What happened to the other three?' I asked. It was difficult to imagine three whole worlds disappearing overnight.

'They merged. As one collapsed it sort of became part of the more stable world that surrounded it.' She put one hand inside the other and opened both hands to create one big circle. 'It's been a long time since Dante's seven levels of Hell has been true.'

As I was considering these odd concepts, Graham appeared and stood with us. He peered out over the empty mud. 'Beautiful, isn't it.' His dry, deep voice sent cold shivers down my spine. Carly gasped, her eyes widening then turned to run. Reaching out a hand he grabbed her arm. 'Don't rush off.' Lucifer turned his head slowly and stared at her. 'Where do you need to go in such a hurry?' He began, ever so slowly, to tighten his grip.

Carly winced as his long slim fingers dug into her flesh. 'I need to talk to my f-father.' Trying to maintain her composure she had caught her lower lip between her teeth. A drop of blood welled up to run along that crease.

'Hey!' I seized Lucifer's wrist and twisted, trying to get him to let Carly go.

Lucifer didn't move. He looked at my hand then shook it off without any effort at all. Grabbing the front of my jacket he picked me up and, with only a slight grunt of effort, threw me away. With a slight smile he watched me struggle to my feet. 'Ah, Joe, my best and finest creation.' He took a step toward me, towing Carly behind him. I noticed there were five small spots of blood where his nails had pierced her skin.

Carly grunted and clamped her lips shut, her face twisted with pain.

'I'm no creation of yours.' Deciding that poorly conceived heroics would be Carly's only hope, I drew my knife and stepped toward him. 'Let her go.'

Lucifer stared at me for a moment then, with a final vindictive squeeze, he pushed her arm away. Bringing his hand to his mouth he gently licked his index finger. 'Tainted,' he said, pursing his lips in disgust. 'Half-angel, half-something else – a mongrel.' He smiled as Carly seized the opportunity to run. 'That one ought to be put down.' He paused. 'Or at least spayed – it really wouldn't be a good idea to breed it.'

'Sorry?' I thought for a moment. 'But didn't you spend a fair amount of time on Earth creating those "mongrels" and half-breeds?'

Lucifer smiled. 'Yes, I did. But a greater power told me that what I was doing was wrong and we have to bow down to those greater than us, don't we, Joe?'

'So I'm told,' I muttered.

Lucifer threw his head back and laughed. 'Oh for pity's sake, say it like you mean it or don't say it at all.' Ignoring the knife he put his arm round my shoulder. 'What did he offer you, Joe?' He beamed down at me. 'Metatron makes all sorts of promises. Did he tell you that you could make up for what you did?'

Before I could answer he glanced over his shoulder and frowned as Carly headed back towards us with Parity in tow. 'She is becoming an irritant,' he said. 'She's far too fragile and needy – brings out the worst in my host.' He gritted his teeth. 'He wants to look after her, but her brother's always there, always in the way. He feels as if he's fighting for her favour.' Lucifer looked down at me. 'Maybe I could stick around longer if I broke the bond, but if I kill her, he'll just put her back together again ... Hm.' He tapped one finger on his lip. 'What to do ... what to do.'

Without giving me a chance to answer, he twisted around and grabbed hold of Parity. Ignoring Carly's pummelling fists he pulled the shocked seer into a close embrace.

Parity, eyes wide, screamed. With both hands on his chest she pushed and twisted. Ignoring her struggles he shoved her to the floor then, dropping to his knees, he splayed his long fingers, placing one hand on her forehead and the other on her heart. Light exploded outward in a blinding blue and white aura. It sparkled and hovered for a moment, then compressed inward to settle in bright globes around Lucifer's hands. He smiled into Parity's terrified eyes. 'Goodbye, Pinocchio,' he whispered as he forced the light into her body.

Parity screamed as she convulsed. Twitching and shaking on her back in the dirt, her heels raised a cloud of pale dust as they drummed and skittered, her arms flailed and her body arched until only her head and feet touched the earth.

'Damn.' Lucifer winced then slumped as Carly rushed over to help the convulsing seer. Farr beat her to it.

'Get out of the way!' Farr screamed. His own blue glow seemed a pale and feeble thing after the light show that Lucifer had just produced. Parity lay on the ground, her clawed hands sunk, knuckle deep, into the earth. She relaxed as his light flowed toward her, but like oil and water, she seemed to repel the advance of the healing glow. It shifted around her form, a billow of blue smoke that eventually dissipated into nothing.

'No, no, no!' Farr cried as he tried again and again to force life into his sister's body. 'What have you done to her?'

he screamed at Graham who stepped back, both hands raised to ward off the furious necromancer. 'I can't get at her. She's not there any more.'

Eventually beaten, Farr sat on his heels and rubbed a hand through his hair. Carly wandered up behind him and put an arm around his shoulders. 'I'm so sorry,' she said.

Silence fell, broken only by Graham's heavy breathing and Farr's occasional sobs. We stood staring at the broken body on the ground. Keril and Belial arrived, both with the same look of baffled incomprehension.

Una dropped to her knees beside the body and, lifting the seer's hand, began to pat and stroke the limp fingers. Parity groaned, sending Una scuttling crab-like to hide behind Keril's tail. Every person standing around must have jumped a good six inches into the air. 'What's going on?' she asked. 'Oh I ache all over.' She rubbed her hand down her arm with a look of pain. 'I never hurt – I can't hurt.' She looked over at Farr with a look of wonder. 'What did you do?'

'Nothing.' Farr, torn between relief and tears, looked down at his hands. 'He did it.' He nodded toward Graham.

'Not me.' Graham held up his hands again.

'No.' Parity sat up, wincing as she moved each limb. 'Lucifer.'

Graham nodded.

'You two really are completely different, aren't you?' She held a hand out for Graham to help her to her feet. He nodded and grasped it like a drowning man being offered escape from a swamp. 'Wow!' Parity rubbed her neck and gritted her teeth. 'I think every muscle in my body just got zapped.'

'He's stopped me helping you.' Farr looked down at his hands; the blue light was fading, lighting up the ground around the miserable man. 'He's put some sort of shield around you and now I can't feed you any more.' Again tears began to roll down his cheeks. 'I'm so sorry, Parry,' he said. 'I honestly don't know how long you can last without me propping you up.'

'Well, as long as I don't do anything stupid, a fair while I should think.' Parity released Graham's hand and began to laugh as she staggered over to hug her brother. 'Of course you can't heal me, you silly arse.' She kicked him gently on the foot. 'You can only influence the dead.' She stretched and winced again. 'I'm not dead.' She giggled. 'I'm alive – I'm real! I feel so different.' She laughed and span in a circle, her bright pink hair swirling above her head making her look like a happy Muppet. As suddenly as she started, she stopped and held herself very still, breathing heavily through her nose as she held onto her head with both hands. 'I'm in a great deal of pain.' She sank back toward the floor.

'Why would he do that?' Keril asked. 'Why would he do something useful – something nice?'

'He hasn't.' Belial lifted one of Parity's eyelids and peered at the rolling eyeball that glared back at him then he pressed two fingers to the jumping vein in her throat. 'Graham worries about Parity,' he said. 'And every time she's near him, Graham gets all flustered and emotional.' Belial smiled at the groaning oracle. 'If there's one thing Lucifer doesn't have, it's empathy, love or any extreme form of emotion. So every time he experiences that he gets confused and Graham can take over. He's hoping that if Parity is human and Farr doesn't have to watch over her like a mother hen any more, he may stop the wild swings of emotion and get a better foothold in Graham's body.'

'Hey!' Farr exploded. 'I had my responsibilities.'

Belial nodded and shrugged. 'Well, now you don't.' He turned toward Parity and Graham. 'I strongly suggest that you two keep this relationship of yours very innocent and new.' He put his face close to Graham's. 'If this becomes familiar or commonplace, we'll have Lucifer back well before we actually want him and dancing naked covered in purple paint won't make him go away.' He raised his eyebrows at a blushing Parity. 'Do you understand? We need to keep him at bay until we get to the Throne Room.'

Graham and Parity nodded in unison before smiling at each other.

'I can't believe I'm saying this.' Belial muttered to Keril as they walked away. 'I'm supposed to represent the carnal desires, the lust, sex and pleasure. All of the kinks and games that man wishes he could indulge in and here I am telling them to keep it clean.' Belial dragged a hand over his face. 'I feel like Mary bloody Whitehouse.'

Keril howled with laughter and clapped Belial on the shoulder. 'Must be a bit of a change of pace for you, old friend,' he said. 'Ah well, it's as good as a rest so they say. You keep this up and they'll change your name again.' He paused for effect. 'So how do you feel about "Ghandi"?' He walked away still laughing loudly and completely missed Belial giving him a single finger. Grumbling, Belial stuck his hands in his pockets and began shouting for everyone to get a move on.

I held my hand out to Farr. He looked at it but didn't move from the ground. 'All this time, I've kept her alive.' He stared over at Parity who was smiling at her own pain and occasionally erupting into giggles. He eventually grasped my hand and staggered to his feet. 'It's taken a huge amount of power. I've had to concentrate, every minute of every day, to keep her mobile and in one piece. To stop the decay, the atrophy – the smell.' He rolled his shoulders. 'So what do I do with all this energy now?' He held out a slightly shaking hand; the blue light dripped from his fingers to scatter harmlessly across the floor. Snaking tendrils burrowed into tiny cracks in the earth and pulled forth the husks of insects that grew flesh and skittered in every direction. As he watched them, expressionless, the ground buckled and a small skeleton of some unidentifiable rodent dragged itself from the dry dirt.

It was as though time had reversed. As we watched, the little skeleton attracted flies, which turned into maggots that leaped out of the re-emerging muscle and tissue then became eggs, which disappeared into more flies. Eventually, the little creature – it looked somewhat like a field mouse but had small white ears and a longer nose – opened button black eyes and looked around. It frightened itself with a sneeze then scurried off over the dirt to disappear into another hole.

'It won't last long,' Keril whispered. 'As soon as this

energy is used up it will die again.' He hung his head as Belial shouted again for us all to move.

After 400 years, to suddenly find yourself free of any obligation must be a fairly scary place to be. I tried to think of something supportive to say but drew a blank. This was one trauma he was going to have to work through himself.

'Come on.' I put a guiding hand between Farr's shoulders and gave him a gentle push. 'Just don't animate anything huge and scary, OK?'

Farr nodded and, with his hands tucked firmly into his pockets, he trudged along lost in his thoughts.

'So how far is this city, Belial?' Keril called after we'd walked for a fair while.

'Not long.' Belial looked around 'We're already in the hunting grounds.'

We followed his gaze. There wasn't really much change in the landscape here than at the waterfall – maybe a few more rocks, but there was still no sign of any life at all.

Belial laughed at our confused expression. 'Each rock marks the entrance to a largas burrow, so we're probably in among the hunting population right now.'

'I'm confused.' Graham looked around. 'Are they invisible? Because even with the best camouflage you couldn't hide out here.'

Belial laughed. 'No, only the Fae can become invisible.'

'Largas?' Keril asked.

Belial nodded. 'They look like large foxes from the front but have the back end of a big rabbit. Odd things – make great eating and they are superb diggers. A family group of about 20 dig out huge round holes. Anyone out hunting gets a meal *and* a dry place to sleep. They leave the rocks on top of empty burrows to warn other hunters that that room is already taken.'

'Fairies can turn invisible?' Now that just seemed too farfetched for even me to swallow.

Belial shrugged, 'Well, sort of – they can phase out. Half in their world and sort of half in the next, so they're here but not.' He frowned at his own explanation.

'So they could be here now?' I imagined a whole race of beings like Melusine could be a lot of trouble.

Belial laughed. 'Skittish, aren't we?' He shook his head. 'No, they can only get into Hell through the Fae Gate in the Throne Room.'

'But Melusine was coming here with us …' I let the question trail away and wondered how she was doing.

'Melusine is different.' Belial scratched his chin. 'She's not human, or Fae or even angel – she's unique. Her mother is full fairy – a water fairy – which is why Mel can change into that mermaid type form that you saw on the boat, but her father was a direct descendant of the original beings that we kicked out of here.'

'Dragons?' I looked around and laughed putting on a querulous incredulous voice. 'There be dragons here?'

'Sorry, Joe, not any more.' Belial looked off to the horizon. 'Like the dinosaurs on your world, they'd pretty much eaten everything available and were dying by the thousand. It's a sad and ignoble death for such a beautiful creature to starve to a sack of scales and bones and then just keel over and die. When Hell was created there were less than a hundred left and humans, having moved ahead of the ice in the lower levels, were attempting to kill them. Neither side were doing very well and we really wanted their land. We offered them relocation for their whole species on the understanding that they never came back here. Well, as you can imagine, they jumped at the chance. Some went to Earth, some went to other worlds. They thrived and learnt to live in their new environments. Over the years they learnt to change shape and mated with the new force – humans – hence Melusine's father.'

'So let me get this straight.' I couldn't stop a giggle from escaping. 'Melusine is part fairy, part fish and part lizard?'

Belial grimaced then nodded. 'Yes, I suppose she is and if you ever decide to point that out to her, please, please tell me first so I can come and watch her reaction, eh?'

I imagined for a moment what that reaction might be and shut up.

'Erm, Dad?' Carly's voice quavered slightly. She nudged Belial and nodded toward a handful of silent forms that waited, armed and watchful.

The small group stood, sat and squatted on top of a large pile of rocks. They studied us in silence as we wandered through the desolate landscape. I wondered how long they'd been there.

'Just carry on walking,' Belial muttered.

Three figures began to climb from the tall black rocks. Two men and one woman walked confidently toward us; they seemed at ease but I noticed all had weapons to hand. Dreadlocks decorated with beads, small spirals of metal, coloured clays and carved bones clinked and clacked as they moved. However, I felt this gentle chiming was deliberate as they approached on absolutely silent feet. The weapons they carried looked handmade – designed to be quick and brutal rather than any attempt at pleasingly aesthetic. Axes, long spears and short, wide knives seemed to be the main weapons of choice.

Rough, woven cloth had been made into simple trousers and tunics; two of them were barefoot, the other sported a pair of ancient green Nike running shoes and a very large, richly decorated watch hung, oversized, from his skinny wrist. It was obvious we weren't going to pass unchallenged. I rolled my shoulders, making sure my knife was loose in its sheath then put my hands into my pockets, threading my fingers through the holes in the 'dusters. Moving to the rear of our little party, I focused on the one that was obviously the leader. Positioning myself for a clear shot I waited to see what would happen.

A small dark man detached himself from the group and, handing his long bladed spear to the woman, he padded across the parched earth, his smile wide and his dirty hands held carefully in plain view.

I sighed. I'd picked entirely the wrong man as the leader. Feeling myself reddening slightly I tried to nonchalantly slide back to stand beside Graham who grinned at me. Damn, I didn't think he'd have noticed.

'Hey, hey.' The little man smiled, his long moustache bending around cracked lips and gnarled dark teeth. 'What can we do for you out here in the dry lands? You lost?'

'No, no.' Belial put his hand up to show that he too bore no weapons. 'Looking for meat – dried meat. We're travelling, don't want to eat in town.'

'Bright man.' The little guy spoke with what seemed to be a Spanish accent. He studied us for a moment as he wrapped a long dirty dreadlock around his finger. 'What you got that we want, eh?'

'Ah, my friend.' Belial stepped forward. 'For a little bit of meat I can make you powerful.'

The rest of the group, confident that nothing untoward was likely to happen, clambered down from the rocks and gathered around the little hunter. They raised weapons as Belial moved. He stopped immediately and held up both hands, palms facing out.

'I am Andre.' The leader motioned for his pack to back off. 'I like anyone who says they can make me rich.'

'I think I mentioned powerful,' Belial said. 'Not rich.'

'Power, riches, they all come creeping out of the same burrow, eh? They each are the other and one does not exist without its friend.' The little man nodded sagely as though he'd just shared some great knowledge. 'So what you got, tall man?' He grinned happily up at Belial. 'A name would be a good start.'

Belial put his hand over his heart. 'Rimmon,' he said. 'We have the urge to head into the ice lands and see what we find.'

The group of hunters laughed until Andre waved a hand at them. 'You'll find it bloody cold is what you'll find.' He rubbed his moustache and, while seeming to watch Belial, flicked glances over the rest of us. 'But I like a fool – even a dead fool – so show me how you're going to make me envied and powerful before you go and throw your miserable life away in the cold.'

Belial made a show of searching through his pockets, eventually bringing out a small leather bag. He shook it enticingly at Andre then poured some of the contents into his palm.

Andre bit his lip. I noticed that the hand stroking his long facial hair moved, just fractionally, faster.

Andre could also act to the crowd. He peered into Belial's hand with a sneer then, shrugging, he shook his head in disappointment. 'Diamonds?' He sounded bored.

Belial nodded then poked them around his palm with a finger. 'Made by humans. These diamonds are stronger, denser and much more useful than anything you'd dig out of a hole.'

The little hunter shrugged. 'Meat's hard to come by out here, and I've got to find a buyer for those.' He shook his head. 'Lots of problems for me, man.'

'Well, I do have one that's a little special.' Belial shook the leather bag until a large white stone fell into his palm. At its heart was a blue star.

'Right.' Andre laughed around at his friends. 'Special.'

Tipping all the other stones into the bag Belial held up the large diamond between his thumb and forefinger. 'This is a memorial diamond.' Belial tossed the stone into the air, then snatched and pocketed it as it fell. 'Created from the carbon in the cremated remains of human bodies it still holds the memories of the one that died.' He grinned at the little man. 'It's so much easier to steal someone's identity when you have their memories being whispered into your head.' He stole a look at Andre then shrugged slowly. 'But I can see you're not impressed. Never mind, we'll chance the food in town.'

'No, no. Wait, wait.' Andre nodded to the woman who sashayed over holding a large package wrapped in an oiled material. She smiled at Belial, looking up at him from under her dusty lashes. Andre frowned, grabbed the package then pushed the woman away. 'I don't really want the diamond, but we've been talking for so long, I almost consider you a friend.' He held his hand out and gave Belial a toothy grin. 'I'll take it off your hands and I'll give you over the normal amount of barter for it.' He weighed the pack of meat in his hands. 'One thing …'

Belial hesitated as he reached for the package and raised his eyebrows.

'You get any more of those diamonds, you bring them to me first, right?' Andre refused to relinquish the package of meat. 'Because I consider you a friend, which round here is almost the same as a brother – man, you're nearly family. I wouldn't want a family member to look bad by offering this rubbish to everyone. Someone might take offence.'

Belial nodded. 'I can see that … I wouldn't want to embarrass family. Deal?'

Andre let go of the package with a grin then spat into the earth at Belial's feet. Belial copied the action.

The niceties and the after-business chat lasted for another half an hour or so and Carly, obviously used to how these things went down in any world, made tea and offered tiny cups of the strong liquid to all members of each party. As she walked by, one man – the one with the Nikes and the bling watch – reached out and grabbed a handful of her bright red hair.

At her startled yelp I headed toward them, but Andre turned and barked an order at the big man, who dropped her hair and shuffled backward looking like a chastised child. 'Fire,' he said quietly.

Eventually, with all the rituals completed, we were on our way again. As the hunters walked away from us Graham called out, 'Hey, Belial, what was that with the diamonds?' Andre stopped dead and turned slowly to watch us walk away.

'Fucking shut up!' Belial turned and swore at Graham who looked confused.

I grabbed Belial's arm. 'Not Graham,' I said. 'He was gone for just a split second.'

'Damn Lucifer,' Belial cursed quietly. 'Why would he do that?' Irritated, he carried on walking, ever so slightly picking up the pace.

Pretending ignorance of the renewed interest from the hunter and his group, we followed him.

# CHAPTER 10

IT WAS THE SMELL and the noise that heralded the real city limits. Carried on the swirling winds, the well-known stink of food simultaneously cooking and rotting, effluent and other, even less savoury smells, made us gag and cough with each pass of the oddly erratic breezes. Repetitive shouts, at first distant, described weapons and foodstuffs, alchemy, whores for sale, true prophesies or fortunes, wards or spells and a thousand other items. It really was bedlam.

The city was black. Not from dirt or neglect – although there was certainly enough of that. Each structure, be it house, store or bar, was carved from the basalt hills that stood in the centre of these levels of Hell. The dull, pitted black rock absorbed all light and, due to the odd column-like formation of the rocks, each building appeared to lean at a distressing angle. Despite the bustling energy of those that we passed, each street seemed to struggle under the weight of its heritage and reputation.

Eventually Carly tugged at her father's arm. 'We need to rest,' she said. 'Parity is finding her new life a bit of a burden.'

I looked back. Parity, her arm over Graham's shoulders, winced with each step, her face contorted in pain.

Belial nodded and turned to the struggling girl. 'Parity, can you tell me where would be safe to stay?'

The exhausted seer took a deep breath and tried to stand upright. 'It's difficult to see,' she said. 'I have to sleep.' Her legs buckled and Graham barely caught her as she fell. 'I've not needed to sleep for over 500 years.' Her voice faded as her eyelids closed.

Keril walked over. 'Let me take her,' he said. 'She'll be no burden to me.'

Belial shook his head. 'Damn,' he said. 'Obviously *life* is not a good aid to concentration.'

Graham nodded vaguely, and although obviously relieved to be able to walk unhindered, his eyes never left Parity's face.

After studying two or three buildings that looked like taverns Belial stopped before a tall door that was only marginally less disreputable than the others around it. A painted plaque on the wall stated this was "The Fat Maggot". A deathly white, rollie-pollie grub stared blankly down at us from the sign; some wag had painted four wobbly stars beneath its distended belly.

Belial stared up at the sign for a moment. 'Well, at least someone's got a sense of humour,' he said.

We pushed cautiously through the tall metal door listening intently for the sounds of shouting or breaking crockery; both were mercifully absent. The inside looked like every cheap hotel I'd ever seen. A faded, red wool runner ran from the door to the desk, behind which sat a woman with fluffy grey hair. After a moment of obvious suspicion she gave us a big smile.

'Hello, hello,' she said, her voice strangely deep. 'Welcome to the Fat Maggot.' Heaving herself to her feet she waved us forward. 'Would you like rooms?'

Belial nodded. 'Yes, one common room if you have it.'

'Certainly.' Her double chin wobbled as she smiled and I noticed that although two or three of her teeth were missing, the rest were white and clean; she wasn't what I'd expected.

'You're lucky to get a room with the festival being about to start. We only have one with a communal bathroom – will that be all right?'

'Yes!' Carly raised her voice from the back of the group. 'Definitely.'

The woman laughed – a great booming sound. 'Been a bit of a trip, has it?' She patted a big book that was open on the desk. 'If you'd like to sign in, I'll get someone to go up and light a fire for you.'

'This is our first visit for a very long time.' Belial stopped her with a hand. 'Are the payment arrangements still the same?'

The woman nodded and laughed again. Her podgy hands rested on her hips and the rings on her fat fingers glittered in the candlelight. 'Haven't ever changed,' she said. 'Tektite, food or barter – which would you like to use?'

Carly dragged over a large rucksack and Belial, after a moment's searching, took out a small velvet box. 'What do you think of this?' He opened the box. There was a slight creak from the snap hinges and the woman leant forward with a sneer.

The owner of the Fat Maggot stared into the box then raised her eyebrows. 'Not what I'm usually offered.' She picked up a single glass lens and, raising it to her eye, peered through it into the box. 'What is it?' She took out the small quartz crystal ball and held it up to the flickering light from the cheap fatty candles that burned in sconces all round the room. They smelt fairly rank and each one gave off a slightly greasy smoke that gathered like the wrath of God near the stained ceiling.

As she moved, the light caught the occlusions and cracks inside the small ball, sending rainbow waves throughout the orb. Captivated by the colours the woman gasped as she spotted the water trapped deep within the crystal matrix. As she tilted the ball it could clearly be seen moving from one chamber to another. Fearing she'd already let her interest show, the woman bit her lip.

Belial smiled and leant nonchalantly on the desk. 'It's said that if you stare into the ball long enough you'll begin to see pictures and from those pictures you can tell the future.'

The woman gave no indication of having heard him and continued to stare mesmerised into the glistening facets deep within the crystal. Eventually she shook her head, placed the lens back under the desk and, with one quick movement, swept the ball into the pocket of her apron.

'I'm Mama Gert.' She was all business once more. 'This will get all of you three nights' sleep in clean beds, hot water and a communal pot.'

Belial coughed and held the open box toward her, ready to take back the ball.

Mama Gert took a step back and smiled. '... and, of course, tea each morning with bread and toppings.'

Belial nodded then, swapping the box for a long quill pen, he dipped it once into a pot of ink that seemed to have a greasy scum floating on the surface and turned to the book. In neat looping writing he signed it "Rimmon". He studied the pen for a moment then shuddered and passed it back over the desk.

Mama Gert noticed his reaction and laughed. 'Not keen on the pen, eh? Got it from our healer, who said he got it from an angel he'd helped. He had no money so he parted with this – a prize possession.' She smiled down at the long white feather, its silver tips glowing yellow in the candlelight.

Carly frowned and moved forward to take a closer look at the feather. 'An angel?' She sounded sceptical.

Mama Gert snorted her big quivering laugh again and reached up to pat a few strays back into her fluffy ring of hair. 'You don't believe in angels, girl?' She ran a fat hand down her flowered apron, pausing just for a moment to check that the ball was still safe in her pocket. 'You're mad if you don't.' Her eyes widened as she caught sight of Una peering, thumb in mouth, around Keril's side. 'You have a child with you?'

Keril put his arm around Una's skinny shoulders and pulled her closer to his warm scales. 'Is that a problem?' he asked.

The landlady stared at the little girl for a long moment, biting her lip. Eventually she gave us a big professional smile. 'No, no, not at all.' She reached behind the desk and came up with a large key. 'It's just so late, she must be exhausted, poor little thing.'

I noticed that her smile didn't quite reach her eyes.

Belial nodded and took the key. 'We all are,' he said. Moving decisively away he brought the conversation to a close. Keril nodded at Graham then at Parity. Swinging Una up onto his shoulder he kept a tight grip on her as he hurried after Belial.

Mama Gert continued to smile.

Belial watched Graham place Parity gently down onto a scruffy chaise then leant over toward me. 'Angels cannot – absolutely cannot – pass the Acheron. She must be mistaken about that feather,' he said. Scratching his head he turned to Keril. 'No one is supposed to be able to get in or out of here. I was expecting to have to make up some fantastic story but she said there's only one room left. How can that be? Who's here and what festival was she talking about? I don't remember hearing about any festivals ...'

'She seemed very interested in Una.' I felt that Belial was missing the important point.

He nodded vaguely and went to stare into the flames.

The room was almost luxurious and the communal pot was not, as I feared, a large bucket in which we were all supposed to pee, but a rather tasty and savoury stew filled with unidentifiable meat, vegetables and herbs.

'I wonder what this is?' Carly poked a piece of meat on her plate. 'It looks like beef and tastes like ...' she pondered for a moment '... I had kangaroo once in a restaurant, it sort of tastes like that.'

I desperately wanted to glance at Keril and wondered how many other people felt the same. I really hoped it wasn't Drekavak stew.

Belial finished his meal then, after pushing the bowl away with a sigh, looked around the room.

There were eight beds, each with matching sheets and blanket. A fire burnt steadily in the basalt fireplace, the soot turning the black stone shiny. The flames, burning through what seemed to be black glass, appeared to be hanging in midair as they flickered and reflected in their own coals; it was an odd sensation.

A thick brown rug had been placed in front of the fire; this was where we all sat to eat. Parity slept on completely oblivious.

'So what's the plan?' Carly asked, staring into the fire.

'I'm just about to go and have a bath – I don't want to miss anything.'

'No plan,' Belial said. 'We'll get ourselves together in the morning and head on out. The sooner we get through the ice lands and down to the Throne Room the better. While we're running around here, we have absolutely no idea what Metatron's up to. As soon as we can sort out Graham's little problem Metatron won't have any claim on him at all.' Standing up he indulged in a huge stretch. 'Shouldn't take that long actually.' He yawned and shuddered. 'We've managed to get through Zephaniah's little set of surprises and if that was the worst that was facing us …' He yawned again and shook his head obviously trying to keep his eyes open. 'Maybe this place isn't as bad as I feared.' Too tired to say more he just trailed off into silence.

Carly grinned at him as he slumped onto the nearest bed. 'I need to soak,' she said. 'I smell.' She took a good sniff, wrinkled her nose then, taking a towel from the piles balanced on the crude shelves set around the room, she vanished through a small door. 'Come on, Una.' She hoisted the little girl onto her hip and, after sniffing at her and making her giggle, she said, 'You could do with a good wash as well.' Within seconds we heard her pumping water from one of the two hand pumps in the bathroom.

'Helpful,' Belial muttered, then looked around the room. 'Farr, can you talk to the dead here?'

There was no answer.

'Farr?' We all looked at each other. The necromancer was nowhere to be seen.

'Well, who saw him last?' Belial leapt up from the bed infuriated. 'Joe, you were talking to him just before we got into town.'

I thought back. 'He was walking beside me when you were dealing with the food.' I racked my brain, trying to picture our conversation. 'I'm sorry, I can't remember. I think that was the last time I saw him … He wasn't happy about Parity's change of circumstances and he was certainly preoccupied.' I shrugged. 'I honestly don't know.'

Belial ran a hand through his hair and sighed. 'Well, there's nothing we can do now,' he said. 'Let's just hope he's gone into a bar, got very, very drunk, got laid, had all his worldly goods nicked and we find him in the gutter with the rest of the dross in the morning.'

'Nice,' Keril murmured.

'Well, believe me, it's a damn sight better than any alternative,' Belial said.

Leaving them all to worry, I stuck my head around the bathroom door.

Carly was padding around in an old T-shirt while rinsing Una's hair. The little girl sat drowsy and soaked in the tub. As I came in she lifted Una out and wrapped her in a rough but clean towel and began to cuddle her dry. 'Hey, you,' she whispered to me. 'Could you put madam here to bed?'

I nodded and picked Una out of her arms. She hardly weighed more than a small dog.

Just as I was sure Una was asleep on my shoulder she lifted her head, yawned and then looked me in the eye. 'You're a bad man,' she murmured.

I nodded. 'I never meant to be.' I whispered at her.

She laughed. 'I still like you.' Then, with another huge yawn, she settled her head onto my shoulder and closed her eyes.

I tucked her up in bed and watched as she cuddled her grubby doll and stuck her thumb in her mouth. 'I like you too,' I said. She smiled round her thumb and rolled over.

I was woken by Parity screaming at Belial. It was a conversation that had obviously been going on for some time. 'Well, where will you look?' She'd been shouting for so long her lips had gone white.

'Everywhere that we can,' Belial said, his voice calm but slightly gritty. 'How about you try looking as well?'

Parity flopped back onto the bed and dropped her face into her hands. 'I've tried and tried, but I don't *see* anything any more. There's been nothing since Lucifer "fixed" me.'

'Well, that's just great.' Belial stood up.

'He has to be somewhere.' Her anger had vanished and

tears ran down her cheeks. 'You will look everywhere, won't you? You have to find him.'

'We'll look everywhere we can and if you shut up for five minutes we might actually get out there and start.' Belial stamped toward the door tapping Keril on the shoulder and beckoning to me as he walked.

Parity shut up.

I groaned and poured myself into some clothes.

Four hours later and we were trying to walk quickly without appearing to run. As we turned down yet another street, I wondered if we'd ever find our way back to the Fat Maggot. A laugh behind me made the hairs on my neck stand to attention.

'Dead end,' Keril muttered.

Putting both hands in my pockets I groped for my knuckle-dusters. As usual I felt slightly sick as I put them on. However, this time it was nothing to do with the slick, greasy feel of the old bone; this time there was no way out, I was really going to have to fight. My heart beat faster and prickles of energy ran around my neck and down my back. Slowly I turned to face our laughing pursuers: there were five of them. Even though I didn't think it was possible, my heart beat just a little faster.

'Now then, gentlemen.' One broke away from the pack. His long greasy hair fell into his eyes and he pushed it back with a filthy hand that was only half hidden by the fingerless gloves he wore. He walked forward a couple of paces and smiled, his ulcerated lips pulling away from grey and brown teeth – those four or five that were left clinging to his blackened gums. 'I think we need you to come along with us.'

Belial laughed. 'Why would we want to do that?' he asked. 'I honestly don't think you scum know any places where we'd want to even walk past let alone frequent.'

I had a sudden urge to punch Belial rather than the rabble facing us. Why couldn't he, just for once, keep his mouth shut? I winced as he went on in a bored tone.

'Just let us pass, keep your grubby mitts to yourself and

you might actually end up seeing the end of the day.' He smiled and leant nonchalantly on the wall.

The men looked at one another. 'I don't think they want to come with us,' one of the other men said as he cracked his knuckles.

Belial laughed. 'Quick on the uptake as well as good looking.' He nodded to the guy who was still cracking his knuckles 'You really shouldn't do that, it'll give you rheumatism – then how will you play with yourself?'

The man roared. As he broke into a run towards the smirking ex-angel, Belial sidestepped and ducked, allowing the man to flow like water over his shoulder to land in a crumpled heap behind him.

'So you're stupid, ugly *and* clumsy.' Belial checked his manicure as he counted off the man's faults on his fingers then tutted as he found a broken nail. He pulled out a knife and quickly pared the injured nail down to the quick. 'Whoever hired you lot must really be dragging the bottom of the cess pit, or perhaps he's as stupid as you.'

All four men ran at us, while the one behind Belial clambered to his feet then, with a leap, hung around Belial's neck. Forced to deal with two attackers of my own I didn't see how he handled them. I was, however, quite gratified when one of my assailants was removed by one of Belial's attackers careering into him. He had obviously been thrown with some force down the alley.

I looked up at the man facing me and wondered where his face stopped and that huge beard began; there was no point going for his throat as I couldn't see it at all. At my half-hearted right hook, the man laughed and caught my wrist. Bracing myself slightly, I raised my left hand and jabbed him in the stomach and abdomen – a quick three punches.

Winded and surprised he doubled over. His hat came off and fell into the mud; I made sure I stepped on it. Staggering backwards, he stared at me for a moment while he got his breath back. I knew I should have hit him then but I just couldn't initiate a punch so I stood and waited for him. It didn't take long; with a grunt he came at me, arms outstretched.

For a moment everything slowed down and I felt completely confident. All my other fights had been staged by Metatron – this was one I'd got into on my own and I was going to come out of it with a smile, even if that smile was missing teeth. I dumped the knuckle-dusters back into my pocket; I didn't need them and I honestly felt like getting dirty with this one.

I sidestepped as my attacker staggered past then, bringing up my foot, kicked him in the back of the knee. He staggered and fell. I heard the dull wet crack of snapping bone as he hit the floor and winced in sympathy. I couldn't feel bad for him for very long though. The man with a tombstone maw was heading toward me and he seemed to have lost his sense of humour. Holding his knife in a grip that suggested he knew what he was doing with it, he approached cautiously, one hand out to the side and the knife held loosely in front of his chest.

It was quite a long knife – dirty, of course, and with a wickedly curved blade. I waited for him to make the first move. Eventually, without a sound, he feinted with his empty hand then brought the knife round at throat height in a sweeping motion. It was slightly high and, as I turned my head, I felt the point zip past my cheek. Carrying on the turning motion I spun full circle. He looked quite surprised as my right foot made square contact with his cheekbone.

Laughing, I hooked his ankle with my foot and watched him go down, his old patched coat fluttering as it hit the mud. I reached over and twisted my fist into his long, greasy fringe then smacked the back of his head onto the ground. With the first contact he grunted, the second he moaned – after the third there was no sound and only the whites of his eyes could be seen. The fourth and fifth bash I gave him really served no fighting purpose but I enjoyed them all the same.

'Nice, but that's probably enough.' I spun, and then grinned as Belial studied my handiwork. He looked as though he'd just stepped from the pages of a men's magazine – calm and serene, with not a hair out of place. I looked down at myself, covered in mud and blood. Obviously, I had a lot to learn.

'Thanks.' I had to admit, I did feel rather proud of myself. 'Where's Keril?'

Belial jabbed a thumb over his shoulder and laughed. 'Looting, I think.'

Looking toward the back of the alley, I could see Keril crouched down by one of the unconscious men. He didn't seem to be going through their pockets and, as I watched, he drifted onto one knee then, so very slowly, fell forward into the mud.

'Belial, I think he's hurt.' I stepped round the surprised demon lord and hurried over to where the Drekavak was huddled. 'Keril ... Keril! Hey, are you hurt?'

The Drekavak winced and pressed a hand to his side. I could see bright blood spilling through and over his scales. 'Lucky jab,' he said, then breathed out carefully. 'Must have had a hidden knife or something sharp.'

'Can you do anything?' I looked up at Belial who wasn't looking so suave any more.

He shook his head. 'No, that looks deep,' he said. 'I could close the skin over the top and heal that but it would just fester. That needs cleaning out – we'd better get him back to the Maggot.'

'Can *I* do something about it?' I took my knife out and cleaned it hastily on my dirty sweatshirt.

Belial's look became thoughtful. 'I honestly don't know,' he said, 'but it's certainly worth a try.'

We gently laid Keril out on Belial's coat and, taking a deep breath, I was just about to attempt some sort of miracle when Keril reached out and grabbed my arm. 'Don't remove a limb or give me two heads, will you.' He tried to laugh but choked on the blood that was now dribbling from the side of his mouth.

'Ha, bloody, ha.' I poked him gently with the tip of the knife. 'Shut up and let me concentrate.'

He nodded then turned his head away.

I concentrated, not on the wound but on the knife; it was

like trying to explain a difficult concept to a cabbage. Every time I managed to latch on to what appeared to be a rudimentary consciousness it would slip away. After five minutes of stern talking, I still didn't feel I was getting anywhere.

'Erm, Joe.' Belial's voice broke through my reverie and I sighed.

'What?' I may have spoken a little more harshly than I intended.

'Are you going to do something with that before it burns all our bloody eyeballs out?'

I opened my eyes then wished that I hadn't. The glow from the knife was so bright that, for a moment, I panicked and was tempted to fling it away from me. 'Argh!' I yelped. Taking a deep breath, I brought the knife down over the wound in Keril's side and gently touched the tip to the demon's bloody scales. Immediately a wash of images assailed me – cut skin, moving blood, something that looked vaguely kidney shaped and other odd bits of tubing and liquids. I didn't understand what it all meant.

Taking a chance I talked directly to the knife. 'I can't make all this out, just fix anything that needs fixing, will you.' I forced the thought toward the knife and watched as the blue-white glow flowed gently into the prone body.

Keril seemed to light up like a Chinese lantern for a moment or two, but eventually the light faded and he opened his eyes.

Exhausted I sat in the mud next to him. 'How do you feel?' I asked.

He sat up and coughed. 'Like I've been run over by a herd of fast-moving caroras.'

'Well, that makes two of us, and I'm not even sure what caroras are.' I leant against the wall and put the knife away. 'Are you all fixed now?'

'I think so.' Keril climbed unsteadily to his feet. 'Oops, maybe not.' His right leg buckled beneath his weight.

'Let's have a look at that.' Belial stared at a deep cut in Keril's right leg. 'This was made by something either cursed

303

or angelic – it's no wonder Joe couldn't fix it. We still need to get you to a healer.'

I staggered to my feet. 'I'm really sorry, Keril, I did try.'

Belial took most of the Drekavak's weight and spoke to me over his shoulder. 'Well, you probably saved his life. It's just a good job this particular weapon only got his leg and wasn't lodged in his spleen.'

I nodded. 'Where did that horrible lot get a good weapon from?'

Belial shrugged. Keril was far heavier than he looked.

Hoisting the Drekavak between us we staggered out of the alley. 'Where the bloody hell are we?' Belial said.

I shrugged then apologised as Keril grunted – he was still losing a lot of blood. 'We've searched so many streets, I've got completely turned around,' I said. 'I have no idea how we get back.'

'Hold him for a moment.' Belial stepped out from beneath Keril's arm and walked swiftly around the corner.

'I've got to sit down.' Keril gasped.

Propping him up by a wall, I ripped off my sweatshirt and T-shirt, replacing the sweatshirt with a shudder as cold wet blood that I knew wasn't mine touched my skin. I ripped two long strips from my Status Quo T-shirt and rolled the rest of it into a ball.

'Sorry, mate,' I warned. 'I think this is going to hurt.'

Keril gave a quick nod then closed his eyes. He only moaned once as I packed my T-shirt into the wound and then bound it around his upper thigh with the strips. It must have hurt like hell; how he managed to stay awake I'll never know.

By the time Belial had returned, the makeshift bandage was soaked through and blood was, once again, running freely.

He stared down at the demon who was now fading in and out of consciousness. 'I've found a healers shop.'

Getting to my feet, I helped Belial get Keril up. 'How much blood does a Drekavak have?'

'I don't bloody know,' Belial answered waspishly as he

looked over his shoulder. 'But he's minus most of a gutter full and I can't see that being good for him, can you?'

'Well, how far is this healer?' I gasped. Keril, who was taking very little of his own weight, seemed to be getting heavier by the second.

'Just around the corner,' Belial said.

'So why did it take you so long to find it?'

'Because I came out of here and went the wrong way.' Belial winced and hoisted Keril into a higher position on his shoulder. 'I didn't see it until I was coming back.'

'Didn't you look both ways before crossing the street?'

Keril came round for a moment 'Will you two just fucking shut up?' With a small groan he passed out again.

Belial frowned and muttered, 'We'd better hurry.'

A nicely kept green door was set well back under a deep porch. As we burst through, almost taking it off its hinges, the man standing at the bench looked up startled. Then, with a jerk of his head, he indicated a cot beside the far wall.

He crossed the room in long strides and within seconds was easing off my makeshift bandage with a look of concern. 'Knife wound?' he asked without looking up.

'I'm not sure,' I said. 'I didn't get a look at the weapon.'

He laughed. 'Bit busy, were you?'

'Something like that.'

Belial had backed into the shadows and was leaning against the wall watching the healer, his head down and his arms folded.

'So can you help him?' I asked.

The tall man nodded. The piercings in his nose, ears and eyebrows and the bright spikes of red and black hair seemed incongruous with his gentle tone and manner. 'I think so.' He laid seven crystals in various locations on Keril's body: one on his forehead, one on his throat then on in a line down his body.

'What are those?' I asked.

'Important.' He began to hum, then stopped. 'Do you always ask this many questions? Why don't you go and sit over near Belial until I'm done here, OK?'

Belial snorted. 'I didn't think you'd recognised me, Galgaliel.'

The man just smiled and ignored us both.

As the humming increased, small items – bottles, jars and other more unidentifiable things – began to vibrate on the shelves at the back of the room. The dust on the floor rose in little puffs then sank back down as the humming rose and fell in both volume and pitch.

Belial winced and headed for the door. 'Come with me if you want to be able to think in ten minutes' time or stick your fingers in your ears,' he shouted as he made to leave.

I was tired; the chair was soft and I really couldn't be bothered to move. I nodded and waved as he headed out the shop.

'OK.' He grinned. 'Don't say I didn't warn you.'

It was an uncomfortable ten minutes or so. By the time Galgaliel had dropped his humming back down to a calm vibration, my jaw ached from clenching my teeth and my eyeballs felt as though they'd been taken out, washed in bleach and put back in the wrong way round. I had a headache which also rose and fell in tone every time I moved and my skin felt as though it had been rubbed down with sandpaper. Even my hair hurt.

'There we go.' Galgaliel nodded with satisfaction and turned to me with a grin. 'Belial bottled it, did he?'

I nodded carefully.

'Headache?' he asked.

Unwilling to nod again I gave him a single thumbs up and kept my eyes closed against the thousands of scintillating scotomas that danced like fireflies at the edges of my vision.

I felt him take my hand and press a rough fired clay cup into my palm.

'Drink that, it'll sort you out. It will also give you back some of the energy you spent doing that healing on your friend here.' He lifted the edge of Keril's tunic and had a look at the long white scar that now graced the demon's back. 'Quite a nice job.' He sounded genuine. 'I bet you feel like shit.'

Careful not to move too fast I gave him a single small nod – then, trying to control my shaking hand, brought the cup to my lips and drank. The thick liquid tasted of aniseed, lavender and had an alcoholic kick to it. A couple of ice cubes, a packet of cheese and onion crisps and a pickled egg or two and me and a bottle of this could easily spend a happy evening together.

Within less than a minute the headache and whirling lights had disappeared only to be replaced with a general euphoria and an unexplained urge to laugh, run and spin. I giggled as Belial stuck his head through the door; his face seemed to be covered in little blue flowers with bells at their centres. I could hear each one ringing independently but they all had a different note and, together, they played *Au Clair de la Lune* as he walked. While laughing at the flowers I noticed that the room had begun to fade.

*I'm in a dirty flat. I wander from room to room, spiders cluster in the corners and cockroaches scuttle over my bare toes. There are other people in the room; I should recognise them but I don't. I walk into the bathroom. Conjoined twins sit smiling in the bath. They are trying to entrap and distract me and smile as they eat handfuls of dried cannabis. Their teeth are sharp.*

'How much did you give him?' Belial bent down to take a closer look at me then pulled his head away quickly as I tried to grab his lower lip.

'Possibly a little too much.' Galgaliel didn't bother turning round from his study of his patient. 'If he tries to walk up the walls restrain him, would you?' He carefully placed a crystal into a bowl of water. Humming a gentle tune under his breath he busied himself cleaning away all the blood from around Keril's tiny pale scales on his abdomen. 'Don't worry,' he said. 'He'll snap out of it soon.'

*I'm standing on a bridge. Three homeless men and a woman are spitting over the sides into the river below. It's a competition. From each laughing mouth comes a never-ending string of saliva – it flares as it hits the water, four glowing strings that divide the water into lanes. Bakeneko tugs at my hand and, dragging me from the edge of the bridge, hands me a PVC cat mask. I shake my head – I don't want to wear it, but he keeps pushing it toward me …*

'How are you able to be here, Galgaliel?' Belial dragged up a plain wooden chair and, turning it around, sat astride with his arms folded across the back.

The tall man shrugged. 'I'd have thought that was obvious.' Galgaliel stared at his hands. 'I chose to fall. I am now one of the Fallen. My name will forever be spat upon by the Host and I'm forced to cure the descendants of murderers and cutthroats to enable me to live.' He paused. 'But life is still better than with the Host. What is it the humans say? "Same shit, different day." What's the difference?' He hummed a little louder and the crystal on Keril's navel lit up for a brief moment.

'Could you not?' Belial pinched the bridge of his nose. 'That humming of yours brings on monumental headaches, you know.'

*Metatron's office is now a gym. I step through the window, as flames lick the sky above the dark city. I need to get home. I'm on a train, people are running from the fire; it pushes them ahead of its boundaries – a flaming sheepdog easily guiding its woolly-headed charges.*

'The question really is, what are *you* doing back here?' Galgaliel leant on the cot and, folding his arms, he stared at Belial.

Belial said nothing.

'Let's ask your spaced-out little friend then, shall we?' Galgaliel said.

*I'm back in the flat and trying to pack. I need to leave with everyone else. My clothes are scattered, ripped into tatters and rags by the twins' sharp teeth. They have eaten all the cannabis and are now drinking long pink cocktails. They pick up crumbs and force them between my teeth. I'm so stoned I can't pack, I can't get away. I look out of the window and laugh at the flames. I'm going to die in the fire.*

Belial yawned and put his head in his hand. 'Well, I don't think you're going to get anything sensible out of *him* at the moment.'

The tall healer shrugged, then pushed himself away from the bed and squatted down in front of me. His eyes whirled in a mixture of amber, silver and gold; his smile stretched literally from ear to ear. He looked like the Cheshire cat. 'I didn't catch your name, my friend?' His smile detached itself from his face for a moment and swung sideways before settling back between his cheeks.

Oh! With his voice the dream flowed away. For a moment I was sad. I'd had an opportunity to escape but the fire had frightened me. I tried to concentrate on the man smiling at me and bullied myself to remember the question. He meant me – he wanted to know my name. Well, that was OK, I could tell him my name. A dark mass pressed down upon me and stopped my mouth. I couldn't think. Which name? Which name should I give him?

'His name's Joe.' Belial frowned over at us. 'Good grief, how long is he going to stay in that state?'

'Joe,' I said. 'Just Joe, that's all I've always been, just Joe. No one else in here, just me, just Joe.' Good God, I was funny, the sounds of "just Joe" fell off my tongue like licking syrup and I laughed and tried to catch some more. 'Just Joe, just Joe. Joey, that's me. Always wanted to be just Joe, never anything else, just Joe.' I felt suddenly sad. 'Never really him though, always tried to be Joe, but that's not me, is it?' I looked over at Belial. I didn't want to talk about names any more. Names were stupid, like labels. They made people treat you in a certain way – made them judge, made them angry. When you looked in a mirror you didn't see a name, you saw the person. What's in a name anyway?

'Joe!' Belial reached for my jacket and gave me a little shake. 'Do try and focus.'

Galgaliel pushed his hand away and smiled at me again. 'You're right, Joe, names aren't important.' He turned to look at Belial. 'Look at Belial – he wasn't always someone that shirked his responsibilities; he wasn't always the person that left an entire group of people to die of starvation and cold. Once he was the best of angels. Once he could be trusted.'

Belial's face twisted in fury and he leapt to his feet. His huge charcoal wings were held high above his head. Picking up his chair he threw it into the wall where it smashed, not only itself but a shelf of glassware. I watched as the deadly shards slowed, glistening and twisting like mirrors in water. I closed my eyes as they fell with infinite grace to the floor, bouncing and tinkling in a rain of deadly bells.

'My responsibilities?' Belial screamed. 'Why were they *my* responsibilities? They were *Lucifer's* responsibilities but he disappeared and I ended up in charge – it was a farce. There were people here that shouldn't have been. They'd done nothing wrong, so I let them go and waited for my punishment.' He shook his head as his wings drooped. 'I would have welcomed punishment – it would have shown that my father cared even that much for me, for the things I did, but none came.'

Galgaliel reached over a gentle thumb and, lifting one of my eyelids, frowned before turning back to the depressed fallen angel. 'You did the right thing, letting them go, but what about the ones you left behind?'

Belial looked up at him and shrugged.

Galgaliel's elegant, bronze-tipped cream wings snapped open as he clenched his fists by his thighs. He closed his eyes then spoke through gritted teeth. 'You condemned hundreds of people to live in a world with no escape, no water, no working government, no food, no structure and no hope.' Galgaliel towered over Belial who refused to look him in the eye. 'You condemned every one you left behind to a slow, lingering death. You walked away to make your new utopia and you left them to die.' The healer howled at Belial, 'How could you do that?' He ran a hand through his coloured hair. 'It's like a boy that doesn't understand the needs of an unwanted pet. So he puts it in a box and forgets about it.'

'They deserved it. They were all walking horrors.' Belial refused to look up from the floor.

'True, they were …' The healer scowled and thrust his face toward the wincing fallen angel. 'But even walking horrors have children, you know. I hope you wake up in the dark and think about those you left behind.' He clutched Belial by the shoulders and shook him, his serene face contorted with rage. 'Do you? Did you?' He shouted. 'Did you think about their children at all while you were building your new city? While you were walking in the sun, while you were buying sweets from your pretty stalls, while you were creating libraries and knowledge and spouting that crap about opportunities and working together.' Galgaliel paused to breathe for a moment. 'Did all that shit get overshadowed by the killing, the cannibalism, the despair, the plagues, the dirt and the madness that you left behind – that you so conveniently forgot about. Did it? Well, *did it*?' He pushed Belial back into the chair and walked over to his workbench where he poured a glass of orange liquid which he carried over to me.

I stared at him. His switches of mood frightened me.

'Come on, Joe,' he coaxed. 'Drink this and everything will be back to normal.'

I looked down at the drink. His long fingers were covering mine and he was gently guiding the glass toward my mouth. 'I promise it will be all right.' He smiled. I believed him and drank.

'I didn't know what to do.' Belial's voice, very quiet and slow, drifted toward us. 'Lucifer had gone, the demons were getting ready to leave, the damned were …'

He broke off for a moment; obviously he hadn't looked back for a number of years.

'God had created Earth, he'd brought in all the humans to populate his little tin town, but they weren't grateful enough, they didn't obey like the angels. They argued and challenged, created things of their own and strived to be more than they were. He didn't want that so he sent his angels down to tell them to behave. It didn't work. A lot of us liked the humans – they laughed and worked and sang. They were irreverent and funny, so some of us got more involved than we should and the Nephilim were born.

'God was so angry that he wiped everything from the face

311

of his play planet with one big storm – washed it up, if you like, and cleaned it out to start again. If I'd been bitter about it I would have accused him of having a tantrum like a spoilt child, but obviously that could never have been true. A group of humans were sent here to be punished and "corrected", but they were just doing what humans do best. It's not in their nature to obey mindlessly – it's almost impossible for them to have faith when they're so busy asking "why?"

'Lucifer was angrier than I'd ever seen him. His children had all been wiped out, the woman he loved, everything he'd enjoyed. All he knew ended up being swept away to make space for another "great plan". He spoke to us all – convinced us that we should complain, say something, do something; just for once we should take a stand.' He broke off and sat down again.

Galgaliel nodded. 'I know.' He raised his eyebrows at me, checking if I was OK. I just nodded – I didn't want to break Belial's concentration. This time I was just going to go with the headache. The room was back in focus and the bell-ringing flowers had all disappeared. It was blissful, I was even enjoying the pain.

'So here we all ended up – out of God's way, and out of his hair.' Belial took a deep breath. 'Most of the angels couldn't take it and just turned themselves off hoping that one day God would forgive them. Lucifer hung around for a while hating everything and then disappeared, which left me as the only archangel in charge. We tried to do what *He* wanted, but it was so hard. The humans that had been dumped here with us didn't deserve what was being done to them, so I let them go. But there were some I couldn't let out: they were so set on revenge – revenge on God, revenge on those that hadn't been put here. I was torn – torn between just letting go. I envied those of us that had chosen the path of sleep and I suppose ...' he hesitated. 'I suppose I was still trying to do as I was told.' He looked up at Galgaliel, his face pale and his eyes wet. 'In answer to your question, the answer is yes. Every night I wake up and wonder what I left behind. It's like indigestion – a pain in your chest – and the

312

guilt weighs everything down. I'm sorry, but I just didn't know what to do. And now Metatron has decided that he could do a better job.'

Galgaliel snorted. 'Now, there's a surprise.'

'He wants to drag Lucifer out of hiding, and remove him from the grand scheme of things, giving his power to his right-hand man.' Belial nodded over at me. 'He'll then take God's power and, with Joe under his thumb, he'll have it all, but we stopped him. We took Lucifer's hiding place and brought it here. I thought if we could get Lucifer to his Throne Room we could separate him from his vessel and that would also bring God back because both of those are better than what Metatron is suggesting, which is the utter annihilation of all worlds, all creatures. Blank slate, start again, and this time humans will be created "properly" – no more questions, no more discoveries: they'll be created to serve!'

Galgaliel dropped the glass he was holding. 'Lucifer's here?' He gasped. 'And obviously you're here.' He looked over at me. 'How many others are there?'

Belial shrugged. 'Lucifer, me, Joe, my daughter and a couple of others.'

'Great, just great.' Galgaliel laughed. 'And let me guess, they all have abilities– they're all "old blood"?' The tall healer dropped into a chair and put his head in his hands. 'What state is Lucifer in now?'

Belial grimaced. 'At the moment he's in human form – a podgy insurance salesman from the soft south.'

Galgaliel groaned. 'Wouldn't be much good in a scrap then.'

'Couldn't poke his way out of a wet paper bag without dropping it and tripping over it,' I piped up. 'What's all this about – why does it matter who we have with us?'

Silence fell for a couple of moments then Galgaliel gave an irritated moan. I couldn't make out the words he used but it sounded like 'Oh bloody hell.'

Shaking himself he got up and began pacing around his surgery. 'OK, the people left here didn't do well in the beginning. Eventually, things became more organised. A crude human council took charge and they worked out that food could be grown over the river, so those with the urge to make a place for themselves went over there and they traded back and forth. Councils changed, governments rose and fell, people had kids and, for about a thousand years, it all worked quite well.'

He paused for a moment. 'But it wasn't enough. As more discoveries were made, this current council took power and decided that they needed more interaction with the outside world. So they worked hard with the materials they had and found a way to open a door.'

Belial frowned and looked up. 'That's impossible,' he said. 'It would take immense power to open a doorway right through the layers.'

Galgaliel nodded. 'Immense,' he agreed. 'This whole world is built on a crystal framework, and the council discovered that certain crystals can hold energy like big batteries – and not only hold it, but increase it. You have to get out of here.' Galgaliel went to check on Keril. 'Although I think this one will have to stay with me.'

'We can't – one of our people has gone missing,' Belial said

The healer looked worried.

'Galgaliel, there's something you aren't telling me,' Belial snapped. 'What's going on?'

Galgaliel started stuffing odd items into a large rough woven bag. 'Does anyone else know you're here?' He didn't bother to look at us – just kept stuffing things in the bag.

'No,' Belial said.

'Yes.' I cut across him.

Both Belial and Galgaliel turned to look at me.

I tried to push my headache away. 'Do you remember that little hunter bloke?' I said. 'He turned round when Lucifer called your name?'

Galgaliel pinched the bridge of his nose between two fingers. 'This little hunter, did one of his mates wear a big watch?'

314

We both nodded and the healer groaned. 'That's Andre. He will have gone straight to the council and you can guarantee your missing friend didn't just disappear by chance. You've already been attacked once.' He waved a hand at Keril. 'It won't be long before they'll be back to try again.'

Belial and I looked at each other. 'Carly,' we said in unison.

'Tall girl, long red hair?' A voice sounded behind us.

We turned slowly to face a vast man that was currently angling his head to get through the door. His shaggy face, gentle eyes and happy smile were entirely at odds with his boiled leather armour and the enormous sword that hung from his belt.

He laughed at our silence – a deep booming sound that actually made your bones ache. 'Don't worry, we're taking very good care of her.'

I'd like to think I was still under the influence of whatever drug Galgaliel had given me to make me act in such an ill-considered manner, or I could have just been overconfident from winning my previous fight but, for whatever reason, I decided that talking wasn't going to accomplish anything. I drew my knife and went straight for the attack.

The huge man didn't even flinch until I came within arm's reach then, with one quick move, he merely reached out a hand and flicked my wrist, causing my knife to sail away into the shadows. Picking me up by the throat he pulled back his other hand and casually punched me in the face.

I saw stars (again), and my head exploded. Lifting me higher, the thug brought me eye to eye with him, smiled and hit me again. At least in this induced darkness I wasn't suffering from a headache any more.


Unfortunately, my returning headache was the first sign of returning consciousness.

'Hey, Belial!' Graham's voice sounded about a quarter inch away from my ear.

I groaned and tried very hard not to heave.

315

'Sorry.' He moderated his voice to a stage whisper and moved away from me. 'It looks as though he's waking up.'

'No, I'm not,' I croaked. 'Leave me alone – I'm dead.'

'You ought to be, you bloody stupid arse.' Belial's voice, beautifully modulated though it was, still sent shards of pain into the back of my skull. I heard footsteps then felt a gentle kick in the backside. 'What on earth possessed you to attack a seven-foot barbarian with a butter knife?'

I cracked open an eye and winced as I noted Belial's split cheek, swollen eyes and bloody lip. 'Ouch,' I said. 'Doesn't look like you did that well either.'

Belial shrugged and slid down the wall beside me. 'We might have been all right if there hadn't been another six outside.'

I coughed and dragged myself into a sitting position. 'Where are we?'

'Take a wild guess.' He leant his head back and stared up at the ceiling.

I looked around. There wasn't really that much to see: dirt floor, rock walls on three sides, metal bars on the fourth. He was right – it didn't take that much imagination to work it all out.

A figure stepped out of the shadows. With his lank hair flat against his head, both eyes blackened and an obviously broken nose, poor Farr looked very unhappy.

'I'm really sorry, Joe.' He gingerly probed his broken nose and winced. 'This is all my fault.'

I nodded, carefully. 'Probably.' I agreed.

He looked up at me with a hurt expression.

I laughed and reached out a hand for him to help me up. 'It's just nice that it's not my fault for once – it's wonderful to have someone else to blame.' I staggered as I gained my feet; he reached out and steadied me. 'Don't worry about it.' I held onto his shoulder. 'They would have got us anyway.'

Farr looked at me for a moment then, with a wry smile, nodded. I looked around the shadowy cell trying to find Carly.

'Everybody?' I peered hard into the gloom. 'Is everyone

all right?'

Belial nodded. 'Carly, Parity and Una are in the next cell. We're all here except Keril. Galgaliel screamed enough to convince the thugs that his injuries were so bad he'd die if he was left alone, so they left him alone and laughed about it.' He sighed. 'He should be OK.'

Footsteps echoing down the stone passage stopped the conversation.

A group dressed in dark clothing came to a halt outside the cell door. Several men and women stared through the bars at us. I felt like a monkey at the zoo.

The silence stretched on – nobody moved or spoke. Belial ignored the spectators and continued his conversation. 'Carly's a little upset though.'

I grinned. 'I'll tell her I'm fine.'

'They shaved her head.' Belial ignored those standing beyond the door. 'I think she's going to be *very* upset when she gets her hands on someone.'

'Vermin.' One of the women outside the cell door had a strong accent. She sounded Swiss or possibly Dutch. 'Long hair breeds vermin in here and, if it's full of fleas, I won't be able to use it.' She stretched her face into what could have been a smile. 'I think I will have it made into a wig.' She stared over at Galgaliel. 'It's just a shame we won't have you around any more. You always made the best soaps.'

Galgaliel stepped forward with a gentle smile. 'Let me out and I'll make that wig for you.' He ignored my yelp. 'Then, I'll strangle you with it.'

The woman looked shocked for just a moment. She snarled and stepped toward the bars. 'It's a shame you won't get the chance,' she said.

Carly's hair had gone: I couldn't believe it – those long red locks, the smell of her watermelon shampoo that always made me think of summer picnics. Hair that I always wanted to touch, to smell. Hair that created a halo around her head at sunset or at dawn.

While Galgaliel and the woman were trading insults I leant on the bars and drooped, coughing and shuddering. She studied me for a moment and then turned to the others.

'Why are we bothering with this one?' She bent down to sneer at me. 'It's nothing special and it's obviously sick.'

I groaned and coughed again, letting a string of drool fall from my lips. She gazed at me with a slightly disgusted look. As she bent her head to study my pain, I reached through the bars and snatched a handful of her long dark hair. Twisting it around my hand, I braced a foot against the bars and heaved backward. There was a wet ripping sound and the woman screamed as her hair and a fair amount of scalp came away in my hand.

I threw the wet handful toward Galgaliel. 'Here, you can use that.' I laughed. The woman, still screaming, put her hand to her bleeding head and fled down the corridor.

A tall man shook his head. 'You really are keeping low company, Belial,' he said. 'Oh how the mighty have fallen.' A thick snake, banded in yellow and green, slithered across his shoulders. He stroked it gently as he glared at the sneering demon lord.

'Andromalius.' Belial dusted himself off and gazed blankly through the bars. 'At least I actually fell and then had the courage to live with it. I didn't need to turn myself off and sulk in a stone box for a thousand years.' Studying his nails he leant on the bars then looked up at those standing on the other side. 'What's the matter? Did you get bored? Were you waiting for our father to come and get you – to forgive you?'

The tall being laughed and addressed the snake which flicked a long mauve tongue in and out as though tasting the air. 'I realised that I wasn't going to be forgiven.' He pulled the hissing creature from his dark hair and turned it to face him. The reptile flicked its forked tongue across his lip. 'There was nothing for me to do but make the best of the situation. I woke up some of the others and we decided that it was better to be big fish in a little pond than servants.'

Belial snorted. 'And who did you choose to help you with this little endeavour?' He nodded to a thin man who was dressed in green. He'd shaved his hair down the sides leaving only a single row of white blond dreadlocks that flopped like a broken picket fence across his bony scalp. Realising that Belial was addressing him, his odd golden eyes flicked back and forth seeking to avoid the other's baleful glare. 'Lerajie … Looks like your daughters finally managed to toss your depraved arse out of Faery then?'

Fiddling with a beautifully carved longbow the ex-angel ignored him, a slight tightening of his lips the only indication that he had heard him at all.

'Rahab, what a surprise …' Belial sneered at a small, muscular angel that glared back at him from beneath eyebrows that were grey and bushy. 'And here we have Caim and Zepar.' Two angels that appeared in the form of teenage boys blushed and looked away.

Belial stared at them all for a moment. 'I would rather be demon and lose my name than be allied with you pathetic lot.'

With a scream of rage, the one Belial had named as Rahab leapt toward the bars, sword in hand. Andromalius, quick to react, grabbed him by the arm and spun him about. 'No,' he said quietly. 'We need them all in one piece.' The tall man smiled at Belial and shrugged. His long silk shirt fluttered in the cold breeze that sashayed through the prison. 'Say what you like.' He stroked the snake which hissed gently and wrapped itself around his wrist. 'When you're gone, you can be sure your words will be taken to heart – they will probably cut us to the quick.'

Laughing, he turned and walked away. His companions followed him without a backward glance.

Graham walked over and picked up the lank handful of hair. 'That is probably the most disgusting thing I've ever seen.'

Galgaliel was leaning with his head on the bars, shoulders shaking. For a moment I thought he was crying. Hurriedly taking the hair from Graham's hands I threw it back through the bars and hurried over to him. 'Sorry.' I reached over to grasp his shoulder. 'I just loved Carly's hair so much. It made me so angry …'

319

Galgaliel raised his face. There were indeed tears on his hollow cheeks, but his big green eyes were alive with laughter. 'You just pulled half of Gomory's hair out,' he spluttered.

I shrugged. 'Who?'

The angel took a couple of moments to get his emotions back under control. 'She's very proud of her beauty.' He took a long look at the hair lying like roadkill on the floor and began to laugh again. 'Her biggest vanity was her hair. She pinned it up with jewels, she brushed it till it shone. She's always coming to me to make her soap or conditioner.' He paused for a moment. 'We're all going to die in agony but at least I'll have the last laugh when I see her wearing a bloody hat!'

Belial shook his head. 'What are they doing here?'

Galgaliel looked up at him. 'Making a little empire it seems.' He put a hand on Belial's shoulder, 'You turning up will have thrown a huge spanner in the works. However calm they appear I'm fairly sure they must be panicking about now.'

'Why?' I kept looking at the hank of hair lying outside the cell. I was a little disgusted with myself. The hank of dull hair lay in a small pool of blood. Thin, limp and dead, it was hardly the great trophy I'd hoped for.

'Because tonight is the festival.' Galgaliel frowned. He looked around at our blank faces and began to laugh. 'You really are here, on the wrong day, the wrong time and in the wrong place, aren't you?' he said. 'Every year, the council puts out an invitation for one child from every household to be awarded the special honour of studying away from here. Each child tells the council what they would like to study and the council pledges to find them a loving family that wants to take on an apprentice to train.' He looked around at us. 'You with me so far?' He glanced at me. 'For you, Joe, I'll try and keep the words small.'

'Thanks a bunch.'

'Anyway, there's a big festival with food, drink, dancing – all that sort of thing. The children get paraded around, they say goodbye to everyone and promise to send letters home then they all get ushered into the bowl with the council.'

'What's the bowl?' I asked.

The angel frowned at being interrupted. 'It's a huge natural pit of moldavite. It's one of the crystals that amplifies and holds power and this is where the gateway has been set up.' He looked down at the dirt. 'Now, where was I ...' he murmured. 'The children go into the bowl and the gates are closed, but it doesn't matter. You can see the glow of the rift when it opens and, when the doors are released, the first traders of the year come through and the children have gone off to pastures new.'

Belial shook his head. 'So what's the problem?'

'Over the last two or three years, it seems as though the birth rate here has dropped.' Galgaliel got to his feet and began pacing the cell. 'So last year there were only about 60 kids who applied to the apprenticeship programme, and when we ran out of power for the gate about three months ago, I began to put two and two together. This year it's worse and there are only 20 children.' He shrugged. 'I know Gomory's worried because she started complaining about my prices. She also implied that I needed to be nice to her, otherwise I could find myself in a sticky situation. She happily informed me that I'd only been left alone because of the services I provide and that the time might come when they don't need me any more. She said that maybe they could find a better use for me. Then you lot come along, leaking power like a whole herd of sieves, just in time for the festival.'

'I don't get it.' I just knew I was missing something.

Belial sighed. 'Kids have the longest life ahead of them, Joe. How much power do you think you'd get if you could take their lives and use them as an energy source?'

He waited patiently for the penny to drop and, when it didn't, he scrubbed a hand through his hair, grimacing as his fingers knocked a bruise. 'I may be wrong,' he said, 'but I think Galgaliel's suggesting that they're managing to extract the children's life energy and transfer it into the crystal, which holds it until they need to open a gateway.'

'That's hideous! They're angels – they wouldn't do that.' I thought about it for a moment and then, finally, the other penny dropped. 'There aren't enough kids for them, so now they want to use us instead?'

Galgaliel gave me a short round of slow applause. 'Give the boy a cigar,' he said. He glanced up at Belial. 'The only thing I can't work out is how they're doing it.' He rubbed his dirty neck then looked down at his hand and sighed.

'Don't let it bother you too much. I think we'll find out soon enough.' Belial settled back against the wall and closed his eyes. 'Wake me when it's all over.'

'Well, I don't see any reason to sit around here and take what's coming to us,' I said. Closing my eyes, I firmly decided that I was in the next cell with Carly. I opened my eyes with a grin and sighed as I realised the same crowd were still around me. They were all looking at me curiously.

Farr ran his hand over the walls. 'These seem to be made of stone, but it feels wrong. It's almost as if it's dead – I've never felt anything like it before.'

Belial laughed. 'Did you really think I'd still be here if I had any choice in the matter?'

There didn't seem much point in talking after that.

Although there were no windows in that cramped, dingy cell, we could tell when night fell. The approaching dark brought with it an almost palpable feeling of expectation.

The sound of a key turning in a lock brought us all to our feet.

Carly, Parity and Una were taken out of their cell and paraded round to stand in front of us. Each had a personal guard who held a long knife to their throats. 'We'd really like to get you there all in one piece.'

One guard ran a rough hand over Carly's shorn head. 'Don't let's have any trouble now, eh?'

I tried to smile at Carly but she avoided my eyes – her shorn head made her look about 12 years old. Parity stared unseeing at the wall. Only Una seemed unfazed by the threatening behaviour of her captors. She gabbled on about the cell and that she was cold and hungry and thirsty.

We walked in a line – one woman at the front, two women at the back – through what seemed to be miles of featureless stone corridors. Most of it had been left to decay. The walls were crumbling in some places and, farther down the passage, rusted cell doors hung askew from broken hinges. The entire place smelt of damp and fungus. Eventually we were brought to a halt before a strong wooden door. It looked out of place in this crumbling ruin. The deep red wood shone and in the candlelight looked almost wet. Someone had spent hours polishing that door.

The guard holding Carly shuddered slightly then wiped his palm down his trousers a couple of times before finally raising it to knock.

Three staccato raps echoed down the corridors.

'Let me go.' A soft whisper swirled around the passage, ebbing and flowing as it stretched away only to be dragged back. 'Let me go, let me go, let me go ...' The words were repeated time and again, one long running monologue of begging and torment. 'Let me go, let me go ...'

Farr straightened and cocked his head to one side. His mouth dropped open and he swallowed hard. Closing his eyes he began to mutter under his breath. Graham stepped to his side and gripped his wrist, breaking his concentration. 'You mustn't do that,' he said in an urgent whisper.

Belial stood upright and stared around trying to follow the path of the unseen whisperer. 'Monstrous,' he murmured.

'What is it?' Galgaliel asked Graham then blanched as he realised the change in the man. He bowed his head. 'Lord,' he acknowledged.

Lucifer, still trying to follow the whispering, leant on the wall with his head on one side. 'Galgaliel.' He gave the healer a huge grin. 'Long time no see.' He tore his attention from the whisperer to peer at the angel. 'Looking a bit rough, my friend. What happened to that fantastic long hair of yours?'

Greatly daring – or getting to the point where I just didn't care any more – I nudged Lucifer. 'I don't think this is the time for *them* ...' I nodded to the guards who were watching us '... to find out you don't know anything about insurance.'

Lucifer laughed; it was a deep and entirely happy sound. 'Who says I don't know anything about insurance?' He turned from Galgaliel to stare at me, his dark eyes unblinking. 'I'm the ultimate insurance, aren't I, Joe?' He snorted and went back to trying to track the path of the whispering voice. 'Keep me with you and you make sure Metatron doesn't bother you – isn't that the quintessential meaning of insurance?' He raised his eyebrows and smiled. 'Of course, no one has bothered to ask what I want.'

'Well, we might get to do that if you hung around long enough to talk to.' I really was getting to the end of my tether. The whispering and the echoes had now joined forces, clashing to form a susurrating cacophony which felt as though it was turning your brain inside out.

'Oh a backbone, how amazing!' Lucifer gave me a wide smile. 'I thought you didn't want me around?'

I figured as I was going to be made into a battery anyway, I didn't really have anything to lose. 'You could get us out of here, couldn't you?'

One of the guards looked over with a frown and I shut my mouth with a snap.

Lucifer put his arm around my shoulders and, leaning close, he hissed into my ear, 'Yes, I could, but you lot brought me here – you dragged my host kicking and screaming out of his life and into Hell.' He bumped my head hard with his own. 'And now you have the audacity to ask me to save your worthless self?' Stepping back he stared at me for a moment then ran a sharp fingernail over my sweating top lip. He held it up for me to look at. 'People sweat for two reasons: heat and lies.' He wiped his finger down his jeans and breathed out and watched his breath condense in the cold of the tunnel. 'Hmm, not exactly hot in here, is it?'

I winced as blood and salt mixed.

'What's the matter, Joe? Don't you have the courage of your convictions? Don't you think you're doing the "right" thing?' He snorted a laugh; there was no humour in the sound. 'Or, by some strange coincidence, are you just going along with what everyone else tells you to do?'

I twisted out from under his arm and glared back at him. 'I was presented with two options – neither of them was great. I went with the one that –'

Lucifer cut across my little speech. 'Suited you best?'

'At least I did *something*.' I was aware that the rest of the group were staring at us. Behind Lucifer's back I could see Belial shaking his head and making "For fuck's sake, shut up" motions. I ignored him. 'Some of us didn't have the opportunity to hide away like a child under the bed. Some of us had to live with the dice that were thrown.'

Belial gave a tiny groan and ran a shaky hand through his hair.

Lucifer just stared at me.

I stared back, arms folded defiantly. Leaning against the damp wall, there wasn't anywhere I could go, so I might as well pretend I wasn't about to need new underwear.

Lucifer's lips whitened as he pressed them together. His almost black eyes narrowed and his nostrils flared.

I swallowed; there seemed to be a lump in my throat.

'Maybe …' The Lord of Hell spoke through gritted teeth, '… I *am* saving your arse despite being dragged around like someone's toy and you're just too stupid to notice.' He took a step toward me and thrust his face forward until it was only inches away from my own. 'And maybe,' he went on quietly, 'it's not *your* arse I'm saving – there are other people here, you know? Believe it or not, the world does not revolve around *you*!'

As I opened my mouth Belial stepped around the angry ex-archangel. He stepped hard on my foot before turning to face Lucifer. 'Is that what I think it is?' he asked.

Lucifer peeled his gaze away from me and stared up at the ceiling as he listened to the begging whispers that drifted about us. Head cocked on one side, he walked over to the polished door. Ignoring the guards who were standing with their hands over their ears, the Father of Lies placed his left hand against the wood of the door and gave it a gentle stroke.

325

'I'm here,' he whispered. 'Be free.'

The whispers grew in force and form; I could now *feel* them as they moved. A warm wind whirled round and round. Dust and small stones rose in a spiral, eventually coalescing into the hazy form of a teenage girl – pale and drawn. Her long hair, once blonde, hung lank and lifeless in a moist mat that stuck to her bony shoulders. I could see the bumps of her spine as it moved against the material of her featureless ivory dress.

She stared at her feet then, with a smile, walked over to Lucifer. Taking his face in her hands she gave him a kiss. 'Thank you,' she whispered. Then, still smiling, she collapsed back into dust and earth. All was still.

'Well, come on then.' Lucifer indicated the door.

One of the guards gingerly reached for the handle.

'Oh, for crying out loud.' Lucifer pulled him out of the way and, giving the heavy metal ring a twist, pushed open the door.

The guard dragged Carly's head back and pressed his knife to her throat. A line of garnet beads appeared livid against her pale skin. Belial and I both stepped forward. Lucifer held up his hand. 'Don't bother threatening me.' He stared at the guard who blinked the sweat out of his eyes. 'Believe me when I tell you that I really couldn't care less if you kill the lot of them.' He stared at the man until he dropped his eyes and focused on his knife. 'But if it's that important to you,' Lucifer carried on. 'Please … after you.' He swept into an elegant bow and gestured for the man to precede him through the door. He remained in this bowed position as we all walked through.

'Liar, liar, pants on fire!' Una sang up at him as she skipped past, ducking beneath his lowered head.

For just a moment I was sure I saw the Morning Star break into a small smile.

As we began climbing the stone steps toward the noisy crowd I turned back to him. 'What was that about with the door?'

Lucifer glowered at me for a moment and then in one of

those mercurial mood swings of his gave me a big grin. 'Have you heard of the wood of suicides?' he asked.

I nodded. 'Galgaliel said something about it being chopped down?'

'Well, apart from being poorly named, I created that wood,' he explained. 'It was so long ago and an odd act of kindness.' He snorted. 'Now you can see what a waste of time *that* was. It really is true that no good deed ever goes unpunished.'

'You have an odd idea of *kindness*.' I concentrated on climbing the slippery stone steps. 'How can it be kind to turn people into trees?'

Lucifer laughed. 'People who want to commit suicide are racked with so many emotions.' He pondered for a moment then went on. 'Guilt because they know they'll hurt their families, feelings of failure and of everything being pointless, terrible feelings of being trapped. Then there are all the reasons they want to end it – that they can't live up to other people's expectations. Depression, illnesses like schizophrenia – it's really difficult to deny those voices, you know. Some of them don't want to die but they really can't cope with living. So the wood offered them a safe halfway environment; somewhere to exist between the states of living and dead. Those feelings don't just go away, you know – they have to be faced, and for some that can take a very long time.'

He climbed in silence for a moment. 'That young girl attempted to starve herself to death, just because she felt it would make her prettier which, in turn, might make people accept some of her other stranger gifts. These people weren't sinners – they were the way they were because of what we did. But it was God's will that if they actually succeeded in killing themselves they'd be denied Heaven.' He bit his lip. 'I didn't manage to get them all. There were some that managed to do what they set out to do. But my tiny forest was made from those that were going to succeed but hadn't managed yet. Forcibly immobilised for a period of time, they would have as long as they needed to work it all out. Some stayed as trees for hundreds of years, some came to terms with their lot and fell with the winter storms, but they were all at peace.' His voice became harder. 'But none of them – not one – were destined to become furniture, or doors or firewood.'

'Oh.' I balked at the idea of a living door, its body mangled and chopped up then reformed into something that suited others – something that had a use. It was the ultimate rape and violation. In a strange sort of way it was exactly what had plagued them while they'd been alive, but in these forms they really were trapped – and for ever.

As I stepped out through the hole I took a deep breath of the clean night air and looked around. Hundreds of faces stared back at me; none of them looked happy.

'Don't say anything,' Lucifer warned. 'Just look stupid.' He paused for a moment, peered at me then grinned. 'Or more stupid,' he amended.

'These people came to take what we have.' The strong voice of a man carried over the crowd. 'They came to steal and to destroy. They don't want us to have a working government and they don't want us trading with the outside world. They want to take us back to the dark ages.' He paused for a moment to let that sink in. 'What should we do with these people?'

Belial shook his head. 'Andromalius – he always could talk a good fucking fight.'

'Send them out! Send them out!' The chants of the crowd became clearer as the guards pushed us along the path toward a huge metal gate.

'Do we want them here?' Rahab called out.

'No!' The crowd roared back.

'Do we send a clear message to those who would try to take our hard-won liberty away?'

'Yes!' The crowd was completely with the speaker. As we walked through the crowd, some reached out and slapped at us or pushed us. Jeering faces and braying mouths covered us with spittle and insults.

I waited for Lucifer to do something destructive, but he just sauntered along with a slight smile on his face. He could have been strolling along a beach at sunset.

Before us, two guards hauled on the handles of the great door. It swung outwards on silent hinges. Through the open gateway I could see a huge empty expanse.

I took a good look around as I was prodded forward. Carved from what appeared to be olive-green glass, I could understand why they called it the bowl. There were no edges or straight lines and the walls curved high above our heads. The illusion that it was leaning toward us was overwhelming. A deep humming tickled my toes and seemed to push upward through my calves. My whole body seemed to vibrate and I felt more than a little nauseous.

Carly was finally released as her captors backed toward the gate. She scuttled over to my side, pulling the hood of her grey sweatshirt over her head as she ran.

I crushed her into my chest and, burying my face in her neck, took the time to breathe in her smell. Reaching up I pushed the hood from her head and ran my fingers through her shorn locks. It looked as though someone had hacked it off with a knife; some of it was less than a couple of centimetres, while other strands were longer. I smiled at her then leant down and kissed her. 'You look like an elf,' I said. 'I like it.'

She kissed me with trembling lips, then, pulling away, she looked down at the ground. 'I know elves,' she said. 'I don't think that's the compliment you think it is.' Sniffing, she gave me a watery smile then pulled her hood up again.

I wanted more time with her but a deep, slow drumbeat began to guide the vibrations. The gate opened again and the five council members paraded through the inside of the huge crystal. They positioned themselves at equal points around the perimeter, standing on five black stone discs that formed the points of a pentacle that had been deeply carved into the crystal floor.

Andromalius raised his hands and began to chant. I couldn't make out any words but it seemed to be a recurring set of syllables that one by one the others took up, repeating the same nonsense sounds over and over to the beat of the drum.

'What was that?' Parity jumped slightly and stared at her feet.

We all looked into the glass floor. Flashes of green-white light seemed to swirl and twist within the crystal. It followed the valleys and hills that were naturally part of the stone, exploding outward in balls of radiance at odd intervals. Some of the lights danced through the walls, backlighting the chanting council members turning them into silhouettes. I felt my legs begin to shake and not just from the vibrations.

I tried to see where it was all emanating from. The lights seemed to flash from nowhere but every time the crystal lit up I could see darkened patches – small human shapes that, like flies in amber, were held deep within the crystal heart. There was layer upon layer of them – tiny used-up husks. That well-known battery rabbit would have cried and changed its career.

Lucifer put a hand on my shoulder. 'Do you trust me?' he shouted above the rising wind and the thundering drums.

'No!' I pushed his hand away. 'I really can't emphasise enough how much I absolutely do *not* trust you.'

He threw his head back and laughed. 'Probably wise,' he replied. His now almost completely white hair began to stand away from his head. I heard Una laugh. 'We need to stand in a circle.' He made motions with his hands as he tried to get his point across over the strengthening wind and vibrations that buffeted our little group.

'Why?' I bellowed back.

'Joe.' He studied me for a moment then shouted into my face. 'You used to trust me, you used to agree with me and you used to just take it for granted that I would *never* let you down.' He stepped forward and grabbed my shoulders. 'I know you don't remember, but you just have to do as I say.' He stared at me. 'Come on, what have you got to lose right now?'

I wanted to shout "No". I wanted to push him away. The wind had now risen to a howling gale and we huddled together, trying to brace ourselves, one against another in an

330

effort to stop ourselves tumbling away across the crystal bowl. Beneath our feet, the lights had now settled into a blanket glow which pulsed with a heartbeat rhythm. As I struggled with my thoughts the glow reached the top of the bowl and shot into the sky, blocking out the strange array of stars.

'I just want to give them exactly what they're attempting to steal.' Lucifer, hidden in the middle of us, sneaked a furtive glance at the chanting figures who had now worked themselves into almost as great a frenzy as the wind they summoned. 'Please.' He clenched his fist. 'I want this to stop as much as you do and, more to the point, Belial needs this to stop. He needs to succeed at something – especially something that saves children.'

Well, whatever he wanted to do, it certainly couldn't be much worse than what the council had planned. With a quick nod I held both hands out and grasped those next to me. Carly gripped my fingers hard, her eyes closed in a pale, unhappy face.

Lucifer physically manoeuvred Farr into the very centre of circle, where he stood alone and small. Lucifer held his shoulders and gave the frightened man a small shake. 'Bring it all back,' Lucifer shouted at him. 'Go as deep and as old as you can and see what you find – then bring it back.' The Lord of Lies gave the quaking young necromancer an encouraging squeeze. 'You don't have any restraints any more. Just let it all out.'

Farr swallowed convulsively then, licking his lips, he gave a single tiny nod.

With a final glance at the chanting council members, Lucifer positioned himself, Belial and Galgaliel at the very outer edge of the group. 'They want our life force?' he screamed above the howling wind and the monotonous chanting. 'Let's give them what they want!'

All three angels spread their wings. Transforming into full Host they stretched and rippled. The most perfect of forms, it was so easy to see that humans were but a poor replica of these incredibly beautiful beings, like a child's drawing next to a Van Gogh. So beautiful they took your breath away. The glow from the bowl highlighted sculpted naked bodies and shining wings that blurred with heat and power: Belial, purple and green tinged like a raven; Galgaliel, bronze and cream; and Lucifer, so dark that even the light seemed to spurn him giving him a dark aura. Each angel rose above us, face turned towards the heavens, mouths open in silent screams. Slowly joining wing tip to wing tip, they created a multi-toned barrier. Belial laid his hands on both mine and Carly's shoulders, Galgaliel held onto Parity. Lucifer loomed behind Una, his long, elegant hands heavy on her shoulders. She gave a delighted giggle. Then they began to draw energy.

Lucifer looked over at Farr who was standing alone, white faced and panicked in the centre of the circle. 'Now, Farr!' Lucifer bellowed.

Farr thinned his lips, stopped shaking, took a deep breath, closed his eyes, raised his hands and began a deep, commanding chant of his own. So totally at odds with that coming from the council, it sent ripples and shudders through the crystal beneath our feet as the stone was bombarded by different tones.

It was an odd feeling, like the sinking feeling of bare feet in sand as the tide tries to take you away. It was a sucking, drawing sensation. None of this really described the loss of life force we were experiencing, but it was the best I could come up with.

Strands of palest pink were pulled from each of us to form a twisted rope that thickened and danced in the centre of the circle. It was like watching a bellydancer sensuously swaying and moving; it gyrated as more and more of our life was forced into the column.

Farr, locked within his chant, didn't even notice that he was standing in the middle of a sparkling column of twisting, humming energy but his voice became deeper, more demanding. Whatever he was reaching out to, he wasn't asking it to obey – he was damn well telling it.

From the sides of the bowl, the reedy chanting of the councillors faltered then stopped as they finally noticed that things were suddenly horribly awry. Cracks appeared beneath our feet, running quietly throughout the bowl. In the odd silences that occurred between Farr's deep chanting and the howling gusts of wind, you could hear tiny pops and cracks as the stressed crystal began to give way under the almost unimaginable pressure of the energies forcing their way into it.

It seemed as though we had stood there for hours, each of us becoming weaker as Lucifer and the other angels used us up. I struggled to turn my head to look at Carly. Huge shadows had appeared beneath her glazed eyes and she shook with the rigours of one who was on the point of collapse.

I stared past Carly's head and frowned as a dark cloud began to form behind Andromalius. It billowed and flowed, reaching upward and outward, darkening and thickening with each second that passed. Struggling to turn my head, I moved my gaze to the angel Belial had named as Lerajie. The same cloud was forming behind him and all of the others – none of them had noticed their own problems as they were too busy watching the other council members.

Slowly the edges of each cloud became defined and recognisable. Five huge dragon-shaped clouds of smoke slowly became the stinking, rotting corpses of dragons, then moved on to become living, vibrant and terrifying creatures. Each animal had a ten-metre wingspan and dead, mother-of-pearl eyes. I watched as the council members finally realised what was standing behind them, then screamed and tried to run. I wanted to laugh but I just didn't have the energy to feel any emotion at all. I felt as if I could see it all happening to someone else and I knew I should be terrified but I just couldn't be bothered.

The dragons screamed into the bowl, their open mouths showing glistening teeth and long whip-like tongues that were suddenly obscured by fire. A thundering, screaming inferno swept across the bowl. I stared, incurious, as it howled toward me. The rolling orange and black wave engulfed the floor of the bowl forcing itself into the minute cracks, ripping them open and giving the fire a million paths through which to burn. All three angels brought their wings to bear, creating a shield which diverted the fire away from our group. Smoking and coughing, the angels reassumed their positions. I stared down at my feet. Below my boots the fire raged, flickering within the crystal, rolling like blood within the veins and arteries of the bowl. Dimly I heard Lucifer's voice.

'Now!' he screamed. The word echoed above the howls of the burning council as they twisted and turned, each trying to escape the fate Lucifer had created for them. That single word echoed round and round the bowl. Louder than the wind, the chanting, the roar of our own twisting creation and the thunder of fire that single word was so intense I imagined it would have been heard across Hell – and perhaps many worlds beyond it.

All three angels leapt for the sky. High above our heads they joined and, catching the pink cascade of energy they'd created, stolen and forged, they blocked its upward path and forced it back toward us. With their wings forming a net they plunged to the ground. Faster and faster they fell, pushing the pink wave before them. The energy moved like water back toward the crystal, the angels guiding it, containing it. With a last push they crushed it into the bowl, forcing it deep into the crystal with the sound of a thousand broken vases. I watched as the pink energy merged with the fire already contained within the crystal heart, ripping it into wheels of red, orange and pink. Satisfied with their dive, the angels waited until the last possible second before altering course. Wings outstretched to their fullest, they soared across the floor of the bowl. Galgaliel, heading straight toward Una, veered to avoid her and caught a wing tip on the ground. He tumbled, a catherine wheel of bronze, cream and exploding feathers to land, broken and twisted on the smoking floor of the bowl.

Parity struggled to turn toward him, obviously intending to go to his aid. However, before she could take a step, the floor began to shake. Gentle tremors began to ripple beneath us. These increased until it became impossible to stand and, still holding hands, we huddled together in a heap.

The explosion, when it came, was almost silent. It certainly silenced everything around us – or maybe I'd just gone completely deaf ... I wasn't absolutely sure.

The bowl bulged in several places then heaved upwards vomiting light, fire and crystal shards in a shockwave that wiped out everything in its path. Cracks and fissures split and exploded; some created deep crevices and some created peaks which snapped and splintered, sending razor-sharp slivers high into the air. These were picked up by the still howling wind and sent slicing across the bowl. I watched, dumb with terror, as the glittering wave of natural weapons swept, spinning and twisting, toward us. Belial and Lucifer pushed us flat and, spreading their wings above us all, created a shelter beneath which we huddled. I firmly squashed the temptation to pray; I doubted it would do any of us any good.

Shards of crystal spun crazily around us until, finally, the whole thing reached critical mass and blasted outward with the roar of a thousand horns, the thunder of runaway animals and deadly soft horror of an avalanche. Then, for a brief moment, there was silence which was shattered by the sharp, single sound of a well-cracked whip. At the sudden sound Carly gasped and screamed as the earth tore itself apart to reveal its very core.

Crystal shards beneath our feet began to vibrate then flow like dry sand into the fracture. A dull red glow suffused the flowing dust, becoming more intense as everything around us was pulled toward the widening crevasse.

'Shit.' Belial flung his wings out and none too gently pushed us away from the sucking chasm.

Lucifer added his wings to the barrier and, between them, they covered us again as we watched every single dull shattered shard, dirt, dust and the blackened corpses of the council members disappear into the ground. Galgaliel, still unconscious, also began to move. Dragged across the stone by the screaming maelstrom he did nothing to save himself. As he slid past, I heard Lucifer swear, then with a lunge he grabbed the healer's ankle and held on tight. With eyes shut and other hand linked with Belial's he held fast until, with another grinding crack, the chasm closed leaving only silence, sparse clean rock and a ringing in all our ears that felt as though it would last for ever.

The two conscious angels furled their wings shut to sit on the ground, both breathing hard. Lucifer was covered in tiny cuts which bled profusely; his eyes were very white in the mask of blood. He sighed, coughed and then fell over to lie on his back. 'That was actually rather fun.' He chuckled occasionally when he could muster the breath to indulge.

'*Fun*!' Belial rolled over to lean on one elbow. 'Once again you failed to tell me what you were going to do. We're lucky to be alive, you inconsiderate, meddling, overzealous, stupid son of a …'

But it was too late. Lucifer had gone and Graham, staring at his own bloodied hands, ducked as Belial screamed at him. 'What did I miss this time?' he wailed. 'What happened? Why am I covered in blood? What did I do?'

Carly began to giggle.

Parity groaned and, staggering to her feet, headed over to Galgaliel. She turned him over, obviously fearing the worst. He, like the other angels, was a mass of bloody cuts and bruises. He groaned and must have said something very unangelic under his breath as Parity looked at first shocked then howled with laughter. Helping him to sit up she gently started to pull crystal splinters from his flesh. He swore at every tug.

Eventually we all managed to get to our feet and turned to face the silent crowd that had gathered at the edge of the devastation.

'What do we do?' Graham asked. 'They don't look friendly.'

Belial stared at him. 'Have you seen yourself?' he asked. 'Take a good look at me, and tell me which of us looks more terrifying: us or them.'

Graham nodded and then, squaring his shoulders, turned to face the sea of shocked faces. We all walked slowly toward the crowd which, in silence, parted like the Red Sea.

Back at the Fat Maggot we each fell into a bed. It didn't matter whose was whose, just as long as we all ended up horizontal.

Keril was waiting for us. He alternated between being horrified at our appearance and irritated that nobody wanted to talk. Still having problems with his leg, he limped over and handed me a package. I stared down at the badly wrapped object in my hands. It was heavy.

I opened it gingerly to find my knife. 'Thanks.' I groaned as I tried to lift my arms high enough to slot it back into its holster. 'I'd have thought you'd be the one person that would be happy to see this weapon lost for ever.'

Keril shrugged. 'It's not the knife's fault you're a complete twat.' He laughed at my hurt expression and clapped me on the shoulder, wincing as I howled at the pain. 'Don't worry, you seem to be getting over it.' He limped across the room to sit down. 'So, come on, you have to tell me what happened.'

'I feel like I've been beaten with a stick.' Parity summed up everybody's feelings. 'Let us sleep, we'll tell you tomorrow.'

Keril pouted.

Parity laughed then leant over to gingerly hug him. 'I'm so glad you're OK,' she said and then turned to her brother with a frown. 'And you.'

Farr laughed. 'I take it I'm still in your bad books then?' He grinned.

Parity yawned. 'I'm too tired to hit you right now,' she said. 'Remind me I owe you a punch in the morning.'

One by one everyone fell asleep. Despite being bone tired, something was nagging at me and my eyes kept opening. I sat up and looked around the room. Lit only by a couple of candles all I could see was covered lumps. One, however, was shaking. Listening hard I could just make out sobbing. I got up.

'Carly?' I sat on her bed and reached out for the covers. 'What's the matter?'

A muffled voice came from under the blankets. 'Nothing,' she said.

'Right.' I tried to pull the covers away from her face but failed when she kept a tight grip on them. 'Come on, Carly.' I leant over and spoke into a little gap I'd managed to make. 'Please.'

She sat up so suddenly I almost jumped off the bed. 'After everything that's happened, it's pathetic, selfish and really stupid.' She glared at me, defying me to agree with her. 'But I'm mourning my hair, OK?'

'What?' I searched desperately for something useful to say. 'Come on, it'll grow back and besides I think it looks really sweet.'

She rubbed the back of her hand over swollen eyes then back again as she wiped her nose. 'It's not sweet. I look like bloody Orphan Annie. Have you any idea how long I've been growing this?'

I shook my head. I honestly had no idea how to be sympathetic about hair.

'Twenty years.' She sniffed defiantly, trying to keep her voice down. She ticked off points on her fingers. 'I know it will grow; I know that in the grand scheme of things it's not important, but I'm tired, I've been frightened and I think I just want to have a good cry.' She stared at me, her big green eyes watery and bloodshot. 'So just push off and let me get on with it. I really don't need sympathy or a pep talk.' She lay back down with a thump and pulled the covers over her head again.

'Carly,' I hissed. 'Carly?'

'Oh for the love of ...' Lucifer threw his covers off and stood up. He was wearing nothing but a pair of grey boxers and a long black T-shirt that had "Come to the dark side ... we have cake" emblazoned across the front in bright yellow letters.

He stamped across the room. 'You do realise that we're trying to get to sleep? That even *I* need sleep, especially after today?'

He ripped the blanket off Carly. Before she could move

he plucked two or three hairs from her head.

'Ow!' she yelped and sat up. 'Get off me!' She stared up at Lucifer and, for a moment, her conviction wavered. Obviously deciding she couldn't care less who he was, she sneered and lay back down again, pulling the covers over her head once more.

Squatting back on his heels Lucifer delicately held one short bright red hair pinched between the thumb and forefinger on each hand. Concentrating, he breathed onto the hair pulling his hands steadily apart as he blew. The hair stretched like elastic.

'Arrgh!' Carly shot out from under the covers once more, her hands clamped to the top of her head. She began to scratch violently. 'Ow, stop! It's like ants – stop it!' She screamed.

Lucifer ignored both her and the mumbled requests to keep the noise down from the other beds. He continued to blow and stretch the hair.

Every hair on Carly's head matched the one in Lucifer's grip inch for inch. It reminded me of those nature films of flowers opening. For a moment bright orange hair stood out like a giant afro before the weight became too much and it settled, flowing over her shoulders and through her grasping, scratching fingers to pool on the bed, then in her lap and then down onto the floor.

Lucifer grinned and then, with a last breath, blew the six-foot hair he now held at full stretch away across the room. 'You look very much like Cousin It.' He patted her on the head and smiled serenely. 'You can thank me later.' Standing up he stamped back across the room and got back into bed. 'Now for pity's sake, be bloody quiet.' Punching his pillow a couple of times he slumped back into his bed with a sigh.

Carly's voice sounded a little odd under the pounds of hair she was now using as a tent. 'That creature has a small tendency to go too far.'

Reaching forward I grasped a double handful of strangely warm red hair and, with only a little difficulty, flipped it up and over toward her back. Her small face stared wryly out at me, framed by what could only be described as a full hairy duvet. 'Hello in there.' I peered into the orange-tinted darkness.

Trying to sit up she winced. 'This is really heavy.' She reached forward and put her arms around my neck then leant forward to kiss me – all sign of tears gone. Pulling away from the kiss she laughed up at me as she tried to unwind unruly hair from around her fingers and wrists. 'Would you do me a huge favour?' she asked.

I nodded.

'Please go and find me some scissors, or a knife or even some garden shears.' We both began to giggle, quieting only when a pillow hit me on the back of the head.

A cold, quiet voice came from the darkness. 'Shut up or I will kill you both right now.'

We shut up.


The next morning I was woken by uproarious laughing from the bathroom. Carly and Parity emerged, both grinning. 'So what do you think?' Parity smiled and twirled to show off her new look. 'As Carly had managed to get her do sorted I asked Galgaliel to fix mine.'

The tall angel edged out of the bathroom, looking more than a little rueful.

Carly's hair had been trimmed and tidied, washed and primped. Now only down to her elbows she looked like her old self and was obviously pleased with the result.

Parity, on the other hand, had gone entirely in another direction. Keeping the chopped, waif look she had bleached the whole lot white then had taken the longest messy clumps and dyed the very tips a bright blue. On one side of her head she had shaved it all down to a white fuzz. The whole thing was finished off with a bright blue silk scarf. With her big boots, ripped tights and tiny skirt, she looked as though she'd fallen straight out of some lost gothic rock band.

The effect on poor Graham was instantaneous and extreme: he reddened, then paled. Gulping rapidly, he couldn't seem to keep upright and sank down onto the bed, his eyes fixed on the punky, laughing seer.

Una laughed and ran over to pat Parity's hair. 'Pretty!' she announced, holding out her arms to be picked up.

'Who did yours?' Parity smiled at the little girl whose blonde curls once more bounced from her shoulders.

Una giggled and struggled to be put down. 'Hungry,' she said.

Carly shrugged at Parity's perplexed look. 'Must have been Lucifer.' She looked over at Graham who, sitting there with his mouth open, seemed to have lost the ability to blink. 'I don't think we can ask him at the moment though, can we.'

Parity seemed pleased by the effect she was having and sashayed across the room to sit next to her brother who was shaking his head with a look of disapproval. 'At least when you were dead I could have a small say in what you looked like,' he muttered.

Parity stared at him. 'Things change.' She laughed. 'Oh, and by the way ...' She leant over to kiss him on the forehead. 'Nice dragons.'

Blushing bright red and stammering horribly, Farr was saved by the arrival of breakfast.

Later, as we were discussing our next move. Mama Gert tapped gently then stuck her head around the door.

'There's some people to see you.' She kept her eyes on the floor and spoke in a respectful tone.

Carly smiled at her. 'Hi, Mama Gert.' She trotted over to talk to the older woman. 'I just wanted to say that breakfast was lovely.' She studied the flustered matron.

Mama Gert raised her eyes and looked slightly hopeful. 'You're going to be the new council then?' She smiled but again it didn't reach her eyes. 'Are you going to carry on with the apprenticeships?'

Carly patted her on the arm. 'We think it's better if the children are educated here, don't you?'

The relief that flowed from the innkeeper was an almost living thing. 'My grandson would have been old enough next year,' she began to gabble. 'And I was so worried. His mam didn't want him to go. He was going to come and work here, but that wasn't allowed so he'd have had to go.' She smiled hopefully up at Carly. 'If they don't have to do apprenticeships no more, can all the kiddies come back then?'

Carly swallowed and glanced at her father who gave a minute shake of his head. 'I honestly don't know yet.' She gave the woman a comforting hug. 'Everything's a little up in the air at the moment.'

Mama Gert nodded. 'Well, like I said there's folk waiting to see you downstairs. I'll make tea.' With that she turned and trotted out the door. 'That can be one of *his* jobs.'

We heard her talking to herself, making plans for her grandson as she clomped heavily down the wooden stairs.

'He can make and carry the tea – it's not doing my back any good, so he can do it …' Her voice faded away.

Parity wiped her eyes on the back of her hand and turned to her brother. 'They're dead, aren't they?'

Farr nodded then closed his eyes, already knowing what the next question was going to be. 'I can't bring them back, Parry,' he said, gently taking his sister's hand. 'Their bodies aren't even here any more, and even if they were I could only animate them. You lived like that – would you wish it on a child? Never growing up, not really feeling anything, just a pretty golem?'

Parity shook her head then gave a shaky smile as Una climbed into her lap. She snuggled up to the seer, one thumb in her mouth.

'You're going to have sticky-out teeth if you continue sucking that thumb.' Parity sniffed and gave the small girl a cuddle.

Una giggled and pulled the thumb out with a wet plop. 'Bunny,' she stated.

Belial heaved himself off the bed and raked a hand through his hair. 'Well, I suppose we'd better go and face the music,' he said.

Drinking tea in sullen silence was a collection of well-dressed men and women. Sitting stiffly, they looked like a group of Amish elders who had just been told they were

342

going to be introduced to the joys of swinging.

Filing in, we all found chairs then sat in silence as we waited to hear what they had to say.

Eventually, one man – broad shouldered and red faced – stood up and, with his hat in his hands, cleared his throat. 'We would like to know what's going to happen now,' he said. He sat down again, the hand that held his hat shaking slightly.

Galgaliel sighed then stood up. 'You all know me,' he said. 'Martin, you've come to me to set bones, Audrey …'

A stick-thin woman with a long face and a sad expression looked up.

'You've brought your children to me – a rather nasty case of insect bites, if I remember rightly.'

Audrey nodded and gave a small smile.

'Well, you have to believe me when I tell you that we don't know what's going to happen now.' He paused to look around the room. 'All we know is that what was happening had to stop.'

'Them kiddies ain't comin' back, am they?' A surprisingly deep voice from a tall, thin man broke the silence.

Galgaliel shook his head. 'No, Sam, they aren't.'

'But why?' An older woman, her hair scraped back into a severe bun, demanded. 'My Alex went away three years ago. He should be finished soon – he said he'd come back.' The woman stood up, hands clenched into fists at her sides. 'You've taken away the gate – they can't come home and you have to fix it so they can.'

'Sarah.' An older man, his hair grey and long, gently took the woman's arm. 'They never went away.'

'That's not true, Geoffrey.' Sarah twisted around to face him and yanked her arm out of his hand. 'They went away to learn a trade.' She turned again to face Belial. 'They did, didn't they? My Alex wanted to learn how to make metal.' She laughed – a shrill and sour sound. 'The council told me he was doing well.' Her voice had risen almost to a scream.

Galgaliel licked his lips and took a breath, but whatever

343

he was going to say was cut across by Geoffrey. 'No, Sarah. You know, deep down, that all those children are never coming back.' He took the woman by both arms this time, forcing her to face him. 'We always *knew* – we just hoped and prayed it wasn't so … But we always knew – deep down inside.'

She twisted and turned, trying to keep from looking at him. Tears rolled down her face and her lips were set as she shook her head in mute denial.

'Sarah.' He shook her very gently. 'You have to understand this, you have to, otherwise you are going to spend your whole life waiting for something that's never going to happen.'

Sarah's lower lip quivered and her face crumpled. 'No, you're all wrong,' she whispered. Sniffling and gulping, she collapsed back into her chair, her arms wrapped around her thin chest. 'Alex … my little Alex.' As her sobbing increased, another woman – also in tears – got up and went to the distraught mother.

'Come on, Sarah.' She wiped her eyes on her grey apron. 'We're going to my place. We're going to talk about our kids and we're going to make sure all the others are all right. Audrey can stay here and fill us in later.'

Sarah nodded, allowing herself to be helped out of her chair. All eyes followed them as they left the room.

We sat in silence for a while, each of us lost in our own thoughts. Finally, Geoffrey turned to Belial. 'So you're back in charge then, are you?' He sounded flat and defeated. 'Full circle, back to where my ancestors were, are we?'

Graham twitched and Lucifer stood up. 'No, I don't think we are.'

'Who the hell are you?' Sam leapt to his feet, chin thrust belligerently forward. 'Him we know.' He pointed to Galgaliel. 'But we didn't know he was a stinking angel. Him we know.' He pointed to Belial. 'His face is on all sorts of pictures and books. Look under "betrayer" or "coward" or "runaway".'

Belial clenched his jaw.

'But who are you?' Sam stalked forward and circled Lucifer.

Lucifer smiled. 'I'm *his* boss.' He nodded toward Belial.

'Yeah? Well, that's where we know you're lying.' Sam snorted. 'Just so you know, he's Belial. Belial the traitor, Belial the treacherous. He doesn't have a boss – the only boss he could have would be …'

It's an interesting experience to actually watch the passage of a single thought cross a man's face.

Sam stuttered and stared at Belial then he winced, took a deep breath and blew it out through pursed lips. By the time he'd turned back to face Lucifer, the Morning Star had changed completely. Wings out, long elegant hands folded calmly before him, he hovered about a foot off the floor, his bare feet crossed gracefully at the ankles. There was a look of expectant amusement on his striking features.

I had to give Sam his due – even with all his senses telling him that his next move was a very important one, he obviously decided that he'd come this far and to give way now just wasn't an option. He'd reached that point where he just didn't care. His worried look vanished and he firmed his jaw.

'Just great.' He turned and squared up to Lucifer. 'You're worse than he is, so now we've got two self-centred, arrogant bastards to deal with. Welcome, Lord.' He swept a theatrical bow toward the floor. 'We have long awaited your return.' He rose again and once more thrust his chin in Lucifer's direction. 'Actually, we really hoped that you'd die in agony before you came back.'

Lucifer raised an eyebrow.

I smiled because despite all of Sam's bravado he had a minute tick in his left eyelid. Lucifer could easily have disassembled the angry man into his component parts; he could have turned him inside out; he could even have made him into something entirely different – a frog, a cabbage, a pair of pants. But there was some small voice in the corner of my mind that quietly remembered another time and, as I sat back to watch the show, I knew, without a shadow of a

345

doubt, that none of these people were in danger. Una, sitting next to me, smiled and patted my knee.

Everybody avoided looking at anyone else as they waited for the certain explosion of anger that was surely going to follow that little tirade.

Lucifer seemed to be at a crossroads. His face switched from murderous intent to having to press his lips together to stop himself laughing. 'Well, I'm truly sorry to disappoint you,' he said. Then, giving in to the less destructive of his impulses, he started howling with laughter.

Galgaliel watched the fallen angel laughing for a moment then sighed, stood up and raised his hands. 'OK, let's just try and find a solution,' he said. He paced around the room as he considered. 'There seem to be a couple of questions that need answering.' He turned to Lucifer who was still sniggering at the belligerent little human. Reaching forward, he snapped his fingers between them. They both blinked and turned toward him.

'Lord Lucifer, is it your intention to take over and make all as it once was?'

The question was asked with a formal tone – obviously this was a deal maker.

'No.' Lucifer turned toward the other angel. 'That's not possible now.'

Galgaliel nodded. 'Belial, are you intending to take up your old position?'

'Hell no.' Belial shook his head. 'Really. No, a whole world of no.'

'I think we get the point.' Lucifer frowned at the other angel for a moment then, with his head on one side and a curious look, he turned toward the healer. 'Galgaliel you seem to care for the people here – will you take on the responsibility of care?'

Galgaliel looked surprised and slightly flustered. 'Erm ...'

Silence fell once more. All eyes followed the angel as he stalked about the room frowning and confused. After he'd walked past three times, Belial snorted and got to his feet. 'Gal!' he called.

The angel stopped pacing and looked up.

'Why not say yes?' Belial looked around 'You could actually do a great deal here. You do care about them – you've already proved that.'

The tall healer examined the floor. 'No,' he whispered then looked up. 'They have to do it.' He turned to the remaining members of the delegation. 'I'll help and guide and do what I can, but they don't want me. They don't need the Host. We've done enough harm here.' He turned to the older man called Geoffrey.

'You're already the head of the blacksmiths and craftsmen guilds.' He turned to Audrey. 'How many years have you been organising the women into a force to be reckoned with?' He paused. 'Martin, you've been building houses and making sure people have places to live, stealing materials from the council, making do, scrimping and reusing? You're all good people despite that you lie, cheat, steal and have, on occasion, killed. But you have managed to hide everything from the council. You've always managed to keep the people together.'

The three delegates stared into the distance, expressionless.

'Sam.' Galgaliel turned back to the little man now standing at Lucifer's side. 'You founded the traders' guild. You stopped a lot of the cheating and you set standards and levels.'

Sam shook his head and clenched his fists as he shouted, 'But there won't be any more trading, will there? The gates are gone, the power has gone.' He obviously remembered where both of those things had come from and flushed bright red. 'And that's a good thing.' He groaned and pushed a hand through his shaggy brown hair. 'But without trade we're locked again. No one can get in or out – what are we supposed to do?'

'Deal with Zephaniah,' Belial spoke up. 'With no danger to her children she should open the Purgatory Gate again.'

'The witch?' Martin shook his head. 'No, she steals those children that she has up there. Trade with her and again we're

347

back where we started.'

Audrey shuffled and coughed. She opened her mouth as if to say something then appeared to think better of it.

Geoffrey stared at her, frowning as he worked things out. 'No, she doesn't steal anything, does she?' He closed his eyes and sighed. 'She keeps them to protect them from our bloody council.' He twisted round to stare at Belial. 'That's what she's been doing, isn't it? The kids have been going to her, sent to her by parents that didn't want them sent away?' He smacked himself in the head. 'The birth rate hasn't been going down. The women have been going to her, having the babies then leaving the kids in her care and coming back to visit them.'

Audrey took a sip of tea.

'You!' The movement caught his eye and Geoffrey twisted to face her. 'You knew about it.'

Audrey nodded. 'I arranged it, but we couldn't save them all. A lot, like Sarah, believed all the council promised, or they couldn't bear to give their kids away – even if it meant them being safe.' She shrugged. 'We did the best we could.'

Lucifer stretched and yawned. 'I think you'll all do a better job than I ever could.' He stared down at Sam. 'I'm in a good mood, so you can count yourself lucky today.' He leant toward the little man. 'If I ever come back this way, I really hope I'm going to see some changes.'

Sam nodded then, greatly daring, stuck out his right hand.

Lucifer looked surprised. 'You have got to be fucking joking,' he said before pushing past us all and striding out of the room.

Audrey came to stand next to Sam and watched Lucifer leave without comment. When the door had slammed behind him she turned to the trader. 'You did see what they did to the bowl last night, didn't you?' she asked.

Sam swallowed and nodded.

'You are the luckiest man alive.' She patted him on the shoulder. 'By rights you should be a smear on the floor. A really flat sticky one that we'd have to clear up with a mop.'

Sam swallowed again; his tic was becoming more

pronounced by the second.

'As you're feeling so brave maybe your next meeting ought to be with Zephaniah.' She smiled.

Sam winced and went to find somewhere to sit down. He seemed to be having trouble holding onto his teacup.

Belial got up and gestured for us all to leave. He stood for a moment head down, deep in thought, then turned to face the townsfolk. 'For what it's worth, I'm sorry,' he said. 'I should have closed this place down completely. I'm truly sorry for leaving you here.'

Martin looked up at him surprised. 'The people you trapped here left a long time ago,' he said. 'They were the first out through the gate when it opened. We chose to stay here. We decided it's better to dictate our own lives than to live by someone else's rules.' He looked around at the others. 'Maybe now I think we can really start.'

Belial nodded. 'Then good luck.' He walked away.

We stayed another night at the Fat Maggot, enjoying the fire and the food. Lucifer had left once more and everything had to be explained to Graham. 'So what now?' he asked.

Farr spoke up. 'The ice lands.' He shook his head. 'Miles and miles of ice and snow, howling winds and the screaming of those still trapped there.'

Graham shuddered. 'Can't we just stay here?'

Parity wandered over and sat next to him. 'How are you, Graham?' she asked.

The question had nothing to do with the conversation we'd been having and we all looked at her, confused.

Graham, his rapidly whitening hair looking odd framing his doughy face, gave her a little smile. 'Fine,' he said.

'But you're not, are you?' Parity gave him a long look. 'What happens to you when Lucifer's here?'

Graham swallowed then closed his eyes. 'It's horrible.' He took Parity's hand. 'I'm just trapped in the darkness. I don't know what's going on and it's all dead in there; there's no sound and I can feel walls on each side. It seems to be getting smaller each time I'm there and I feel like I'm there for days.' He drew a shuddering breath. 'It's like being

349

trapped in a living coffin or maybe like something has eaten you and you're still alive in its stomach.'

Belial shuddered and shook his head. 'We have to get you to the Throne Room. We need to stop all this for your sake and, if we don't, these people are going to rule themselves for about a week. As soon as Metatron finds out they've opened the Purgatory Gate he's going to come in here and flatten the lot. We really need to separate you and your passenger.'

Graham frowned. 'And have you worked out exactly how you're going to do that yet?'

'Not quite,' Belial admitted. 'But I've got a theory.'

Graham leant back against the wall, folding his arms and raising an eyebrow. For a moment I had to double-check that it wasn't Lucifer that had come through.

'And that theory is?' he prompted.

'Still under construction,' Belial growled.

Graham nodded and turned away.

'You do have a plan, right?' I asked as I watched Graham stuffing things into his rucksack. It was the first time I'd seen the man get angry.

'Yes, I have a plan.' Belial sighed. 'But it's a really shitty one and I'd like to come up with something better,' he said. He rubbed his neck – a movement he favoured when he was stressed or under pressure. 'Preferably one that doesn't require me to murder either Lucifer or Graham, because that's all I've got at the moment.' He began checking the packs that were piled around him. 'But it's OK, it's going to take us ages to cross the ice and find the door to the Throne Room so I've got some time.' He fell silent for a moment. 'And of course we could all die of cold so that would be an outcome of sorts.' Carly sauntered across with some more packs. 'Is this it?' She huffed as she looked at the pile on the rug. 'Is this the last of them?'

'It's probably the last of everything.' Belial shook his head and then went to talk to Parity.

'What's up with him?' Carly stared after her father.

I shrugged. 'Too many options and none of them right.'

Carly glanced over at Graham and nodded. 'That will drive Dad crazy,' she said. 'He hates it when things aren't completely black and white.'

'OCD?' I grinned at her.

She snorted. 'Let's hope it doesn't run in the family, eh, or our kids could be completely screwed.' She laughed at my expression and, after giving me a quick kiss, walked away.

'Kids?' I hurried after her.

# CHAPTER 11

THE NEXT MORNING, WE headed away from the city of Dis and began walking toward the horizon. The party had become used to warm fires, soft beds and good food, so none of us were in a particularly happy mood. For the next three days the conversation was minimal, each of us unwilling to share our misery with the others. Nights were cold and sleepless, days were cold, filled with the need to put one foot in front of the other and meals were scarce. I felt as though I could no longer tell day from night. My legs ached, my hands and feet became steadily colder as we headed out into a blank wasteland and, like everyone else, I was miserable.

Graham, trudging along beside me, was particularly unhappy.

'I want to go home,' he grumbled.

I was curious; it wasn't something he'd said for a good while now.

'Why?' I asked.

'Because I didn't know how good life actually was,' he explained. 'I went to work, I had a nice house, a good car, money in the bank and I could do what I liked.'

'And what was that?' I pressed. 'What did you actually *do*?'

'Well, I …' Graham frowned and fell silent. We carried on walking for a while then he burst out. 'Damn it all, I must have done something!'

'Girlfriends?'

He shook his head. 'Too much trouble.'

'Hobbies?'

Again, he shook his head.

'Fast cars, motorbikes, strip clubs, internet poker, role playing, horse racing, decorating, an odd collection of antique pince-nez or fuzzy teapot warmers?' I stopped for breath. 'Surely you must have done something – everyone has *something*.'

Graham looked miserable. 'Well, what did *you* do?' he asked.

'Books.' I remembered my exploded lounge and felt an odd frisson of pain beneath my ribs. 'I had lots and lots of books.'

'So you didn't really live your life either.' Graham sighed. 'But at least you vicariously lived other people's, even if their lives were pure fiction. I didn't do anything, nothing at all. The most boring man on the planet. I drifted through my days, making money, going to work, sleeping and eating.' He turned to look at me. 'What's that sin with the really odd name?'

'Which one?' I racked my brain, trying to remember them all.

'The one about not living life to the full – being apathetic and listless,' he said.

'Acedia?'

'That's the one.' Graham nodded. 'I am the embodiment of acedia. I'm acedic, if there is such a word.'

I watched him walk away then laughed. I *had* lived my life. For goodness sake I'd lived a hundred times longer than he ever hoped too. How many bloody lifetimes was I supposed to embrace? He'd made it sound like my life was as bad as his; all he ever did was sit around and wait. Death would have crept up on him and he never would have done a thing to stop it, whereas I …

I felt uncomfortable. I certainly didn't sit around waiting for death – I didn't need to wait for it: it chased me around with an axe and usually caught me. But had I done everything I could have? At one point I'd picked up a job lot of self-help books and had actually read one or two of them. I'd found them irritatingly awash with phrases such as "positive thinking" and "visualisation for success". Dismissing them, I had unceremoniously boxed them all up again and given them to the local charity shop. Thinking back I couldn't remember whether they'd been boring or guilt inducing; either way, I certainly hadn't taken the messages on board.

I stared over at Graham as he tucked a thick blanket around Parity like a poncho. Acedia, eh? Well, maybe I was acedic too.

As we walked, I noticed that the ground was beginning to crunch and crackle under my boots. Being so dry the land had cracked and split; everything around us was divided into uneven hexagons of baked grey dirt. The cracks between each ranged from a few millimetres to a few centimetres in width. But now, within the bigger cracks, I could see the shining darkness of ice. I shivered and dragged my huge parka around me; I wished I'd put another pair of socks on.

'So it will be OK, won't it?' Graham was trotting beside me again.

'What?' I looked over at him. 'Sorry, I was just noticing that ice was beginning to form.' I pointed down at the cracks. 'Look.'

'I was saying that I can't see any way of Belial separating me and my passenger.' Graham was definitely not going to allow himself to be sidetracked. He kicked a loose bit of frozen earth and watched as it skittered and bounced across the featureless frozen plain. 'If he wants Lucifer, he's going to have to dig him out like a winkle out of its shell.' He pursed his lips and looked over at Parity. 'I'm the shell and that's the bit that gets thrown away.' He coughed and rubbed a hand across his eyes.

'Not necessarily,' I lied.

'Don't worry, Joe.' He continued to stare at Parity. 'I actually wanted to thank you. It's just a shame it has to end now that I've found something to live for.' He wandered over to the punky woman, who greeted him with a big smile. Looking up into his face her expression changed to one of concern.

Shit! He was right. Belial wasn't having any luck coming up with a decent plan. As we plodded along I racked my brain, coming up with scenario after scenario and rejecting each one. I thought for so long I didn't even notice that ice and snow had covered the cracks and my feet were now so cold I couldn't feel them any more.

'Cold.' Una said, teeth chattering. Warmly wrapped in what looked like a small duvet, mittens on her hands and wearing a hat with a kitten face on it, she looked up at me then slipped her hand into mine. 'Cold nose.'

I looked down at her with a smile. Her little nose was very red, as were her cheeks.

Bending down, I pulled her scarf away from her neck and up over her nose. Her big blue eyes stared at me; it was like staring at something down a hole and that something was staring back at you.

'Warm,' she said.

I nodded.

We looked at each other for a moment before she patted me on the hand – that odd little movement now so familiar it had become part of her personality. 'Everything will be all right,' she said. And with that she skipped back across the snow, her boots kicking up little flurries as she went. I stared after her. That sentence had actually made sense.

That night, exhausted from walking all day, our feet frozen from being ankle deep in snow, hands and faces stinging and wet, we huddled in silence around another small, ineffectual fire.

'Where did you find the wood, Belial?' Parity held her hands out toward the fire, rolling her eyes in exasperation as Farr pulled her hands away from the heat.

'You'll burn yourself,' he warned.

Belial opened a bag and threw another small log into the centre of the blaze. 'I brought it with us.' He stared into the tiny fire. 'There's nothing up here to burn, nothing to eat, nothing to drink.'

'Where's the river?' Carly asked.

'We're standing on it.' Belial stared out into the darkness. 'The ice has crept up over the years. This once was the Lethe, the last river of Hell – the river of forgetfulness.' He tapped his foot; it made a hollow sound. 'Now it's just ice along

355

with everything else.'

'How far do we have to go?' Keril, still occasionally troubled by his knife wound, looked odd wrapped up in a quilted jacket; he looked a bit like a children's comic book character. His tail hung out from beneath the jacket and his scales were dull.

'A long way,' Belial murmured. 'We have four regions to get through.' He stared into the flames. 'All the murderers and traitors were held here, but only the very worst were completely submerged in the ice. Those that had used magic for betrayal and self-gain were only in the ice up to their necks.' He frowned. 'But it looks as though those that were left are now buried deep within the ice. It's going to be a very long, boring and cold trip.'

Parity stared at the snow. 'Do they know?' she asked.

Belial shook his head. 'No, they're alive, sort of, but they're frozen in the waters of the Lethe. They forget everything.'

Graham looked up from where he was tying his laces. 'And what shall we do when we get there, eh, Belial?' He stood up, his hands fisted at his thighs. 'What exactly are you dragging me towards?'

At the pregnant silence, Graham gave a disgusted snort then, wrapping himself in his blankets, he lay down and turned his back on us all.

Belial stared at the dark hump on the ground and sighed.

During the night, the fire had died and I was surprised we hadn't died with it. We could hardly move it was so cold. Ice made our blankets crackle as we staggered out of them; no one had bothered to undress. Parity and Carly were pale and couldn't stop shivering. It was frighteningly difficult to wake Keril at all – his body temperature was different from ours and the cold affected him badly.

'What's the point of this, Joe?' I looked up to see Lucifer standing beside me as I was debating whether the cold coffee still in the pot was preferable to none at all. I didn't have an answer for him and we stood and stared out over the huge white expanse. 'My host is a little anxious – he's fairly sure

356

he's walking to his death.' He looked unblinking at me then stretching luxuriously and yawned. The cold didn't seem to affect him at all. 'And I'm getting bored with listening to him worry – he always worries.'

I shrugged. 'This is Belial's show,' I hedged.

'Ah, come on.' Lucifer reached down and picked up a mug. Pouring cold coffee into it he brought it to his lips and blew on it; steam immediately began to rise from the cup.

Greatly daring I held out mine.

Lucifer regarded me for a moment then, with a shrug, warmed my drink. 'Is it so important to get me there?' He sipped his coffee and made a face. 'This is really terrible, you know.'

I nodded. I was fairly sure the stuff was strong enough to strip enamel from teeth. 'We have no other choice.' I cupped my hands around the hot mug. 'You and Graham are sort of attached and we only get one of you at a time. We need to stop Metatron getting his hands on you. We need you to sort all this out.'

Lucifer frowned. 'Hang on a moment.' He took my mug from me, placed it on the snow with his own then picked them both back up and handed one over. 'Here, try that.' He paused. 'Sort what out?'

I took a wary sip of my coffee. Mocha with cinnamon and a really good shot of some alcohol – it tasted so wonderful I almost cried. Sometimes it was difficult to remember exactly who this was. Just as you were getting used to the easy-going smiling side of him, the treacherous, nihilistic personality would suddenly surface and you would be forcibly reminded just what was standing next to you. I cradled my cup for a moment then looked up to find Lucifer grinning at me. 'We need to go back to the way things were,' I said, trying to ignore the delicious smell rising from my mug. 'If we bring you back, then God comes back and he can deal with Metatron. It's got to be better than Metatron wiping the board clean and starting again.'

'Bring God back?' Lucifer laughed. 'Back from where? Just because he won't answer the call of some psychotic megalomaniac …' he snorted a laugh. '… whatever makes you think He went away?'

'Metatron said that you two were linked and, as you faded, so God faded as well.'

Lucifer looked surprised. 'Now, that's an interesting theory.' He stared off over the ice for a long moment and then, with a sudden movement that made me jump, poured the last of his coffee down his throat. 'Let's test it out, shall we?'

Reaching up into the air he began to draw a rectangle with one outstretched finger. The shining outline began to glow and fill with steam. 'It's a lot of fun to go for a walk in the country,' Lucifer shouted over the sounds of cracking and grating. 'But now I think I have things I need to do.'

The steam became darker and the swirling clouds slowed to become whorls and knots in a perfectly ordinary, heavy wooden door.

'I'm sorry to disappoint you all if you're enjoying this little expedition.' Lucifer studied his handiwork. 'But I can't take the time to faff about and watch you lot die of hypothermia. As incredibly funny as it would be.' He kicked the door open and peered inside. 'Shall we?' He indicated the darkness inside.

It may have been dark but it was also warm and damp. The sounds of dripping water echoed around the long stone corridor. It gave us the opportunity to disprove a theory. Cold people move slower than warm people – isn't that the accepted maxim? Well, it's wrong. It took only seconds for the whole party to rush through the door. Packs were hastily filled and many things just got left behind as everyone scrambled to get away from the cold. Keril staggered through last– he could barely put one big foot in front of the other; Farr was holding him up. Once through the door he slid down the damp wall and lay on the floor, still and quiet.

Lucifer pushed hard on a small grey stone that protruded slightly from the wall.

Lights hanging from the high ceiling began to glow. Small three-bulb chandeliers stretched as far as the eye could see –

little triplets of light that reminded you of the effect of looking into two mirrors, one directly facing the other: it was like looking into infinity.

'Still a bit of a way to walk.' Lucifer stuffed the torch back into the bag. 'But it's easier than slogging through all that white stuff.'

He began to walk away, his thick boots making no sound on the pale wet sand that covered the floor.

As we staggered after him the sounds of dripping stopped and the walls became dry. The only sounds were the scuff of feet through velvet sand.

Lucifer shook his head. 'Can't you lot go any faster?' He turned with a frown. 'It's like parade day for the old people's home.'

Belial handed him a huge backpack. 'Carry this if you have the energy,' he said.

'Just leave them.' Lucifer turned to face us. 'There's nothing in there you'll want. They won't go anywhere. You can always come back and get them if you really feel the need.'

We set the packs down, repacking food and water into smaller bags and distributing them among the group. Bags of blankets, cooking utensils, clothes and other unnecessary rubbish made a tall pile on top of which Una gleefully placed her kitten hat and mittens. 'Snowman,' she announced.

Carly laughed and gave her a hug. 'Bagman,' she corrected. Una giggled.

With our loads lightened, warm and dry – and in much better spirits – the party walked on.

'How long is this corridor?' Belial hailed Lucifer who was leading the way.

'As long as you need it to be,' came the enigmatic reply. 'Have you talked yourself into believing that your plan's good yet? Are you reconciled to what you're about to do?' Lucifer swung round and faced Belial. The group staggered to a stop. 'Because that's an entirely innocent man you need to dispose of. His only crime is to have been born in the wrong line. He's never done anything wrong – in fact, he's spent his whole life battling against my influence and because of that he hasn't enjoyed any kind of life at all.' He gave Belial a cheerful grin. 'So if you need a little more time, we can just keep walking.'

Belial faced Lucifer. 'I know what has to be done,' he said.

'Good for you, well done.' The Morning Star clapped the irritated demon on the shoulder, then turned and walked on, whistling.

I'm not sure what I was expecting to find at the climax of this journey but I think it was just *more* than we actually got.

I couldn't help myself. 'Is this it?' I did try very hard to take the sneer out of my voice.

Belial nodded, looking pale and unhappy.

The doors ahead of us were impressive enough in their own way: ancient blackened oak bound by iron rods and nails which had rusted and pitted over the eons. Etched deep into the wood was a huge symbol – I recognised it immediately. It looked like the symbol of Lucifer that you find all over the internet and, although the basic shape was there, certain additions made it uncomfortable to look at for long.

An open eye stared malevolently from the centre of the sigil. The downward strokes formed the leaf shape of that well-known blade and the tops of the "X" in the centre swept upward in tall rams-horn curves. Even if you had never seen this particular collection of sweeping lines before, there's no way that you'd go through this door with a happy heart.

I could feel Graham trembling at my side.

'You OK there?' I looked over at him, just to check who I was talking to, and when he didn't reply gave him a nudge. 'Graham, are you all right?'

'Home again, home again, jiggety, jig.' The trembling stopped suddenly and the dry, tired voice of Lucifer echoed around the passage.

Parity who had been having a long and quiet chat with Belial sighed and stepped forward. 'Hi, Graham,' She gave him a little girl gaze, looking up at him from under her lashes.

'Wait …' Carly reached out to stop her but it was too late.

The man at my side turned slowly. His gaze lingered on her face for only a second before he looked away to study the hand she'd laid on his arm.

'You know …' Parity continued, '… when this is all over maybe you and I ought to go out and see the sights – get a little mad and see where we end up, eh?' She smiled, putting as much sex appeal as she could into that gaze. (I have to admit, you'd have to be three years dead not to be affected by it).

Graham lifted one side of his lip. 'And why,' he paused, 'witch, would we want to do that?' He pulled his arm from under her hand. 'Not this time.' He looked up at Belial and took a deep breath of the old air. 'Not here, not now and thankfully not ever again. Oh, and do remember, dear heart, just because I had the whim to keep you alive last time we touched doesn't mean I can't change my mind.' He smiled at her and leant in close. 'So, do you want to repeat that interesting offer you were making?'

Parity blanched then, shaking her head, dropped her hand and backed away. Apparently, Graham had gone for good and there was nothing that could be done now. Lucifer was back, his human vessel submerged for ever; we'd got exactly what we wished for.

The Morning Star laughed. Closing his dark eyes he placed one slim hand on the door. From his back smoke began to rise, spiralling and twisting up into the air above his head. The dark matter coiled and turned in on itself as it thickened and curved to a point above Lucifer's head.

'Black spirits and red, old spirits and grey, mingle, mingle, ye that may.' Lucifer sang gently to himself as he pushed the door open and took a step into the darkness beyond.

He stopped just past the door and looked back at us. 'Well, my escorts, my little troop of troublemakers, will you just stop here, cowering and clucking like abused chickens? You that have come so, so far just to make sure I get here – just to make sure that I'm *safe*?'

The sneer was back and it didn't sound like an invitation anyone with any sense would accept. I certainly wasn't going into that room with him.

'Well, thank you for walking me home.' Lucifer smiled around at us all. 'You can go now.' He closed his eyes; his wings solidified and became muscle and feather. He'd had wings before but these were different – bigger, thicker, more real – as much a part of the man as his white hair and dark green eyes. Black as a raven's, his primary feathers brushed the floor. The tips pulled the dust into small sand devils that twisted and danced behind him as he moved, drunken worshipers doing the conga at a bacchanalian feast. Above his head the huge wings faded into smoke at the very apex.

Stretching like a man awakening from a very deep sleep Lucifer unfolded them, bringing them up as high as he could then snapping them downwards with a deep smile of pleasure. His little dusty worshipers jumped and span, flattening themselves against the floor only to leap high a moment later.

I noticed that his shirt and boots had disappeared and, as he gripped the stone floor with his toes, the stones beneath the sand buckled and cracked.

Without another word, he walked away from us into the darkness, wings spread wide, chest bare save for a slight sheen of sweat.

'What do we do?' Carly, after making sure Parity was all right, came and stood beside me.

I shook my head – I had no idea. I don't think any of us really thought we'd get this far and now that we had, well, what happened next was completely out of our control. We'd done exactly what we'd said we'd do. We'd unleashed Lucifer and brought him home. It didn't really matter what he was going to do next because, quite frankly, this incredibly powerful ex-angel could do anything he damn well liked and there wasn't a thing we could do about it.

Belial, his wings wide, pushed us aside and headed for the doorway.

'Father!' Carly screamed. 'Don't!'

Belial ignored her and, with sword drawn, rushed after Lucifer. He ended up across the passage, against the far wall, in a heap of smoke and feathers. His sword clattered to the floor; he had literally bounced off the darkness.

'Embarrassing.' Keril, finally warm enough to function again, stood beside Belial and reached down a hand to help him up.

I pushed at the darkness –, it pushed back. Gently holding my fingers to the barrier, I stroked it, there seemed to be some give. Reaching for my knife, I concentrated hard then, pushing so gently I was hardly moving at all, I inserted the tip of the blade, pulled it downward and, using the knife to keep the long tear open, I stepped through.

'Joe!' Carly tried to follow me through the rip I'd created but was thrown into her father's arms. Both hit the wall and down they went again in yet another pile of feathers.

Farr regarded me from the other side of the barrier. 'He's done this on purpose, you know,' he said. 'It's only ever you he talks to. It's only ever you he needs a reaction from.' He cocked his head to one side and regarded me curiously. 'Why is that do you think?'

I shook my head. I didn't know why and I didn't want to know. I could feel my memories beginning to crack every time I studied them. All I knew for certain was that the past was a place I did *not* want to revisit.

'You be really, really careful in there,' Keril said, joining Farr at the doorway.

I still had the knife stuck in the darkness and, moving slowly, I reached back to take the large torch that Parity offered me. It seemed that it was only inanimate objects and me that the darkness would allow entry.

'Well, thanks for that.' I looked around at the group. They stood together like 15-year-old girls at their first disco, nervous and uncertain. Even Una was staring at me with a hopeful look.

Twenty steps in and the torch was completely useless. All I could see were the stones beneath my feet – there was nothing else but darkness. The room through which I slowly walked was huge and empty. The space around me pressed down and I found myself having to deliberately place one foot in front of the other to keep moving. My brain was telling me to lie down and crawl.

'Joe, thank God.' A well-known voice whispered in my ear.

'Metatron?' I jumped and turned to find my ex-boss standing behind me.

The little angel nodded. 'Where is he?'

'Who?' I knew full well "who".

'Lucifer'. Metatron was sweating, his eyes darting left and right as he peered into the absolute darkness.

I shrugged. I really wasn't sure what was going on. 'In here somewhere, I expect.'

'You've changed, Joe.' Metatron peered up at me. 'Really taken charge – and you've managed to get this far. I'm so proud of you.' He gave me a huge smile. 'I'm so sorry I had to do this to you but you had to do this of your own free will. But look on the bright side, you've paid your debt in full. You are completely free of sin.' He paused, obviously waiting for me to start celebrating.

Something didn't feel right. 'I haven't done anything except run,' I said.

He laughed. 'Oh, you've done far more than that.' He put an arm around my shoulder. 'Hell's torn down, Belial's back in the inner circles and Lucifer ...' He stared around at the darkness, '... well, he's back where he's supposed to be. Really, really well done. I knew I could rely on you.'

I nodded. Well, that wasn't really what I'd aimed for, but I supposed when it was put like that ... I shook my head, a little nagging voice somewhere deep inside was telling me that all of this was way too convenient.

'You tried to kill me. You sent Michael to kill me.'

'No!' The little angel laughed. 'He's a good actor though, isn't he?' Metatron smiled; his hand was still on my arm. 'Michael's job was to act as sheepdog. He needed to chase you through purgatory and get you over the river.'

'Oh.' I guess that sort of made sense ...

As I stood there in the darkness I had an image of Michael being attacked by goats; the way he'd dragged himself, battered and bruised away from Zephaniah's god to chase down Belial; standing in the cathedral kicking Zephaniah as she lay on the ground in front of the altar. The wet thump as the head of that lad that had opened the door to him hit the floor, smoking and looking surprised. The look on Raphael's face as he'd walked through the door.

Metatron tightened his grip on my arm. 'Come on, let's get out of here. You have a life to live now. What are you going to do first – now that it's all over?'

I looked down at him. His eyes had completely lost that maniacal glint I'd become accustomed to over the years. Indeed, he seemed relaxed and happy.

I smiled back. 'I honestly don't know. I'll have to think about it,' I said.

Metatron nodded and grinned. 'Come on, we'll think about it together.' He turned and stepped back the way I'd come. 'Come on,' he called over his shoulder. 'I have a really great single malt we can work our way through.'

I laughed and moved to follow him. 'Did you ever forgive him?' I called toward his back.

'Who?' The angel glanced back over his shoulder.

'God. For the whipping you received when that visitor to Heaven stated you must also be a deity.'

'Oh yeah, of course.' Metatron carried on walking. 'That's what we do: forgive.'

As I stepped up behind him with my knife in my hand I felt a slight regret. It would have been so nice to just play along with the charade. If I'd lasted long enough I might have got that holiday to Hawaii I was always promising myself.

As the blade slid smoothly into his back Metatron screamed. The scream continued on and on echoing around me until it just switched off. The sudden silence was unnerving.

The impaled angel turned. The knife met no resistance, just seeming to cut through his body until, as he faced me, it was embedded in his chest. He looked down at the knife then up at me. He smiled. 'It seems you know Him better than I these days.' The figure before me began to fade until I was left standing alone, my knife in my hand.

Silence and darkness. I continued forward; with no sort of landmark, I could only hope I was heading in the right direction.

'What are you doing, Joe?' A voice off to my left, gentle and questioning, made me jump. I twisted around and thrust the torch toward the sound. No movement – just motes of dust hanging in dead air. 'Why is it always *you* they call upon to do their dirty work?' The voice paused as though thinking and then continued. 'But it's not just theirs, is it?' A low laugh. 'It's everybody's.'

I forced myself to keep walking, one slow, rhythmic foot in front of the other. Eyes fixed on the edge of the torchlight. 'Keep counting.' I whispered into the darkness, '1 … 2. 1 … 2 …' I kept step to my counts – not too fast and not too slow. Just try to stay in a straight line.

'Do you *like* being everyone's lackey, Joe?' The voice now came from my right. 'Should we change your name to Igor?' A laugh from behind me and a sibilant 'Yeth mathter.'

I concentrated on my steps.

'Is it hard to think for yourself? Following orders all the time? The perfect little servant – lose one master and find another.' The voice fell silent for a moment, then with a sigh continued. 'It's pathetic how much you need to be guided and controlled. Everything you've ever done was forced upon you by someone else and you love it.'

'1 … 2. 1 … 2 …'

'All that free will.' Another voice, deeper and ahead of me. 'Free will that you were allowed to keep – all of you disgusting creatures, you mud walkers, you fornicators, you hypocrites.' The voice hardened and rose in volume. 'Allowed – no, *encouraged* – to aspire and grow. Look at what you've managed to achieve, and in such a short time. Almost total destruction; everything you touch turns to shit and decay.' The voice dropped away.

I couldn't breathe. My chest felt compressed and it took every ounce of willpower I had to just keep moving.

'You have no master now, Joe. Even if that wasn't Metatron you just skewered, you still severed any tenuous links to a relationship.' A female voice right by my left ear made me jump and stop for a moment, but only a moment. I pressed on, my head pounding, my eyes burning from staring ahead into the pitch black. I could feel tears running in a continual stream down my cheeks. My heart seemed more sensible than I and, without permission, was working itself up into getaway frenzy. The darkness pressed ever closer, causing my circle of light to contract. I could feel its physical presence, like an oil slick, flowing around a small island. The pressure became painful.

My knees buckled and I felt stone beneath my hands. As the torch rolled to a stop only inches away I felt the darkness pressing on my back – my own personal demon, deep, silent and uncaring. My chest heaved and I heard a sob. I wondered who was crying so hard.

'Poor Joe.' A child's voice from just in front of me.

I raised my gaze from the floor but there was nothing but darkness.

'What will you do now? What will you do when you have to take responsibility for your own decisions – for your own actions? There's no one to blame except yourself now.' A pause. 'Do you like it?' The voice changed to an old man's, querulous and hoarse. 'It's not good, is it, not as good as in the old days.' Another pause. 'I'll do you a favour. I'll take it all away and you can release yourself to my care. You won't have to make a single decision. I can make you do such things and you won't have to take responsibility for any of them – just do them in *my* name.'

I had a huge lump in my throat and couldn't swallow. My eyes were glued shut. The effort to even try and open them was just too much.

'Metatron made a mistake when he gave his own power to you.' The voice drifted to my left. 'You're so scared; all that power and you don't use it. You don't need me, you could take him on all by yourself. Let me teach you how.'

I felt stone on my forehead, then the same cold on my chest and thighs as I lay down and just listened to the offer.

'Work with me and think of all you can do. You know what it would take for humans to properly grow – to give up their vicious ways. All you would have to do is tell them how. You could be in charge and I can guide you. They'll bow down to you and you bow down to me. Everyone's happy.'

It was a good offer; just do as I'm told and life would be easy. I liked an easy life – it was all I'd ever wanted. I hated having no direction; I could never be sure if what I was doing was right – better to leave the decisions to those greater than I. The darkness put its boot between my shoulders and pressed me to the floor. I smiled.

'We'll do wonders, you and I.' The old man was gone, replaced by someone young and vibrant, sexless and enthusiastic. 'We don't even need the humans to obey. Together we'll rid the world of its parasites and start again. This time we'll do it right and you'll be there at the beginning, watching me wipe out the old and you'll be there to welcome the new!'

I nodded. He was right of course. 'Yes, Metatron.'

'No!' Pain lanced through my shoulder down my spine. I screamed then hugged the floor again. 'I think we need to start with the basics. That *angel*, that secretary, that unimaginative pawn.' The words were spat into my face. 'He will be your first target. You can make him scream – I can give you that whip that God used on him. After I've finished with him there will be nothing left to name. We'll wipe it from everyone's lips – his name will be proscribed. You of all people should understand how that feels.'

I tried to hang on to the hazy aftermath of my discipline. I deserved it; I deserved more. I tried so hard to agree. I nodded and sank flatter onto the stones, abasing myself, trying desperately to keep my inner eye away from the sickening mental image I had of myself, prostrate in front of yet another psychotic angel that wanted to use me as a weapon.

Lucifer was right: I really had no willpower at all, but – try as I might – I just couldn't seem to get into that master-servant role that I so desperately thought I needed. I tried to imagine my life as he described it: adored and worshiped. Well, that would be nice. The faces of all those I knew stared at me. Carly, no fight left, would just do as she was told – she'd never twist my ear again. Keril, I could get Arden and Alice back for him, re-create their old world somewhere. They'd be happy, they'd never need to work or worry. I almost laughed as I imagined the Drekavak's reaction if I made that sort of suggestion. Michael, prostrate before me and Raphael ... In my mind's eye he just looked disappointed.

No, this was never going to work. It all sounded good in theory, but in the end, if I followed this path, I'd be alone – unloved and despised ... I'd be Metatron.

The darkness lifted from my back and, sighing, I stood up. Dusting myself off I reached down for the torch. I was in a dark room – a dark, dusty room – and quite frankly I was sick of it. I was sick of my life; I was sick of being used and there was nothing – *nothing* – that Lucifer could do to punish me that was worse than what he'd just offered as a reward.

I looked around at my little ball of light – the only thing keeping the darkness at bay. Looking back over my shoulder I couldn't see the door beyond the torchlight, but I hoped that Carly could see me. I blew her a kiss then, taking a deep breath, turned the torch off. Let the darkness come; let him do to me as he would. I just didn't care any more, but I wasn't going to be used again. 'Thank you, but no,' I spoke calmly into the void.

I stood in the darkness and waited. There was no pressure, no voices and no hope.

Ahead of me a figure appeared, tall wings reaching toward the unseen ceiling. Lucifer sat on the fabled tourmaline throne and studied me. The light increased and I could finally see the whole room; it really wasn't that big at all. About 30 square foot, a chunky, dusty cave, every surface showing vertical ridges where tools had cut deep into the rock. I studied the crystal formation and decided that I was wrong. The cave was natural – every surface black tourmaline; the ridges were a natural property of the crystal.

In the very centre of the cave, a huge black block thrust in blunt hexagons toward the ceiling. Lucifer sat, as though on a comfortable sofa, staring at me from a vast seat, worn shining and slick from unimaginable eons of use.

He nodded and raised an angular eyebrow at me. 'Man has changed.' He gave a small shake of his head. 'No, scratch that, *man* hasn't changed at all.' He rolled his eyes. 'But you have.' He smiled – the first real smile I'd seen since I dragged Graham Latimer down from his crucifix in Metatron's office. 'Somewhere over the last huge number of years you've managed to pick up a spine from somewhere.' He laughed. 'Did you steal it or did you grow your own?'

'Flat pack from Spines-R-Us.' I wasn't going down in silence.

He laughed. 'It doesn't matter.' Lucifer, Morning Star, The Antichrist, Lord of Lies actually managed to look a little regretful. 'I don't really need you. I'll still change the world and I have the horrible feeling that you might just be the one thing that could stand in my way.' He stood up and stretched. 'I genuinely like you, Joe and I really don't want to get rid of you. We had some good times together.' He gave an elegant shrug. 'But there you go, choices, choices – and you don't remember them anyway.' He stretched again. 'There has to be a balance, but if it's going to tip one way or the other, I want to make sure everything goes my way.'

Reaching over my shoulder I pulled out my knife. 'I don't think so,' I said. The weapon hummed in my hand. This was the knife that Metatron hoped would annihilate Lucifer. I hesitated. If I went through with this, would I be doing Heaven's will or Metatron's, or Lucifer's, or just mine? They seemed to have become all mixed together.

Lucifer moved so fast. Before I even had the knife fully in my hand, he had captured my wrist and twisted hard; the knife flipped out of my hand and careered across the floor. I watched as it bounced and clattered, cartwheeling and rolling, changing direction as it hit every lump and bump on the ground.

'Sorry, I really don't want that thing anywhere near me.' He frowned. 'You, on the other hand, are susceptible to all sorts of methods of murder and, despite any recuperative powers that Metatron imposed upon you, this time, I don't think you'll be coming back.' He stretched out a hand toward me.

My mind a complete blank, I shut my eyes and waited. I wouldn't even dare to hope that he might not be able to do what he promised. I just hoped that whatever came next was over quickly and my future existence was dark and quiet. I waited for the end ... I waited and waited. Eventually I got bored and cracked open one eye wondering why nothing had happened.

Lucifer's hand wobbled and he frowned. Taking a deep breath he ducked his head and tried once more. Again the hand trembled and there was nothing.

'Don't be stupid,' Lucifer muttered. He stared at the wall and seemed to be struggling to move.

Graham's blue eyes focused on me. 'Joe, get your fucking knife,' he screamed as his eyes flashed blue, then dark, then blue again. His body pulsed as it morphed between buff ex-angel and flabby insurance salesman.

Well, I wasn't going to hang around and marvel – I dashed over and grabbed the knife. With the weapon held loosely in my hand I stood shifting from one foot to the other as I tried to work out when would be the right time to strike. Graham and Lucifer were changing back and forth so fast it was difficult to tell which was which and this was one thing I couldn't mess up.

For a moment the changes slowed and Graham, sweating and gritting his teeth, managed to hold his own form for longer than a split second. 'It has to be me,' he whispered. 'Stab me. The body's still mine. Get rid of the body and Lucifer has nowhere to go. Then when he splits away kill him, but you have to stab me first.'

371

I hesitated. Over the last week this man had almost become a friend. I didn't want to do the wrong thing once again.

'Now, Joe.' Graham closed his eyes and opened his mouth in a scream. 'I can't hold him. Now, Joe – now!'

I stepped forward. 'I'm sorry.' At the very last moment I hesitated then, gritting my teeth, I plunged the knife deep into his chest. It stuck for a moment on a rib or some other hard object but then shifted and dived, without my help, into his heart.

I opened my eyes as Graham opened his. I stared into one light blue eye and one almost green-black. They both closed as Graham Latimer choked and convulsed.

Sickened, I tried to pull the knife from his chest but it was well and truly stuck. Graham fell away from me, the knife still embedded in his ribcage. I released the hilt and just watched him tumble.

Reaching down to the body I tried once again to remove the weapon but it moved within my palm. Alarmed, I pulled back; the knife had been warm and soft. It felt almost alive.

I watched in horror as first the crossguard then the hilt and finally the pommel slid, without help, into Graham's body. The knife was gone. A pool of dark liquid crept from beneath him and made the crystals in the floor shine and shimmer.

'What have you done this time?'

A voice I hadn't heard for what seemed a lifetime rang in my ears and I spun to look up into Nessus's long face. He hauled me up in a bear hug.

'Have you just killed Lucifer?' Nessus dropped me back onto the ground and, bending down, stared at the body. 'What happened to the other guy – the insurance salesman? He is dead, isn't he?' He looked around the room. 'Where's everybody else? They're not dead, are they? Are you the only one that made it through?'

'Whoa, whoa.' I waited, poised, for Lucifer to free himself from the rapidly cooling flesh. 'Everyone's fine, they're outside. In fact, the one person that was dead now … erm … isn't.' I shrugged at Nessus's blank look and changed the subject. 'Are you all right?'

Nessus snorted. 'Don't ask, I hate that place – it shifts and changes on someone's whim. One minute you're slogging your way through a hailstorm, the next it's a blazing summer's day.' He shuddered as he stared down at the white-haired corpse. 'So what was this supposed to accomplish?'

I didn't want to look any more. I could feel the blood, sticky and still warm on my hand. 'Lucifer.' I shook my head. 'He managed to subdue Graham.' I shrugged. 'It's all got a bit confusing since you left.' I looked up at the tall centaur, then grinned and walked over to him. 'It's really good to see you. What happened to the green dog?'

'It's good to be here.' Nessus nudged me. 'Faery's in a right mess. Cu Sith managed to get me to the door, but then he had to run and if he's got any sense at all he's still running. The latest laws over there are that anybody who deals out of realm, with either angels, demons or half-breeds, is almost guaranteed to be put to death.'

'So how are we going to get back?' I didn't fancy the idea of going back the way we'd come.

Nessus didn't respond and we stood in silence for a moment. 'What are we waiting for?' Nessus laughed. 'Are you expecting him to get up again?' He reached out a cloven hoof and gave the body a prod. 'I don't think he's …'

There was an odd sound like a child hitting a pudding with a spoon and Nessus finished his sentence with a word that sounded like 'huggpfpf'.

'What?' I dragged my eyes away from the body and turned to look at him. 'You don't think he's what?'

Nessus stared at me, his huge eyes showing white. Slowly, like a toppling oak, his legs gave way and he fell to his side. A long white stick decorated with feathers protruded from just behind his front leg. It quivered with every laboured breath the centaur took, his fingers flexing and scrabbling at the stone beneath him.

'Hello, Joe.' Michael stepped casually out from behind the throne and, slinging a short bow up onto his shoulder, walked over and prodded Nessus in the chest with one silver toenail. He smiled at his handiwork then looked over at me. 'Don't you go away now. I have someone who wants a word with you, and he's very upset that you just left. He's waiting for some sort of proper resignation.'

Michael wrapped his hand around the shaft. He slowly dragged the bloodied barbed monstrosity out of Nessus and casually wiped it on his flank. The blood made a dark sticky mark across the shining hair, matting and dulling it almost immediately. The prone centaur shuddered and gasped.

The dour archangel looked down at Graham's body then waved the arrow at me. 'Looks like you did what you were supposed to after all.' He walked back behind the throne.

'Shit!' I knelt down beside the wheezing centaur. 'Nessus, keep breathing – just hold on.'

It seemed a lifetime ago that I'd healed Keril; I tried desperately to remember what I'd done. Reaching for my knife I felt a cold hand grip my heart. I didn't have it any more. It was gone – hidden somewhere inside Graham's rapidly cooling body. With no other option available I attempted to heal him without its help. Holding my hand against Nessus's ripped, bloody side I tried to see it whole and sleek again. I closed my eyes against the morbid scene and my ears to the sound of the laughing angel and finally felt the skin on my hand begin to tingle. 'Come on,' I whispered, 'we don't need that bit of old iron. I can heal him. The power comes from me.' I poured all the energy I could into the centaur's labouring lungs and kept my hand hard against Nessus's side. I could feel his breath becoming more rapid and shallow. I desperately poured as much as I could into his body.

'What are you doing?' Michael laughed. 'You really are stupid, aren't you?'

I felt his hand wrap around my throat and he pulled me bodily to my feet. I retched and coughed as his long fingers wrapped around my throat, alternately squeezing then letting go just enough for me to take a short breath.

He tapped me between the eyes with the tip of the arrow. 'Angelic weapon.' He punctuated each word with a squeeze from one hand and a tap from the other, then dropped me to the floor. 'You have to use this weapon to heal any wounds it's responsible for. There wouldn't be much point if any piece of low-class shit could just hold up his hand and use a little bit of stolen power to just say "heal" now, would there.' He held up the arrow. 'I'm not going to let you do that.' Taking the arrow in both hands he casually snapped it, then, lining up the two pieces, snapped it again. He threw the four pieces carefully around the room. 'There, unlike being eaten alive by stinking goats and burnt by noxious poisons, there really is no coming back for him.'

Grabbing my knuckle-dusters from my pocket I lunged toward him, aiming for his chest. Twisting, he brought one of his great grey and white wings down onto my arm. I heard a scream and felt the sickening crack of bone then lost all the feeling in my fingers. One of the 'dusters flew from my numb hand and bounced, skittering off to stop against Graham's thigh.

'And then there was one.' Michael ignored the flow of blood from where I'd managed to graze his wing. He drew his sword and the flames lit up the crystal room. Exhausted, I sank to the floor, one hand on Nessus's back, not really caring what Michael had in mind. I watched the dying centaur through a veil of tears, gasping each laboured breath in sympathy with my dying friend.

'I don't think so.' Belial and the rest of the group appeared at my side. The angry fallen angel had also drawn his sword and the black smoke smothered Michael's flames. The room quietened again.

'Belial.' Michael dipped his head. 'How are you, brother? Still picking the wrong side I see. Still picking the wrong fights – still championing the underdog.' Michael rearranged his face into an exaggerated pout. 'Oh dear, still failing.'

Belial stared down at Nessus and swallowed. Carly joined me at his shoulder and, running her hands over and over his dulling hair, sobbed. I wanted to hold her, to comfort her, but because of my broken arm my hand hung heavy at my side and I just couldn't stop the other from stroking the centaur.

'We really ought to talk about this, you know.' Belial didn't look up from the dead centaur. 'Why don't we do it over a meal? There's a Caribbean place in Birmingham that does an excellent goat curry.'

Michael sneered. 'Maybe I should sell them the rest of this chap then – for ingredients.' He reached over his shoulder and brought out his arrow bag: a tall goatskin bag, the head was still attached to the flap cover.

I winced. Bright, laughing blue eyes had been replaced with jewels and stared at me in silent accusation.

'I like to stroke it when I'm thinking of you two,' Michael said.

I looked over at the others. Keril had his hands on Una's shoulders; Farr was next to his sister who appeared to be having trouble breathing – her brother was holding her and whispering urgently into her ear.

Belial smiled. 'Little brother,' he said, approaching Michael. 'Seen Gabriel recently?'

Michael's smile fell away. 'My family is such a disappointment to me,' he said. 'One brother a traitor, the other a raving psychopath.'

'But you get on *so* well with raving psychopaths.' Belial leant on his sword, his tone conversational. 'After all, you take orders from one.'

'That's a little harsh.' Metatron, in his little professor guise, stepped around the throne with Raphael in tow. 'I do love a family get-together.'

He glanced at Nessus, snorted then looked over at Graham's body. 'Joe, I see you've screwed up yet again.' He gave a delighted laugh. 'You are without doubt the worst, most useless human I have ever had the misfortune to meet.' He wandered over to the body and kicked the bare foot and then waited for a reaction; there wasn't one. 'However, every time you screw up, it works for me. I've been doing it wrong all these years. I should have gifted you to Hell right at the very beginning – you'd have probably taken the whole thing down by yourself and I wouldn't have had to lift a finger.'

He perched on the black throne and studied me. 'And now

we wait.'

I winced. My neck and back felt as though they were on fire, while my head felt as though it was stuffed with cotton wool. All I wanted to do was lay down and sleep.

'He's dead.' Reaching out, Michael gave Graham's body another vicious kick.

Metatron shook his head. 'No, only the body is dead. Lucifer's still hiding in there desperately hanging on but he can't hang on for ever. All we have to do is wait for his power to transfer to Joe and God's power to transfer to me. Then we pick Joe up and he'll be joining poor Gabriel in chains.' He smiled and glanced my way. 'I would have left you free and worked with you, but you make bad choices, Joe.' He looked down at the body. 'Very bad choices. You can't help turning on those who love you.' He looked around the room. 'You take up with scum and demons, traitors and harlots.' His eyes settled on Carly. 'And other abominations that should have been left in the cold to die ... You.' He pointed at her. 'You are against God's will and should be put down like a feeble kitten.'

Belial roared with rage and, swinging the great black sword, rushed at Metatron.

Expressionless, the Voice of God leapt toward the ceiling, his great grey wings cracking like thunder as he twisted nimbly out of the way. His long white hair swirled around his head and in his hands appeared a long black staff from which streamed a green light.

'Nice to see you've managed to get your balls back at last, Belial,' he said. 'But I am still the Voice of God.' He laughed as he blocked each of Belial's smashing blows. 'And as soon as Lucifer has the guts to emerge from that corpse, I will *be* God.'

As the two angels fought above our heads, crystal shards shattered and fell. Metatron aimed bolts of light toward the enraged archangel but Belial was fast and most of them exploded into the walls. The two beings traded blow after blow and it seemed as though Belial was finally getting the upper hand as he drove Metatron back toward the tourmaline

377

throne. He obviously intended to shove him back through the Fae Gate that was still open in the far wall.

Raphael, ducking out the way of some falling crystal, shot across the room and snatched Una from where she stood, looking frightened amid the noise and glittering shards of smashed stone. Wrapping his arms around her he scuttled back behind the throne.

'No!' Farr leapt forward obviously intending to drag the child away from the angel.

Michael stood in his way. 'If you love death so much, necromancer,' he said. 'Let's see if we can let you experience it firsthand, eh?'

Farr slid to a halt and began backing toward Parity. He wasn't fast enough. With a shout Michael raised his sword and began a slow sidestep toward the suddenly sweating man.

Keril growled, locked his claws into Michael's arm then, swinging him into an arm lock, he attempted to force the angel's sword arm back and up between his wings.

Michael sneered and, with a slight shudder, picked Keril up and threw him easily into the throne. There was a sickening crack and Keril slid, unconscious, to the floor.

Farr watched the advancing angel and, with his hands glowing blue, he closed his eyes.

'There's nothing here.' He turned toward his sister. 'There are no dead here.' He sounded panic-stricken

'There's always *something* there!' Parity shouted. 'Be creative.'

Farr gritted his teeth and, ducking Michael's sword, plunged his glowing fingers into the soft white sand that carpeted the Throne Room and began to chant.

Spiders, beetles, centipedes and a huge array of other insects – some I didn't even recognise – heaved themselves from the sand and crashed in a black wave toward the enraged angel.

Michael, after one incredulous look at the oncoming tide, took to the air in an effort to avoid the plague of resurrected insects. It didn't work. The ones that could fly merely took off after him, coating his face and neck until, screaming, he tumbled to the floor, where the thousands of others advanced.

Even over the clash of the battle raging above me I could hear the dry whisper of thousands of wing cases and stick-thin legs brushing against chitinous exoskeletons. I pulled my legs in but the advancing wave of undead insects seemed intent only on Michael.

Raphael, still bombarded by falling, dagger-sharp shards of black crystal had thrown a wing over Una's head. She didn't seem to be too worried and was peering through his feathers at the fighting taking place all around her.

Michael, almost invisible under the blanket of humming, buzzing insects, held up his sword. As the blue fire cascaded like water down his arm, then on down his body, the crackling fire turned him into a nightmare form of flames and smoke. He grinned with satisfaction at the layer of tiny smoking corpses that littered the ground around his feet. Shaking off a layer of soot he glared at Farr. 'I hate goats and I hate insects.' He shuddered and brushed a hand through his hair.

Metatron shot around the throne and landed beside him. As Belial followed him down, the Voice of God tapped Michael gently on the hand and pointed at the demon. 'Stop him,' was all he said.

Michael leapt toward Belial, barrelling into the demon and knocking him away.

'Michael No!' Raphael looked so tired; Una seemed to be holding *him* up.

While both Michael and Belial were struggling, Metatron aimed carefully and knocked the black sword from the demon's hands. It flew in a short graceful arc into the wall where it shattered like glass.

Belial, enraged beyond all reason, screamed again and, with hands hooked like claws, shook off Michael and went for the Voice of God with nothing but fury and fingernails.

Almost casually, Metatron swung the staff and, catching Belial across the ribs, knocked him into the throne. He bounced off and landed in a crumpled heap next to Keril who, twitching and retching, was just beginning to come round.

'No!' Carly leapt up and ran toward her father.

I tried to put out a hand to stop her but my broken wrist, still healing, twinged and I drew it back, gasping as I cradled it against my chest. Taking as deep a breath as I could and, uttering a quiet apology, I placed a hand on Nessus's back and began to push myself upright. A weight fell on my arm and pulled me back to the floor.

'Dad!' Carly knelt and placed her father's head on her knee then looked at Metatron. 'You are shit!' she screamed at the sneering angel. 'How can you think of yourself as God when all you do is destroy and torture.' She sobbed as she stroked her father's hair away from a horrific gash in his temple. 'You're worse than the Morning Star ever was – he had a reason to hate. At least he tried to change things. You, you're just a pathetic, power-crazy warmonger. *You* should be the Antichrist.'

Metatron's eyes dulled with every word. Finally he couldn't take it any more. 'You have no idea what you're talking about, half-breed. I wanted nothing more than to sit at God's right hand – to be His voice, His scribe.' The furious angel bent down and thrust his face into Carly's. 'I'd done nothing wrong but He punished me – 60 lashes just to prove that I could be disciplined, just to prove I wasn't a god.' He stood up. 'Is that fair?' Metatron reached up and, snatching at the front of his tunic, began to pull. 'He didn't love me. I was nothing, I was a tool. He loved the humans – they were like toys to a spoilt child. I tried to do my best. I loved Him and wanted nothing more than to spend eternity doing His will.' With a final jerk Metatron ripped off his tunic and, holding it tightly in his fist, continued to rant. 'And do you know what His will was?'

Carly reached over her father to prod Keril who had managed to pull himself up until he was slumped against the throne.

Metatron had expanded to over 15 feet tall. His wings brushed dust and dirt from both floor and ceiling, causing all of us to cough and splutter.

'That I should always suffer – that I should *know my place*!' Metatron turned away from Carly and screamed into the air.

His back was, quite frankly, a mess. Long lines of lava ran as it bubbled and hissed within the 60 lines that crisscrossed every exposed piece of skin. From little scratches on the back of his neck to long, weeping gashes that disappeared beneath the waistband of his trousers. Some were thin and some were wide as though two or more strokes had landed in the same place. The skin around the lash marks was burnt black, bubbling up in blisters that burst, continually spattering fluid and necrotised flesh onto the ground. Where the boiling liquids fell, they hissed and caused little grey smoking pits in the shining perfection of the crystal room.

No wonder the angel was insane – that sort of pain would unhinge anything.

Metatron turned slowly to face Carly again. 'Are they the actions of a forgiving God?' He took a breath, obviously forcing himself back under control. 'We have a lot more in common than you know.'

Carly shook her head and gripped her father's shoulder. 'I don't have anything in common with you.'

'What about your people?' Metatron raised an enquiring eyebrow. 'God decided that you were an abomination – half-human, half–angel – all were destined for destruction. You had the power of the angels and the free will of the humans – you were dangerous. So he decided you were vermin and tried to drown you all.' Metatron smiled. 'Well, most of you, anyway.' He rolled his bleeding shoulders. 'But that's OK, we'll now take care of the rest.'

Carly glanced up at him from beneath her brows. 'God was right, you know, you're just a secretary. You should really learn your place because it doesn't seem as though the whipping taught you enough.'

The hand moved to my broken arm and I looked down at Graham Latimer whose face was lying close to my thigh. Lying completely still, he winked one dark blue eye, and then closed it again.

I gritted my teeth as my arm healed faster than ever before. Heat and pain rushed through me and, copying the Light Bringer's example, I forced myself to stay slumped over Nessus's body.

At Carly's words Metatron's face went white. 'You know nothing, you're pathetic.' He snarled and stepped away from her. 'Every road toward change has to start somewhere and I think I'll start by removing you. Time to go.' Metatron raised his staff and pointed it at Carly.

'Go, now!' Graham pushed my missing knuckle-duster into my hand.

As everybody watched Metatron. I leapt over Nessus and rushed toward Carly. Out the corner of my eye I could see Raphael heading toward me. Sidestepping, I ducked but belatedly realised that I wasn't Raphael's target. Drawing his sword, he aimed it at Metatron's staff and, with a huge downward sweep, he shattered the glowing weapon. The two separate pieces went dark and fell to the floor.

'No!' Metatron dragged his sword into being and, with one quick movement, spun so that he was standing behind the confused angel. One casual swing severed Raphael's wings from his shoulders and hurled him toward Michael. 'I'm surrounded by traitors,' Metatron screamed.

I stared at the twitching wings as they slowly turned to smoke and then vanished leaving only the smell of burnt feathers behind. Una peered out from behind the throne, tears streaming down her tiny face.

Michael howled in fury and caught the screaming Raphael as he fell. 'Why?' he bellowed at Metatron.

Metatron turned, his face impassive. 'His actions marked him as fallen. I just made the changes permanent.' He spoke slowly and smiled. 'Any action against God – me – will be punished.'

Gently placing Raphael onto the ground Michael stood up, his normally stern face white with shock; tears streaked his cheeks. 'You're not God. He was acting as per his nature – the nature that God gave him. You took his wings. He didn't fall – he was pushed.'

The Voice stared at the weeping angel. 'I *am* God, and if Raphael loves humans and abominations so much, he can spend the rest of his short time with them. I did him a favour.' He turned to face me. 'Leave Raphael alone, Michael, I'm going to let you do something you've wanted to do for a long time. Now you can kill Joe.' Metatron smiled. 'You can do what you like – this time I won't stop you.'

'I don't think so.' Michael brought his sword into existence then, holding it up for a moment, dropped it casually to the sand where it lay, cold and dead. He knelt and, gently lifting the newly created human into his arms, spread his wings and disappeared through the Fae Gate with a crack of displaced air.

'This is why everything needs to be cleansed.' Metatron laughed. 'Everything is flawed. I will make it anew – perfect – and there will be no more questions.'

A movement caught my eye and I turned to see Parity helping Lucifer to his feet.

Metatron's happy smile fell away and his eyes widened. 'You're dead.' He screamed as he stared at the pair.

Lucifer twisted his neck to get out some cricks. 'No, I'm not dead. I'm not actually sure what I am. If anything …' He smiled as he stretched. '… I seem to be more than I was, I don't really know.' He shrugged and cracked his knuckles before concentrating on Metatron. 'But I do know that you're not God.'

Silence fell. Lucifer stared down at Nessus's body. 'These acts of spite and stupidity show the world how flawed you are.' He gazed calmly at Metatron. 'You're a long way from being God.'

'I didn't kill him,' Metatron said.

Lucifer walked over and sat on his throne, staring down at Metatron who was almost purple with rage. 'You need to go now.' He spoke in a bored tone, and raised a hand. 'I can help you on your way if you wish.'

Metatron stood his ground, unimpressed by the being sitting on the throne, blinded by anger and hatred.

'You're not Lucifer.' He spoke slowly, defiantly. 'I'd know if you were – I'd feel it.'

'I am Lucifer.' The being stood up and glared at the sputtering angel. 'Star of the Morning, the Antichrist, Abbadon, Father of Lies, first among God's creations.' He paused for a moment and frowned. 'Or at least the important parts of him. I also know a huge deal about insurance and I'm quite keen on digestive biscuits too.' He shrugged. 'Not the same – different, new and improved.' He raised his hand again and began to push the walls of the room outward, changing the black tourmaline to a dazzling white quartz that ran in thick ropy veins down clean brick walls. 'I'm still learning.' He reclined into a huge wooden chair that had taken the place of the dark crystal throne. He looked comfortable on the padded tapestry seat, illuminated by the candles that had suddenly appeared on the walls. 'But I'll get there. In the meantime ...' He looked pointedly at the door.

With a laugh, Metatron raised his sword and began stalking toward the throne. 'You're just another fucking useless half-human with a bit of stolen power and ideas above his station.' He matched his words to his steady walk.

Lucifer watched him approach, his face impassive. When the angry angel was within striking distance, Lucifer merely held him fast. Metatron struggled, then, as Lucifer picked up a sword and walked around to stand behind him, sweat broke out on the angel's red face and he began to shake.

The Morning Star spoke gently into the straining angel's ear. 'Hear me, Metatron. I *am* God's first creation and I will be here to the last. You, little scribe, little scribbler, creator of lies and stories, you're not worthy and have no right to judge the world and now you will do as you are bid.'

After a moment's struggle, Metatron bowed his head and became the podgy little professor once again. Grabbing the lapels of his jacket he settled them firmly on his chest. With one last vitriolic look at Lucifer, he turned away from the throne.

'I look forward to working with you,' Lucifer called as the angry scribe stamped through the Fae Gate. We all watched him walk away into the dappled sunlight until he disappeared among the trees.

Lucifer sighed and slumped back in his throne. 'I must put a lock on that gate,' he muttered. He closed his eyes and rested his head against the back of the big wooden chair. 'I do believe I have a slight headache,' he said.

Carly looked around the room. 'Is it over?'

Lucifer snorted as he sorted out new clothing for himself. Eventually, after a dizzying series of quick changes, he settled on a well-cut pair of jeans, robust black boots and a deep green silk shirt which hung open over an old Eagles 1994 tour T-shirt. On one of the arms of the throne hung a dark leather coat with toggles and a hood. 'How can you ask that?' he said, running a hand through his white hair which grew shorter and spikier as he did so. I noticed a tattoo on the inside of his forearm. A long, slim sword ran from the crook of his elbow to his wrist – from its tip seven stars cascaded into his palm.

'Better?' He glanced at Parity who swallowed hard and nodded.

I noticed that in his hair there were two or three dark stripes that ran from his temples and through his fringe.

'You've made huge changes to the world, to me, to everything.' He hopped down from the throne and walked toward the body of Nessus. 'There have been some losses that we really can't afford.'

Lucifer stood for a moment in silence as he studied the huge body. 'I didn't know him at all.' He chewed his lip.

With a sudden movement that made us all jump he swung round to look at me. 'What do you think, Joe?' He looked back at Nessus. 'Did you know him? Did he have a good life? Did he enjoy himself? Did he have a good childhood?'

'I … I … I don't know,' I stammered. 'I only met him recently.' I had to smile as I remembered Nessus in the lift, his confusion outside the gates and his general good humour. 'But I think he liked life – he certainly laughed a lot.'

'What about you, Carly?' Lucifer turned to watch Carly helping her rather dazed father to his feet. She jumped as he addressed her; he'd never used her name before. 'Is he going to be all right?' Lucifer nodded toward Belial, whose eyes were still rolling in different directions. 'Maybe he ought to sit down for a bit.' Lucifer nodded toward the throne.

Carly's eyes widened and she nodded. As she helped her father sit down she spoke over her shoulder. 'Nessus was always there. He drank too much, he laughed too much and he loved a good fight.' She turned back to the huge body on the floor and sniffed, blinking hard to stop new tears. 'When I was little he taught me to ride.' She wiped her face and pulled in a shuddering breath. 'He was one of my first models for my painting. He stood in one place for three hours and didn't stop complaining once.' She laughed through her tears. 'He was a really good guy to have around but he told the most terrible jokes.'

Lucifer laughed, and the group stopped what they were doing and stared at him in amazement. 'Do you think he'd appreciate the opportunity to carry on with life?'

Carly nodded. 'Yes, I really think he would.' Making sure Belial was upright and mostly awake she walked over to the Lord of Hell. 'Can you bring him back?'

Lucifer's grin widened and he put an arm around her shoulders.

Carly stiffened at his touch. She paled slightly then relaxed.

'I couldn't bring him back if he was dead.' He poked at Nessus's rump with his boot. 'Come on, you're fine. I healed you about 15 minutes ago – now you're just playing possum.'

Nessus cracked one eye open and grinned. Heaving himself to his feet he shook himself back to order then grunted as Carly flung herself at him.

Lucifer laughed.

'What happens now?' I reached forward and laid a hand on Lucifer's arm.

Pulling his arm away to place it round my shoulders, I really wasn't sure I liked this new relaxed version of the Adversary.

'I don't even know who I am yet.' He looked down at his hands. 'I'm someone entirely new – half-human, half-angst-ridden fallen angel.' He rolled his eyes. 'Actually the angst-ridden angel thing is wearing off, thank God. I'm actually feeling quite ...' He paused. 'Happy? Excuse me.' He grinned down at me. 'I have to go and collect a debt that should cause some consternation.' He gave a wicked giggle and wandered over toward Parity who shrank back against the wall.

Carly stood beside me still trying to get her ribs back in order from where Nessus had hugged her. 'Did he just giggle?' She watched with a smile as Lucifer began asking Parity when she was going to make good on all her suggestions of the last week. He stood next to her and leant one arm above her shoulder, all smiles and flirting.

'I think he did and it's quite unnerving.' I turned to look at her. 'Is it time to go home now? How do you fancy a holiday?'

Carly stepped back and held me at arm's length. 'What are you suggesting?' She laughed and turned away to grin at Una who was trying to follow the lines of glittering quartz in the wall. Una looked back at her, her little face sad, tears in the corners of her eyes. 'Una?' Carly called over. 'What's the matter?' She stepped toward the little girl and said over her shoulder. 'I think we could all do with going home.' She sighed 'But what do you think the angels will d –' Her eyes widened and her mouth opened but no sound emerged. The world stopped in a gasp as Metatron's blue sword blade erupted through her chest, covering me in blood.

I stared, open mouthed, as the glistening point disappeared and she fell away from me to land where Nessus had so recently lain.

Parity screamed and everyone turned to watch as Metatron appeared from behind Carly's falling body. 'Whore, abomination – one less of you now.' He screamed then turned to Lucifer. 'Do you think you can just order me away like a child?' He stepped over Carly and headed toward the Morning Star, his wings unfurling and his eyes glittering, dark pinpricks of insanity that were fixated on his foiled plan. 'Don't you know who I am?' He raged as he stood in the middle of the room. Then, taking his sword in both hands, he first bent then snapped the blade. 'Plenty more of these around.' He grinned. His hands dripped Carly's blood in a small trail as he stalked toward the expressionless Prince of Lies.

I dropped to my knees beside her shuddering body. Blood trickled from the corner of her mouth and she looked somewhat surprised. Holding her on my lap I watched as the blood stained her blue and white striped shirt first red then black. She reached up and tried to grip my arm but her hand fell away. I shook my head, hard. I needed to stop crying; I couldn't focus on her face and I needed to look at her for ever.

'I love you. I had to say it before I leave.' She gasped, her hand turned red and wet as she attempted to cover the wound. 'No more coffee cakes.' Forcing a smile, she coughed and I wiped away the fresh blood that cascaded over her lower lip. 'I'm so sorry,' she whispered.

'What for?' I had trouble getting the words out and choked as I stroked her hair away from her face. It was dark and wet and stuck to my fingers.

'I'm sorry we won't get to have all the fun together that we should have had.' Her words were becoming slower and quieter. 'I'm sorry we won't get to fill your fridge with real, edible food together.' She coughed again.

I tried to sit her more upright 'Don't be silly. Lucifer will fix you. We'll have plenty of time for you to turn me into a good useful member of society.' I looked around for Lucifer. He was currently at full stretch, battling with Metatron high above us.

'I'm sorry we won't get to decorate my house, since yours got knocked down and I'm sorry we'll never get to combine our book collections.' Her voice trailed away to the barest of whispers. 'I'm sorry we won't be able to buy a puppy or have huge arguments or irritate Mr Morris. Tell Dad I love him.'

Then, with a last shallow breath that whined through her

stripped lungs, she was gone.

Placing her head carefully on the floor, I stood up and walked slowly over to where Michael's sword still lay on the ground. Both angels had expanded in size as they grappled. White and black wings created the sound of gunshots as they slapped the air into compliance, each fighting for dominance. Lucifer had hold of Metatron's throat with one hand and a huge grey sword in the other; it dripped slow purple fire which rolled and tumbled away into the air every time he swung it.

Metatron had no weapons but full armour which he used to block each blow. Eventually Lucifer landed a blow and Metatron sprawled across the tiles, but not before he'd managed to thrust Lucifer away from him and into the wall with a sickening crack.

This was my chance. I picked up the sword, grunting at its weight. Despite my best endeavours I couldn't get the tip from the ground. For a moment nothing happened then slowly the sword became lighter and a small trickle of white flame dribbled down the blade. Moving quickly I stepped toward Metatron, sword held high. I chose not to acknowledge Una's shout of warning. 'Joe!' Intent on plunging that sword deep into the prone angel I carried on toward him.

Metatron turned to look at me. 'You'd kill me, Joe?' He laughed. 'After all I've done for you?' Shrinking to his normal size he laughed and easily blocked my wild thrusts. 'You always wanted to stop doing this. Always wanted out.' He paused and shook his head. 'You never really committed to all this, did you? Just going along for the ride and getting away with doing so very little.' He stepped back easily as I swung a clumsy backhand swipe at him. 'You have tainted me.' He spat onto the floor. 'Even being near you for all these years has left a greasy mark.' He blocked another slash with his arm.

Lucifer grunted as he dragged himself to his feet, wincing as one of his wings faded to smoke then remade itself straight and whole.

389

'You didn't even realise how much we hated having you around.' Metatron stepped back out of reach as I tried a direct stab. 'I should have let Michael have his way with you. He really wanted to dismember you and throw some body parts into the river and feed others to the pigs. He wanted to see if you could come back after that.' The angel skipped aside as I screamed at him and tried another wild swipe.

'He was so angry when he learnt that I'd given you all these abilities, I thought he was going to have a seizure.' Metatron laughed. 'But you were so useless I just couldn't be bothered to waste myself healing you each and every time you finished a job. I had to spend time doing it and I had to look at your stupid, ugly face.' Metatron was beginning to froth.

Avoiding yet another stab, he glanced over at Una who was calmly walking toward us, talking rapidly to Lucifer. Metatron ignored her. 'I always keep my promises, Joe, and I promised that this would be your last job and then you could have darkness and peace. I promised you could have your life back.' Metatron raised his hand and deep red whorls of light began to spiral toward me. 'Enjoy your reward, Joe.' Metatron's voice seemed to be fading. 'I know I will.'

'No!' Una's thin scream was the last thing I heard.

The room went silent. I could see Keril and Farr bending over me, their mouths moving, but I couldn't hear what they were saying. I watched as the scene played out in silence and wondered what was going on as Una reached up to hold Metatron's hand. There was a burst of sunshine as they both disappeared into a bubble of darkness.

# CHAPTER 12

'… OO! NOOO! NO!' I stumbled as, suddenly upright, my feet found themselves dealing with uneven rocks instead of smooth stone floor. I staggered for a while and wondered why I seemed to be wearing a dress.

Looking around, I had no idea where I was but it smelt so familiar. It was one of those teasing scents – possibly from childhood, possibly from a dream. I peered into the night, trying to make out the features of the figures around me. Eventually my eyes adjusted to the gloom and I realised I was standing in a grove of small trees – an olive grove to be precise. I got to my feet and racked my brain trying to work out why this place seemed like home and why I felt the need to run away so very strongly.

At the sound of footsteps I turned. The long robe wrapped itself around my legs again and forced me to stumble. A strong hand caught me as I fell and lifted me to my feet.

'Do try and be more careful.' A tall angel smiled into my face. 'You can't play your part if you brain yourself on a rock now, can you?'

'Gabriel, how did you get away?' I couldn't think and, every time I tried, my mind veered away on to some ridiculously benign topic. I desperately wanted a coffee and, strangely, I realised I never did do anything about those weeds in my front garden.

'Get away?' The angel looked at me closely. 'You seem a little confused, are you all right?'

'I was with Metatron. He killed Carly and tore the wings off Raphael. He wants to be God …' I gabbled. If I could talk about it all, it would stay with me.

'Whoa, what?' Gabriel stared at me. 'When did he start this?' He grabbed my arms.

391

I sat back down on the rock. 'I don't know when it started but I've been with him over a thousand years.' I grinned up at him; it seemed easier than crying. 'So sometime before that, I should imagine.'

'You've been with him for a thousand years?' Gabriel frowned. 'This is the second time you've been back here, isn't it?'

I had no idea what he was talking about so I just shrugged.

The beautiful angel stared into the distance. 'Damn, I don't have much time.' He gave me a little shake. 'Why does Metatron think he can be God?' He shook me harder. 'Quickly now.'

'He thought that God disappeared when Lucifer vanished and, if he can turn me into the Adversary and kill Lucifer, then God's power will transfer to him.' I gritted my teeth; Gabriel was gripping my arms fairly hard.

'What? That makes no sense.' Gabriel shook me again. 'Did it work?'

'No!' My voice was becoming strangled. 'You gave me the wrong knife.'

'I did?' Gabriel frowned then dropped my arms and sighed. 'Look, I have to go. I've got important things that I need to do tonight and so have you.'

'I ... I ... don't know.' I look around again. 'I know you, and I feel I should know this place, but ...'

Gabriel's eyebrows headed up into his long fringe. 'You *feel* as if you should know this place?' he mimicked. 'Really, I wouldn't have thought you'd ever forget it.' He turned again and checked the darkness. 'Damn it all, I have no time.' He nudged me with his elbow. 'Is everything all right with me though – am I happy?' He looked as if he already knew the answer.

I swallowed hard.

'Damn.' Gabriel winced. 'I have to go.' He smiled. 'Just one quick hint?'

'Don't go anywhere near Brazil.' I patted him on the hand. 'Not ever. If you're even thinking about it, put it out of your mind. If you want a holiday go to Spain or Portugal, or Cornwall's nice.'

'Brazil?' Gabriel frowned. 'Somehow I don't think I'm going to get in trouble for doing something in Brazil.'

A gentle voice full of humour and empathy spoke quietly from the other side of the trees. 'Ah, the spirit is willing, but the flesh is weak.'

'That's my cue.' Gabriel reached out and grasped my shoulder. 'Sorry, Joe, your turn soon.'

I watched him walk toward the unseen speaker, my stomach churning and my throat tight. I couldn't breathe. I knew where I was and I knew who I was. I knew, finally, exactly what my sin was and I couldn't go through this again, I just couldn't. As my breathing shortened and I began to sweat, a heavy hand clapped me on the back. My heart leapt for the second time in as many minutes.

'Joe. Hm – nice frock.'

I turned and stared, bewildered, into Lucifer's eyes.

'Come on, snap out of it.' He gave me a little shake. 'Here, I brought you one of those awful drinks you like so much. Holding out a cream cardboard cup with the familiar green mermaid design emblazoned on the side he gave me a nudge with the cup. The familiar smell finally gave me something "normal" to concentrate on.

'How are you here?' I stared at him.

He turned and stared out over the grove. 'Time can be got around pretty much as easily as distance,' he said. 'I'm already here, or I was, so I have a place here and I can use it at any time – just like you.'

'I never wanted to come back here.' My hands were shaking but I managed to hold on to my coffee. 'Carly?' I asked. I ripped off the plastic lid and threw it to one side, before taking a huge mouthful of mint mocha with cream.

Lucifer shook his head and reached into a pocket from which he produced a tiny jade woman. He held it up to the starlight between two fingers and stared into its depths; it seemed to be full of stars. Grinning at me he leant over and picked up the lid of my coffee cup. 'I don't think that's a good idea, do you? There would be a legion of archaeologists wetting themselves over that little find.' He put the lid in his pocket. 'Come on, snap out of it,' he said, snapping his fingers in front of my eyes. 'You look like a bush baby on smack.'

'I won't do this again.' I finished the coffee and crumpled the cup in my fist. 'It all hinges on me – again. I spent a thousand years dead then another thousand thinking that I was paying for what I did that night ...' I paused and tried again. '... am going to do tonight – am *not* going to do tonight.' I felt sick and lost in the time differences. 'I won't do it again.' It was a feeble finish.

'You have to.' Lucifer gathered his leather duffle coat around himself and sat next to me. 'If you don't, it won't happen and then everything goes tits up.' He paused and frowned. 'Everything depends on you and that damned kiss.'

'Please, there must be another way.' I stood up and felt my fists hit my thighs. 'I don't think I can even speak the language any more.'

'Don't worry, you can. You already are.' Lucifer leant back on the rock, resting on his elbows. He stretched his long legs out then, crossing them at the ankle, stared at me. 'Metatron was right, wasn't he? Isn't this what you wanted? You've always asked to stop working for him. Well, he's given you exactly what you asked for: he's put you back where you started, right at the beginning of all this. Unfortunately you have to live it all again.'

I could feel a lump in my throat. 'I thought I wanted my life back, but I had no idea what I was asking for. I didn't actually want *my* life back. I just wanted *a* life – one where I didn't work for bloody angels. I don't want to go through all that again – the grief and the guilt.' I stared up at the stars. They'd changed quite a bit over 2,000 odd years. 'I made myself the most hated man in history. I'm a bloody noun, an insult – something you call someone when there's no other insult hideous enough.'

I shook my head and tried to breathe. 'I'm not that man. I don't think I ever was.'

'So,' Lucifer gave me a smile. 'If I offered you a way out would you take it?'

Alarm bells began to ring and I forced myself to keep my mouth shut. This wasn't a mate I was talking to, whatever it felt like. On the other hand, he seemed far more genuine than the angel that called itself my friend.

'Maybe – what have you got in mind?'

The look on my face obviously tickled Lucifer and he let forth a bellowing laugh. 'The act still has to be done. But I'll do it for you,' he said.

'How?'

'I can make myself look like you.' He frowned. 'Although you do seem a bit heavy on the dirt – were you really this messy?' He shook his head and dragged himself back to the subject at hand. 'I'll do all that needs to be done.'

'And what happens to me while all this is going on?' I imagined being in Lucifer's body – a sort of exchange programme.

'Nothing, you'll be asleep.' He got to his feet and stared over his shoulder for a moment. 'Come on, time is running out.'

I dithered. I still couldn't think straight.

'I need you back, Joe.' Lucifer shrugged. 'I need someone on Earth. The place is a mess. I need you to do your old job but for me.'

'Can't I just die now?'

Lucifer smiled. 'If that's what you really want.' He paused with his head on one side regarding me. Fishing in his pocket he brought out the little figurine again. 'But I think you might want to think through all of your options. You of all people might want to watch this one grow up again.'

I stared at him then the penny dropped. 'You can re-create her? I thought that once someone was dead, they were dead.'

Lucifer nodded. 'There was an intervention.' He frowned and placed his hand on my chest. 'This is a captured soul. I have been given permission to find somewhere to put it.'

'Couldn't you just put it back into her old body?'

Lucifer shook his head. 'That body was damaged beyond

repair, even if it could exist without a soul, which it can't. That's why it was so funny when people kept trying to sell them to me.'

Lucifer watched me as I ran it all through in my head. 'I need you to *want* to do this,' he said. 'Trust me, I think you'll be happy with the terms but …' He tilted his head, listening. 'Here we go. Come on – yes or no. I have to know *now*.'

A voice whispered loudly in what is now the predawn gloom. 'Judas?'

Lucifer stepped quietly back into the darkness beneath a tree then raised his eyebrows, widened his eyes and spread his hands in the universal gesture of a question.

'Judas Iscariot, are you there?'

That name – that terrible, terrible name. I won't be known by that again. Turning toward the shadows I nod quickly. 'Yes,' I whispered. 'I agree.'

There was a deep chuckle and then, once again, the floor fell away.

I woke up with a headache and had never been so pleased to see the damp patch on my bedroom ceiling. On the bedside table stood a pot of tea, a small jug of milk, a mug, three digestive biscuits and two paracetamols on a plate. There was also a small folded piece of paper, with "Joe" handwritten on the outside.

Puffing my pillows up onto my headboard I made myself comfortable and poured a mug of tea. Downing the painkillers, I began to happily dunk the biscuits. Only when they were reduced to crumbs did I finally reach for the note.

*Women's Hospital, Maternity reception, 3.30 p.m.*
*ps Hope you like the changes I made.*

It was signed just with the letter "L".

I looked over at the clock: 10.45 a.m. I had at least three free hours, downing the last gulp of tea. I turned over and, with a big sigh, snuggled back into the pillows.

It was only seconds before my eyes opened again and I realised that Carly was dead and my house, by rights, should be a pile of smoking rubble.

Leaping out of bed, I threw on some jeans and a pair of scruffy trainers. Hesitating at the top of the stairs I finally forced myself to walk down them. Peering into the kitchen, it looked the same as it did when I left: washing up still to be done, a couple of cupboards open where I was hunting for Carly's chocolates.

Ignoring the pain in my chest at the thought of her, I resolutely opened the door to the lounge. It was a mess.

But it was my normal mess – the mess that was there *before* I brought Graham back from Metatron's office. As I stared around at my books and weapons, I noticed that there had been some small changes. Lots of wooden ornaments now peered at me from between the books; I now had a tall lamp on my dining room table and cushions on my sofa; a big green rug snuggled up to the front of the fireplace; and in one corner of the room a group of large canvasses had been carefully placed against the wall.

I walked slowly toward them. They were all here: every single painting that Carly kept at her house was now in mine.

Leaving them where they stood, I walked out of the front door. The young rowan tree now growing in my front garden flashed as the discs and bent silver forks that hung from its branches spun in the late summer breeze. Slumped glass sculptures rubbed shoulders with stacked rusty tins and artfully placed mosaic structures hid among the long grass, nettles and decorated rustic boxes of bolted herbs. I noticed that students had thrown a couple of beer cans into my garden.

At the sound of a door closing I stared over the fence toward my neighbour's house. The drive was neatly paved to create a parking space for a small city car. The woman, blonde and dressed in a conservative suit, nodded to me as she climbed into the car. With a smile and a short wave, she reversed onto the road and was gone.

'This isn't a garden, it's a bloody rubbish tip.' I snapped around to face Mr Morris who was leaning over the opposite fence. 'This really is unacceptable.' He glared at me. 'You do realise that you're bringing the price of the houses down around here.'

I grinned at him. 'I don't care.'

'What?' He pulled himself up to his full height. 'Now listen here, young man, I don't know who you think you're talking to, but I say this lot has to be cleared.'

'No.' I turned and wandered over to the fence. 'I like it. I can do what I like with my garden, and I love it the way it is.' I leant toward him. 'It will be staying, so suck it up.'

'I'll call the council!' He blustered, pulling away from me.

'Do what you like.' I headed for the door. 'As I said, I don't care.' I could hear him spluttering impotently as I shut the door – hard.

Sitting on the sofa, I held the painting that I loved so much. The girl on the dock seemed to echo my feelings of loss and longing. I stared at it for so long my tea went cold. Eventually a strange clunk-flap-clunk sound brought me back to the present. I frowned and looked around for the source.

A small black cat with two tails regarded me steadily from the rug. After a moment it turned and jumped on to the sofa where it changed into a young Japanese man.

'Bakeneko.' I went back to looking at the painting. 'What are you doing here?'

There was silence from the man beside me.

'Look, I'm sorry about the bin thing.' I put the painting down and turned to look at him. 'You tried to warn me and I ignored you, I'm sorry.'

My apology obviously took him by surprise and he blinked at me. 'Well …' He lifted a foot, remembered he was human and used his finger to scratch his ear. 'I suppose I didn't really give you that much to go on.' He glared at me. 'But you definitely owe me a new pair of jeans and my boots were ruined.'

I nodded and shuffled as the silence stretched on. 'So, what can I do for you?' I was having trouble forcing my gaze away from the painting in my hands. 'I'm sorry but I'm not really in the mood for social visits.'

'I'm your new housemate.' The words were forced out between gritted teeth.

'What?'

Getting up, the cat demon wandered backward and forward on the rug, occasionally stopping to study the ornaments. 'Lucifer has given me a job,' he explained. 'You're going to be stuck with me for a while.'

My head hurt. 'I really don't care.' Picking up the painting I heaved myself to my feet. 'I'm going back to bed. You do what you like.'

He nodded and looked around. 'Maybe I'll tidy up a little, eh?'

I shrugged. 'Just don't touch the paintings.'

I knew I had to deal with them. They needed hanging – they were too good to just heap in a pile. Maybe I should decorate – that colour Carly had in her room was nice, I'd try that.

Carrying the painting with me I headed back upstairs. Kicking off my trainers I got back into bed and, curling protectively around the picture, I closed my eyes. It was lucky that Carly used oil paints; tears wouldn't damage it.

It took me a long time to fall asleep.

# INTERLUDE

*METATRON STANDS IN HIS office staring up at the painting of Lucifer who actually appears to be enjoying his fall. He looks away and, clenching his fists, sits at his desk. There are no papers, no letters – the surface is clear. Even his mugs have gone. There is nothing left to do.*

*A knock from the city scene window breaks the silence. Metatron's blood leaves his face at the sound and, after a quick glance, he puts his head down, hands cupping his eyes, and stares wide eyed at the surface of his desk. This moment had to come, all he ever had to do was wait, but – try as he might – he just can't summon the strength to face it with dignity. He has never been quite as terrified as he is now.*

*'No, no, no, no ...' His voice trails away to a meaningless mumble.*

*A girl, tow headed and smiling, pushes her hands through the glass and onto the sill in the office. Easing herself gently through the window her curly blonde hair, momentarily pushed back from her forehead, flops back into the big blue eyes as head and neck enter the office. As her foot hits the floor she changes into something older, neither male nor female, but full of power. A golden youth.*

*'My speaker.' The deep, rich rolling tones echo around the room.*

*Metatron clamps his hand to his nose – it comes away bloodied. Refusing to look at the child, who is now through the glass to the waist, he stands and begins to back toward the door. Keeping his eyes on the floor he reaches behind him to the handle. There is nothing there; what was previously a door is now no more than a thick wooden wall.*

*The child steps over the sill with an innocent, beatific smile then places its second foot onto the carpet.*

*'What have you done, my voice?'*

400

*Hands clasped over his ears, eyes squeezed tightly shut, Metatron sheds his human form and at full force puts his shoulder to the wall. It hardly even quivers with the blow. Wings flaring he rises from the floor and flees toward the other window. Smashing into it, he slides like a stunned sparrow to the ground, his wings dimming and whirling in slow arcs. Black blood bubbles copiously from his ears, down his neck and runs down his arm.*

*'Where will you go, my son?' The youth walks slowly across the room to stand in front of the crumpled angel. 'You, who have professed to speak for me for so long, will you leave now that I actually have something to say?'*

*The stunned angel moans and opens his eyes to stare at the feet of the being before him.*

*Its voice hardens. 'Speak, Metatron, and tell me why you have forced the combination of human and angel.'*

*Blood falls from the angel's eyes like tears. It erupts again from his nostrils and pulses through his skin, running freely, to pool in the delicate hollows behind his clavicles.*

*He opens his mouth but all that emerges is nonsensical sounds. 'Gah, pluh, pluh.' Blood bubbles up his throat as his organs collapse. It gushes over his chin and runs down his neck, joining the thin streams from his ears to form a flood that paints his naked chest a ghastly shade.*

*The youth considers the stricken angel for a long moment. 'My congratulations.' Its voice takes on a ringing tone. The muscles in Metatron's throat begin to jump and twitch, his facial muscles spasm and tighten to form a rictus grin. 'You have managed to achieve what I never would dare – a truly independent angel with all the power of the Host and the empathy and arrogance of the humans. Lucifer is now completely without any form of control or sanction: an angel with true free will.' The child bows its head and sighs. 'He has human feelings, human concerns. If he questioned orders before, now there will be no stopping him. He has what he wanted all along – an equal footing and a loyal following – and it's all down to you.'*

*The youth crouches, as though finding a better position*

*from which to study the agony it's causing. Its elbows rest on its bare knees, the short white shift settles in folds across pale slim thighs. Tilting its head to one side the child considers its work.*

*Metatron tries to speak, but again fails as fresh blood erupts from between his clenched teeth. He gags and heaves, clawing at the floor.*

*The youth sighs. 'I would have stopped you, but you made it impossible. You of all my sons are my voice, you are a representation of* me. *To change your decrees makes all pronouncements suspect – all of them, right back to the beginning. My sons would have flocked to Lucifer's call. There would have been war the like of which is unthinkable. Not just Earth but all worlds would have been destroyed. But that is what you hoped for, isn't it?'*

*The angel digs his fingers into the deep carpet and shakes his head in denial. Blood flies in a fine fan to decorate the elegant walls and sumptuous furnishings.*

*'Oh yes, but you knew that, didn't you? You knew I would have to watch all this play out and not lift a hand to stop it – and what if you had succeeded?' The youth shakes his head sadly. 'You would have become "I". You would have taken all that Lucifer is and joined with him. With that sort of power you would have been able to stand against me and would have cut off my voice for eternity and the Host would never have known. You would have made yourself Creator.'*

*Bands of fire arise from the floor and encompass the angel. He is forced to a standing position as his skin blisters and blackens. Burned blood first fries then vanishes into black dust. His wings dim further, flicker, then vanish.*

*'I have spent the last seven days studying demons. The fallen – those who turned from me – and it was you – you who have made this so.' The youth frowns. 'And it is I who have learned much about them, much about both species.' It gives a short laugh. 'Humans, demons, goats and dragons.' The child stares at the floor and smiles. 'There is far more to them than I ever imagined.'*

*The angel's silent screams cause the air to shake. The*

402

*office and all its contents shimmer and vanish. There is nothing but one small blond child and an angel in agony.*

*The youth sighs. 'Right at the beginning, he told me this would happen. He warned me that if I tried to crush them they would just flow away from me. I told him he was wrong. Now there is nothing to be done except to see where this will lead us.'*

*Raising a hand the youth pushes aside reality and opens a window to the world; it hangs blue and green, peaceful in the darkness. The youth regards it for a moment then returns to the angel. 'Should I destroy it? Should I start all over again, or is there still time to hope for change?' There is silence as options are weighed. Rising, the child continues to stare at Metatron. 'No. I am old enough to accept that there may be a different way.' He regards the world once more and speaks gently toward it. 'If you think you can do a better job than me, I'm willing for you to try. I have other problems to attend to. So, first of my creations, I hand the world to you. Do with it as you will.' Closing the window the child turns to regard the angel again. 'However for you, my son, my voice, my traitor. From here on in there is nothing for you to do. You have already done it all and done it well.'*

*With a raised hand the pain stops and the fire drops away. Metatron remains hanging in space, his face a contorted mask of blisters, blood and tears.*

*'Let there be sleep.'*

*The angel's eyes close and his ravaged body finally relaxes and there is sleep.*

*'Let there be, once again, perfection.'*

*The blood and burns vanish along with old scars and punishment and once more there is perfection.*

*'Let there be time to reflect.'*

*Behind the sleeping angel a door opens and the body moves silently into the darkness beyond.*

*A child stands in the void. No voice, no contact, isolated and alone, he sees that, for now at least, it is time to leave.*

# AFTERWARDS

'JOE.'

I was staring at the pictures of the babies that had been born on this ward over the last five years – there seemed to be hundreds of them. I turned around quickly and nodded to Lucifer. He stood in the doorway of the maternity unit, hands, as usual, deep in the pockets of the black leather coat he seemed to favour.

'Come on.' He indicated a corridor with a nod of his head. Placing his hand on the lock he opened the door to the ward and walked on through. 'This way.'

A nurse in green scrubs passed us in the corridor then stopped, unsure. We were obviously not supposed to be there. Looking surprised as he bowed his head to her, she smiled back and then continued walking. Making sure she'd gone, we entered the room she'd just vacated. It was small and most of the space was taken up by the large wheeled bed. In the corner was a transparent plastic crib; a tiny, wrapped form could be made out through the transparent plastic side.

'What's going on?' I wandered over to the crib and, smiling, offered my finger to the little person inside. The child was wearing pink and had a pink bunny propped up at the bottom of the crib. From the many cards scattered around the room I decided there was no doubt it was a girl. She gripped my finger with that almost defiant hold that new babies have. Big blue eyes stared unfocused at the world around her.

'Carly.' Lucifer indicated the baby.

'Really?' I pulled my finger away from the baby then 'own to have a better look. There was no outward sign ⸴ she was older than about three hours. She already ⸴emark orange hair, even though it was no more ⸴n fluff around her head. 'Are you sure?'

'Yes, I'm bloody sure.' Lucifer perched on the edge of the bed. 'She's fairly unique, you know.'

I stared down at the little pink lump. 'I know.' I couldn't help smiling at her. 'She won't remember me, will she? She has human parents so she's going to be completely human?'

'I don't really know. This has never been done before.' Lucifer rubbed the back of his neck. 'Carly will grow up like any other child, but what will happen when she reaches adulthood ...' He shrugged. 'This child was destined to die at birth so I have merely replaced the damaged cells with a set of my own, like little cuckoos.' He shrugged again. 'After 15 , 20 years, give or take, something may bring her memories back or she may go through this entire life completely oblivious. This isn't really an exact science, you know. I can't speed her growth – she's going to have to go through childhood and puberty again.' He frowned. 'Actually it's probably a good thing that she won't remember until after that: no one in their right mind would want to go through that twice and remember it.'

Standing, he approached the crib and placed his finger in her hand for her to grasp. She obliged with what looked like a smile, but was probably just wind. 'Anyway, I've got enough to keep you busy for a while.'

I stared down at the baby – 20 years seemed longer than the 2,000 I'd already pulled.

'Come on.' He grasped my shoulder and turned me toward the door. 'I can only keep the mother out of here for so long and, quite frankly, I'm too tired to deal with *that* conversation if she finds us with her baby.' He stretched, looking like a cat that has just been dragged unwillingly away from the fire. 'Do you know what?' He rolled his shoulders and neck with a small wince. 'I think I might actually need a holiday – maybe I should have taken Keril up on his offer to go with him to find his sister.'

I took a long final look at the baby then hurried after him.

'So?' I said, once we were out the room. 'What now?'

Lucifer frowned. 'Well, I've got to deal with Zephaniah. I need to have the city cleansed and all that pipework removed

405

so that everyone can move back. Belial needs time: he's struggling with returning powers and the loss of his daughter, but Melusine's sorting that out.'

'She's all right?' I'd wondered how the dragon was doing.

'No,' Lucifer shrugged. 'Not many could dive into the Acheron and live.' He smiled. 'She's tough as old boots, that one, though not as pretty as she once was.' He paused, thinking. 'Maybe I should get Raphael to have a look at her.'

I spluttered. 'Raph's OK?'

Lucifer winced. 'Well, he's not an angel any more, but ...' Lucifer shook his head, '... he decided that was a good thing. The last time I heard he was working in an alternative therapy centre and spending a lot of time on a beach in Cornwall. And before you ask, I have no idea what's happened to Michael.'

'I had a dream about Metatron this morning.' I tried to remember what I'd seen.

'No, you didn't.' Lucifer stuck his hands in the pockets of his coat. 'I saw it too. It was just God's little way of telling us that he didn't go unpunished.'

'Why?' I couldn't understand why God would do anything for us after all the trouble we'd caused.

'Oh, I don't know.' Lucifer ran a hand through his mad hair. 'Maybe it was a thank you for all the chocolate and piggybacks.'

'What?' Images of Una cascaded through my mind and I gulped. 'That was ... Oh my God.'

'Exactly.' Lucifer laughed. 'Take some time off, Joe.' Lucifer stared out at drizzle that fell from a slate-grey sky, wrinkled his nose and pulled his hood over his head. 'I'll call as soon as I need you.' He grinned. 'Hey, maybe you and your new houseguest should take up gardening or at least experiment with those powers of yours. You really aren't using them very well yet. Ask Bakeneko for some pointers.' He turned to go then turned back with a snap of his fingers. 'Damn, I nearly forgot.' Putting his hand in his jacket pocket he pulled out a white box, its sigils still bright and fresh. 'See what you can do with this,' he said.

I opened the box and there lying on its bed of velvet was the *other* knife. I recoiled and shut the lid with a snap. 'What the hell am I supposed to do with it?'

'Well, you can teach it some manners for one thing.' Lucifer frowned at the box. 'It really is very unpleasant and quite contrary. I asked Parity to talk to it for me and she passed out. Farr is a little grumpy about the whole thing so I thought I'd let you have a go.'

'Gee, thanks.'

He turned away again. 'I'll see you soon, Joe.'

Then he was gone, walking unnoticed among the pedestrians as they hurried, heads down and umbrellas up, along the wet city street.

# Here endeth the Gospels of Joe

*I WANTED TO COMPLETE this chronicle before starting anything new. Lucifer wants his own works published so I suppose I shall carry on writing but what these will be called I have no idea. Dark Gospels? Demonic Gospels? The Gospel according to Hell? I don't know – everything sounds like a bad role-playing game and I dread suggesting that to him because he'd find it really funny and do it just because it makes him laugh.*

*Everything is such a mess at the moment and, as I've got 20 years to wait, I have no doubt he'll have me running around soon enough.*

*Meanwhile life goes on and, as usual, the humans didn't even notice that it was touch and go there for a while. I'm still getting roasted for my "garden art" by Mr Morris and I've met my new next-door neighbour;, they're nice enough, but I don't think I'll be going round for dinner anytime soon.*

*Bakeneko and I are existing in a sort of malevolent harmony. I discovered that his species is Bakeneko and his name is actually Haruna, which means springtime vegetable. Life got a lot better after that little discovery.*

*I keep waiting for my next job but all is silent. Maybe "L" really did go on holiday; just thinking about him scuba-diving in Hawaii freaks me out a bit. The Devil in shorts, just hanging out by the pool, enjoying blue drinks with glittery umbrellas in them – well, it's a little odd.*

*I enjoyed the first week – I really needed the rest. The second was a little tedious, but I managed to catch up with all the little jobs I never get around to doing. We painted my living room and the stairwell; it looks good – much more cosy and homely. I suppose I ought to find some more jobs to do around the house; Haruna tells me he has a list but I'm ignoring him.*

*I have tried to do what Lucifer suggested and use my powers a little more, but every time I try, I either blow something up or it quietly disintegrates. It's a lot harder than it looks and I've pretty much given up, much to the Bakeneko's disgust; although he has been a lot quieter about my failures since I managed to remove a sizable patch of fur from his arse with a rather wild attempt at moving him from one place to another.*

*Quite frankly I'm getting a bit bored.*

**www.accentpress.co.uk**

Printed in Great Britain
by Amazon